A
Drop
of
Ink

ALSO BY MEGAN CHANCE

The Visitant

Inamorata

Bone River

City of Ash

Prima Donna

The Spiritualist

An Inconvenient Wife

Susannah Morrow

YOUNG ADULT FICTION

The Fianna Trilogy

The Shadows

The Web

The Veil

A
DROP
of
INK

A Novel

MEGAN CHANCE

LAKE UNION
PUBLISHING

Text copyright © 2017 by Megan Chance
All rights reserved.

Published by Lake Union Publishing, Seattle

www.apub.com

Amazon, the Amazon logo, and Lake Union Publishing are trademarks of Amazon.com, Inc., or its affiliates.

ISBN-13: 9781503940994
ISBN-10: 1503940993

Cover design by Shasti O'Leary Soudant

Printed in the United States of America

But words are things, and a small drop of ink,

Falling like dew upon a thought, produces

That which makes thousands, perhaps millions, think;

'Tis strange, the shortest letter which man uses

Instead of speech, may form a lasting link

Of ages; to what straits old Time reduces

Frail man, when paper—even a rag like this;

survives himself, his tomb, and all that's his.

—*George Gordon, Lord Byron*

Don Juan, Canto 3, Stanza 88

For my sisters,
Robyn, Amy, and Tonia
With much love

In the summer of 1816, we visited Switzerland, and became the neighbors of Lord Byron. At first we spent our pleasant hours on the lake, or wandering on its shores . . . But it proved a wet, ungenial summer, and incessant rain often confined us for days to the house. Some volumes of ghost stories, translated from the German into French, fell into our hands . . .

"We will each write a ghost story," said Lord Byron, and his proposition was acceded to . . .

I busied myself to think of a story—a story to rival those which had excited us to this task . . .

—*Mary Shelley*

Introduction to 1831 edition of *Frankenstein*

Love, fame, ambition, avarice—'tis the same,

Each idle—and all ill—and none the worst—

For all are meteors with a different name,

And Death the sable smoke where vanishes the flame.

—*George Gordon, Lord Byron*

Childe Harold's Pilgrimage, Canto 4, Stanza 124

LAC LÉMAN, GENEVA, SWITZERLAND—LATE MAY, 1874

ONE

GIOVANNI

Bayard Sonnier—writer, luminary, genius, and my illustrious employer—leaned back into the bow of the rowboat and gazed out at the twilight. The Jura on one side was shadowed and dark, Mont Blanc a looming gloom, the trees and houses onshore only just visible through a glowing mist that turned the lake into a rimmed bowl, the sky an oval dome spangled with just-emerging stars.

"We'll need to throw out the last twenty pages," he said.

Which I had just spent the morning transcribing. I paused in my rowing. "Why?"

"It won't do. It was wrong to have Juan leave for Coppet. He's got to stay. Otherwise Ianthe will do something foolish. She's too volatile. And she needs to be thinking about the life she's been promised at Monteverde. She won't consider it if he's gone."

As if they were real people dictating events. As if he were help-less against the demands of these characters, these figments of his imagination. I'd never felt that way about any character I'd written, and once again, I despaired at how far short I fell by comparison.

Was that what made him such a genius? Or was it simply a weakness, a flaw in an otherwise formidable talent, that he could not turn the characters in the direction he wished them to go? I had no idea. I longed to know. In any case, I didn't know how to emulate it, or even if I should. *"Everyone goes about it differently,"* he'd said to me once. *"Stop trying to do what others do. Do what* you *do."*

If only I knew what that was.

He went on, "No matter. I'll have it worked out by morning."

I didn't know which was more annoying, his smugness or his certainty. It hardly mattered—his tone made it clear he didn't need or want my help. He was staring again at the sky. I was already forgotten—no, more than that, nonexistent.

Just so.

I laid into the oars more forcibly, and soon our destination, the Orsini château, came into view. It was on a slight hill that fronted the shore, across the lake from the Villa Diodati, which Bayard had rented for the summer. Rose pink, gray stone pillars, a turret on one side, and a mansard roof sheltering dormers. The lights from the windows glowed through the blue shadows of the trees, reflecting in rippling gold stripes across the water, made hazy by the mist. We had been here several times in the two months we'd been in Geneva. Orsini's Thursday night salons were nearly the only society Bayard could bear, though we attended more infrequently than I liked. Tonight, he'd torn himself away from work only because a friend of his—Madame Lester—was visiting.

A frog croaked as we went ashore; the smell of woodsmoke from the château chimneys clung to the damp air. I took up my coat from the seat beside me and put it on, smoothing my dark hair before I put on my hat, which brought a teasing smile from Bayard.

"Oh for God's sake, it looks fine. By the way, if Madame Lester asks you about your education, 'a Benedictine monastery' is not a good answer. She despises Catholics, and she's happy to let everyone know it."

"What should I say then? It's the truth."

"I don't care. Say you were a scholarship student. Let her assume whatever she wants. Or even say you're self-educated—no, don't say that, on second thought. They'll only think you a poor street Arab."

"I never lived on the street. My father was a—"

"—poverty-stricken cobbler who sacrificed everything for his only son, et cetera, et cetera. Yes, I know. It's nearly the same thing. Listen: just smile and look pretty. And Vanni . . . I don't want a repeat of last time. If it happens again, I'll stop bringing you. I don't give a damn what I promised."

Last time, when I'd challenged Monsieur Delavergne to a duel over wine I'd spilled on him. He'd been the one who stumbled into me— I'd only just managed to keep from dropping my glass, but I couldn't keep it from splashing his shirt. He was drunk, and he'd blamed me for stepping into his path, and things had escalated from there. Bayard had to drag me out.

I was grateful that he'd smoothed things over. It was something else to admire about Bayard—he kept his promises, and he had promised to introduce me to the society that could help me in my own writing career. It helped that he liked me—or at least, he claimed to, though there were times I was not so sure. What I did know was that he believed I had talent. Otherwise he would never have wasted his time with me. Bayard was a generous mentor, but he was not entirely selfless. If I succeeded, he would be sure to take the credit. On those days when I contemplated leaving his service over one of his innumerable mockeries or slights, I had only to remind myself of that.

From the lake there was a small stone pathway to the house, lit only by the reaching incandescence from the windows, which were uncurtained. We could see people moving about. Several carriages waited out front. We were not late, but there was a crowd already.

Bayard sighed; he hated being in society at the same time he loved the adulation. It was the reason he never tried to put a stop to the telescopes the owner rented out at the Hôtel d'Angleterre, which had a superior view of our rented villa. It was an affirmation that he still held the world's attention. I wondered what would happen if that attention ever went away. A ridiculous notion, of course. Bayard would always find a way to command it.

The butler showed us in and took our hats. From the salon came the sound of talking and laughter.

Bayard grimaced and murmured, "'Once more unto the breach.'"

I followed him into the room, which was very large, with clustered gatherings of chairs and settees throughout. A fire leaping voraciously in the hearth made it too hot, so the various scents of heavy perfume were cloying, and clouds of tobacco smoke turned it as hazy as the mist on the lake, and made my eyes water.

The crowd dazzled—women in expensive silks and satins, glittering with jewelry, bracelets and rings on gloved hands, tiaras and earrings, sparkling necklaces. Men with watch chains more lavishly ornamented than mine, and boots shined so brilliantly they reflected the light. Sherry and champagne made the rounds, borne by servants in deep blue and gold livery, along with hors d'oeuvres that I knew from experience would be wretched: soggy toast spread with anchovy paste, eggs stuffed with caviar so salty it burned one's tongue, underbaked cheese puffs, and limp shrimp with some kind of bitter sauce I'd never been able to identify. Orsini had the worst cook on the lake, but either no one ever told him that, or he didn't care.

"There she is," Bayard said to me in a low voice, nodding toward a woman talking animatedly to a crowd of men at the far side of the room. She was gowned in solferino, and the purple-red color touched her pale skin with rose. Her blond hair was piled on her head, ringlets falling in the latest fashion. "Remember, if you talk to her of priests, I shall disown you."

But there was no opportunity to speak to Madame Lester of priests or anything else. The moment she saw Bayard, she gestured him over with an exuberance that told me she was half in love with him—as was seemingly every other woman—and turned to the other men, exclaiming, "Oh, but you all must know the sublime Bayard Sonnier, do you not?" They all nodded and exclaimed, so that when Bayard introduced me, my name got lost in the brilliance of his splendor, and after a few polite smiles, I was promptly cast into shadow.

Of course. As always. I stood there drowning in insignificance, imagining the day when I was the one they would gasp and fawn over, but the familiar daydream had lost its luster. Winning the job as Bayard's secretary had been a coup I'd scarcely dared to hope for, but over the last year and a half of serving as both servant and companion, I'd come to realize how difficult it was to shine standing near him. I struggled to push aside my resentment and searched the crowd for a friendly face.

Across the room, there, Edward Colburn, the publisher of a no-account London magazine, but a publisher of a no-account magazine was better than no publisher at all. He was talking to a woman I'd never seen before, petite, dark haired, and extremely pretty. Spanish ancestry, or perhaps Italian, like mine. As was most of the crowd here, she was older than I—perhaps ten years beyond my twenty-three. Colburn was laughing, and it didn't look to be a romantic tryst, and so I grabbed a glass of champagne and went over to them.

"Ah," he said as I approached. "Madame Brest, may I introduce Giovanni Calina."

She looked at me with eyes as dark as my own, and then swept me a head-to-toe glance that was so obviously assessing and interested that I nearly choked on my champagne. Her interest was not so surprising—women tended to like the look of me—but her boldness was.

7

"Mr. Calina," she murmured, pressing a glass of sherry to charmingly reddened lips. Her voice was accented; I couldn't place it. Spanish, as I'd thought? Something else? "What a delight it is to meet you. Are you one of Edward's writers?"

Edward. More intimate than I'd thought. So perhaps this was a romance.

"Not one of mine, no," he said.

"I'm a novelist," I explained. Colburn was notorious for disliking fiction. "I've written some poetry too."

"Calina is Bayard Sonnier's secretary," Colburn said.

Madame Brest seemed unimpressed. "Who is he?"

Either she was being disingenuous, or she didn't read, or she'd been lost in the Amazon for the last five years. Well, perhaps the Amazon was not a good excuse, as Bayard had received an admiring letter a few months ago from a missionary there.

Colburn seemed equally startled. "You don't know of Sonnier?"

"Should I?"

"You see that crowd over there? He's in the middle of it. He's the most famous writer in Europe just now. You've not heard of *The Temptation*? Perhaps it's not as popular in Portugal, but—"

"Oh, that." A shrug. "Yes, I've heard of it. But I must confess it has not interested me enough to read it."

Colburn laughed. "No? Everyone's talking about it."

"People talk, talk, talk." She made a chattering motion with her hand. "What is it about? Some exploring man . . . What do I care for such things?"

"It's very entertaining," Colburn said. "And somewhat philosophical. With a truly decadent protagonist."

"Decadent?" She turned to me. "Is your employer decadent as well, Mr. Calina?"

Judiciously, I said, "He would caution you against confusing an author with his characters."

"That is not an answer."

Colburn chuckled. "Sonnier's well known for his exploits. Even more so lately."

Thanks to Marie Arsenault. The reason we were in Geneva, where Bayard hoped to lick his wounds, and where I hoped to shake him out of his depression so we would not have to stay long. I had not thought I could dislike anything more than those last months in London, when the drama of it all had turned him into a recluse who never left his rooms, but Geneva was not much better. I had no love for the city, or at least, not so far. Beyond these salons, there was nothing to do. Bayard was content to sit moping and writing in the villa, but one could spend only so many hours floating on the lake, and even the brothels were no distraction, the girls there as boring and staid as the rest of the town.

But at least he was writing again, and thankfully, blessedly away from the cursed, dewy-eyed, all-too-available women who'd longed to comfort him in the aftermath of the hurricane that was Marie.

Madame Brest asked, "What exploits are these?"

"You've an eyewitness standing right before you." Colburn glanced to the crowd, which was still entranced by whatever tale Bayard was relating. "In fact, I was hoping to see you here tonight, Calina. I have a proposition I think might interest you."

"Oh?" I took another sip of champagne, hiding my excitement, pretending to be unimpressed. A proposition? Or a commission? Perhaps a story or even a poem—I imagined my father's delighted boasting when he saw my name in print, *I told you he would be famous!*—but no, Colburn's dislike for fiction meant he never published it. His interest was in philosophical and political tracts. I'd never tried my hand at either, but I could surely think of something . . .

"Everyone wants to know about Sonnier," Colburn said. "I think they might pay a tidy sum to satisfy their curiosity, don't you?"

It was a moment before I understood. It wasn't me he wanted, but Bayard. Why had I expected anything else? I stared down into my champagne, too disappointed to speak.

"What do you say? You're in a prime position to tell us everything we want to know. I should think it would be worth . . . well, I'd pay you five hundred pounds. All you'd need to do is keep a journal of sorts. Tell us what he does, who he sees, that kind of thing. Personal details."

"The more scandalous, the better," I noted dryly.

He shrugged. "The world is curious about his life. You would merely be writing it down."

"Can I be hearing this, Edward?" Madame Brest asked him. "You mean to turn the *Colloquy* to gossip?"

"Not the *Colloquy*, no," he said. "I'd thought to publish this separately. And I've still no interest in fiction, Calina. I want truth. Nothing made up. Sonnier is depraved enough that it shouldn't be difficult to find what's suitably shocking. Are you interested? I think we could sell several thousand. Perhaps more. With your name on the cover, of course."

Several thousand. The whole world would know of me then, wouldn't it? But only because I had written a gossipy piece about Bayard Sonnier. It wouldn't really be mine, and not only that, there was the dishonor of it to consider. When Bayard had hired me, discretion had been part of the agreement, and while he could be arrogant and sometimes difficult, I liked to imagine we were friends. My father had raised me to be a principled man, and I prided myself on my loyalty. Besides, if Bayard lived up to his promises, I would eventually have what I wanted without resorting to this. All I needed was patience, not a trait I had in abundance, or at all, really.

I shook my head. "I don't think I'm the man you're looking for."

"You are precisely that man," Colburn said. "Come, Calina, what other offer have you? I don't see publishers beating down your door."

That stung, not just because it was true, but because he knew it. I snapped, "I'll have you know that—"

There was a burst of laughter from Bayard's acolytes, as if they meant to save me from myself, and Madame Brest set aside her sherry and put her hand on my arm. "I would like a breath of air. Would you take me to the garden, Mr. Calina?"

It was just enough to distract me from my irritation. "Of course."

She said, "You will not mind if I drag him away for a few minutes, Edward?"

A slight nod of acquiescence. Then, "You will think about my offer, Calina?"

"There is nothing to think about."

His expression hardened, but he stepped back to let us pass, and Madame Brest and I went into the garden. It was a beautiful night. The stars against the deep blue sky, the shrouding mist creeping up onto the shore, the air faintly chill and smelling of reedy, fishy Lac Léman and smoke, tinged with the ever-present, earthy stink of cows and manure from surrounding fields.

She shivered. I said, "Can I bring you your wrap? Or perhaps, find your husband—"

"My husband is not here. He could not leave Portugal, and he has no patience for illness."

"Illness?"

She wrapped her arms around herself and looked out at the lake. "Elizabeth Orsini is my very dearest friend. Tomas does not like to say it, but she has not been well."

"I didn't even know Madame Orsini was here. No one ever sees her. I assumed he'd left her in London."

"She finds the lake restorative, though she never leaves her rooms. She likes the noise of his salons. It's why he holds them so often. It makes her feel less alone." She twisted, half facing me. "It is quite chilly, yes?"

"I'll get your wrap—"

"No, no." She stopped me with her hand. "Just stand closer. Ah yes, there. You are very tall, Mr. Calina."

"You're very small," I noted.

"A mere mouthful. That is what my husband used to say. Of course, he does not say such things any longer. We have been married too many years."

I had never met a woman so forward. Or honest. It was disconcerting. There was a faint splash, a leaping fish, and then the lake was quiet again but for the gentle lap upon the shore.

"Tell me about yourself, Mr. Calina," she said.

"As Colburn said, I'm Bayard Sonnier's—"

"Have you naught else to recommend yourself?"

I was nonplussed. The truth was, it was the best I had. As much as I wished otherwise, it was, so far, the only thing about me that caught people's attention. I struggled to think of something to impress. "Well . . ."

"What is your novel about?"

"There's a mystery in it. And a love story, I think. An old house, a tragic past . . ."

Her smile was quiet and beguiling. "A love story?"

"I know it's not the fashion, but—"

"You're a romantic. I like that in a man. Do you really mean to refuse Edward?"

I should not have been surprised. That she and Colburn were intimate was obvious. Of course she was his conspirator. "I see. Is that why we're here in the garden? So you can convince me?"

"A book such as he is proposing would help you, yes? Is he right when he says you have no prospects?"

"I haven't written much lately," I explained. "There's been no time—"

"Ah. You are devoted to Mr. Sonnier, is that it? He is a friend to you as well as an employer."

"Yes."

I expected her to keep pressing, but she only put her hand again on my arm. "We should go back inside, I think, but you will not leave the party? You will come talk with me at least once more before the night is over?"

"As you like," I said, surprised by her insistence. Perhaps I'd been wrong. Perhaps she did have an interest in me beyond Colburn's proposal. "Whatever you like."

She said, "If I were to ask you to supper tomorrow, would you come?"

Her smile made me forget Bayard and Colburn and everything else. "I am your servant completely, madame."

Fortunately, I did not have to work hard to convince Bayard to stay. He was actually enjoying himself, basking as he was in Madame Lester's admiration. "Why not?" he said when I cornered him. He was half swaying from drink.

I flagged down a waiter bearing wilting cheese puffs and took a handful. "You should eat before you fall over."

Bayard grimaced, but obliged, popping one into his mouth. "Whatever would I do without you?" Impossible to tell if he was sarcastic or sincere, but he grinned at me as he moved off. I went back to the party, though I kept an eye on him, ready to depart at the merest hint of his discomfort. But Bayard was in a good mood tonight, and we stayed until dawn, when others began to leave.

Madame Brest gave me a quick kiss on both cheeks in good-bye. "Supper tomorrow. Don't forget."

"I'm already regretting the hours until then," I said.

She laughed. "Do not disappoint me, Mr. Calina."

I did not plan on doing so, whatever the excuses I might have to make to Bayard.

As it turned out, I did not have to make any.

"I saw you talking to Colburn," he said as I rowed us back across a lake skimmed with mist that swirled away at the touch of the oars, the deep blue water ribboned with the lavender and pink of sunrise. "And the lovely Madame Brest."

"You know her?"

"I'm surprised you don't. She's been here two weeks at least. Watching you from across the room."

I was too swarthy to blush easily, but I felt the heat move into my face. "Watching me?"

"Last week when we were at Orsini's. I'm surprised your ears weren't burning." Bayard let his arm dangle over the side, trailing his fingers in the water. "But then again, you're not that perceptive when it comes to women—no, don't get your dander up. It's true."

"I had thought she might have an attachment to Colburn."

Bayard made a dismissive sound. "Last summer's attachment. Long over."

That was reassuring. "She's asked me to supper tomorrow—or, no . . . I suppose I mean today."

"You'll go, of course. She'll do you good. You're so damned rigid. Those brothel visits of yours only make it worse. Have you ever had a woman you didn't pay to take to bed?"

I regarded him stonily. "You're the one who says it's never free. You say all women are whores, because their love always requires a payment of some kind. You wrote that."

Bayard rolled his eyes. "That's what I *wrote*, yes. You can't be so stupid as to mix up an author's real thoughts with those of a character. Don't tell me I have to change my estimation of you."

"I know the difference," I retorted, stung for the second time tonight. "But you said the same thing. You, only a few weeks ago, regarding Marie Arsenault."

"Don't mention her name to me."

14

I started to argue, but then I saw the boats looming out of the morning mist as we approached the harbor, and it was so surprising I forgot what I'd been about to say. It was my habit to go out in the rowboat at dawn, before Bayard was awake, and float about aimlessly for a few hours, and it was not unusual to see fishing boats with their split sails and trailing nets so early. But these were not fishing boats, and they were bustling with activity.

I slowed. "What's going on?"

Bayard sat up, frowning.

There were men in the water too, swimming and shouting, and men standing on rowboats and swirling poles about like cooks trying to fish a soup bone from a pot of broth.

"Go closer," Bayard ordered.

I maneuvered us next to one of the boats, where a group of men watched with grim interest.

"Hey there!" Bayard shouted. "What's all this?"

They looked at us questioningly, not understanding. Bayard spoke no French, though he read it fluently, but I did, so I translated.

"A drowning," one of them told me.

It was then I noticed the upturned rowboat bobbing just beyond. When I told Bayard, he said, "A drowning? So early in the morning?"

The man pointed to the hill of terraced vineyards rising to the crest where the Villa Diodati sat. Even among the other villas, it stood out with its appealing, blocky symmetry of three stories and a colonnaded patio, its well-kept lawn and gardens shaded by ancient chestnuts and hedges. The sunrise glowed on its cream-colored walls, turning them nearly as pink as Orsini's château, and winked blindingly off the three sets of windows across its front. The man said to me, "Some famous writer lives in that house. The boy came out to see him swim."

We were always besieged by those trying to catch a glimpse of Bayard. If it wasn't the spyglasses at the hotel across the lake, it was people rowing over to picnic on the shore while they watched him take his daily swim, women giggling as they tried to climb the path to the villa, or stepping from their carriages on the road to stare. I had banished several dozen in the weeks we'd been here.

I told Bayard what the man had said.

He looked stunned. "A boy? But I never swim this early."

"We warned him not to go out," one of the others went on. "Too much mist. The lake is treacherous."

I knew it to be true. I'd seen a waterspout only a few days ago. The currents could be formidable. Winds rose without warning. "You knew him?" I asked.

One of the men said, "He hired a rowboat, but he wouldn't pay a boatman."

I relayed all this to Bayard, who said, "Christ," and sank low into the bow, looking sick.

"Shall I go ashore?"

He shook his head. "The least we can do to stand witness."

So we did. I kept the boat in place with a steadying stroke now and again, and we watched in silence as the sun eased higher and a breeze stirred the mist tangling about the shore so it wisped away, clinging only to the trees, slate blue and pink giving way to a gold that seemed nearly obscene as the men continued their grisly search, swimmers popping to the surface and then diving again, those on boats churning the water with their long poles. A small group of people gathered, watching, on the rocky shore.

It was an hour or more before a swimmer came up with a shout, waving. "Over here! I've found him!" One of the boats full of searchers hastened over. With a combination of poles and swimmers, they brought up a limp body of such a bloodless white it didn't look real. That it was too late to save him was evident. No one even tried. Instead they bundled him into a blanket, wrapping him like a mummy. Someone righted the rowboat and rescued the oars from where they floated free, and then, with no more ado than if they'd been out fishing for *felchen*,

16

they left the harbor. It was easier to sail to Geneva, a little over two miles away, than to haul the body up to the road.

The night at Orsini's seemed forever ago. The dawning day was appallingly bright, the sun soft and warm, the treacherous lake so sublimely blue and clear near the shore I could see the pebbled bottom, schools of minnows dashing about. From one of the villas I heard a dog bark, from another, children shouting. Birds fluttered and played in the sweet chestnut and magnolia, and the leaves of the terraced grapevines shivered delicately in a breeze wafting with the Arcadian perfume of new-mown grass. A man had drowned, and yet the world had hardly noticed.

But I was unsettled, and the feeling only grew worse when I realized that three people still stood on the shore, awaiting us. More fanatics that I would have to send away, and God help us both when they realized Bayard was actually in the boat with me.

And then, as I brought us closer, I realized who one of them was.

I should have turned around.

TWO

ADELAIDE

When they pulled the boy from the lake, lifting him from the mist and the water like a sacrifice to some long-ago god, Julian's pale blue eyes went distant and far away. It was a look I knew too well. My chin began to itch; with effort, I ignored it.

The man who'd brought us from the hotel that morning had advised that we wait onshore. *"He travels everywhere by boat, and hasn't yet returned from his cavorting about last night."* He scowled as if his disapproval justified such intimate knowledge of Bayard Sonnier's comings and goings. Spying on Sonnier had seemed to be the sport du jour at the hotel. But distasteful or not, we had taken his word and not gone up to the house, and now I wished we'd ignored him.

The boats, with their funereal burden, made their slow way out of the harbor, but for one, which came toward us. My sister, Louisa, stood on tiptoe to see, brushing impatiently at the long green feather on her hat when it dipped before her eyes. "I think that's him," she said breathlessly. "Oh, yes, it's him!"

Julian stepped close and put his hand to the small of my back in a show of reassurance. I forced myself not to pull away. The rowboat came slowly into view. There was a bundle of something in the bow, and a dark-haired man rowing.

"He's coming!" Louisa's voice hushed. She smoothed her skirt and settled the feather, composing herself. "Don't embarrass me."

"How would we embarrass you?" Julian asked, amused.

She didn't answer as the man lifted the oars and put them aside, letting the forward movement of the boat carry it ashore.

I said, "He's very handsome, isn't he? But darker than I expected."

"That's not him," Louisa said impatiently. "He's in the bow. That's his servant rowing. Mr. Calina. He might be handsome, but he's quite annoying."

"How so?" Julian asked.

The bundle in the bow stirred, taking shape as a man, Bayard Sonnier, who stared at us with an expression I could not decipher. Mr. Calina jumped out, splashing in the shallow water as he grabbed hold of the boat to steady it.

"Well, well," Bayard Sonnier said, stepping out. "Look who's washed ashore."

His eyes were vivid and deeply blue, and his hair dark and wavy, touched with copper by the sun. While he was as attractive as his servant, it wasn't his looks that awed, but the sheer force of him. Bayard Sonnier simply eclipsed everything. I understood why Louisa had been so taken.

My sister broke into a brilliant smile. "I told you I would come."

His tone was not exactly cold, but distant, as he said, "You must pardon me for doubting. It's a long way from London to Geneva."

"I was quite determined. And I didn't travel alone, either. I followed your orders, so you needn't be upset. I brought my sister, Adelaide. And Julian Estes."

"Estes!" Sonnier's curious look changed to one of admiration. He extended a hand to Julian. "Louisa gave me your poem, 'Cain in the Garden.' Spectacular. Truly."

Julian shook Sonnier's hand, looking entirely pleased. "I'm gratified you took the time to read it."

"I admire one who shouts his principles, whether I agree with them or not. It's a pity it did not get a wider readership, but perhaps it's for the best. You would have been torn to shreds, you know. They hate anything that smacks of a taste for reform, but atheism especially."

Atheism was only one of the reasons the world hated Julian, but none of us said that, and Julian only smiled and said, "I confess I have a taste for causing discomfiture."

Sonnier laughed. "There's an understatement." He turned to me, taking my gloved hand, bending gallantly over it. "Miss Wentworth. Your sister tells me the two of you had a most singular upbringing in Massachusetts. Utopian farms and half raised by Emerson himself—it's quite astounding."

"You said you didn't believe it," Louisa teased.

"I don't," he said. "But if your sister tells me it's true, I suppose I'll have no choice."

"You'd believe her over me?"

"She has a more honest face. I hope that's no illusion, Miss Wentworth."

His attention was a force, like standing next to a too-hot fire.

"She's more honest than most like," Julian put in.

"Is that so? How wonderfully challenging. I've forgotten what it's like to be so engaged. Vanni and I have been left to ourselves for so long we're stagnating."

Mr. Calina glanced up from mooring the boat. A flash of annoyance crossed his face, but he said nothing.

"My secretary," Mr. Sonnier introduced him. "Giovanni Calina."

Mr. Calina only nodded an acknowledgment and turned back to the ropes. It was not rude, though it bordered on it, and it was strangely dismissive. I wondered why.

"You'll come up to the house, won't you?" Sonnier asked, starting toward a path that led up the hill. "I'm a bit disenchanted with the lake this morning."

"We saw them bring up the body," Louisa said, falling into step beside him. "How awful! And right in front of your château. How will you ever manage not to think of it every time you look at the view?"

Sonnier grimaced. "I had not thought of that. Thank you for bringing it to my attention."

"What happened?" Julian asked quietly. "Do you know?"

"He was hoping to catch a glimpse of me during my daily swim. Unfortunately I'm not usually up so early." Sonnier's voice was heavy with regret.

"What has you up so early today?" Louisa asked, a bit too casually probing.

"I haven't slept. We were at a salon."

"I suppose society here keeps you quite busy."

She was smiling like a daft thing. It was so obviously desperate, but I understood. Everything depended on Bayard Sonnier now.

"Busier than I like," Sonnier replied. "I came here to work."

"We should not wish to keep you from it," Julian said.

Bayard Sonnier said, "Nonsense! I'm looking forward to your conversation. You'll spend the day, won't you?"

Louisa beamed. "Of course we will! Why wouldn't we, when I've come all this way to see you and introduce you to my family?"

Julian glanced at me. I shrugged. There was nothing to do now but leave it to Louisa. I was unused to trusting her, but I'd seen no hint of overexcitement when she'd suggested this, and what other choice did we have? Even if Bayard's invitation were the delusion I suspected, we were no worse off than we'd been in London, crawling as it was with bailiffs, arrest warrants for debt in hand. Not only that, but we'd been unwelcome even in the homes of Julian's oldest friends. Society, it seemed, was not ready to accept our philosophies, and then, of course, to make everything worse, there had been Emily, and the hell of Venice . . . We were exiles, snubbed and reviled. His father had disowned him, and would not even speak my name. "Cain in the Garden" had not brought the funds we'd hoped, but only more notoriety. Bayard Sonnier was our last hope, and we had nowhere else to go. With any luck, Julian could gain Bayard's friendship and his patronage. Certainly Julian's charm was compelling to those who did not have to live with it.

The path was steep and tortuous as it wound its way upward through the vineyards. I lifted my skirts to keep them from dragging on the mist-dampened dust. Lizards scrambled into hiding as I passed. The curling tendrils of the vines clung to my sleeves; broad leaves sheltered clusters of tiny yellowish nubs and threadlike flowers. The air smelled of dust and grass, along with something sweetly ephemeral: unripe melon, perhaps, or pears. Underlying all was the pervasive, not unpleasant stench of ordure.

The Villa Diodati stayed hidden until the path ended at a short expanse of lawn on the ridge, though we'd seen it from the Hôtel d'Angleterre. It was a square, elegant house built into the hillside and topped with a red mansard roof, with pillars around three sides supporting a main-floor terrace with a cast iron rail, and large, mullioned windows with dark shutters. The gardens surrounding it had the look of generations, gnarled trees and twining clematis and huge bunches of lavender swaying on either side of the patio, not yet in bloom, though the hint of its perfume teased.

I paused, trying to catch my breath. The climb had been difficult even without the corset that neither my sister nor I wore. "This is where Byron stayed?"

Bayard Sonnier nodded. "And where *Frankenstein* was conceived, or so the story goes."

"How lovely it must be to live in a house possessed of such ghosts," Louisa said.

"I wish I felt them more than I do," Sonnier said. "I keep waiting to be inspired by them, but sadly they seem to be avoiding me."

"You don't need them to inspire you. Your own genius is so formidable," my sister said affectionately.

"It was at least half the reason I took the house."

I hoped he was joking.

Julian said, "Perhaps you haven't harnessed their spirits correctly."

Sonnier raised a brow. "Spirits? How does an atheist believe in such things?"

"I don't believe in God," Julian told him. "But that there are spirits, I'm certain. I see them."

I tensed, waiting for Sonnier to laugh. He didn't. "You've seen them?"

"Just this morning, in fact," Julian went on, so passionately sincere it could not occur to anyone to ridicule him. It helped that nature too seemed to favor him, turning him ethereal as the sun filtered through his fine, thick hair and gilded it so it was a lion's mane about his chiseled face. It was hard to look away. "I knew that boy was dead before they brought him up. I saw his spirit rising. Joining the mist." He spoke the last almost too quietly to hear.

Bayard Sonnier stared. I could not tell what he was thinking. Finally, he said, "I don't really doubt it, you know, but I've never met anyone who could say for certain. How is it that you're not a believer?"

Julian laughed. "That would take at least an evening to explain, I'm afraid. And probably a great deal of wine."

"As it happens, we have both," Sonnier said with a smile. "Come inside. Perhaps you can tell me if you see Byron or Shelley hovering about."

He led Julian across the patio between the great columns, and inside. Louisa started to follow, but I held her back. "He was not expecting us, Loulou. You said he would be."

She shrugged off my hand. "I told him I was coming. It's not my fault he didn't believe me."

"The hotel bill will take nearly all the money we have left."

"We won't need to pay it." She was so confident. "We won't be going back to the hotel."

"He didn't seem overjoyed to see you."

"He can hardly play the lover in front of my sister and the man who is charged to protect me and guard my reputation."

I didn't say what was true: that Julian had done more to destroy her reputation than Bayard Sonnier might ever do. Though, of course, it was not Julian's fault alone; I was equally to blame. In the eyes of the world, more so. "That's what you've told him?"

"Why not? It's the truth, isn't it?"

"He hasn't heard the talk? Are you certain? He was in London."

"But he never left his rooms, Addie. He was avoiding everyone but me. He had no idea who Julian was until I told him. Don't worry. He's heard nothing. How would any of it follow us here? Who in Geneva knows us?"

But I was not reassured. Louisa's affair with Sonnier in London had been a godsend in one way. A man of his popularity had the power to change Julian's literary fortunes, which we desperately needed, yet I had not been sanguine about following him. It had taken weeks to settle my sister after the fit she'd thrown when he told her he was leaving. I supposed we were lucky he hadn't taken one look at her and ordered us to perdition. He had fled to Lac Léman to escape the rumors that dogged him, though I suspected that escaping her might have been in his mind as well. He would not welcome anyone who destroyed his peace, and peace had left us so long ago I could not remember what it felt like. Bringing him trouble was just one more thing we could not afford.

Louisa insisted, "Bayard already admires Julian's daring—did you hear his compliments? I'm so glad I gave him a copy of 'Cain' before he left London. And I've talked to him of Julian's genius often—he'll help us. You'll see. He so cares for me, he'll do whatever I ask."

"I hope you're right."

"You're just jealous, Addie. Why can't you believe that he might want to do things for me? Why should you be the only one to inspire a great man?"

"He went off without you," I said meanly, unable to help myself. "Clearly he didn't find you inspiring enough."

"At least I'm not trying to destroy him, as you are Jules."

I jerked back in hurt surprise. "That's not true."

She glared at me, but my words fell into a place neither of us wished to look at too closely. Louisa flounced away into the house, and slowly, feeling enervated and spiritless, I followed.

The ground floor held the kind of silence that bespoke empty rooms. I heard Julian's voice, and Sonnier's, carrying from the main floor above, and so I went down the hall to the stairs. They were in the salon, which ran the length of the house. The dark, parqueted floors were softly burnished by the light from the windows that opened onto the terrace, overlooking the lake, the Swiss Jura range, and to the west, the spires of Geneva.

"This is a view that would inspire anyone," Julian was saying.

"Or distract anyone," Bayard noted. "But I do see why Rousseau and Voltaire and the rest found the lake so mesmerizing."

"One cannot help but lean toward philosophy here."

"You, perhaps. I am rarely of a philosophical bent."

"Oh, but you are," Louisa put in, sparkling in that way I had always been envious of. "I defy you to say *The Temptation* is not philosophical."

Bayard Sonnier looked at her as if he could not help himself. I thought he seemed to fight the impulse, but it might have been my imagination. I was so disposed to think this disaster.

"I have to agree with Loulou," Julian said. "A man running from his own nature, traveling the length and breadth of the world to find serenity—how could it be anything but?"

"I had not thought weary dissipation philosophical, but then, I don't seem to see the book as others do. At the time, I was simply wondering how a man who was done with the world and everything in it might learn to change his mind. A pure flight of fancy." Sonnier laughed shortly. "A bit too prescient, it turns out."

"Well, we are here to make you merry again," Louisa said. "Do you see how I try to please you? I've brought the best people I know to ease your dark thoughts. Adelaide and I will regale you with our life in Concord, and Julian has many amusing tales."

"Thank God. I could use some distraction after this morning." Bayard Sonnier glanced around. "Where's Vanni? Did we leave him back on the shore? Ah, never mind, I'll fetch the wine. We should sit on the terrace, don't you think?"

"I'll go with you," Louisa said, following after him.

When Louisa's chatter and Sonnier's monosyllabic replies faded, Julian asked, "How was it that she met him, again?"

He'd heard the story before, though he was clearly skeptical, with good reason. I rubbed at my itching chin, but my hand was gloved, and it eased nothing. "She went to buy you the Keats, remember? He was in the bookstore. He took her to tea."

"Yes, the bookstore." Julian frowned. "Just after all the hubbub with—what was her name? Anderson, or . . . Argot—"

"Arsenault," I reminded him. "Marie Arsenault."

"Curious that he was out in public, don't you think? He would have been better hiding away than traipsing about London."

"Well, you did not hide away, did you?" I said, goading, baiting, telling myself not to but doing so anyway. "Why should he have any more reason than you?"

"Mine was not a moral failing. The world isn't yet ready for our ideas, but one day it will listen, and we'll no longer be reviled for simply speaking the truth."

"He had an affair that went badly," I said. "That is not a moral failing either. And you should know better than most that one can't believe everything one hears."

"I do know that, but even if only half of what they say is true, he's a debauched libertine. I know Louisa insists they are only friends, but he hardly seems the kind to be content with friendship, and she is so trusting. She would be ill equipped to manage Sonnier if he tried to seduce her."

I almost laughed at Julian's assessment of my sister. I wanted to ask if she had been equally ill equipped when Julian had seduced her, but he would only look shocked at my question, and that would lead to a hundred defusings and misdirections, and in the end, I would be no closer to knowing the truth than before, and I supposed that was best. I didn't really want to know if he and Louisa had found solace and happiness in each other's arms during the short months of my pregnancy, as I suspected. It would only increase my own bitterness, which was already overwhelming.

"Well, you're here to protect her, aren't you?" I said.

He frowned. "You don't seem to be worried, when you know very well her propensities. You will have to be vigilant, Addie."

The words hardly needed to be spoken. I had always been the ballast in the shallow-keeled hull of my family. I did not know how else to be. "Yes, of course."

He went quiet. Beyond the windows, the lake was a lovely indigo, rippling gently, and very clear. There was no more mist. I noted the slight tremble of his hand.

He reached into his inside coat pocket, as I knew he would, and brought out the small chased silver flask he carried everywhere. Quickly, he uncorked it, took a sip of the laudanum inside, tucked it back.

"Don't give me that look," he said, though he had not taken his eyes from the view.

"Seeing spirits?" I asked.

If he heard my sarcasm, he didn't respond to it. "I knew he was dead before they—"

"Yes, so you said."

"If I could help it, I would. Do you think I enjoy this?"

Yes, I thought he did enjoy it. Whether it was true that he saw these things, I didn't know. There was a time when I had believed he did, when I believed it was what made him special. He was a prophet, a visionary, a man destined to enlighten us all.

But he had not seen the souls I'd needed him most to see. And so I did not believe it anymore.

THREE

VANNI

They no doubt forgot my existence before they reached the path. I did not know whether to be insulted or relieved. Relieved, I decided. The less I had to do with Louisa Wentworth, the better.

I upturned the boat and stowed the oars beneath. I was starting to feel the effects of a sleepless night as I started up the path to the villa. I heard them upstairs in the salon, and so dodged into the kitchen, where the maid, Lise, was pouring cream into a pot at the stove. She relaxed when she saw it was me, and not Bayard. She was wary of him, not that I blamed her. He'd fallen on more than one maid in the time I'd known him, and that he was a demon looking to corrupt every respectable daughter in Geneva was common knowledge—at least to the locals.

I grabbed some of the strawberries she'd been hulling and sat at the table, gesturing for her to go about her work and ignore me, and wondering just how long I could hide here before Bayard called me on some pretext or another—though I knew better than to leave him with

Louisa Wentworth, didn't I? I should be beside him now, reminding him that he disliked her as much as he wanted her. That he'd been glad to escape her. *Bedlamite,* he'd called her, more than once.

All the stories she'd told . . . Raised in a utopian community in America? Hobnobbing with Transcendentalists? Emerson her godfather? Hawthorne a family friend? Bayard hadn't believed anything she said. As for me . . . well, you could not have convinced me a woman like Louisa Wentworth existed until I met her. And remarkably, by the looks of things, everything she'd said was true.

I was reaching for another berry when I heard Bayard's voice, along with hers. He never came to the kitchen; management of the maid was strictly my purview. Before I could make any escape, they were there, in the doorway. Louisa was clinging to his arm, and no longer wearing her cloak. I'd forgotten she was a dress reformer. Corsetless, bustleless—it really was an unfair weapon to use against someone like Bayard, for whom resistance was difficult enough. Her gown was a pink that complemented her brown hair and eyes, the sleeves elbow length, and beguilingly slashed to show the soft flesh of her upper arms. The skirt was caught up to reveal a purple petticoat embroidered with pansies. With it, she wore a fringed sash of bright green. It was all very colorful, and cut to show that she was rounded in all the right places, and I knew in that moment how this would end, and had no doubt at all that the dress was part of her calculation.

Her admiring gaze for Bayard became scornful when she noticed me.

Bayard gently unwound her arm from his and said, "There you are. Why are you down here instead of with our guests?"

"I was informing Lise that we had some," I lied.

Lise cast me a reproving glance over her shoulder.

"I came to get some wine," Bayard said. "Where is it?"

I went to the sideboard and opened the cupboard beneath, where there were enough bottles of wine to sink us both into oblivion every day for a year. I pulled out two and handed them to him.

"Bring the glasses, will you?" he asked Louisa, and then, to me, "We're on the terrace. Join us."

There was an urgency in his expression that told me he knew very well her effect, and wanted interference. I nodded, and he departed with the wine, leaving Louisa looking confusedly about for wineglasses.

"The shelf over there," I pointed out.

"So you're still with him."

"Why wouldn't I be?"

She twisted to sweep me with a glance that told me exactly what she thought of me, if I didn't know it already. "I've heard he's been taking you about in society. So nice of him, really, especially when he knows how they laugh behind his back."

It was uncanny, really, the preciseness of her aim. "No one's laughing, and I don't need him to take me about. They're my friends too."

She gathered the last of the glasses. "I worry at how tender-hearted Bayard is. He feels such a sense of responsibility that he doesn't always realize what's best for him. He probably believes that all your fancy vests and watch fobs disguise what you are, but no one is the least bit fooled."

"I seem to remember a time when they fooled you." *Yes, goad her, you idiot. It's always turned out so well.*

"You're mistaken."

"Am I? You may want to think on it again."

"I imagine it must be necessary for a man like you to delude yourself." Such a perfectly innocent countenance. She almost made me disbelieve my own experience.

Curtly, I said, "When do you return to London?"

She gave no answer, but stepped over and grabbed up some strawberries, plunking them into a glass, and then she walked out with a smile.

To think that I'd once wanted to do something other than throttle her. I had no doubt the day ahead would be unbearable. Not only would she make sure of it, but Bayard would be wavering—God knew

31

he'd never once, in the time I'd known him, turned down a woman who made herself available, unless she was a gorgon. Louisa Wentworth was far from that, at least physically, with those large and soulful eyes beneath a tall, pale forehead, an elfin chin, and an enchanting smile that made one forget she was a lunatic. He would never forgive me if I didn't at least try to talk him into sending her on her way. I would never forgive myself.

I went upstairs. They were on the terrace. Louisa laughed as she handed the glass with the strawberries to her sister—whose name I'd forgotten already—with a delighted "Look what I found for you! Your favorites."

Bayard poured the wine. Was it even nine in the morning? I glanced at the clock on the mantel, but both Bayard and I had forgotten to wind it again, and it was stopped at six, which was at least a respectable time to start getting drunk, especially when one had already been up all night.

I joined them, pulling out the chair from the small marble-topped table where Bayard often worked. Louisa's sister sat stiffly on the cast iron bench with Estes, who was lounging, one arm stretched along the back, dangling near her shoulder, though they didn't touch. The strawberries she tipped from the glass into her hand, eating them with a delicacy that didn't disguise that either they were indeed her favorites, or she was hungry—or perhaps both. I had the sense that she would have gobbled them in a single mouthful had she been alone. She was very like Louisa, but her coloring was more extreme—very white skin, and very dark hair and eyes, a study in contrast. Her face was longer, her mouth fuller; and she was both taller and more slender. Pretty in a cold, untouchable way. She scratched absently at a red patch on her chin. Bayard finished pouring the wine and sat on the bench, and Louisa took her place beside him, very proper, not too close, which was odd given how she'd been wound about him in the kitchen.

Bayard raised his wine in a toast: "Here's to what I hope will be a long friendship—where's your glass, Vanni?"

"Oh, I'm sorry. I didn't bring one for him. I didn't realize he was staying," Louisa said.

I gave her a thin smile. "You know how much I enjoy your company. How could I possibly leave?"

"To friendship," Estes said. They echoed him, clinking glasses, Bayard and Louisa enthusiastic, the other Miss Wentworth—Alice? Annabel? Something with an *A*—rather less so.

Bayard said, sipping his wine, "I've thought often of going to the States. Americans love me more than my own countrymen. They seem much less judgmental. Is that so?"

"Well, Concord is certainly progressive," Miss Wentworth the older said. She had a low voice, and a quiet one too. Very serene. Hard to imagine it might ever be raised. "As you might think, given its nature."

"You really were raised in a Fourierian phalanx?"

"They all shared the work," Estes put in. "Both Adelaide and Louisa can cook, chop wood, build houses . . . they can plow the back field too, if you wish it. Really, they can do anything. I'm quite overwhelmed by their accomplishments."

Adelaide—her name at last—Wentworth said, "It was very hard, and we were only children, and the farm was hardly a farm."

"But the utopian community, the experiment—was it successful? How many people were there?" Bayard asked.

Louisa laughed. "Well, it was us, and Mr. Simpson and his wife, and two men—what were their names, Addie? Mr. Cotton and . . ."

"Mr. Prescott," Miss Wentworth answered. "And Miss Jessup."

Louisa grimaced. "She smelled of linseed oil."

"She was a painter."

"We were there a year and a half," Louisa said. "Mama refused to stay longer. I think Papa would have, but—"

"Mama insisted." Adelaide Wentworth finished the sentence in a rush, as if she were afraid her sister might say something else.

"Were they all Transcendentalists?" Bayard asked.

"Every one," Miss Wentworth said. "Self-reliance was my father's motto. He taught us to believe that anyone can change the world, and that it was our responsibility to do so."

"That seems a heavy burden," Bayard said.

"It's no burden to offer enlightenment," Louisa said. "It's a beautiful obligation. A gift, really."

I wished for Bayard's interest to exhaust itself so they would leave. I was having trouble keeping my eyes open. The sun was beginning to stream through the trees to the east. It was going to be a warm day. Too bad it would also be a wasted one.

The conversation wound on, skipping from utopian communities and Transcendentalism to the tenets of Free Love, of which they were all adherents, and suddenly I remembered something. Rumors about Estes, and some horrific thing . . . what was it? It was at the far reaches of my mind, something I couldn't quite grasp . . .

"Your father was a teacher?" Bayard asked.

"He helped Mr. Emerson formulate his lectures for years," Louisa said. "But then, well—"

"I'm certain we're boring Mr. Sonnier," Adelaide Wentworth said.

"Not at all," Bayard said. "And please, call me Bayard. We should not stand on ceremony here. Tell me, how long do you plan to stay in Geneva? What arrangements have you made?"

Julian Estes glanced at Louisa, who gave Bayard a smile of such brilliancy that I had to squint.

Time to interfere. I asked, "What hotel have you taken? There are several I can recommend."

Louisa ignored me and said to Bayard, "We're at the Hôtel d'Angleterre. It's nice enough, but I do think it's lost some of its luster since Byron's time. It's just so cramped and small."

"I could suggest the Hôtel de l'Ecu or the des Bergues," I said. "They're both right on the lake. I'd be happy to help you make the change."

"Do you know the owner of the d'Angleterre rents out telescopes to spy on you?" Louisa's voice rose with indignation. "I told him I thought it was unconscionable."

Bayard chuckled. "I think they half hope to catch me holding orgies in the salon."

"It's terrible. I'm surprised you have not tried to stop it, Mr. Calina."

"I keep them off the property as best I can," I said, irritated at her criticism, even as I knew to expect it. "Every now and then someone escapes my best efforts. Now, as to another hotel—"

"Everything is just so fearfully expensive," Louisa said to Bayard. "The d'Angleterre is at least reasonable, but even that is a strain—"

Miss Wentworth said, "Loulou—"

"But such things are easy to endure when it means spending time with you." She put her hand on Bayard's arm, setting her back to her sister's protests.

From where I sat, I could see Louisa's expression clearly, how she licked her lips to glistening, the way her brown eyes shone—tears? Truly? I resisted the urge to applaud.

She went on, "I only wish there were more of it. I fear we've only a day or two before our expenses force us to move on. Why, it's hardly enough time for Jules to get your advice on his latest work—you would love it, Bayard. You've been wasting your talents on those who have none, but here I've brought you another genius, and there are so few hours to spend with him! And I have missed our friendship these last weeks. You know how it breaks my heart to see you so despondent. Do you remember when you said I refreshed your spirit? I would wish to do so again, but alas . . . Ah well, I suppose we shall all have to make the best of it."

Bayard stared at her, struck and incoherent. She was the most unsubtle creature I'd ever known, but she also had formidable weapons, and she knew how to use them. Given his expression, her "refreshment of his spirit" had something to do with his more carnal one.

He'd lost the fight; I knew it already. Really, I'd known it the moment I'd seen the dress. I settled back against the uncomfortable cast iron, hoping—uselessly—that I was wrong.

Bayard turned to Julian Estes. "You've new work?"

"It's splendid," Louisa said. "But he won't listen to me."

Bayard looked at her sister. "You've been quiet, Miss Wentworth. Do you have an opinion?"

She seemed surprised to be asked. She rubbed her hand through her glove as if it itched. "Julian is a genius. But if you've read 'Cain,' you know that already."

Her directness took Bayard aback, but he was impressed too. He always liked honesty. Unless it was too honest.

Estes looked abashed. "Adelaide is the best of muses. Thanks to her, I've been working a great deal, but I wish I were more confident. I'm too close to it. I confess I would like another writer's opinion. But I fear I left everything back at the hotel."

"Vanni will fetch it," Bayard said, nodding to me. "Along with your luggage."

"Our luggage?" Louisa asked hopefully.

"Why not? We've plenty of room here. I'd like you to be my guests."

It was all I could do to keep from groaning aloud.

"You should probably leave now," Bayard told me.

"But I've been up all night," I protested.

"As have I. I don't feel the least bit tired."

Thanks to Louisa Wentworth, of course. All that work getting free of her in London, and here she was, back again, and like a barnacle, sticking fast where one least wanted her. Instead of crawling into bed and dreaming of my little Portuguese, I would be rowing and hauling luggage. Probably they had a dozen trunks on top of it.

"As you wish," I said, rising stiffly. I gave the others a nod of farewell.

I was halfway through the salon when I heard footsteps behind me. Bayard. "You needn't act so annoyed."

I glanced toward the terrace. "You wanted to be rid of her, remember."

He drew me farther into the room, away from the open door. In a low voice, he said, "Well, why not keep her awhile? She'll be a good distraction."

"That's what I'm afraid of. You don't need any distractions. Hanson's expecting the manuscript in August, or have you forgotten? You asked me to make certain nothing interfered, and you're already behind. You wrote nothing those last months in London."

Bayard's expression tightened. "Don't remind me of London."

"You told me you'd sworn off women completely," I pushed on.

"I'm tired of abstinence." It had lasted barely a month.

"And she's the one you choose to break it? She was half the reason for it."

"She has perfect breasts," he said. "Now that she's here, I can't stop thinking about them. When she unbuttons her bodice, I lose my head."

"This will only make the gossip worse, you realize."

"Then we'll give the spyglasses something to see."

I bit back my exasperation. "Just remember that I warned you."

He clapped me on the shoulder. "I won't forget. On your way out, tell Lise that our guests are staying. If you hurry, you'll be back in time for supper."

"I already have a supper engagement," I protested.

"Cancel it," he said. "I'm certain the fine Madame Brest will understand. God knows she's been pining over you long enough that another day or so won't hurt."

Bayard went back to the terrace, and I went to my rooms to shave and change. Damn Louisa Wentworth and her wretched relations. Not only was I now obliged to be their servant, and having to give up the one thing I'd looked forward to in months, but they also made my job much more difficult. Bayard treated his deadlines far too casually as it was; it was my duty to keep him on schedule, and no one was more aware than I of the consequences of not doing so. If Bayard didn't write, he didn't get paid, which meant he could not pay or keep a secretary— me. I could not allow his liaison with Louisa Wentworth to collapse everything I'd built so carefully.

My rooms were next to Bayard's—his were small, but he'd chosen them because there was a door to the balcony, where he liked to sit. Mine were smaller still, closet rooms meant for a maid, only big enough for a bed and a nightstand and a single chair, and an adjoining room that was not much larger, but had at least a window and a desk. Despite the fact that there were several large bedrooms upstairs, Bayard wanted me close enough to call at all hours of the day and night.

I took off my coat and then my waistcoat. As I set it aside for another, I thought of Louisa Wentworth's nastiness in the kitchen about my clothes not fooling anyone. The fine purple and bronze embroidered silk looked well on me, I knew, and it was one of several I'd bought when Bayard had hired me, along with a watch fob dangling with orna-ments, and a real beaver hat. It had put me in debt to do it, but I felt I deserved them, and yes, I believed they made me look the gentleman I yearned to be. When I wore them, I could pretend the foul stink of Bethnal Green did not still live in my nostrils, or the accent I'd fought to lose wasn't lying in wait to twist my tongue whenever I was tired or drunk, or that my natural short temper had not been honed by hourly fights and provocations.

As a child, I had looked at my father's gnarled hands—a lifetime of labor in those hands and that perpetual stoop—and been afraid of what I would become even before I'd had the words to explain or understand my dread. I was not ashamed of my father—I had never been ashamed of him or that life, but I had never wanted it. Nor had he wanted it for me. He had watched me so sadly and so carefully, and the day he'd sent me to the Benedictines was one of sorrow and relief for both of us. I had worked hard to make him proud, and to become the man we hoped I would be. All my days at school spent studying not just Latin and languages, art and science, but the other boys—most of whom were from good families. Changing myself to imitate them, so that gradually, bit by bit, I erased the boy who'd run wildly in the street. And now . . . now, *"I hardly recognize you, Gio-Gio,"* my father said each time he saw me, and his pride only fed my own.

I had thought the change to be seamless and complete; I'd thought there was no longer anything in me to show what I had been. But then . . . well, it wasn't quite true, was it? Something must give me away. I had no idea what it might be. A misstep? A flaw I didn't know to spot? A stain on my skin? Whatever it was, Louisa had found it. With a stroke, she had turned me again into the son of an immigrant cobbler from a London slum—one more reason to dislike her, because she reminded me that, for all my efforts, this too was only pretense, and all the yearning in the world could not change it.

FOUR

ADELAIDE

We spent the night talking before the fire, the conversation leaping from the dangers of wolves in the mountains to the moral obligation of poets, and dashing about a hundred things between. I did not contribute much to the conversation; the long journey and the relief of having arrived made me feel muddled and stupid. I was only glad we'd moved from the subject of our lives in Concord. I was too tired to be clever; I could not concentrate well enough to parse my answers. My mother and father had espoused Free Love and Transcendentalism, but that had not stopped them from casting off both Louisa and me when I'd fallen in love with Julian.

God is in everything, my father had once said, and as his delusions grew worse, I'd seen him kneeling to the tulips to whisper "hello, God"; to the forsythia, "hello, God"; and "hello, God," to the wheelbarrow. But the day I'd told him that Louisa and I were leaving with Julian, he had been sane enough to be furious. I was only following my conscience, I'd said, but he'd ordered me from his sight. *"I can no longer see God in you, Adelaide. God has abandoned you."* The letter I'd received from my mother only reaffirmed his words. *We have no daughters. We will deny that you have ever belonged to us.* Concord's charms had faded until they felt very distant indeed.

By midnight, Giovanni Calina had not yet returned with our luggage, and Bayard was visibly vexed. He took us on a tour of the villa and let us choose our rooms upstairs. Julian and I took the one that fronted the house and looked over the lake, and Louisa took a smaller one down the hall, though I had no doubt she would be spending little time within it.

"If he's not back soon, I shall poison him," Bayard said, coming out of his bedroom bearing a mound of nightshirts and a robe. "Surely something here will do for you until he returns."

Louisa took a blue-and-green robe, and made a great show of taking it to her room. "Good night! Good night!"

Bayard watched her go with hungry eyes. I wondered how long it would be before he tapped on her door, and then realized, no, of course not, she would go to him. She would want to put a full floor between us, with no one near enough to hear.

Julian was so consumed with trying to impress Bayard that I didn't think he noticed any of it, thankfully. We took the nightshirts and said our good-nights, and once we were in our room, Julian went to the window to look out at the lake. He wore the rapturous expression that evidenced his elevated mind, his finer sensibility. I'd been beguiled by it when we first met on my father's porch that humid summer day, everyone glowing with sweat, batting at the constant fog of gnats. My father, his eyes too brightly lit, signaling a change that would come within days and cause him to be locked in his bedroom, had brought Julian up the stairs. *"My dears, I would like to introduce you to someone. This is Mr. Julian Estes, just come from London."*

Julian had come to Concord to speak to our neighbor, my godfather, Mr. Emerson, which was unfortunate, given Mr. Emerson's dementia; and also Mr. Alcott, unfortunate as well, because that old man spent most of his time sitting beneath an elm and handing out apples to passing travelers in the hopes of conversation, pontificating until one either went mad or deaf. But that afternoon, Julian had forgotten them both. His gaze had been fastened on me, and mine was equally glued, and our future together had been sealed before we'd spoken three sentences to one another. I had loved him beyond all sense; my only hesitation in running away with him had been at the idea of leaving Louisa behind, and in the end, I had not been able to. I had dragged her with us, the habit of responsibility impossible to shake.

"So many stars," Julian murmured now from the window. "Every one of them is a soul. That's why there are so many."

I tore off my glove to scratch the dry, scaly skin on the back of my hand, reminding myself of my vow and my obligations. Louisa relied on me. Julian needed me so desperately. I could find my way back to him. I had to try, and it was not only because my sister and I had nothing else. "You're thinking again about the boy who drowned."

"I've thought of him all day. I know it must have troubled you too."

It was gratifying that he'd noted my state, proof that he was not as oblivious to my sorrow as he sometimes seemed. "Yes. But I didn't know him."

"That mist this morning . . . it was the spirits of all those who died today. They were rising to become stars."

"What a morbid thought."

"I rather think it beautiful. So does Louisa."

"Louisa thinks so only because you do. Ask her tomorrow, and she'll say something different."

"Don't be cruel, Adelaide."

"I'm only saying what's true. She is changeable as the wind." That was an understatement, and we both knew it. At thirteen, Louisa's already tempestuous nature had turned into something much more dangerous. We'd been reading a book of folk tales one evening, and she'd dashed out of the room in her nightgown. *"Let's go find a fairy ring, Addie. I shan't rest until I find one!"* I'd rushed after her as she ran out the back door and into the woods bordering the yard, trying to keep up, but she was only a splash of filmy white in the near darkness. *"Louisa!"* I'd called. *"Louisa, come back! What are you doing?"* She'd only laughed at me, dancing through the trees, spinning and spinning, *"Not until I find one!"* and then suddenly she screamed and collapsed near the edge of the wood. When I went to her, she looked up at me with a stricken expression, and a terror so palpable that the benign woods I'd always known became sinister. *"I found one,"* she said hoarsely. *"Oh, Addie, I found one!"* It was all she would say as I dragged her home. She went straight into Mama's arms, sobbing piteously. *"I wish I'd never seen it."*

She was in bed for two days, not eating, not sleeping, stricken with a horror she could not explain, but on the third day, she was herself again, and it was as if it had never happened. *"I don't know what you're talking about, Addie. It was only a nasty bunch of toadstools."*

But my own life was upended from that night. My sister became as unpredictable as our father. I never knew when the fits would take her, and I was the one who stayed alert to Louisa's every change; it was I who watched over and protected her. I had not trusted Mama to manage her, not when Mama already seemed so undone by Papa's madness, and I feared that Louisa too would soon become unable to tell dreams from reality, governed by every shift in mood, no matter how unreasonable.

But it was those very shifts that enchanted Julian, I knew. He had not been raised, as I had, with ominous silences and locked doors. His life had not been ruled by manias and rages that were not his own, where a too-loud footstep or a wrongly placed laugh could cause a tempest. Perhaps Julian was too much like Louisa to understand. He was as tempestuous as she, equally quick to laugh and self-indulgent. I was none of those things. What a trickster was the fate that had made me love a man with so many of my sister's traits, that made Julian see in me a muse. Had it meant for us both to suffer as we did? What had we done to deserve it?

I said softly, "I wish we had gone somewhere else."

"To your idyllic small village to hide? There's no such thing, believe me. Even if there were, none of us would be happy there."

He would not, certainly, nor Louisa. But I would have reveled in the quiet. Sometimes the thought of speaking a single hello exhausted me. A day passed in silence and anonymity, the slow creep of uneventful, even-tempered hours . . . how lovely that would be.

He went on, "And Louisa wasn't wrong about Bayard's welcome."

"No," I said, though the extent of it remained to be seen. Julian knew nothing of Louisa's affair with Bayard in London, or how she hoped to resume it here. He thought them truly the like-minded friends she'd described them to be. Nor did he know just how upset she had been when Bayard left. Otherwise, Jules would have worried as I did. But Louisa had bound me to secrecy, and I had obliged for the simple reason that I did not want to see the evidence of Julian's feelings for my sister when he discovered the truth.

"Did you hear him say he admired my work? I hadn't expected that. I confess I wasn't certain at all about this plan of Loulou's, but I like Bayard better than I thought to, and she's right. He has a great deal of influence. If he chose to champion me, it would change everything. A word from him, and people would read my work. What do critics and reviewers know? Nothing. It's the people who will start the revolution."

How his lack of success chafed at him. He had been genuinely surprised when the critics had lambasted "Cain in the Garden." He had expected everyone to understand, to immediately turn to atheism and Free Love once he showed them how we suffered beneath the tyranny of religion and the yoke of marriage. It startled him anew every time a critic called him immoral. *"They're the immoral ones! Is it not immoral to defend the status quo? Ignorance is our greatest enemy, and they are its guardians."*

The lamplight touched the mass of his hair with a faint gold sheen. His eyes were mostly iris from the laudanum he'd drunk tonight, all through the evening, surreptitious sips from his flask when Bayard tended the fire or went for more wine, and now they looked ghostly and strange. "Come here." When I hesitated, he said, "There was a time when you were eager."

"It's been a very long day. I'm tired."

"Where have you gone, Addie?" He spoke nearly in a whisper. "Why have you left me in this cold world alone? I miss you, my love. I wish you would return to me."

The poetry in the words held the memory of my love for him, but it had no force or resonance, because now I also heard in them the selfishness that had caused the breach between us. He did not understand why I blamed him.

I looked away.

He sighed. I heard in it his disappointment, but I could say nothing to ease it.

The lamp flame sputtered, at the end of its oil, and went out, leaving us in darkness, so the only light was that of the stars and the shimmering lake, a lambent, eerie glow that touched him but did not reach me, and I felt again the weight of my mistakes, and his, so that every motion and sight and sensation held the shadow we lived beneath, that burdened everything we did.

He sat straight up, waking me. "No."

"Jules?" I asked, trying to unglue myself from sleep.

"No." He shoved off the blankets, leaping from bed. "No! Get away from me!"

The realization of what was happening cut through my grogginess. My heart sank. He was already across the room and to the door.

"Jules, no!" I shouted.

He jerked on the knob as if he could not remember how to work it, then again, shaking it in frustration. "No no no! Help me! Help me!"

The knob turned. He threw the door open so hard it cracked against the wall, and ran into the hallway, which was lit only by moonlight streaming through the windows at one end, that strange white glow that chased everything with shadow and silver, turning the world into something unreal, so I felt I moved within a dream as I raced after him.

He was already at Louisa's door, pounding on it, screaming, "Help me!" and all I could think was that he must not open it. He must not see that she wasn't there. In panic, I grabbed his shoulder.

He twisted, screaming, and threw me off so violently I fell and hit my head, and then he dashed down the hall, stopping at the end of it, whirling around, his hair flying, nightshirt flapping at his shins. He scrambled to another door, pounding, rattling the knob, screaming, "Let me in! Let me in, damn you! They're coming for me! Let me in!" That door opened; he darted inside.

I heard someone run up the stairs. It was Mr. Calina, fully dressed. "What is it? What's going on?"

I gestured limply to the bedroom Julian had disappeared into. "He's not himself. He's not awake."

Mr. Calina frowned. "What?"

"He's having a nightmare."

From inside the bedroom came a cry, high and pathetic, like the mewling of a child.

"A nightmare? You mean he's sleepwalking?"

"I'm afraid he'll hurt himself." Two months ago, he'd smashed a chair to pieces. Before that, he'd broken a window at a hotel and threatened to cut his own throat. "Please."

I had no idea what I was asking him, what the *please* was for, but Mr. Calina went into the room, and I followed, tenderly probing the bump on my head, relieved that there was no blood. Julian cowered against the far wall, cringing to avoid imaginary blows.

Mr. Calina grabbed his arm, and Julian turned into a dervish of biting, scratching, and hitting. "Go away! Stay away, foul spirit! I won't go with you! I won't!"

Mr. Calina swore beneath his breath, grappling with Julian, trying to gain hold.

I heard a commotion at the door, and turned to see Bayard in a dressing gown, with Louisa in that green-and-blue robe standing behind him. "Oh, Addie," she murmured. Julian had these spells several times a year; it seemed a cruel twist that he might have one now, our first night with Bayard, when we needed so to stay.

"What is it?" Bayard demanded.

"Night terrors," Louisa said. "He has them sometimes."

"Christ," Bayard said.

I looked for irritation, impatience. I expected dismissal.

"He sees what others cannot," Louisa went on with that admiration I resented. "A higher realm."

Julian twisted again in Mr. Calina's hold, trying to escape. Mr. Calina's hand slipped, and Julian tried to bite him. Calina cried out, shoving Julian brutally against the wall, then slapping him so hard that Julian's head snapped around.

"What are you doing?" I cried. "Don't hurt him!"

Mr. Calina released Julian too abruptly, so he stumbled. I rushed to him before he fell.

Julian blinked, suddenly awake and confused. He grabbed at me for balance. "What? What is it?"

"You were sleepwalking," Mr. Calina said.

Julian rubbed his jaw, puzzled, hurt, like a child. "Did you *hit* me?"

I glared at Mr. Calina before I studied Julian's cheek. It was hard to tell in the moonlight, but I thought it was bright red. "I told you I didn't want him hurt."

"He tried to bite me," Mr. Calina said.

"Don't be so hard on Mr. Calina, Addie," Louisa said. "He doesn't know to do anything different." When I looked at her in question, she explained, "He grew up in the slums—with gang boys, no doubt. You can't blame him for doing what comes naturally."

Louisa had never mentioned Giovanni Calina before this morning, when we'd seen him on the boat. Until then, I had not known he existed. But she seemed to know a great deal about him. Then again, he was Bayard's secretary. She would have seen him every time she'd visited Bayard.

Mr. Calina's expression was stony. "Forgive me. I thought only to help."

I said, "I don't know what you learned with your gang boys, Mr. Calina, but I assure you that in civilized society, such barbarism is not in the least acceptable."

"It is not," agreed Bayard. "I had no idea you had such a fearsome right, Vanni. Remind me of that the next time I'm asked to put forward a contestant for a boxing match. How do you feel, Estes?"

Julian was still rubbing his jaw. "I hope I still have my teeth."

"If I'd meant to hit you hard, they would be on the floor," Mr. Calina said.

Louisa laughed. "My, how wonderfully crude, Mr. Calina! You do make my blood run cold. Tell me, did you often play at fisticuffs in the gang? I suppose you stole things too. I hear that gang boys even commit murder for pay."

"I couldn't say." He bit off the words. "I was never a gang boy. I was in a monastery."

"A monastery?" Julian asked with a frown. "You meant to take vows?"

"You? A monk?" Louisa laughed again. "You do seek out the impossible, don't you, Mr. Calina? A monk, a secretary, a writer . . . I suppose that next you'll tell us you intend to be king of England."

"The British have lost their taste for papist kings, Loulou," Julian said. "Even they know better than to put their faith in a man who wears a pointy hat."

"Like a witch!" Louisa taunted.

Mr. Calina's jaw tightened. "You should take that back, Estes."

Julian snorted. "If you choose to be offended by the truth, I cannot stop you. I've no patience with men so intellectually crippled that they make incense and idolatry a god."

Mr. Calina started toward Julian, and I came between them quickly, pressing my hand to Calina's chest, pushing him back. "We are not in the streets of London, Mr. Calina."

"Temper, temper, Vanni." Bayard's voice was light, but I heard the threat beneath it. "Keep going, and it won't be Julian you'll be fighting."

Giovanni Calina glanced at Bayard, and then obediently, and obviously resentfully, stepped back.

"My pardon," he said tightly. "Your luggage is downstairs."

"Well, bring it up," Bayard said, and I was relieved that he said nothing of our leaving. "You can't expect the ladies to carry their own trunks."

I could almost see Mr. Calina's hackles rise. "As you wish."

He went out of the room. Bayard shouted after him, "What took you so long anyway? You were to come right back."

I heard a murmur of an answer. Bayard scowled.

Louisa said, "No doubt he stopped in a tavern along the way."

Bayard shook his head. "He has a new ladylove, but I told him not to visit her tonight."

"A ladylove?" Louisa asked. "I can hardly believe it."

"I hope he manages his temper better when he's with her," I said.

"He can be hotheaded," Bayard admitted. "But he means well. And for all his sins, he's the only man I've known who can consistently read my handwriting, so . . . well, I suppose it's late. Are you all right, Julian?"

"Exhausted," Jules said. "I'm afraid I'll collapse if I don't get to bed. I apologize for disturbing you. It's a damnable affliction, but I've had it most of my life."

"You mustn't apologize." Louisa glowed with that reverence she reserved particularly for him. "Not all men have the sensitivity for such feeling."

I had no patience for it tonight. I took Julian's arm. "We should say good night—"

"What were you seeing?" Bayard asked Julian. "Was it a higher realm, as Louisa said?"

Julian perked at Bayard's obvious interest. "I believe so. Sometimes I see angels. Other times, demons or ghosts. Often it's quite terrifying. But it can be splendid as well."

"Can you visit it at will?"

"Sadly, no. I confess I've spent a lifetime trying. I've caught mere glimpses of it, but I'm convinced it is the realm where all our mysteries might be known. If I could find a way to see more, to stay . . . I believe I would find the same transcendence that Coleridge and Shelley found."

"You're saying they saw it too?" Bayard asked. "How do you know that?"

"You can tell by their poetry. It's obvious they've communed with the sublime. Such a thing hardly exists in this world, but in the other—I think it the realm of poets."

"What of Byron?"

"Byron is too much of the earth. He cared more for men than spirit." The words seemed to leach the last of Julian's strength.

Bayard pressed, "I have a hundred questions—"

"Tomorrow," I told him, though I was grateful that he was fascinated instead of horrified. If Julian did not sleep after this, the next days would be unbearable for his depression and irritability. "For now, I think it best that Julian rests."

Bayard bowed his head in agreement. "Tomorrow, then."

I led Julian away. I had no idea if Louisa went with Bayard back to his room or to her own. I was too tired to care.

I crawled into bed, and Julian curled into me, burrowing into my arms. He was asleep within moments. But I lay awake, listening to the rhythm of his soft breathing, holding him close against the demons in his dreams, which, despite what he'd said tonight, had never seemed benign or angelic. Nor had I ever heard him say that these terrors belonged to any realm of poets. I would have thought it all simply talk meant to impress Bayard, but for the expression I'd seen on my sister's face that told me she had heard these things before.

There was a time when Julian would have confided such ideas to me, when we had talked far into the night of ideals and philosophies, and of his belief that poets were the conduit to the divine. But now my despair bewildered him. Neither of us knew how to move past it. He'd said it earlier tonight. *Where have you gone?* The problem was that I couldn't tell him. I did not know the answer.

FIVE

VANNI

Usually, I was awake at dawn to keep my daily appointment with Lac Léman and the rowboat, and an hour or so of drifting lazily about the sunrise. Bayard was rarely up before noon, preferring to write until the wee hours, and then fall into a stupor of a slumber. But I'd been awake for nearly forty-eight hours by the time I lugged the trunks of our guests upstairs—two of them, and two carpetbags, which I'd had to haul on my own to the boat because every porter at the d'Angleterre was somehow miraculously busy, and that only after I'd spent two hours haggling with the desk clerk. Estes had not yet paid the bill, and they wouldn't release the luggage until I'd signed Bayard's guarantee. The trunks were so heavy that the rowboat nearly swamped when a breeze came up, and so, for my own safety, I'd put in at Orsini's to wait out the wind.

I was there for hours. Well, what could I do? The breeze was still stiff, and it would have been churlish to refuse supper, especially as I'd previously accepted the invitation. When I realized I'd been seated next to Colburn—who was disagreeably persistent about his proposition—I wished I'd done as Bayard requested and stayed away. But then came Madame Brest, and her delightful voice and light hand on the pianoforte, and I admit I lost track of time. I could not leave in the middle of her recital. Nor could I resist her invitation to walk in the garden, especially as it had been offered with a winsome, wistful gaze.

It was nearly one by the time I arrived back at the Diodati, and later still when I finished half dragging, half hoisting the luggage up the hill to the villa. Then, of course, there was Julian Estes's sleepwalking, and all the rest . . . the memory of it still irked the next morning as I lay in my narrow bed, staring at the ceiling. I'd been shocked to realize that Miss Wentworth and Estes, though obviously unmarried, were sharing a room. I'd seen a great deal of scandalous behavior since I'd been in Bayard's employ—married men with mistresses and wives cuckolding their husbands, and a multitude of other combinations—but never such an unapologetic and unrepentant flaunting of sin. They were Free Lovers, I remembered, but I'd never met one before, and I had only a hazy idea of what it meant. Something about abolishing marriage and making love to whomever you wanted whenever you wanted, wasn't it? The monks who'd taught me would be horrified to find me in such company. I wondered how long they meant to stay, and then wondered if I could feign illness and keep to my bed all day to avoid them.

I was studying a crack in the wall that did not bode well for winter, when there was a perfunctory knock—really just a rattling of the knob before it opened—and Bayard pushed inside. I don't think he had ever bothered to wait for me to say "come in." The only boundaries Bayard respected were his own.

He was wearing his burgundy dressing gown over shirtsleeves and trousers, and his feet were bare. In his hand, he carried a sheaf of papers. "Still abed? It's nearly noon."

"I was up late. Why are you awake? Were you swimming?"

He shook his head ruefully. "Better to abstain from that for a while, I think. I want no one else to suffer that boy's fate, and besides, Louisa is exercise enough. You'll need to manage the maid, by the way. She heard the screaming last night. I think she believes us all madmen."

"She half believed it already."

"Well, reassure her, will you? You're good with her, and she looked at me as if I were a monster this morning when I grabbed the vacherin for breakfast." He threw the papers onto my chest. "There are fifteen pages for you to transcribe and send off to Hanson. That should ease your deadline concerns for a time."

"*Fifteen?* You're not human, you know. Did you make a deal with the devil when I wasn't looking?"

A laugh. "He and I are boon companions already. But this time, it so happens that I was inspired."

"I see." I sat up, grabbing the papers before they could spill to the floor. "Are her breasts still perfect?"

A lifted brow of assent. "Fuller than I remember, too."

I glanced toward the wall separating his bedroom from mine. "Is she sleeping?"

"Returned to her room with the dawn," he said, idly picking up my hat from where I'd left it on the dresser, turning the brim in his hands. "Actually, I kicked her out so I could work. She was none too happy about it."

"Yes, I remember her 'none too happy.'"

"She didn't throw anything this time."

"She's no doubt still on her best behavior."

"About behaviors—" He paused, distracted, frowning at the hat. "Is this real beaver? Do I pay you enough for that?"

"I bought it on credit."

"Ah." He put the hat aside. "You should be careful, you know. Debt collectors are persistent as gnats, but more pernicious. Did you have to hit Julian so hard last night?"

"He tried to bite me. What else was I to do?"

"How about watch your damnable temper. He was sleepwalking."

"I was tired."

He accepted that. "Try to keep from further offending them, will you? I've never met anyone like Estes. I actually like listening to him, which may be a first. And by the way, he doesn't know about me and Louisa. I'd like to keep it that way for a time."

"If she keeps coming to your room it won't be long before he finds out."

"She's nervous about it. He's very protective, apparently. Thinks of her as a sister. And he's very high-minded—"

"I thought he was a Free Lover."

"Yes, well, apparently it's one thing to espouse such beliefs, and quite another to live them. Louisa's worried he won't approve, and given my reputation, she thinks it's possible he may form a dislike—or even an enmity—for me, which I'd rather he not. I don't wish to be fighting duels with him. Neither should you."

I nodded.

"In any case, I don't wish it to affect my friendship with him."

"You've just met. How is there a friendship?"

"I think it could be a fast one," he confessed. "So . . . keep quiet about it, will you? There's no harm in waiting until he and I know one another better."

"As you like," I said.

"What kept you last night? Why were you back so late?"

"The wind was up. I was afraid I'd lose their luggage—and myself too. I kept thinking of that drowning. So I sheltered at Orsini's."

"Hmmm." He regarded me skeptically. "I thought I told you there would be other nights to make love to Madame Brest?"

"The wind—"

"Given how inconvenienced I was, I hope it was worth it. Tell me you at least kissed her."

I couldn't admit that I hadn't, and so I said nothing, which, of course, was answer enough.

Bayard made a sound of exasperation. "Have I taught you nothing? The moon was out, I recall. Or weren't there enough stars to inspire you?"

"I was distracted by my obligation to bring the luggage."

He laughed. "Well, at least you amuse me." He turned to the door. "I'm going to get some sleep. Get to work on those pages, will you? We're going out on the boat this afternoon. Wake me if I'm not up by four."

He left, closing the door behind him, and I looked down at the pages, which were covered in his cramped, ill-formed scrawl, j's looking like t's that sometimes looked like fs, his mind working too fast to fully capture every word, so there were abbreviations, things half spelled out that I had to guess at. Transcribing it was like unlocking a puzzle that had a precious jewel at its center—and one that revealed how well my own writing suffered in comparison. *"Don't be so hard on yourself, Vanni,"* he said on the days he was feeling magnanimous. *"You've more than enough talent, if you weren't so lazy."*

Which only meant that I wasn't scrawling fifteen pages a night after spending most of it making love to my mistress. I barely wrote that amount in a week.

But my goal was to learn from him as well as to gain by his association, and the study of his writing was both fascinating and illuminating, so I sighed and hauled myself out of bed and got to work. I was glad of the excuse to leave our guests to their own devices too, because there was no doubt I was going to have to apologize again, and I was in no mood for Louisa's gibes—or Adelaide Wentworth's, for that matter. I'd preferred it when she was a quiet nonentity with a name I could not remember. I was coming to dislike her as much as I disliked her sister.

I had finished half Bayard's pages, and was writing a letter to my father—*my work is going well. Bayard and I are the closest of friends, and he respects my opinion on many things. You will be pleased to know I am learning a great deal*—when I heard voices in the hall. It was nearly four. My bedroom door opened, and Bayard called in, "Come on! We're going out."

I supposed there was no way to excuse myself. I wiped the pen and capped the ink and went to meet them just as Julian Estes and Adelaide Wentworth came down the stairs. The sight of them raised the memory of last night, provoking me all over again, until I remembered Bayard's admonition and ruthlessly tamped down my anger.

Louisa was already in the salon with Bayard. She went rushing to Estes. "Are you quite all right today, Jules?"

"Never better," he said, patting her hand affectionately. "I slept like the dead."

"Possibly a poor choice of words," I commented.

He frowned at me. "Why do you say that?"

My damnable mouth. Could I never just keep quiet? "Last night you said some spirit was chasing you. So the dead weren't sleeping, were they?"

"Is that what I said?" Estes asked Miss Wentworth. "I never remember."

"It was all that talk of the mist and the drowned man," she answered. "You're so sensitive about some things."

I didn't think I imagined the edge in her voice. Reluctantly, I said, "I apologize again for striking you, Estes. My temper sometimes gets the best of me."

"You mean often, don't you? It often gets the best of you," Bayard put in, very droll. "My friends, shall we go? The boat awaits."

"Can we all fit?" Louisa asked. "It seemed quite small."

"I don't mean the rowboat. I've rented a sailboat for the summer. It's moored a short ways out. It will be tight, but I think we can manage."

"Perhaps someone should stay behind." She looked pointedly at me.

Bayard ignored her and glanced out the window. "We should hurry, before those clouds over the mountains decide to descend."

The day smelled of the budding lavender near the door, and squirrels chittered warnings as we went across the lawn to the trees that signaled the start of the path, their leaves rustling in the very stiff breeze. It would be a good day to sail, as long as those clouds Bayard had mentioned kept to their sentry over the Jura. We hurried down through fluttering, swaying vines and the sun-warmed pear scent of blooming grapes. The sky was a plummy blue, the water choppy and deep indigo. The cottager who lived below waved as we passed, calling out, "You'd best be careful! Looks like a storm!"

Bayard made a dismissive gesture. "We'll be back long before it starts. Unless any of you has an objection?"

"None at all," Estes said. "Lead on."

I rowed us out to the sailboat, and we set off. Bayard was an experienced sailor. I knew where all these ropes went when it was time to coil them up and put them away, but I had no idea what they actually did when they were in use, or how to manage them, and so all I could do was sit and enjoy the ride, which was fast and exciting, so that Louisa squealed and made a pretense of clutching Bayard's arm in delighted fear and then blushing like an ingénue embarrassed to have done so. No doubt for Estes's benefit, though I could not believe he didn't notice her infatuation with Bayard. If she wanted to keep it secret, she was doing a poor job of it. Estes and Miss Wentworth sat in the bow, and never were two lovers more determined not to touch each other. I wondered what was wrong between them, and again, uselessly, tried to recall that bit of gossip about him.

Bayard glanced measuringly at the sky. "We'll make it a short trip today."

Adelaide Wentworth lifted her face to the wind so the scab on her chin was obvious, as was the way it was spreading up her jaw. She clutched the ribbons of her hat to keep it from blowing off her head. "Must we really? I quite like it."

"You and your storms," Louisa said affectionately. "Do you remember that terrible thunder when we were crossing to England? Jules and I went to the cabin, but Addie stood on deck until the crewmen forced her to go below."

"I like the wild of it," Miss Wentworth confessed—which was a surprise, given her placidity. Then again, she had not been so placid last night when she confronted me.

"I like it myself," Bayard agreed. He stood, one hand on the rudder, so the wind blew his dark hair from his face.

"How Byronic you look," Louisa teased. "Why, you could almost be the man of all the rumors."

"The rumors don't know the half of it," he said dryly.

"Oh, tell us!" Louisa said, laughing. "Tell us which of them is true."

"I don't know them all," he said.

"Very well, I shall list them. Let me think . . . oh, here's one! They say you killed an army captain in the middle of the street while his wife looked on."

"True," Bayard said. "It was a duel, and he insulted me greatly. He asked his wife to witness because he thought I might forgive him if she was there. I didn't."

"You kept a live tiger in your London house."

"Just a cub, and only for a few days, until its owner rescued it."

"It didn't want to eat you?" Estes asked.

Bayard grinned. "Of course it did. I'm very tasty, or so I've been told."

Miss Wentworth blushed. Estes laughed.

"You had a masquerade and invited only women. Two dozen of them, and they had to dress as harem girls, and dance with swords, and then you had . . . Oh, I can't say the rest," Louisa put her hand to her eyes as if the very thought of it were mortifying.

Bayard made a face. "No, but I wouldn't mind it being true. Though two dozen is too many even for me. One must take exhaustion into account."

"And jealousies," Estes joked. "One should not encourage women to fight when they are armed with swords."

Bayard laughed with him, the way I heard him laugh sometimes at the salons. Joyfully and freely, with men of his own station. He had never laughed like that with me, no matter how amusing he claimed to find me.

"Another one," Louisa went on, this time in challenge. "You seduced Marie Arsenault's sixteen-year-old daughter."

Bayard stilled.

"Loulou," Miss Wentworth admonished. "That is really too much."

Louisa seemed not to sense her misstep. "It's what Arsenault says, you know. She tells it to everyone, or so I've heard."

"You should not believe all you hear," I said quietly.

No matter that it was true. And it wasn't Marie's daughter, but her stepdaughter, whom she'd offered up as a prize in one of the stupid games she and Bayard used to play, each trying to outdo the other for outrageousness. *"She was no virgin,"* Bayard defended himself when Marie decided to be incensed over it, though it was clear he was troubled and ashamed by the whole thing, and he couldn't deny—at least not to me, who'd been his confidant throughout—that he'd lusted after the girl for weeks.

Estes said, "Well, I don't believe it."

"I think you are far less wicked than everyone says," Miss Wentworth said, very stalwart.

Bayard threw me a glance and smiled thinly. "You should not be so certain. I have a perverse nature. The depths to which I have sunk would horrify anyone. God knows I've danced with demons more often than I like to say."

"Jules used to try to summon demons," Louisa said, then, when her sister gave her a startled look, "Hasn't he told you, Addie? Tell her, Jules."

"I did," Estes admitted. "When I was young. I had grimoires and incantations."

"Did anything work?" I asked.

He shook his head. "I should have known you then, Bay, as you and Satan seem to be on a first-name basis. But I did almost blow up my room at school in trying."

Bay. It was the nickname used only by Bayard's most intimate friends. I had never dared it. I had missed a great deal of camaraderie last night, it seemed.

"You blew it up? Truly?" Bayard asked.

"Nearly. I was inspired. A few nights before, I'd seen the will-o'-the-wisp. When I was a child, I fancied it the calling card of demons."

"The souls of unbaptized or stillborn children," I put in. "That's what I've heard."

"Not that." Miss Wentworth spoke with quiet horror. "That would be too cruel."

Estes sobered; he and Louisa exchanged a glance, and Louisa said, "Of course it's not true, Addie. Is that what your pope tells you, Mr. Calina? That innocent children should be punished for eternity?"

"I only meant that perhaps Estes was not calling exactly what he imagined," I said, irritated.

"Vanni, let Jules tell the story," Bayard scolded.

My face heated. I looked out toward the mountains. Those ominous clouds were sliding quickly down the slopes and over the water. Too quickly. The air held the moist, heavy feel of just before a storm. But I said nothing. It wouldn't be welcomed in any case.

"I decided that if I could duplicate the phenomenon, it would draw demons to me—a calling card of my own, so to speak," Estes continued with a mischievous smile. "I had a laboratory of sorts in my room, which quite alarmed my schoolmates. What can I say? They had no spirit of adventure. I was trying different combinations of gases and *boom!* A ball of flame! It made a wreck of the ceiling, as well as melting my eyelashes and my eyebrows, and burning off all the hair on my arms."

Bayard chuckled. "You must have looked a proper madman."

"You could say that. Certainly my father thought it was so in truth. He tried to have me committed."

"Committed? You mean to a madhouse?" Bayard asked.

"Must we speak of him?" Miss Wentworth asked. "I don't wish to ruin the day."

Estes ignored her. "I confess that during my experiments, I half feared I might summon my father instead. It wouldn't surprise me to discover he's a demon."

The wind gusted, and the boat heeled hard enough that I was almost thrown over. Miss Wentworth cried out. Louisa lost her balance, sliding off the seat, across the cockpit. I grabbed her just in time to keep her from falling over the side.

Bayard swore and loosened the line. The boat righted. Louisa gasped, "Don't touch me!" and scrambled out of my arms as if I were one of the devils we'd been speaking of, instead of a man who'd just saved her from plunging into the lake.

"You and I have something in common then." Bayard took up the conversation again as if he hadn't just nearly tumbled us all into Lac Léman. "But it's not my father who torments me—though I won't forgive him for dying young and leaving me to the mercy of my mother and my British relations. Pious Protestants, every one. Nothing worse. My mother never tried to have me committed, but she did a great deal of praying for my soul. I suppose it's good that someone does."

As if to accent his words, lightning zigzagged across the peaks. A crack of thunder made us all jump.

Bayard's good humor died abruptly. "We'd best head back. Coming about—watch the boom!" He swung the rudder, turning us into the wind, which gusted again just at that moment, slamming into the boat and grabbing the sail. As before, the boat heeled, water coursing over the side, soaking my trousers. I cursed and pulled back, bracing my feet to keep from falling. Bayard gained control and gave the sail more slack. It eased slightly.

The clouds were moving fast, churning, rolling furiously over themselves in an attempt to erase every inch of blue in the sky. The storm arrived with the kind of speed for which Lac Léman was famous. Again, I thought of the poor boy who'd drowned in a quiet harbor clouded with mist. This was more dangerous by far.

Louisa looked frightened, Estes terrified.

"Are you taking us *into* the storm?" he asked.

"It's the quickest way back," Bayard explained.

There was another flash of lightning, which lit the pines of the Jura eerily, and then grumbling thunder that seemed to ricochet and echo from every peak. The sail grabbed with another gust; again the boat heeled.

"Hold on," Bayard said. "Vanni, see to Louisa."

"I don't need him," she said, instead grabbing the side of the boat with a death grip.

Lightning struck again, turning the lake into a blinding glare. Thunder cracked, just overhead, followed by a roar as the clouds opened up. Rain drenched us all within moments, pocking the water and turning the sail into sodden, snapping canvas.

Bayard's eyes gleamed, demonic, flashing, so it was suddenly hard to believe he *hadn't* trafficked with Satan. He lifted his head and laughed, letting go of the ropes and the rudder, leaving the boat directionless as he leaped to his feet, howling like a madman—a primal sound that made my hair stand on end. He dragged off his coat, throwing it to the deck. His shirt was immediately plastered to his skin. Again, he howled, and then he raised his arms, shouting, "Do what you will, you merciless monster!"

He had a talent for the stage. I admit even I felt the drama of it.

Estes and Louisa looked stunned. Miss Wentworth's already-pale face was white, and with her very dark eyes and hair, she seemed drained of color. But she didn't look afraid. She looked . . . enraptured, caught in the spell of him.

"Julian can't swim," Louisa said urgently, grabbing Bayard's arm.

Bayard spun around. "Jules! Have no fear. If the boat overturns, I'll save you!"

Estes shouted back, "I'd rather drown than have you drag me to shore like a child!"

Again, Bayard laughed. The air pulsed with energy, and he was both its source and its worshipping congregation, an excitement that was catching. I felt it surge in my own blood, and then—astonishment of astonishments—Adelaide Wentworth broke from Estes's arms and leaped to her feet as Bayard had done. She threw back her head and screamed at the clouds, but there was no exultation in it. Only a heart-wrenching grief and anger, a kind of piercing, impossible rage that startled me. What would cause that kind of pain?

Bayard howled again. Then Louisa—of course, of course she would be next—did the same, leaving me and Estes to stare, and then Estes joined them, and finally . . . well, it became too much to resist. I jumped to my feet, and screamed out to the heavens, raging at everything I was and everything I wanted, everything I feared I would never be, so we were a boat full of lunatics shouting into the rain while the lightning and thunder raged and the waves crashed against the sides and the treacherous lake threatened to take us under.

SIX

ADELAIDE

We raced back to the house in darkness and pouring rain, blundering through dripping vines and slipping on the muddy trail. At the crest, the villa was a hulking, menacing shadow.

"'Quoth the Raven, "nevermore,"'" said Bayard in a spooky voice that made the rest of them laugh. It only raised a shiver up my spine and made me feel more intently the lingering fragments of rage and grief that had overtaken me on the boat.

Mr. Calina opened the door and turned on the gas, but its light did not stretch beyond the sconce; the voluminous emptiness of the room beyond swallowed it. We tromped inside, skidding in our wet, filthy shoes, dripping puddles on the parquet.

"We'll meet in the salon once we've changed," Bayard announced, clapping his hands together, rubbing them like some king with a nefarious plan. "I've got a surprise."

"What is it?" Louisa asked. "Do tell me!"

He shook his head; I wondered if he had forgiven her yet for her question about Marie Arsenault. How foolish she was sometimes.

"Ten minutes!" Bayard said. "Jules, as you did not drown out there, you can thank me by bringing up some wine. Vanni, fetch our dinner. I think there's a strawberry tart too. We'll have a picnic next to the fire."

Outside, the wind screeched. Rain dashed against the windows, and beyond, the lake was a tossed shadow touched with bits of glowing white foam, roaring with the crash of waves on the rocky beach.

Julian went to fetch the wine, and Louisa and I went upstairs.

I said quietly, "What were you thinking, to ask him about Marie Arsenault's daughter?"

"I thought he loved me enough to tell me."

"Perhaps he might have if you were alone, but why would he admit such a thing in front of all of us?"

"Because he likes Jules so much already. Don't you see? He wants to be his friend, and friends confess their sins to each other."

"Not always," I said.

She gave me a puzzled look. "Of course they do."

"They've only just met, Loulou. It's early for confession."

"Only because you keep Julian from being himself." At my frown, she explained, "He is too anxious about you."

I would have said that Julian was as much himself as he had ever been. He had not changed in the least, was that not the problem?

"He hardly laughs," she went on. "He's always watching for your reaction. He is afraid to upset you."

"Truly, it amazes me, Louisa, how quick you are to take his side."

"I'm not taking any sides. But your melancholy will drive him away and then what will we do? You should be glad that I'm here to remind him why he should keep us."

We had reached the top of the stairs. She gave me an apologetic look and hurried to her room before I had an answer. I stood in the hallway, staring at her closed door. Louisa was not given to reason; that she saw this so clearly surprised me. Or was it simply another one of her rationalizations, an excuse for behavior she did not want to admit was wrong? I no longer knew. Since we'd left Concord, I felt my sister sometimes as a stranger. We had always balanced each other, but the balance now was off, swung sideways, flung upside down. I no longer knew what equilibrium felt like; I could not find it in either of us.

I went to my room and peeled off clothes that clung wetly and persistently, changing into a dry chemise. I looked down at the sodden pile, wondering idly what to do with it, if the maid would take it or if I should hang the clothes to dry, and then the door opened and Julian came inside. He looked at me, standing nearly naked as I was, holding my gown. The walls rattled with thunder. Lightning flashed. The storm again, offering release or succor or rage, and I thought: *Just take me. Don't let me resist. Make me feel something. Make me want you again.*

"I was afraid out there," he said with a weariness that made me want to cry, and I waited for him to reveal his fears so I could reveal my own. I waited for him to ask me what I'd felt when I'd screamed on that boat. More than that, I wanted him already to understand, and to offer me comfort.

But he did none of those things. He took off his coat, his shirt, letting them fall to the floor. It was so familiar, so many times we'd left a trail of clothing strewn across the room, too impatient to be in one another's arms, and I wondered if he thought about that too. But no, he went to his trunk and fumbled with the lid, his fingers trembling, and I knew the storm was in his head, the waves splashing over the side, the boat rocking, sails useless, the boy who'd drowned.

"Julian—"

"Only a little," he assured me as he took out the laudanum. The bottle was opaque brown, and I could not tell how much remained, nor did I know what he would do once it was gone. We had so little money, surely he would give it up then? He took a sip and then another, and then he returned to where he'd left his coat on the floor and rifled through it for his flask, which he refilled.

I waited for him to change. He put the flask in his pocket, then helped me with the buttons on my gown, both of us silent, his knuckles warm as they brushed my back, a touch that made me shiver with something I didn't understand, the memory of desire, perhaps, or perhaps revulsion; I was no longer good at telling them apart.

A fire leaped in the hearth. The gas was turned down low, so the room was mostly dark, but the flames sent our shadows cavorting along the walls. A pot was on the tea table, and the room smelled of thyme and butter. There was also a loaf of bread and a glistening strawberry tart that made me think of Louisa's gift of the berries yesterday, one of those little gestures that reminded me that my sister loved me, and at the same time made me feel churlish that I never thought of such kindnesses.

Wine had already been poured. Mr. Calina sat in a chair flanking the fire. Bayard poked at the logs, raising sparks. Louisa watched him too avidly from her place on the settee. I thought of cautioning her, but I would only draw attention to it, which I did not want, given my promise to keep her affair with Bayard secret.

The light played eerily over Bayard's prominent nose and Louisa's shining forehead, Mr. Calina's gleaming dark hair and the jeweled and gilded baubles on his watch chain. I'd rarely seen one so heavily decorated. As Jules and I entered, Bayard turned and smiled. "Good, we're all here. Come, have some of Lise's veal stew. Apparently it's her specialty."

Mr. Calina spooned up the stew, chunks of veal in a creamy broth studded with carrots, and I took a bowl each for myself and Julian. Louisa refused hers, and she was restless, tapping her foot. I knew the signs. The last time she'd evidenced them had only been a few weeks ago, and I'd had to beg the dressmaker not to call the police. It had taken all my persuasion, and a half day of cleaning the shop, as well as a promise never to return, to make the woman forget Louisa's destruction. All because the clerk had refused to order one hundred gross of ribbon, another of Louisa's ruinous fancies. One hundred gross, ridiculous by any measure. What would we have done with such an amount?

"You should eat, Loulou," I warned.

"Oh, I could not. I'm too impatient for Bay to start."

"Start what?" Julian asked, sitting next to Louisa. There was a time when he would have drawn me down beside him, unable to keep from touching me even a moment. But there was no room with the two of them; I had to sit on the settee opposite.

Bayard put the fire poker aside and reached for a book on the mantel. "I have here the very ghost tales that inspired *Frankenstein*. The *Fantasmagoriana: Tales of the Dead*."

As if in response, there was a sudden dash of rain against the window. We all started.

"The very same?" Louisa asked.

Bayard's blue eyes looked black in the dimness. "Close to it, anyway. This is the English version. Most of the stories are the same. None of you object, I hope. No one's afraid of a few ghost stories? I doubt they're nearly as frightening as Julian's visions."

Louisa said, "Oh please! Read them."

"Absolutely," Julian agreed, his own eyes gleaming in anticipation.

I had no idea if Bayard knew already of Louisa's fondness for ghost stories, if he'd done this to please her. She and Julian were alike in that, which I'd always thought odd, given his very real night terrors. He and my sister often spent hours together, shivering and laughing nervously over some macabre tale or another, making spooky voices, jumping at shadows until the early hours. It was not a game I liked. The world was full enough of horrors; I wanted no others. I'd often gone to bed tense and wary, listening to them terrify one another, waiting for disaster.

Bayard turned to me. "Adelaide?"

"Oh, don't say no, Addie," Louisa begged. "You've three strong men here to protect you from any ghouls."

I gave her a thin smile. "Then how could I possibly object?"

Bayard flipped the book open, scanning the first pages. "Where shall I start? Which story strikes your fancy? 'The Death-Bride'? 'The Family Portraits'? Or perhaps 'The Spectre-Barber'?"

"I have a horror of portraits," Julian said with a shudder, glancing about the walls, which held gory landscapes. Against the far wall was one of a bullfight; over the mantel a scene of men charging into battle.

"Really? Remind me to show you the portrait gallery down the hall," Bayard said.

Julian laughed. "You mean to terrify me, my friend, I can see that. So by all means, read 'The Family Portraits.'"

"Gather close," Bayard said.

He stood with the fire behind him, which cast his shadow huge and flickering against the opposite wall while the windows also reflected his image, so his dark shadow seemed to have a heart of a man caught in flame.

The night flashed bright and blue with lightning, a pealing crack of thunder made Louisa shriek with delight, and Bayard smiled and began the tale, lowering his voice and infusing it with feeling and inflection, a powerful delivery that held us all in his spell.

He told the story of an ancient house, of a large and terrible portrait that hung alone, and the family tradition that said it had been painted by the Dead. They had tried several times to plaster over the picture, but by the next day, the colors came through again, rendering it as distinctly as it had been before, vibrant and untouched. The ghost of the portrait roamed the house. A kiss from it in the night sealed the fate of those who received it, and that fate was Death.

Louisa and Julian hung on Bayard's every word. Mr. Calina was listening, but he was also staring into the fire, seemingly unmoved. Now and then, a clap of thunder had both my sister and Julian jumping.

Louisa's frightened giggle held the too-familiar touch of hysteria. I watched her warily.

The story wound to a close, the mystery solved, a piece of parchment found behind the painting that presented the means to end the curse: two families must be joined. As it was a circumstance already in progress, the daughter in love with the neighbor's son, the curse was lifted, and as for the portrait: "'. . . it was no longer perceptible; the colours, figure,—all had disappeared; not the slightest trace remained.'"

Bayard's voice fell into hushed silence. He was as good reading a story as he was writing one; he knew just the right effect.

The wind and rain whipped against the window.

Louisa clapped her hands, breaking the spell, and Julian laughed. "A happy ending! Though it was quite horrifying until then."

"I had not thought curses ever had happy endings," I said.

Julian's laughter died abruptly. In the next moment, he looked so sad it startled me, and his voice was soft when he said, "You only torment yourself, Addie. And I cannot stand to see it."

How intimate were his words. What had he been thinking to say such a thing in company? It was unlike him. No doubt the laudanum had played some part. Then I realized that both Bayard and Mr. Calina were staring at us, obviously confused, and I was embarrassed at what they must be wondering.

Louisa spoke up quickly and brightly. "I shall not sleep a wink!" It was a deliberate distraction for which I was grateful. "Read another, Bay!"

Bayard obliged with "The Death-Bride," a tale about a lovely specter who roamed the land, trying to seduce men into betraying their lovers, so much unhappiness, such a thirst for misery, and suddenly I was no longer listening, but instead thinking of how Julian had told me that the lake mist was made of spirits ascending to become stars. But there had been no mist in Venice that morning when I found Emily floating in the canal, her dress tangled around our mooring post, caught as if she'd meant for me to discover her. And there had been no mist two days later, when I'd staggered home to our rented rooms, exhausted and undone, still swollen from the child I'd miscarried. I had never seen those ghosts, but I knew they never left me.

The clock on the mantel chimed midnight.

I started from my thoughts. "Where did that clock come from? It's never rung before."

I realized too late that I'd interrupted Bayard in the middle of a sentence. They all looked at me in surprise.

"I wound it when I built the fire," Mr. Calina said. "Usually neither of us remembers."

The chime faded into spooky silence. The room felt alive, as if it waited for something.

Then, sudden and loud, came the heavy creak of a tree branch, a *crash*.

Louisa cried out.

Julian leaped to his feet. "What was that? Did you see it?"

"See what? A tree branch breaking?" Bayard asked.

"There was a movement—" Julian hurried to the window. "There! Someone's out there!"

"No one would be out there on a night like this," Bayard said.

"Who is it?" Louisa raced over to Julian, clutching his arm. "Where?"

"It's gone. No—"

"It's a ghost!" Louisa cried, too sensitive always. "Oh, no . . . no, it's a demon! We were talking too much of it today. We've called it. I can feel how evil it is!"

This was what I'd feared might happen. "Louisa! Loulou, calm yourself—"

She screamed, which made Julian start and cry out as well.

Julian backed away from the window with a shriek, seizing the curtains and jerking them shut so fiercely the rings clattered on the rod. He grabbed Louisa and shrank against the wall.

"It's probably just one of those fanatics trying to see inside," Bayard said reassuringly. He looked pointedly at Mr. Calina, who protested, "It's pouring. No one's out there. You know it as well as I."

"There is someone out there. I saw it too!" Louisa's voice rose. "You must go out and send him away. What if he means to kill us in our sleep, or . . . or what if it's a ghost? Like the one in the story?"

"How am I to send a ghost away?" Mr. Calina asked in exasperation.

"I'll get my pistol," Bayard said.

"You don't mean to go out, do you? No, you mustn't. It wants you!" Louisa twisted in Julian's arms, pulling him closer.

Mr. Calina said, "For God's sake, there's no one out there. Enough of this. Bayard, you know how she is—"

Bayard glared at him, quite effectively silencing Mr. Calina, who turned away with a gesture of impatience.

"Oh, I know! I know what we should do! We'll all go together." Louisa lifted her chin bravely. "Yes, we must all go together. Otherwise, it will sneak in when someone's alone. Someone will be killed."

"Yes, all right," I said in my calmest voice. All I cared about was soothing her. I knew how well her hysteria could turn. Fighting would only make it worse. Once she had a notion in her head, there was nothing to do but agree. "All right, Loulou. We'll all go."

"Yes." Julian pushed from the wall, releasing my sister, who would not let him put her aside, still wrapping her hands around his arm, pressing into him. "Let's see what's out there."

The shadows in the room pulsed with fire, elongating, misshaping. My sense that the room was expectant heightened. The anticipation of danger was heady and catching. When Bayard went to his bedroom and emerged with two pistols, handing one to Julian, Louisa grabbed his arm too, so she was between them, and though her face was pale, her fevered excitement warned me not to stop this drama. Who knew what she would do? I would not risk it.

I followed them down the stairs. Bayard stopped abruptly when the maid appeared in the hallway, clutching a brass candlestick. She spoke to Mr. Calina in rapid French.

"She's heard the screaming," he said with a peeved glance at my sister. Then he answered the maid in French. It surprised me that he should know it.

Louisa said something to her too, short and impatient. My sister had a gift for languages, and had studied long after I'd given up.

Mr. Calina said, "You're not helping."

"We have to *go*," Louisa answered sharply. "Reassure her when there is something to reassure her about."

Mr. Calina murmured to the maid, who stepped back, not relinquishing the candlestick, and Bayard opened the door onto the patio. "Stay close."

The wind whooshed in, spattering us all with rain, nearly extinguishing the flame in the oil lamp Mr. Calina held. We went into the noise of the storm: the lashing waves of the lake, the squeaking branches, fire smoke heavy in the wind whistling through the eaves. A branch crashed to the ground before us. Louisa screamed and jumped back, and then laughed breathlessly. My heart began to pound.

We crept around the corner, staying close to the house, the light from the lamp barely visible in the darkness, illuminating nothing beyond ourselves. We were wet within moments.

"There!" Julian flung himself away from Louisa and fired. The world narrowed to a cloud of smoke, the smell of gunpowder, the whistle of the bullet into the trees. We all fell back into the wall, shocked, silenced. The hysteria that had gripped us dissipated as suddenly as it had begun. What were we doing but getting wet, traipsing out in the middle of a storm?

Mr. Calina wrenched the pistol from Julian's hand. "There's nothing there. No one's out here."

Julian bristled. "I tell you I saw something."

"A branch moving. The wind."

"There was someone," Louisa insisted. "I saw it too."

Bayard said slowly, "Well, whatever it was is gone." He took the gun from Mr. Calina. "Let's go back. It's madness to be out here tonight."

When we were safely inside, Louisa said in a trembling voice, "Lock the door." Mr. Calina obediently shoved home the bolt.

Wet and shaken, we went back into the salon, where the fire still burned.

"The book," Louisa said, pointing to the *Fantasmagoriana*. "It's moved!"

We all looked. The book was on the settee, open and face down.

"It was closed and on the table!" she insisted, turning to Julian. "Wasn't it?"

Julian said slowly, "I believe it was."

"Louisa," I said, squeezing Julian's arm hard. "No one touched the book."

Her gaze came to me. "No one?"

"No one," I confirmed.

I felt her weighing my words, a tremor of hesitation fighting with her longing to believe. Finally, she closed her eyes and took a deep breath, nodding.

It was over. I was relieved she'd listened to me, but at the same time I felt a growing impatience, that anger again that the burden of Louisa was mine.

Bayard laid both pistols on the table.

"It will be impossible to sleep now," Julian said, reaching for a glass of wine, gulping it. "Bay, read another story."

"Haven't we been frightened enough tonight?" Mr. Calina sank into the chair.

"Yes, another one!" Louisa's laughter was choked and half despair. "Let's not part from each other yet."

"Expecting a deathly kiss from a spirit?" Mr. Calina asked.

"Be careful, Vanni. The one who mocks is always the first to end up dead." Bayard picked up the *Fantasmagoriana* from where it splayed on the settee, snapped it shut, and laid it aside. "Does it occur to any of you that tonight mirrors that which inspired *Frankenstein*? The storm, the stories . . . even our own composition. Two women, three men."

"It must be a sign," Louisa said.

"Don't say that," I said tiredly. She'd caused enough drama for one evening. "It's not a sign."

"Perhaps we should do what they did," she went on, ignoring me.

"Drown in the Gulf of Spezia like Shelley? Or die at Missolonghi like Byron?" Mr. Calina asked. "Thank you, no."

"Oh, I don't mean that, of course. They had a contest, didn't they? A writing contest."

"None of them finished but for Mary Shelley and Byron's doctor," Bayard said.

"Mary Shelley clearly won," Louisa said. "No one remembers the doctor, or even what he wrote."

"'The Vampyre,'" Julian said. "He wrote 'The Vampyre.' Though everyone thought Byron had done it."

"How do you know that?" I asked.

"I read it. Long ago. What was his name? Poly-something. Pollydolly . . . Pollydorry . . ."

"Polidori," Bayard said.

Julian said, "Yes, that's it. The tale was interesting. He had some talent."

Mr. Calina glanced up. "Whatever happened to him?"

"I've no idea," Julian said. "Disappeared into obscurity."

"We should have a contest, just as they did." Louisa's insistence surprised me. The most writing she had ever done was in the journals we showed to our father once a week so he could correct our impressions and urge us always and forever to never settle for the commonplace. *"See what isn't there, my darlings,"* he would say. *"Look for what others do not notice.*" I'd been the one who'd longed to be a writer, but it had been years since I'd written poetry on the banks of the pond, my youthful ambitions suffocated by responsibility and obligation. They had been so unrealistic anyway. As a woman, what kind of life could I possibly have made of them?

"Why, Louisa?" I asked.

She gave me an impatient look. "For fun, Addie. For the sheer joy of it. Or is joy quite beyond you now? We'll all write a ghost story, and whoever wins gets—I don't know. What should the winner get?"

"We all know already who will win," Mr. Calina said gloomily.

"Bayard," Julian agreed. "It will hardly be a contest."

"I'll write with one arm tied behind my back if it helps," Bayard offered. "Go ahead, Jules, I dare you."

"What about me?" Mr. Calina asked. "Do you think me not worth challenging?"

Bayard shrugged. "Well, as you hardly ever put pen to paper . . ."

"I've been busy."

"Yes, with your little Portuguese," Bayard teased.

"Perhaps it will be me who wins," said Louisa. "Another woman. Just like Mary Shelley. Or Addie—oh, but no, Addie won't compete. She must be Julian's muse."

Her casual assumption that I would be content to be so, rankled, though it should not. She was right; it was what I must be, what Julian expected and needed. Any lingering wishes of my own had fallen away when presented with such a worthy substitute. Only a few months ago, I had wanted nothing more than to be his muse, especially as it had been coupled with his admiration and desire.

I forced myself to turn to Julian with a smile. "I shall do my very best to inspire you with this too."

He seemed taken aback. Had I really smiled so seldom that it should be shocking?

Louisa said, "There should be a deadline, don't you think? Should we say—oh, two months from tonight? We'll present our finished stories then."

It was so presumptuous that I could not believe she'd suggested it, at the same time I admired her daring.

Clearly, Mr. Calina felt it presumptuous too. "Two months?"

"Is that not enough time for you?" she asked archly.

"Why not? Two months it is," Bayard agreed.

Louisa smiled with satisfaction. I was relieved, and also astounded at what she'd won us. Two months in this house. Two months with Bayard Sonnier.

"We shall all start tonight," my sister said.

"I think it can wait until morning, don't you?" Bayard said, and she dipped her chin shyly and glanced away. Julian did not seem to note it.

Mr. Calina took up the empty bowls. "I'll put everything away and tend to the fire."

"Good night, then." Bayard got to his feet with a grin. "I'll see you all in the morning. Or possibly much later."

Louisa and Julian and I made our way up the stairs. I felt her excitement, her flurry to be in her room, to wait the breathless moments until everyone was settled, that she might fly back down the stairs and into Bayard's arms. Disaster averted, at least for tonight. I suspected she had no intention of writing a word. She only wanted the credit of it. From now, and for all time, she could say, *I'm the one who gave Bayard Sonnier the idea for his ghost story. He wrote it because of me.* A muse to his genius.

The only competition Louisa had entered into was with me.

Julian sat on the edge of the bed and pulled off his shirt. "Well, at least we're settled until the end of July. I cannot believe Louisa tried it, or that it worked. Sometimes I think she has missed her calling. She has an eye for opportunity." He didn't look at me as he went on, "I'm relieved you didn't take up the contest. It's better for us all, I think. Especially a ghost story. It might remind you of . . . unpleasantries."

Unpleasantries. The past was neither as trifling nor as easily banished as the word implied. I struggled every moment to keep from drowning in it. But I stopped myself from a nasty retort. A fight was not what I wanted. I had promised to try. "I'm content to be your muse."

He nodded as if he'd expected nothing less. "This contest could be what we've been waiting for. All I need is the right idea . . . In two months, I can surely impress him enough that he recommends me to his publisher."

He sounded excited, inspired, something I'd not heard in some time. I should not resent that it had been Louisa, and not me, who'd brought it about.

"Did we bring the Plato?" he asked.

"It's in my bag."

"Will you read to me tonight? Your voice and his words are just what I need. That argument between Diotima and Socrates . . . there's something there, don't you think? Or . . . perhaps the other realm? A demon in this world who finds his enlightened twin in the other . . . Doppelgängers, yes, of course. Perhaps there's something to work with in that—what do you think?"

This was what had drawn me in the beginning, this leap of ideas, the man Julian was when he was inspired, when he believed all things possible. I was reminded of the days we'd spent beneath the willow at the pond, when I'd read to him as he laid his head on my lap, and I'd woven my fingers in his hair, made gold by a sun dappling through swaying branches. He was never still for long; I would see a sudden flash in his eyes and feel his pulsing energy as he jumped to his feet, responding to something I'd read, speaking so quickly I could hardly understand him, arresting my laugh by falling to his knees before me, pushing me to the spongy bank. *How you inspire me. How I love you. I cannot live without you, surely you see that.*

Now I felt a shiver that told me I was not wrong to think I could reclaim what we'd had. It was still there in some measure. All it needed was this. All I must do was keep him in this mood . . .

"I'll get the Plato," I said, going quickly to my bag, finding the book. When I sat beside him, he leaned his head on my shoulder as I opened it to the pages he'd mentioned, and as I read I felt his excitement and his inspiration twist into desire.

He kissed my jaw, and then pulled me down to meet his lips. His arm went around my waist, pulling me close almost desperately. "This is what we are, Addie," he whispered. "With you, I feel I can do anything."

I struggled to dissolve into his touch as he stroked my hair, and when he dragged me back to lie beside him, I forced myself to relax, to let him do as he would. He was gentle, almost hesitant, every moment a question: *This? This?* And I let myself answer, *yes* and *yes*, though I was aware of a growing urgency within me, a rage that matched the fury and grief that had burst from me in the boat, responding not to Julian's touch or his urgings but to the whistling and screeching of the storm beyond the windows, which pushed and prodded as if it knew something I should know, as if it wanted me to look at something I could not face.

SEVEN

VANNI

The next morning, lying in the rowboat and listening to the caws of gulls and ducks as they dived for food, looking up at a dawn sky washed brilliantly clean by last night's storm—of which nothing remained but broken branches and leaves flung across the yard, and flotsam washed up on the lakeshore—I tried to think how to turn my novel into a ghost story for the contest. Then I realized: add a ghost, of course. Of a most miserable and moaning sort. Until now, Bayard's brilliance had inhibited my own, but now, well—why shouldn't I win the contest? I imagined Bayard's praise so well I could almost hear it: *"I knew you had it in you. I saw it from the start."*

It was almost enough to make me forget my irritation with Louisa's manipulations last night, and the way she'd managed two months of leeching off Bayard. How very clever. But I didn't mind the idea of a deadline. Perhaps it would serve as the prod I needed.

I hurried back to the villa in a flurry of excitement, scattering the birds poking through the storm's debris into a fluttering, flapping frenzy. I meant to go directly to my room to work, but I heard talk from the kitchen, Lise's high and panicked babbling, and Bayard's low-voiced answer. Why the hell should he be talking to the maid? She barely spoke English. Surely it couldn't be for carnal reasons; he'd been with Louisa all night. God knows I'd heard them into the wee hours—but then again, when had that ever stopped him before?

When I reached the kitchen, I was surprised to find that instead of Bayard opportuning Lise, it was she who had him backed into a corner.

"Vanni. Thank God," he said in relief, looking both haggard and provoked. "She's being damnably difficult. I've been trying to explain things to her, but I don't understand half of what she says."

"Explain what?" I asked warily.

"She says she's quitting. I came down this morning and she was packing." He gestured to a bag on the floor.

Lise said in heavily accented English, "I leave today."

"Why?" I asked her, but I already knew. Estes's night terrors. The screaming and shooting last night. She'd been ready to level us all with that candlestick when we came down the stairs. I had barely managed to soothe her.

But her answer was not the one I expected. "I will not work in a house of"—she struggled to find the right word—"a brothel."

"It's not a brothel, for God's sake," Bayard said. "They're friends of mine. Do you understand that? *Friends.* There's no whoring going on."

"She doesn't mean brothel," I said quietly. "She means indecency." I translated the word for her.

She nodded fervently. *"Oui."* She added, in French, "Screams in the night, and drinking and godlessness and women half-dressed . . . everyone knows what is going on in this house. My papa says I am not to work here anymore."

Bayard looked at me in confusion. "What's she saying?"

I sat at the table, noticing for the first time papers strewn next to last night's strawberry tart. "There's talk in town. Her father won't permit her to stay."

"Talk? Oh, for Christ's sake. They'd create a scandal of my eating a plum—I'll never escape it. How I hate all this gossip."

I didn't point out that he surely liked the fame that brought it well enough. "She's frightened too. I don't know how you could blame her. That first night, with Julian's screaming, she thought we were being murdered in our beds. Now, after last night . . . well, you saw her. She was nervous about working for you to begin with."

He let out a sound of frustration, and motioned Lise toward the door. "Go then, get out."

I translated—though I was a great deal gentler, and I told her I'd send her wages to her father. There was no point in unpleasantness; being frightened was hardly an offense.

She said to me, "I am very sorry, monsieur. You are kind." Then, with a quick curtsey, Lise grabbed her bag, hurrying out as if she feared Bayard might drag her back.

"Well, that's fine," I said, watching her go. "How are we to keep a houseful of guests without a maid? And for two months—you were mad to agree to that. You can't want Louisa here for that long."

"Why not?" he asked. "She's a passionate little piece."

"Your deadline—"

"Can you cook?"

"What? You aren't serious?" I could, but I was damned if I would tell him that. I refused to spend my days as more of a servant than I was already.

Bayard exhaled heavily, sitting across from me. He broke off a piece of crust from the tart, nibbling on it as he said, "No. Not really, anyway. Do you think we can find another girl?"

"It was hard enough to find her. They aren't clamoring to work for you, you know."

"Yes, I know. The demon seducer." He was morose. "I'm growing tired of that reputation."

"Think of how many admire you for it," I said, trying to make light of it, though I knew how it all troubled him: his bitch of an ex-mistress spreading nasty rumors, and his idiotic response—bedding every woman who came knocking—making everything worse, our hasty exile. We'd come here looking for quiet, but he wasn't good at it, too easily bored, too quickly melancholy when there was nothing to engage him. "I think there are special clubs for the horribly debauched, aren't there? You'll probably be invited to join."

"I've already been invited," he said, and then, at my raised brow, "I have. I went once. It was boring. Rich men playing at being dirty. Some whores in togas. A lot of sagging flesh and pretending to be harem lords. That kind of thing."

"I have no idea what 'that kind of thing' is."

"Count yourself lucky. When one starts relishing the thought of such scenes, it means there's no longer anything in the world that can please you."

There was weariness in his eyes as he said it, something I'd only just begun to see. Not for the first time, I wondered what he was searching for. Those early days with Marie Arsenault, I'd seen a happiness in him that told me that perhaps the famous, decadent Bayard Sonnier was simply hoping for what we all hoped for: love. Even, perhaps, a savior. His disillusionment when it was over had been so complete—and so shocking, given how cynical he was—that I had no choice but to believe it so.

He would laugh if he knew I felt sorry for him, and say something cutting, which was why I offered no comfort. "I'll see if I can find another maid, but it may take weeks. It was bad enough when it was just us. Now, when you add Free Lovers and godless madmen to it . . ."

"I'll admit it's a curious thing about Julian," Bayard said thoughtfully. "But I don't think it madness."

"Probably laudanum," I suggested. "Have you seen his eyes? I think that's what he keeps in that flask of his."

"Is it a curative or a cause? That's the question. He is a man of uncommon sensitivity, that's certain. I admire him for it."

I had never before heard him speak that way of anyone else; certainly such admiration had never been directed at me, as much as I longed for it.

Bayard rose and gathered the scattered papers into a neat pile. "Here. I was writing all morning. Not the novel, which I know you'll complain about, but I'll get to that. I had an idea for the contest. I came down to give this to you when you came in from floating about—yes, of course I know you're out there, don't look so surprised. Half the time I'm awake and staring at the damn ceiling. Anyway, I came down and that's when I found Lise shoving knives and things in her bag."

I forgot my jealousy. "She was stealing?"

"Metaphorically. Certainly there were knives in her eyes when she looked at me. I can hardly read the pages myself, so good luck with it. Now I *am* going to sleep."

I nodded, taking up the papers as he left. Twelve pages. Twelve! All of them filled with scrawl over scrawl, additions spiderwebbing across the page, down the margins, sentences crossed out and then circled, with *stet* written above them, though the original words were nearly impossible to read through the heavy overlining. Even so, I was caught with the first sentence. He'd used an epigraph from *Macbeth*: *"By the pricking of my thumbs, something wicked this way comes . . ."* and the story was of witches. *Macbeth* was his starting point, but nothing after belonged to Shakespeare. It was brilliantly warped into a tale that made me race through the pages. It was unfinished, ending just where I wanted more, every word perfect. Each one burrowing into my brain like some kind of worm, settling itself there in blazoned, taunting perfection.

How could I possibly write anything to compare with this? The morning's inspiration seemed childish and stupid. As much as I studied

Bayard Sonnier, as much as I tried to discern the reasons for his every deletion or insertion, to follow the train of his thought in the hopes that one day it would inform my own work, I was growing to believe it never would, that whatever talent I possessed—*talent!* What a joke!—was so inconsequential as to be nearly an illusion.

The knocker at the front door cut through my depression. No doubt one or another of Bayard's followers who hoped to be admitted to the chambers of the sacred author—well, I was in no mood for it. I went upstairs and threw open the door, angry words already on my tongue, before I saw it was a young man wearing Orsini livery.

He held out an envelope. "For Mr. Calina, sir."

For a moment, I wasn't sure I'd heard him correctly. No one from Orsini's ever asked for me. But that was my name, not Bayard's, written clearly upon the flap.

"I'm to wait for an answer, sir," the boy said.

I opened it, both confused and hopeful at the unfamiliar handwriting, my gaze dodging to the signature. *Vera Brest.*

I couldn't help smiling like an idiot. The message was short:

> *Please come to tea today. I shall be the most desolate*
> *of women if you decline.*

The boy waited.

"Tell Madame Brest that I accept, with pleasure."

He nodded and hurried off, and I went back downstairs to retrieve Bayard's pages from the kitchen.

Louisa Wentworth was already there. That she had just come from Bayard's bed was obvious. Despite the fact that I'd nearly killed myself hauling her trunk up a hill and two flights of stairs, she wore his blue-and-green robe, which was too big. She had rolled up the sleeves into fat cuffs that nearly swallowed her wrists. The lace of a chemise peeked at her slippered feet. She'd braided her hair, but it was loose and lumpy, as if she'd speedily tugged it together. She was also holding the pages.

"What has you looking so pleased with yourself?" she asked.

I tucked the letter into my pocket. "Walking about dressed like that is probably not the best way to keep Estes from suspecting where you spend your nights." I reached for the papers. "I believe those are mine—"

She swept them from my grasp. "Julian's seen me this way many times before. He won't think it unusual."

That surprised me—and shocked me too. "He has?"

"Traveling is expensive," she said impatiently. "Sometimes we all must share a room." But she didn't look me in the eye.

"I see."

"Bayard says the maid is gone."

Which reminded me that I didn't have time to bandy words with Louisa Wentworth. "Yes. Last night frightened her, and you didn't help by ordering her to quiet down and run off to bed." I gestured to the papers she still held. "Now, if you don't mind . . . I have a great deal of work to do before I go."

"Go? Where are you going?"

"I have an invitation for tea at Orsini's, so if you will please give those to me—"

"But Bayard promised to walk with me this afternoon."

"He's not going. The invitation was for me alone."

"You?" She was so incredulous it was insulting. "Oh, that's right. Your new love is staying there."

I wished to hell I hadn't said anything.

She tilted her head, surveying me critically. "She's Portuguese, isn't she? That's what Bayard said. That explains why she finds you appealing."

"What has that to do with anything?"

"She must be used to men like you where she comes from."

"Men like me?"

She shrugged. "Well, so dark and common and . . . *Catholic*. She probably doesn't realize that you're not really respectable."

I struggled to keep my temper. I held out my hand. "The papers, Louisa."

"You should call me Miss Wentworth."

"Why? We know each other better than that, don't we? And really, you're hardly respectable yourself, are you? Throwing yourself at debauched writers. Following men about whose names you don't know—"

"I did know your name," she protested, coloring. "Or I thought I did."

I snatched the papers from her hand. "It was days before you thought to make sure."

"You were happy enough about that," she countered. "You knew I thought you were Bayard, and you let me just believe—"

"You wanted to believe it."

She jerked back as if my words repulsed her. "You took advantage."

I laughed. "Not as much as I could have."

"You are the most disagreeable man I've ever known."

"I'm wounded. Truly I am."

"I have Bayard's ear, you know. I could make things very difficult for you, if I wanted."

As if she hadn't already. "I think you overestimate your charms."

"Poor Vanni, so desperate for his master's approval. So *devoted*. Like a little dog."

I glared at her. "Let me pass."

"He loves to throw you a bone now and then just to see you slaver. We've laughed about it many times."

This time, when I pushed by her, she allowed it.

"Are you leaving so soon?" she taunted. "I'd hoped you would make me breakfast. Bayard said you would. He told me that you could serve as our maid until you found another."

My step stuttered. The words pricked; I had no doubt Bayard had said them. "Go to hell. Make your own bloody breakfast."

"Oh, now I see the real Giovanni Calina revealing himself at last! You're just a vulgar cobbler's son. I wonder how long it will be before your new love sees it too?"

I clenched my teeth to keep from responding. Better not to let her see how her jab met its mark. It was all I could do to get up the stairs without a word.

Once I was in my room, I threw Bayard's papers onto my desk, staring at them sightlessly as scenes of a drippy and charmless London winter tripped before me like an endlessly tormenting magic lantern show. A steamy café, pages slipping from my hands to scatter over the floor—Bayard's name, my transcriptions—and Louisa Wentworth rushing over, kneeling in a billow of green-and-cream stripes, purple silk grapes jiggling on her hat with her every movement. *"Oh, let me help you."* Walking her home through an oily and stinking coal-smoke fog as the streetlamps faltered to sickly yellow life. Helpless in the face of her admiration, bewildered by the force of my hope and desire as she said, *"I would so like to see you again."* Trying to be honorable, forcing the words I didn't want to say, *"Perhaps you don't know who I am—" "I know everything I need to know."*

Better to forget it, to not think about what had almost been. I sat at my desk and took up Bayard's pages. But I was never good at self-control, and the memory continued to taunt me until it was time to dress for Orsini's and tea with Vera Brest.

I had mistaken many other things in my life, but it was impossible to misread the welcome in Madame Brest's eyes. It was a relief to know that, in this parlor, everything was as I knew it to be.

She took my hands. "I am so happy to see you, Mr. Calina." She led me to the tea table, where an enameled flowered tray held a silver teapot and two bone china cups, a plate of petit fours decorated with sugared rose petals.

"Am I your only guest?" I asked.

"You are nearly the only friend I have made here," she said. "Does it trouble you to be unchaperoned? If you like, I can call Tomas to join us, though he is quite busy with his account books."

Orsini and I had barely exchanged a dozen words in the time I'd known him, so I shook my head and said, "I promise to be on my best behavior."

"Oh, I do hope not," she teased. "It is one of the benefits of being a married woman that few care any longer what you do."

I would have taken the chair opposite, but she sat on the settee and patted the cushion beside her, and so I sat, maintaining a proper distance. "I imagine your husband cares very much."

"He is busy with his own pursuits." She was not the least self-pitying. "If I am happy, he is happy. And he is in Portugal, and far away, which is how I like him best."

She poured tea. We sipped companionably. The petit fours were layered with marzipan, but I hardly tasted it. I tried to think of something to say that wouldn't sound like desperate and fawning gratitude for her attention, to remember something—anything—Bayard had said about her, or about how I should approach her. As a motherless, sisterless boy, women had been to me the most mysterious of subjects. My notions of them had been formed by romantic novels and poetry—laughable, I know, but what else is one to do when surrounded by other boys and monks? I was nineteen, and home for Christmas, when I helped the widow Leporello with her bags and ended up in her bed. She had taught me a great deal about how to pleasure a woman, but as to wooing one . . . I had no idea how to go about it. Louisa Wentworth had been proof enough of my fumbling ineffectualness. I'd been so easily misled. So foolishly expectant.

Madame Brest said, "You seem distracted this afternoon, Mr. Calina."

"It was a chaotic morning. Our maid left rather abruptly."

She set aside her tea, putting her hands in her lap. "Maids can be so difficult. Who knows why they do anything?"

I could hardly tell her the truth. "In this case, it was because her father wished her at home. But she's left us with guests and no maid. I shall be hard-pressed to find another."

"Oh? Why is that?"

"Bayard's reputation is . . . difficult."

She laughed. "Yes, I've heard! But I did not know you had guests."

"The spyglasses at the d'Angleterre must be quiet lately. Julian Estes, the poet, is staying with us. Do you know of him?"

She shook her head. "Is he famous?"

"Not very. He's an atheist."

"Ah. How very bohemian!"

"He's brought with him two sisters from America."

"America? I have never met an American. Are they much different?"

"I should say so. They have rather strange notions. They're Free Lovers."

Her fine brow furrowed. "I do not know this thing."

"They believe that people should love whoever they wish. They don't believe in marriage."

"Strange, you say? It sounds sensible to me."

"Yes, I suppose it is. Estes is half-mad, I think, but Bayard admires him. It will be interesting to see if he's as good a writer as he thinks. We've decided to hold a writing contest." I was babbling, but I couldn't seem to stop talking. "We're each writing a ghost story. Bayard's already done twelve pages. I had hoped to do something to beat him, for once, but—"

"He's written something new? What is it about?"

I frowned at the enthusiasm in her voice. "You sound excited."

"Who would not be excited about a new story from Bayard Sonnier?"

"But I thought . . . you said you'd never read him. When we met, you said it."

"Yes, that is true," she agreed. "But you work for him, yes? I wanted to know more about you. So I read *The Temptation*. It was very wonderful."

I should not feel disappointed that she was no different than anyone else, but I was. I had liked that she was ignorant of him. I had liked that, in her eyes, I did not disappear in the glare of Bayard's talent and fame. "Yes, I suppose it is."

"Is this story wonderful too? Tell me about it."

I wished I'd said nothing. But she was staring at me so eagerly, and obediently, I told her what it was about, finishing with "I can't do it justice. If you could read it, you would see what I mean. I can't compete."

She leaned closer. A hand on my knee. I tried to pretend I wasn't astonished. Or that I wasn't immediately aroused. "I do not believe that. You are only despairing."

"Despairing and realistic," I said with a self-deprecating laugh. "I had hoped this contest would be the answer. All I want is for people to actually notice what I can do."

"But when you had the chance to show them, you refused it." A light caress.

I was having trouble keeping my thoughts together. "When I had the chance?"

"Edward Colburn's offer." Then, at my blank look, "The journal he asked you to keep about your time with Mr. Sonnier."

"Oh, the gossip."

"Would it not bring you the attention you wish for?"

"Undoubtedly. But I could not betray Bayard that way."

Her dark eyes were mesmerizing. "Would he feel the same sense of honor toward you, I wonder?"

It was a good question. "I would like to think so."

"Hmmm." Her hand traveled higher, resting now on my thigh. "Such a book would make you famous, Mr. Calina, and would that not give you everything you wish for?"

"But it's only because of Bayard that anyone would read it. It would not really be mine."

"I think it would be yours enough. Your name will be on the cover; it would be your words they read. And if you do it well, they will buy your next book. It matters not how they find you, does it? Only that they wish to read you again."

I hadn't thought of that. But then again, it was difficult to think of anything but her hand, and my wish that she would move it higher still.

She went on, "Such opportunities do not come one's way often."

"I would have no time to work on it anyway," I told her, too distracted to argue. "Bayard will probably have me taking on maid duties now too."

"Oh, but that is something I can help you with. I will send you a maid."

"I don't wish to inconvenience you—"

"It is no inconvenience."

"I think you can't know what an impossible task it will be."

"Ah yes." A tilt of her head, a coy underlook that made my mouth go dry. "The gossip. Something to write about, I would say to you, but no . . . of course I understand. If I do send a girl, I would have your promise that she will be safe."

"You have my word."

Her hand slid higher. "You will keep her from Mr. Sonnier?"

"He's got Louisa to keep him bus—" I bit off the word, too late.

She drew away with a delighted little gasp. "You mean one of the Americans?"

I winced. "I should not have said it. It's a secret." Though why should it be, especially here? It was only Julian who was to be kept unsuspecting. What harm could it do that Vera Brest knew?

"I will not say a word," she promised. "How scandalous!"

She was hard to resist. I liked her flirtatious horror, her mock outrage, the glow in her eyes. Mostly I wished she would put her hand back on my thigh.

Her sideways glance hit me hard. "Has Mr. Sonnier corrupted you with his bad habits? Perhaps you don't wish to write of such things because you are afraid to admit that you participate. Perhaps it is you I should worry over. Should I be jealous of a maid?"

I heard myself say, "My affections belong only to you."

She smiled, coming close, breasts pressing into my arm. Her fingers at my thigh again, caressing, a captivating, sensuous tease. I fell into her eyes. "Then you will let me help you, yes? You will let me send you a maid, and you will bring me Mr. Sonnier's story, and think about Edward's offer?"

She kept returning to the story. My suspicions rose, but her hand . . . those eyes . . . I would have promised her anything. "Yes. Yes of course." Too fervent, but she did not seem to care.

Before I knew what she was about—because I would not have released her—she jumped to her feet and held out her hand. I was half in a daze as I took it and let her lead me to the doorway.

"You must go." She whispered in my ear, hot breath against my skin. "Madame Orsini waits for me. But we will see each other soon. When I send the maid, she will tell you when we shall meet again, yes?"

Her lips grazed my cheek, a quick, chaste kiss that left me tingling. She giggled and waved me off, and I found myself going out the door, walking down the path like a blind man. I was hardly aware of leaving, only of being bereft, longing, the burn of her hand and her kiss. I was halfway across the lake before I came to myself again.

EIGHT

ADELAIDE

I had dreams of lightning flashing over the mountaintops, of curses and ghosts, and I woke disoriented and sad. For a moment I could not remember where I was, but then I saw the wet and dry clothes scattered on the floor and I remembered last night, the storm and the contest, making love, falling asleep in Julian's arms. He was nowhere to be seen.

The sun peeked through a crack in the curtains. I opened them, blinded briefly by the brightness, and then my eyes adjusted; the shadows standing on the crest overlooking the lake became solid. It was Julian, wearing only shirtsleeves and trousers, his hair a frizzled halo in the morning light. Cradled in his arms was my sister.

She leaned into him as if he were her only strength, and he gripped her tightly, resting his chin upon her hair. How dare they do this now, here, after everything? Did last night mean nothing to him?

But then . . . no. Louisa twisted in his arms and stepped away. She spoke animatedly, spitting words. Her fingers curled into her palms. This was not a tender moment between lovers. Louisa was angry.

My fury faded, leaving behind heat and tingling nerves. I scratched at the rough skin on my chin and hand. Julian was trying to calm her, but he could not do it as well as I. She would need me. She always needed me.

I glanced back at the bed longingly. I wished only to crawl again beneath those blankets and disappear. Instead, I dressed quickly, pinning up my hair as I hurried down the stairs. They were no longer in the yard, but I heard them in the kitchen, which surprised me. Julian was at the stove, stirring something in a skillet, while Louisa stood next to him, slicing onions.

"I'm making the famous Estes eggs," he said as I came inside, and his smile for me was warm and affectionate, of a kind I hadn't seen in some time. "People have been known to line up for miles to taste these, so consider yourself lucky."

"My, my. I didn't realize you had so many talents," Louisa teased. "Poet, conjurer of demons, scrambler of eggs—is there nothing you can't do?"

"Nothing," he assured her, winking at me. "But the eggs are my real gift."

"Where is the cook?" I asked.

"She quit this morning," Louisa said. "Rather suddenly."

I thought of what I'd seen earlier, Louisa's clenched fists and her anger. Cautiously I asked, "This didn't . . . it didn't have anything to do with you?"

"Why should you always assume that I'm to blame? No, it had nothing to do with me. Last night I did tell her to go to bed and stop her blathering, but why should a maid quit over that? Mr. Calina said she was frightened."

"No doubt my terrors had something to do with it," Julian said, seemingly unabashed.

I had not considered that when we'd decided to come here. Julian's family had lost several servants over his fits. They had occasioned a great deal of gossip, just as they would now. Hopefully there would be no more, and the maid would not talk of this one. Even if she did, she was only a village girl. There was no reason for anyone in society to hear of it. Still, I couldn't banish my apprehension.

"Stop scratching," Julian said to me. "You'll only make it worse."

I gripped my hand as if pressure could stop the constant itch, and sat at the table.

Louisa spilled the onions into Julian's pan.

"Wait! I wasn't ready for them yet," he protested.

"It's not your fault the maid left, Jules. Nor mine, whatever Mr. Calina says."

"What did he say?" I asked.

"Among other things, that I could make my own 'bloody breakfast.' Really, he's such a bore. I can't think why Bayard should have him as his secretary. It doesn't reflect well on him."

Julian said, "He does seem a strange companion for Bayard. Rather out of his class."

"It's not our concern, and we shouldn't intrude. We're guests. You and I barely know Bayard." I had my doubts that Louisa knew him any better. The time she'd spent with him in London had been so short.

"Perhaps, but I think we will be great friends, and friends have a duty to be honest. I feel bound to tell him that having such a fractious servant doesn't help him."

"Nor, I think, do guests running from invisible demons," I commented. "If that maid tells everyone what she heard . . ."

"You make too much of it," Louisa said.

"We cannot cause him trouble," I said quietly to Julian, whose mouth had thinned. He concentrated on stirring the eggs as if it were the most important task he'd ever undertaken. "He'll throw us out, and then where will we go? What have we gained? Everything depends on your winning his favor, and—"

"Do you think he finds me a fool?" Julian's voice was chill. "Is that what you're saying?"

"No, of course not, but I think—"

"Bayard has a mind to equal Julian's," Louisa said. "He'll understand that we're only living our principles. He'll admire us for it."

"Will he? I suggest you think about what he would hear, Louisa, and then say that to me again."

"Enough," Julian said. "You speak as if the fault is entirely mine and Louisa's. Perhaps you might remember your own part in all this, *my love*."

He threw aside the wooden spoon, took the pan off the stove and slammed it on the cutting board, and stalked from the kitchen. All the tender intimacy I'd managed to earn last night lost after only a few words.

Louisa said, "Really, Addie, why must you torment us? Why must you keep nagging about all this?"

Again, I scratched at my hand, which set up a corresponding itch at my chin. Irritably, I rubbed them both. "Because you cannot seem to control yourself, and you only feed Jules. You can't just give in to hysterics whenever you please, Louisa. You've seen what happens to Papa often enough that I'd think you—"

"I'm not like him!"

I said nothing.

"I'm not."

"I see. So I'm imagining the times I've had to lock you in your room to keep you from throwing yourself in front of a carriage? Or drag you from some shop or another because you had a notion you couldn't put aside? What about that incident at the dressmaker's with the ribbons she couldn't order? Was that my imagination too?"

She paled, but she came to the table and planted her hands firmly on the top. "If I'm as mad as Papa, it's because you've made me so with all your warnings and worry. You never let me forget and just live! I think you would prefer it if I were the one wearing a straitjacket."

"Don't be absurd," I said wearily.

"In fact, I think you half want it. Then I would be out of the way."

"I want no such thing."

"You are making us all miserable. You and your stupid fantasy of a curse—"

"Tell me the truth, Loulou: It wasn't Mr. Calina you were upset with this morning, was it?"

Louisa's expression shuttered.

"It was Bayard," I prodded.

"I couldn't tell Jules, of course."

"How long do you think you can keep this affair from him, Louisa?"

"Just a little more time," she said softly. "Jules would think it his failing. You know how responsible he feels for me."

Yes, he felt responsible, though it was my fault that Louisa was in this position, with no father or male relative to support her. Who else was there but Julian to assume the role of her guardian? He took the duty more seriously than I'd expected, but how could I complain of it? We must rely on him for everything.

Louisa went on, "He would spite himself out of anger and make us leave, and that would ruin everything. Bay could help him so much, but Jules half believes all the rumors. All he needs is to know Bayard better. They'll become the best of friends, I know they will. Then he'll be happy for me."

I had nothing to say to that. Everything she said was true. "What did Bayard do to upset you?"

She sank onto the bench opposite. "He has this way of looking into the eyes of someone who loves him and then saying, 'Get out. I'm tired and I want to sleep.'"

"Perhaps he resents that we've all descended upon him."

"He invited me."

"Did he? Did he really?"

"I told you he would miss me. How could he not? As long as we were together in London—"

"It was only a month and a half, Louisa."

"You saw his face when we arrived. You saw how happy he was to see me."

I tried to remember exactly what I had seen, and couldn't. I'd been too consumed with the drowning boy, Julian's faraway stare, the disaster I sensed looming with every passing moment.

She said, "It's Vanni who doesn't want me here. He's poisoning Bayard against me."

The familiarity took me aback. *Vanni?*

"Mr. Calina," she corrected impatiently.

"Why would he be doing that?"

She jumped to her feet, turning nervously about. "I don't know. He's never liked me."

There was more here; I knew her too well. "Why? Did you do something to him?"

"Stop blaming me. I've done nothing!" Her eyes blazed, again those clenched fists.

"Then I don't understand why he would malign you to Bayard."

"Because you don't know him as I do. He was always hovering around in London, always watching." She was pacing now, her agitation coalescing. "He's jealous of everything Bayard has, and I think he even fancied once that he might step in when Bayard was done with me—as if I would have him!—but Bayard's never going to be done with me. He's going to love me. I know he is."

I rose, stopping her with a touch, keeping my voice low and even as I said, "Loulou, take care. You're getting upset over nothing."

She jerked away. "It's not nothing! You didn't see him. He told me to go away, and he meant it. He did not want me to stay even though we'd just . . . he'd just—"

"I'm certain he was only tired. Or perhaps wishing to write," I said soothingly, cutting her off before she could go into a detail I had no interest in hearing. God knew I'd heard enough of it in London.

"He'd written all night," she said. "We went to bed and made love and then he was up again, writing and writing. I swear he never stops. He said it was the story for the contest. He was inspired. That was because of me, Addie. It was my idea, remember? He was still writing, and I asked him if he wasn't tired, and he said no and came up behind me while I was washing and made me bend over the desk—"

"Louisa, please."

"—and he just . . . we were both . . . How could he have wanted me to go after something so blissful as that?"

"You said he was up all night. Perhaps it was just as he said. He was tired. He wanted to sleep."

She paced again, ten steps, turn, ten steps. "But I've been so good to him. I came all this way. What other woman has done that? What other woman thinks of him as I do?"

"Louisa," I said, taking her arm again, leading her back to the bench, pushing her gently until she sat down. "You really must calm yourself before you end up as disturbed as you were in London."

"Yes," she said, taking a deep breath, trying to relax, failing, looking up at me plaintively. "Do you think that was why he left?"

"You said you destroyed his globe and several books. Was that not true?"

She put her face in her hands. "Oh, Addie."

"Perhaps he had some reason to leave you behind," I said, sitting beside her, stroking her hair. "So you must not give him a reason now. Do you understand?"

Her head bobbed beneath my hand.

"We have no place else to go," I whispered. "This was your idea, so you must remember how Jules needs this. *We* need this, or . . ." I could not finish the words, even in my head.

"I know," she whispered back. "I know."

NINE

VANNI

Over the next weeks, we fell into a kind of routine. Mornings we avoided each other, each of us tending to his own affairs. Sometimes I saw Estes on the cast iron bench on the lawn, his open notebook on his lap, staring transfixed at the lake, a pencil poised in his hand as if his thoughts were too sublime to record. Whatever Miss Wentworth did with her mornings, I did not know. I transcribed pages from the pile on my desk, which was rapidly diminishing, as Bayard had stopped writing. When I reminded him that his publisher was waiting, he snapped at me, "If I wanted a scolding, I'd get a wife." But I was used to his temper, and had no intention of ignoring my duty to keep him on schedule. My livelihood depended on it.

It would help to be rid of Louisa and Estes, of course. Louisa because she went to him at all hours and never failed to engage him, and Estes because he too easily embroiled Bayard in pseudo-philosophical conversations that lasted an eternity. That Estes still seemed ignorant of Louisa's real relationship with Bayard was a testament either to grave stupidity or a blindness so profound I was surprised he wasn't walking into walls.

Whenever we met, the questions abounded. "How are you doing on your story?" "Will you make it?" No one ever gave more than a vague reply. I had no idea who was writing and who was not. I hated to admit that anything Louisa Wentworth suggested might have merit, yet the deadline was the spur I needed. I was certainly trying to meet it, but Bayard's abortive effort had left me cursing my own lack of imagination.

In the late afternoons, we went out on the boat, excursions which had become occasions for Estes to hold court, gesticulating so that his cloud of hair jumped about his face, seeming almost alive itself. He told one story about how he'd spent the night in his family crypt to see if ghosts really did come out at midnight, and he'd awakened to see that one of the skeletons had extended an arm, a bony hand reaching out for him "with her fingers curled about a button that she'd torn from my coat."

"I've always suffered from curiosity," he'd said another day, in preface to a tale about how he'd climbed the roof of his family home, some four stories, in the middle of a storm to test if lightning could reanimate a dead cat—I could only assume he'd been drunk on laudanum. He dropped the cat, tried to rescue it and lost his balance, but managed to catch hold of an eave, where he hung until his mother spotted him dangling outside her bedroom window. "She thought I was a thief or a murderer," he said with a laugh. "I told her I was only a philosopher, and that her cat was still dead."

Bayard laughed so hard at the story his face turned red. Even the somber Miss Wentworth smiled.

I wondered if lightning had actually struck him that night—it would explain both his idiocy and his hair.

My only solace was in knowing that sooner or later Estes and his companions would leave, and I would have Bayard to myself again. In the meantime, Bayard's lack of output meant that I had some time to work on my story, especially because the maid that Madame Brest had promised materialized like a miracle. I had no idea how she'd done it, but the girl, Sylvie, showed up the next day, and seemed competent enough, and I liked her if for no other reason than she was a connection to the woman I could not stop thinking about. She also brought a note from her mistress: *Please come for tea. Bring Mr. Sonnier's story!*

Bayard teased, "Well, your Portuguese has come in rather handy, hasn't she? She's rather clever too, sending a pockmarked girl."

"Why is that clever?"

Bayard shook his head and sighed. "What am I to do with you? Clearly she doubts your fidelity. She sends an ugly girl so she doesn't have to worry that you might be tempted to stray."

"Even if she'd sent a pretty one, it wouldn't have mattered. I would not betray her in that way."

"Don't act so affronted," Bayard said. "Sometimes you astound me. Have you taken the woman to bed yet?"

I tensed. "I would hardly tell you if I had."

"Which means no," he said. "Very well, keep going to your whores if you like, but why are you paying for something you can get for free?"

"I haven't been to a brothel in weeks."

"Weeks? Good God. Well, fortunately you have a hand." He laughed and went off, no doubt to look for Louisa.

Bayard was right; why was I so hesitant to take what I wanted? I resolved to at least show Vera Brest how much I desired her, and thought of all the ways I might when I went to tea and read his story to her, making excuses for not bringing my own—it was only a few pages; I hadn't had time to get to it; I would bring it the next time—but in truth, she seemed not to care. I chose not to be offended—what did it matter that she was as enraptured by Bayard's prose as everyone else, including me? She was beautiful and exciting; if it bought me her affections, I would deliver a hundred Bayard stories.

Not only that, but she believed I had influence with my employer—which I took as the highest of compliments. "He listens to you. They all say it. Can you not press him to finish?" When I demurred, she kissed me, chastely, but with such sweetness I promised her I would bring the rest of the story with my next visit.

She said, "Edward is returning tomorrow. Will you reconsider his proposal?"

I told her again that I could not dishonor myself, as Bayard not only trusted me, but had given me opportunities I'd never dreamed of, and I owed him my loyalty and gratitude, and she ran her fingers down my shirtfront, tangling them in the decorations of my watch chain, rubbing a jeweled key between her fingers as she said, "What opportunities are those? How has he helped you with your dream? Do you not wish to be known?" and I went off as befuddled, aroused, and frustrated as before.

I was determined to please her—at least when it came to the story—and to show her too that my influence with Bayard was as great as she believed it to be, but when I asked Bayard about finishing, he only shrugged and said, "I'll get back to it when I can," as if it didn't matter in the slightest, as if the tale had already burned itself out for him. He didn't care that he'd left the reader hanging—the only reader was me, as far as he knew, and in fact, I think he liked that I suffered.

"Oh, I know how it ends," he said, smiling sadistically. "But you'll just have to wait."

"You haven't much time if you mean to compete, and you'll have to fit it in with the novel, too."

"That will hardly be a problem."

In that moment I hated him. I hated him for being brilliant, and I hated how little effort it seemed to take him. I hated that I wanted to know the ending of the story he'd written for a contest he found so trifling that he didn't bother to finish.

But mostly I hated the knowledge that I could never, never beat him. What brilliance did my own story have? The ghost was a pathetic addition to a moldering mystery that even I was uninterested in. As the days passed, I labored over it, doggedly putting one word after another, spinning out mediocre prose, and the more frustrated I became, the more my story fought me, my own brain refusing to play by the rules I'd set it.

Yet in the face of all this, I still could not bring myself to give up. The contest became a test of my mettle. If I failed it, I must admit that my dreams were only useless fantasies, that I was not a writer but a fraud. I would have to face my father, who expected any day to hear what a success I'd made of my life.

No, I could not admit defeat, not yet.

Bayard had brought four bottles of wine onto the boat. He was in one of his melancholias, no doubt thinking of Marie and hating himself for Louisa. I knew these moods too well, and I was tense, waiting for him to find fault with me. The wine didn't help; it only made him more morose and irritable.

Julian took a swig from his flask—I'd stopped counting how often he did so, and he made little attempt to hide it—and got to his feet, holding on to the mast and gesturing to the mountains ringing us about, so close at this part of the lake that they seemed to rise from the shore. "Look—don't the Alps seem some majestic choir? Mont Blanc is their conductor—do you hear them sing?" Then he burst into a jocular, full-throated song about puny man and nature surpassing all gods—who knew what the hell he was talking about?

It was obvious he meant to brighten Bayard's mood, which only annoyed me more, first because he thought he could, and second because I wasn't sure he couldn't. Finally, as the song wound to a blessed close, Bayard smiled, and Estes gave me a smug glance that said, *do you see how he loves me?* and broke into a corrupted Paternoster. "Our father, who art nonexistent, hallowed be our liberty, from psalms that enslave, and priests that chain our thoughts with ridiculous sophistry. Release us to our consciences, as we are well able to manage them ourselves (except for men like Calina, who were corrupted early by monks), and—"

I was on my feet, halfway across the deck, before I knew it.

Bayard shouted, "Vanni!"

Louisa laughed. "Oh, do sit down, Mr. Calina."

Miss Wentworth regarded me with a tired gaze, as if the very thought of motion was beyond contemplation. She turned away to look at the mountains, and I felt her uninterest like a scold, and sank back into my seat, burning, imagining heaving Estes overboard and watching him flounder and gasp and sputter until someone—not me—decided he was worth saving.

But Bayard said, "'Release us to our consciences.' Do you really believe that would be wise? Without God to manage us, we would be at the mercy of our passions."

I closed my ears to Estes's reply, which was some nonsense about freeing us from our inhibitions to make a more just world. It was always like this. Always such ridiculous ideas that I was surprised each time that Bayard did not laugh Estes off the boat. But it was clear that Estes still fascinated him, as did the Wentworth sisters' Transcendentalist upbringing. I found myself often left out of the conversation. It wasn't because I didn't try, but any contribution of mine was usually met with Estes's dazed and blank expression, as if he could not fathom who I was or why I should be talking.

Just so.

It had become our habit to sit around the fire when we returned from the boat, eat dinner, drink, and continue whatever mind-numbing conversations we'd had on the lake. That night was no different. I slumped in the chair, still chafing from Estes's insult, and listened to him boast idly about how *very well* his story was progressing. "Then why not show us?" I goaded.

"Show you?" Estes asked.

"Yes, why not? If it's going so well?"

"There isn't much of it," Estes demurred.

"Brilliance often shows itself best in brevity," Louisa said.

"It's a thoughtful piece," Estes explained. "I don't think I'm quite ready to share it. I'm having trouble getting the words just right."

Louisa said, "You should show us what you have too, Bayard."

"You think so? What about yours?" Bayard asked her.

"Mine?"

"Have you not been writing away? Why, this was your idea to begin with."

"I haven't—"

"You said you meant to beat us all," Bayard went on, taunting, settling languidly into the settee, the very picture of indolence. "You were going to be the next Mary Shelley. Or have you forgotten?"

Louisa's cheeks pinked.

"You shouldn't go about issuing challenges you have no intention of meeting." He sipped at his wine. "But then again, I suppose it's too much to hope that you could. It's not your fault, of course. It's a failing of your sex. I don't think I've ever met a woman who was particularly good at scribbling."

I had seen him this way before. I had no idea if he believed the things he was saying, sometimes he said them just to be contrary.

Louisa said, "No? What of Mrs. Radcliffe? Or . . . or George Sand? Or Margaret Fuller—"

"Pot-boiling, overly romantic, and humorlessly didactic," he said, numbering the flaws on his fingers. He sat up, poured another glass of wine, and leaned back again. "Any other examples you wish to throw my way?"

"Harriet Beecher Stowe," Louisa offered.

"Sentimental and self-righteous. Melodrama is the province of women, of course, so"—a shrug—"I suppose you could always write what you know."

Louisa threw back her shoulders and lifted her chin. "What are you implying?"

This I had also seen before. I'd spent more than one afternoon cleaning up after it. I said, "Bayard," at the same time Miss Wentworth cautioned, "Louisa."

Miss Wentworth seemed as surprised as I by our unison.

Estes said idly, "I'm certain that if Bay had seen your poetry, Loulou, he would not be so cavalier about it."

Miss Wentworth's attention turned from me. "Poetry?"

Estes said, "She's been writing poetry since we left Concord. Before that even. I've been tutoring her."

Miss Wentworth's gaze narrowed. "I had no idea. Loulou, how bad of you not to say anything."

I savored my wine, gratified that for once not everyone was enamored with Julian Estes.

"You've had so many other things to concern you, I didn't want to mention it," Louisa said. "But I did have hopes that Bayard might take a look. As a favor."

The requests for such favors were constant; I wrote at least a dozen letters a week in response to some poor soul or another who believed he was possessed of a talent for the ages, begging Bayard to take a look, to write a review, to speak a kind word of puffery. It was Bayard's least favorite thing to do.

He sipped his wine, considered Louisa with a thinly veiled testiness, and said, "Of course."

Louisa's smile was brilliant. "Would you really?"

Usually, what happened was this: he would say yes to a writer he could not avoid for whatever reason, hand it off to me, I would read it and tell him what to say, and he would never lay eyes on it unless I told him it had merit. Though he might have to handle this differently, given that she was spending every night in his bed.

Bayard said, "Give it to Vanni. He'll see I get to it."

No, no different after all.

Louisa looked stunned. She glared at me. I gave her my most angelic smile.

Then, with dismay, I realized Bayard was watching.

"What about your story, Vanni?" he asked. "You've been working on it so much you've been scarce lately. I've been like a proud papa. How many pages have you? Sixty? A hundred?"

"Twenty," I said guardedly.

"Well, I suppose a story needn't be long." Bayard poured more wine into his glass, as self-satisfied as any emperor. "Let's see what we all have, shall we? Who will begin?"

Estes and I were both silent. I should never have started the damn conversation to begin with—what the hell had I been thinking?

Bayard said, "How do you expect to find that fame you long for, Vanni, if you never allow anyone to read your work? That's just playing at being a writer. Pretenders litter the steps of John Murray. They'll tell anyone who listens that they're a novelist or a poet, but real writers show the world what they have to say and be damned. Don't tell me you're a pretender too. And after all the time I've lavished upon you. Come, let's see what you've managed to wrest from the nothingness."

It was as if he knew all my insecurities. I hadn't thought myself so transparent. I tried, "I don't think—"

"Don't you want my opinion? I'm offering it now. You won't get another chance."

I wanted to argue that it was only fair that we wait until the deadline so I could perfect my pages, but it was best not to test him in this mood. Reluctantly—and irritated that I had to prove myself so early—I went to fetch my pages. I was nervous now, almost sick with it, but I confess there was a part of me that hoped to impress him. I knew the pages weren't good enough, but it was impossible not to hope I was wrong.

I brought them back and sat down to expectant silence. My hands were actually shaking as I took a large gulp of wine. I cleared my throat and began to read. I was aware of nothing but my own voice and the ticking of that damn clock—why had I wound it?—on the mantel. I stumbled over words, trying not to wince in some places, and when I was finished, I gripped the pages so tightly they wrinkled beneath my fingers.

"Well," drawled Bayard finally, "certainly it doesn't suffer from a surfeit of originality."

Estes barked a laugh. "All it needs is a witch on a broomstick, and you'll have the perfect Hallowe'en tale for children."

"Or a scarecrow, perhaps," offered Louisa.

Bayard said, "Really, Vanni, a ghost? When do the cloven-footed devils arrive? Page twenty-two?"

Estes laughed again. "Come, come, Bay. There were some redeeming qualities."

"Oh, yes, there were," Louisa said. "I had not thought you such a good mimic, Mr. Calina. Why, the villain is so *very* like Robert Lovelace it seems as if you lifted him from the pages of *Clarissa*." Louisa's eyes fairly glowed with enmity.

I had tried to expect such criticism, but this was worse than anything I could have prepared for. Angry, hurt, I leaped to my feet. "If they're worth so little—"

I flung the pages into the fire.

Adelaide Wentworth yelped in alarm, nearly falling from the settee in her haste to retrieve the papers. Bayard too rushed forward. She yanked them from the fire and tossed them, smoking, to the hearth. Bayard stomped out the flames.

"What the hell is wrong with you, Vanni?" he demanded. "We were joking."

"Partly," Estes amended. "But yes, mostly we were joking."

"Go to hell." I swept the wine bottle from the table. It flew across the room, smashing against the wall, wine splashing up the wallpaper.

Miss Wentworth said, "Dear God, I have had my fill of bad behavior."

"No doubt you have," I shot back, nodding toward Louisa. "But it's not me you should be blaming for that."

"How dare you!" Louisa cried.

"Watch your tongue, Mr. Calina." Miss Wentworth shoved the papers at me, edges blackened, some half-burned.

I smacked them away, sending the whole pile fluttering to the floor. "Go ahead. Laugh at me all you want."

I stalked from the room, ignoring Bayard's "Vanni!"

I rushed downstairs, outside. Without thinking, wanting only to escape them, I stumbled down the path in the darkness. I tripped over the jagged rocks of the shore, falling once and bruising my shin, silencing a choir of frogs with my cursing as I dragged the rowboat into the water and rowed out into the black lake, into the shadows of the mountains. Bayard's face jeered at me from the starry sky, and suddenly I heard Vera Brest—*"would he feel the same sense of honor toward you, I wonder"*—and I realized how stupid I'd been, how naive to think he cared for me at all. I was a joke to him, to all of them.

The faint light of Orsini's château glimmered in the distance. Edward Colburn was there now. I'd refused his offer out of my misplaced loyalty, but no longer. Bayard deserved it. They all deserved it. *Bad behavior,* indeed. Why should I not take advantage of theirs? What did I owe them? Nothing. Nothing at all.

I set my course for Orsini's.

TEN

ADELAIDE

Bayard strode to the window and stared thoughtfully out into the darkness. "Damn, he's gone out on the boat."

"He'll be safe enough," Louisa said. "He's on it every morning."

"There's no wind, and the sky is clear," Julian agreed.

Still, Bayard looked worried.

"I didn't think he would react so poorly, but it only shows the kind of man he is," Julian said.

"I have never known anyone more objectionable," Louisa agreed.

Perhaps Louisa and Julian did not feel guilty, but I did. Mr. Calina had a right to his anger tonight; his work had showed talent and imagination. To humiliate him that way had been beneath all of us, and yet I had played my part as well. He had lashed out at us, and I had lashed back, but he was not the cause of my anger. It had been easier to rage at him than to acknowledge my frustration with Julian and my jealous surprise at the news of Louisa's poetry, but Mr. Calina could not know that. I had behaved badly, and I was ashamed.

I glanced at Julian, who tended the fire, looking barely chastened. He was disappointed with his own writing, and I knew that was at least part of the reason he had taunted Mr. Calina. The contest story was supposed to be Julian's opportunity to win Bayard's support, and yet he had managed only a few pages. *"They're not good enough, Addie. They must be stellar to impress a man of his talent, and I fear I haven't the right idea."*

I went to stand beside Bayard. Quietly, I said, "We should not have mocked him that way."

Bayard took a deep breath. "He'll need a thicker skin if he means to be a writer. I've tried to tell him so, but . . . yes. You're right. I suppose I'll have to apologize." He turned back to Julian and Louisa and said, "Who'd like to hear another ghost story?"

My sister clapped her hands like a child. "Oh yes!"

I could not stay to listen. The evidence of how little my sister and Julian cared about what they'd done to Mr. Calina was too much to bear. I picked up his pages, patting them into a neat pile, and took them to his room, which was spartan in design but cluttered with his things, a coat abandoned on the back of a chair, his hat on the dresser, along with a hairbrush and jumbled silk ties, papers spread across his desk, both his and Bayard's. The surface was also spattered with ink, so much that I wondered how often he threw his pen in frustration. Quite often, it seemed.

I set the papers neatly on top and stared down at the words, my guilt returning, and with it, a grudging admiration. Mr. Calina had come from nothing, according to Louisa. He had none of our advantages, and yet he had talent and faith enough to persevere. Passion too, as I'd once had. I envied him that.

I rejoined the others. It was nearly one in the morning when we decided to retire. Bayard looked again out the windows toward the lake.

He said nothing, but his concern was obvious. I saw how Louisa wanted to go to him, but he seemed oblivious of her.

Julian went upstairs, but I followed slowly, and so I heard Louisa say something coy and teasing to Bayard, and his terse answer, and then an argument, and Louisa rushed up the stairs, ignoring me, her fury spinning in a tornado about her. She ran into her bedroom and slammed the door.

I closed my eyes in exhaustion, knowing I should go to her. But I could not make myself. Not tonight. I had spoken the truth to Mr. Calina. I was so tired of bad behavior, weighted as I was with a hundred other tempers, vacillating moods, ungovernable delusions.

"Oh, to go to some island far away from here," my mother used to say to me, her smile wistful. *"You and I could go together, Addie, wouldn't that be nice? To have peace all day long?"*

There were times, like tonight, when I longed for such an island so intently I wondered that sheer yearning hadn't made it real.

In the bedroom, Julian said, "There's no need to feel guilty over Calina, Adelaide."

"How do you know I feel guilty?" I asked.

"Because I know you."

"His work showed some promise."

"Now there's a commendation."

"You're being sarcastic."

"Not at all. I think you've a gift for spotting talent. After all, you saw mine immediately."

I eyed him, uncertain of his sincerity.

Julian took the laudanum from the bedside table and uncorked it to take a large sip. Again, I wondered how much was left and what he would do when it was gone. "Did Louisa meet Calina before we came here?"

I tensed, trying to remember the details of the lie Louisa and I had decided upon. He knew, of course, that Louisa and Bayard were friends in London, and that was the reason we'd come. But we had been careful not to make him suspicious about their real relationship. Julian should have already sensed the truth, yet his ability to be willfully blind when he didn't wish to see had often surprised me. "Why do you ask?"

"He seems to irritate her unduly."

Something I'd noted as well, but I had no idea why. She'd never mentioned him until we arrived at the villa. I made up something that sounded at least plausible. "I believe he was in charge of Bayard's schedule in London. You know how she is; she has no sense of moderation. Apparently Mr. Calina didn't like her just popping in whenever she wanted to."

"He certainly doesn't seem to keep her from Bayard now."

Again, I could not interpret his tone. Was it out of jealousy or responsibility or simple curiosity that he asked the question? "I doubt he could," I said with more bitterness than I'd intended.

"You should not begrudge her his friendship, Addie," he chided. "She's suffered, you know, from our affection for one another."

"She's suffered?" I was incredulous that he would use that word with me.

"Sometimes you seem not to understand how alone she feels."

"But you do. Did you learn that by helping her to write poetry? Why did no one tell me about that?"

"She's trying to be helpful. It troubles her that she does nothing to contribute to our family. She dislikes being so dependent."

"She's never said that to me. What confidants you are."

"Who else should be her friend when you decided you could no longer bear her company?"

I thought of that bare, cold room in Venice, Louisa at my bedside looking impatient and annoyed, and I said angrily, "She did not even try. None of it was her tragedy, and so she didn't care."

Julian sat on the bed, rubbing his forehead. "That's not really true, you know. She's very sensitive."

"Indeed. God forbid she should not feel *everything* more than everyone else."

"You knew this when you asked her to run away with us. You begged me to allow her to come. Don't you remember how afraid you were to leave her? You said then that she was fragile. You said she needed you. So you cannot now blame her for being what she has always been. I wish you wouldn't forget that you love her."

"Of course I haven't forgotten." How could I? Who was more responsible for what Louisa was than I? Who knew better the terrible sense of obligation that had made me bring her, or my fears of what might happen if I did not? I did not miss the irony that I was again listening to Julian chastise me for not being kind enough, or accepting enough, when everything I'd done was to help her. Even now, all I'd been trying to do was keep her damnable secret from him.

But I could not let this keep coming between the two of us. I could not admit that I'd made a bad decision in Concord, that running off with Julian had not been best for me or for my all-too-vulnerable sister. We had no money of our own, nor any means of making it, or at least none that the world would allow. All the philosophies we'd been raised upon, all those arguments that women deserved lives of our own choosing . . . We could not eat philosophy, nor could it clothe or house us. There was no support that we could provide for ourselves, and so we were completely dependent upon Julian. I could not allow him to stop needing me, not for myself, and not for Louisa. I had to love him, because I could not do otherwise. I forced myself to sit beside him. "I don't know why we're talking about her now anyway. It's late."

The wretched laudanum was already working its magic; I was not certain Julian would have been able to follow our conversation even had we continued it. We undressed and got into bed, but I didn't sleep. As Julian's soft, even breathing filled the room, I tried to dream of those early days with him, when everything had been so promising, when I had been giddily in love for the first time, hungry to share every part of myself with a man who listened so ardently. But my thoughts turned stubbornly away as if to say, *not here, not now,* and I found myself thinking instead of Mr. Calina's story, and the ghost he'd written, who'd moaned and howled, whose miserable presence was so corporeal. Nothing like the ghosts I knew, who flourished in words that could not capture the depth of my feeling, though they were the only words I had. Regret and grief and sorrow.

I felt uncomfortable and unsettled, and I got up again and pulled on my dressing gown. The night was very dark beyond the windows, and there was no moon, but the lake seemed to gleam as if it emanated its own light. I saw no sign of the rowboat, or Mr. Calina, and it surprised me to realize I'd been searching for him. I could not stop thinking of what he'd written, of his pain and chagrin when he'd thrown his papers into the fire.

I lit a candle and quietly left the bedroom. I made my way to the ground floor, but as I approached the kitchen, I stopped short at the faint light from within. Mr. Calina was back. I no longer had to worry. When I went to the doorway, I was surprised to see not him but Bayard sitting at the table, his pen scratching as he wrote in a notebook by the light of an oil lamp turned down low.

He caught my movement and looked up. "Couldn't sleep either, could you?"

"I didn't know you were here. I'll go back upstairs."

"No need. I'm only writing down my thoughts. Sometimes it helps me to make sense of things. But it's nothing to disturb."

I sat across from him and blew out my candle, quiet, uncertain what to say.

"Would you like tea?" he suggested. "I'd say wine, but it's done enough damage tonight, I think."

"You're waiting for him?"

He nodded. "Best to broach him just when he gets back. He'll be tired and perhaps more amenable to an apology."

"I'm glad to hear you say it."

He smiled wryly. "Do I seem like such a monster to you that I can't admit when I'm in the wrong?"

"No. It's just . . . you employ him and . . ."

"And I treat him abominably much of the time."

"That is not what I was going to say."

"It's what you should say. It's true. I confess that sometimes I want to throttle him. We aren't a good match, you know. He's like a wounded bear, and I can't seem to keep from poking him. I knew it when I hired him. But I like him despite all that. He can be very engaging. And now you've heard his work, and . . ."

"You think you could make something of him."

"I *am* making something of him, Adelaide," he said. "Or at least I'm trying to. He fights me at every turn. I blame his father and his priests. He was precocious as a child, I understand, and instead of beating it out of him, his father encouraged it. If I could get his pride pruned to a manageable level . . . ah, but that's the trick, isn't it? You can't change someone who doesn't want to be changed."

I thought of Louisa, of Julian. "No, I suppose you can't."

"But I have hopes. He's still young. Perhaps he's capable of learning." He sighed. "Or perhaps he'll insist on being a fool the rest of his life. It's hard to tell at this point. Frankly, I may not survive him long enough to beat any sense into him. He could use a muse, I think. Someone like you for Julian, or . . ."

"Louisa for you?" I suggested cautiously.

His expression went bleak. "I've never loved her, Adelaide, nor pretended to. If she tells you differently, she's lying to herself. Vanni will tell you I'm incapable of resisting a woman who offers herself, and he's right. But I'm done with love."

Louisa would be devastated to see what I saw now in Bayard Sonnier's eyes. "Did Madame Arsenault really wound you so terribly?"

"I had never felt that way for anyone," he said frankly, "and I am entirely certain I never will again. If I do, you have my permission to shoot me. At close range. Do not miss."

"I wonder if love is ever what we expect?"

"You sound as one equally wounded."

"When I left Concord with Julian, we were so besotted with one another that I thought nothing terrible could ever happen. I knew he would never let it."

"But something did."

I nodded.

"Do you blame him?"

"Yes. I suppose I do."

He didn't ask why, for which I was grateful. I was not certain I could have told him. "What do you mean to do about it?"

"I don't know," I said. "Every day I think something different."

"You'll excuse me, but . . . I confess I don't much understand this 'affinity' idea you Free Lovers talk about. What exactly does it mean?"

How to explain such a transcendent thing? A memory came to mind: the firelight in the sitting room at Concord, and the way it seemed not to cast Jules in its light but to radiate from him as he bent close to me on the settee, his hip and his thigh against mine, his hair brushing my shoulder as he read from Hume, a fervency in his voice and his eyes that inflamed me in turn. Who could know why such things happened? Why we chose one person over another, or what alchemy was in our bodies that made them wish to unite? It would require a different kind of language than I had to translate the feeling, but I tried. "Julian would say that it is only by allowing ourselves to freely love that we can find the one who possesses the soul of our soul. When laws chain us to one lover, we are proscribed from seeking those who would make us better people."

"I see. Well, that's convenient, isn't it? Though it seems a better theory than practice. It's difficult to juggle lovers. Believe me, I know."

"That's not what I mean," I said. "It's the *free* in Free Love that is most important. It's not orgies or communal marriages, as people think. We believe in devotion to one person at a time. It's the freedom to choose that matters, the freedom to leave. My parents say that being forced to live with someone you don't love is a prison, and one should not be bound if love dies, but . . ."

"But?" he pressed.

"But it's not so simple, is it? Other things than love keep people together. Habit. Friendship. Dependence. Do they not matter? Must love trump everything, or is obligation not important too?"

"You don't mean to leave Jules, then."

"He needs me. What he has to give to the world is too important. I could not be responsible for spoiling that. Julian and I have lost our way, but I believe we can find one another again. I'm . . . trying. Louisa and I have nothing without him."

Bayard gave me a thoughtful look, as if he saw something in my words I did not, but whatever he would have said was forestalled by a noise at the patio door. The soft click of the latch, the open and the close, quiet footsteps. Then, a pause loud with bewilderment, and there was Mr. Calina in the doorway.

He straightened. Exhaustion crossed his face, exasperation, and he said quickly, turning away, "Pardon me. I've seen nothing."

"Of course you haven't, because there's nothing to see," Bayard said, his voice booming in the quiet. "I've been waiting for you."

"Why?"

"I wanted to apologize for tonight. It was uncalled for. I'm sorry."

"An apology from the great Bayard Sonnier. A rarity, isn't it?" Mr. Calina gestured to me. "And lo and behold, a witness to prove it."

"Oh for God's sake. You make me want to take it back."

"Now you will make me angry as well, Mr. Calina," I said.

"Well, that's hardly unusual, is it?"

"And here I'd hoped a few hours in the cold might make you less objectionable," Bayard said.

Mr. Calina's expression hardened. "I accept your apology. Now, if you don't mind, I'm to bed. By the looks of it, I'll have some work to do tomorrow."

"This?" Bayard glanced down at the journal. "No, I'm afraid I'm only writing thoughts to myself."

"Nothing?" Mr. Calina asked. "Not even the contest story?"

"I've been too busy."

"So you have. With that little—" Mr. Calina glanced at me, and bit off whatever he'd been going to say. I guessed he meant my sister, and I realized that of course he must know about Louisa and Bayard, and was keeping the secret as well. Perhaps my obfuscations about his guarding of Bayard's schedule were more apt than I'd known. It explained the animosity between them. "Well, you'll do whatever you like. Good night."

He left.

Bayard said, "You see? Poking a wounded bear, as I said. It's astonishing, isn't it, how much he makes one want to annoy him?"

I rose. "He never let me say I was sorry."

"Go on," he said, waving me off. "See if you can't smooth his fur a bit. God knows I can't."

I hurried after. He was halfway up the stairs when I called, "Mr. Calina, if I might have a word with you."

He stopped. "It can't wait until morning? It must be nearly three."

"I've waited up."

He looked as if speaking with me might be the last thing he wanted. "What is it?"

I went up the stairs, closer, not wanting anyone to hear. Louisa would only mock me. Julian would not understand. I was uncertain I understood myself. "I wanted to apologize."

He gave me a quick nod. "Very well." He turned to continue up.

I touched his arm to make him pause. "I also . . . I thought you might want to hear what I thought of your work."

"Well, I suppose you didn't really get your chance at ridicule, did you? Go ahead. I'm listening."

"I didn't wish to ridicule you at all," I said. "I wanted to compliment you. You've talent, and what's more, Bayard and Julian think it too, though I don't know if either of them would say it."

He had his mouth open, ready to retort, but when my words registered, he closed it again, frowning. "What?"

"The story isn't very good, that's true. They were right when they said the characters were cliché, and the ghost is truly a problem—"

"I think you misunderstand the definition of 'compliment.'"

"—as I said, the story could be better, but it shows promise. You've the bones of an intriguing plot, and it was very suspenseful even with its flaws. Your characters speak with such real feeling, even as hackneyed as they are."

My words fell into an awkward silence. He looked to be completely lost. I didn't know what else to say. I hardly knew why I'd felt the need to tell him any of it.

Finally, he said. "Who put you up to this?"

"I don't understand."

"You didn't wait up until three in the morning just to discuss my story. What happens now? Does everyone jump out and laugh at me for wanting so to believe you?"

"No, no, it—"

"Then what? Why are you here?"

I didn't know how to answer him.

Again, he started up the stairs. "Good night, Miss Wentworth."

I heard myself say, "Ghosts don't appear the way you've written them. They don't moan and flit about. They don't give you any way to fight them."

He stopped, turning again to face me.

"They aren't in the world, but they . . . press. They're memories and . . . and shame. They're regrets you can't escape, even if you want to."

He was quiet. Then, "What is it you want from me?"

"I don't know," I said, and suddenly I felt like crying. "I don't know."

He hesitated, and then he came down the two steps between us and took my arm, and I felt so tired, so inestimably tired, that I leaned into him.

"I'll take you to Estes," he said softly, with a kindness that was almost unbearable.

"No." It came out more fervently than I intended. "No, not . . . not yet. If you'll just . . . I'm fine, truly. I'll be fine. I just need a few moments."

He took me to the salon, to the settee. The fire was dead. He went to prod it back into life, and I said, "Please don't bother."

Again, he hesitated, glancing toward the hallway, the bedroom he must want to go to, and I said nothing to forestall him, though I was glad when he decided not to leave me. He sat at the other end of the settee, and we said nothing. Usually he closed the curtains at some point during the evening to shelter us from the prying eyes at the d'Angleterre, but they were open, everyone having forgotten, and there was the lake, still with its otherworldly gleam, even though we were in the darkest part of the night.

I said finally, needing distraction, "What do you do out there?"

He had been staring out the windows as well, and so he understood. "Float around mostly. Let the currents pull me about."

"I think that must be very peaceful."

"It is. It helps me settle myself to just lie there and think of nothing."

"Do you often need settling?"

"More often than I like to admit. Though I'm not sure it worked very well tonight."

"I am so sorry," I said again.

He looked down at his hands, and I knew the evening still pained. My apology, or Bayard's, did not go very far toward what must be a cruel hurt.

I did not want to be like Bayard. I did not want to keep poking a wounded bear. I let the apology drop; he would accept it or not, and I could do nothing about it. I said, "I'm keeping you from your bed, and you must be exhausted yourself, and you probably think I'm half-mad. You're kind to sit here and tend to me, when I'm certain you'd rather be anywhere else."

He only watched me, saying nothing.

"It's only . . . I confess I'm afraid to sleep. I've been having nightmares, and your story only reminded me of them."

"It was intended to remind you of nightmares. It was supposed to be a ghost story. Though perhaps the hackneyed characters were the biggest horror." He smiled when he said it, making me smile in turn. "But I appreciate your insight. I'd been having trouble with it. Now you've shown me I needn't waste any more time."

"I didn't mean to discourage you from writing."

"I wonder if anything can do that. What about you? Did you change your mind and decide to write for the contest? There's still time."

"Oh no. What would I write about?"

"Perhaps ghosts," he suggested. "As you seem to know so much about them."

How little he understood, after all, though I had not expected him to, had I? I had only meant to apologize. "I'm sorry for keeping you up so late. You've been very good to keep me company, Mr. Calina, but now I think it time to say good-night."

I left him there. I went to my bedroom and slid into bed, and Julian sighed in his sleep and shifted away when I touched his back with hands I didn't realize until then were cold.

ELEVEN

VANNI

When I woke, it was already afternoon. I was still tingling from the pure eroticism of the dream from which I'd just awakened, where Madame Brest had cornered me in Orsini's darkened ballroom, and I'd spoken the name I had not yet dared to use. *Vera.*

And another one as well. Adelaide.

I frowned. She had been in my dream too, I remembered, standing in the background, watching, her dark hair falling all about, wild and almost pagan looking, the Adelaide Wentworth who'd howled at the storm, her eyes full of the pain I'd seen then and again last night, on the stairs.

I got out of bed, stumbling to the other room, to my desk. The five hundred pounds Colburn had given me after I'd signed his contract were on top of my singed pages, which stank of smoke, along with the journal I'd started to write for him—a fine one clad in oxblood leather, another indulgence bought months ago, though I hadn't used it until last night.

How elated I'd been when Colburn had shaken my hand. Everything in my favor at last. Five hundred pounds would easily pay off the debt I'd amassed buying clothes and hats and fine pens and journals in London, with plenty remaining. It was the most money I'd ever had at one time. Then there had been Vera Brest's encouraging smile—and yes, we had been in the ballroom, as in my dream, and yes, she had pressed against me, whispering in my ear how glad she was that I'd taken Colburn's offer, how famous I deserved to be, and had Mr. Sonnier finished the story yet? *Come to tea the day after tomorrow,* she'd said. We would sit in the garden, which was abandoned in the afternoon, and read. The promise in her eyes had left me bedazzled.

But now, this morning, the anticipation I'd felt, that sense of fortune's favor, was gone, replaced with disquiet and shame. Uneasily, I opened the journal.

> *Marie had no sooner broken with Bayard than he began entertaining a string of actresses and singers, along with a maid or two or three, sometimes at the same time, until his rooms had the look and feel of a badly kept brothel. And then, one day in early March, Louisa Wentworth, the goddaughter of the famous American Transcendentalist, Ralph Waldo Emerson, followed me from John Murray's publishing offices under the misapprehension that I was Bayard, and wishing to tender her admiration . . .*

It went on and on, pages of it, not just about everything I'd witnessed in London, but about Louisa's brazen arrival here in Geneva to continue their affair, and Estes's ridiculous night terrors. I'd been angry when I'd written it, but now, I could only think of how chagrined my father would be to read this. He would accuse me of behaving disgracefully, and he would be right. I would be embarrassed to see this in print, especially now, after Bayard's apology and Adelaide Wentworth's compliments. The contract with Colburn was petty and wrong and ill advised.

I picked up the money and the journal and put them into the drawer of my desk, locking it and throwing the key into a box of pen nibs. Tomorrow, when I went to see Madame Brest, I would return the money to Colburn and ask him to tear up the contract. It had been a mistake, just as everything last night had been a mistake. I picked up the pages of my story and dumped them unceremoniously into the trash. Weeks of work gone, and the contest deadline moving inexorably closer, day by pitiless day. Nothing worthwhile had come out of this time in Geneva. Only Bayard's unfinished tale, painstakingly copied out, still sitting on the corner of my desk. He cared so little that he had not even asked to see the fair copy.

I sat down, staring at the pages, remembering Miss Wentworth saying that I had talent. That she'd seen promise. Bayard had said such things to me before, but somehow, coming from someone who had no stake in me at all, it seemed different. Now that my temper had passed and I could think again, I realized that her criticisms too had been useful. She'd made me see something I hadn't seen before.

I'd never actually laid eyes on a ghost, but I believed wholly that they existed. The Benedictine monastery where I'd gone to school had rooms that fairly stank of them. At ten, I'd played with the notion that the nave there was the center of purgatory. After all, it must be somewhere; why not in those vast stone halls and arched ceilings? Sometimes, during prayers, I shrank against the sense that the spirits were swimming in the air above me, staring down, glowering with judgment. It had been terrifying—I'd felt God's power resided not in heaven but in the nave, and that it was there I would be measured. When the incense smoke swirled and drew itself out, I imagined the ghosts weaving it through their unseen fingers; I heard their voices—*we are the ones you must worry about, Giovanni Calina. We are the angels of God, and we shall be your jury.*

They had pressed, as Miss Wentworth had said, and I too had known there was nothing one could do to fight them or make them go away.

Why had I not written that?

I picked up Bayard's story, skimming it again, searching for answers. When I'd taken this job, I had been so certain Bayard was the opportunity I needed. I'd been so determined to learn from him.

I turned to the last page, the final line. *Who can say what might have happened had I not gone to them, or what horrors I might have escaped?*

Suddenly I remembered Bayard telling me that, as a boy, he had taken the tales he loved—Rousseau's *Julie*, Byron's *Don Juan*, Dumas's *The Three Musketeers*—and rewritten them for his own pleasure. *"It taught me how to write. Though of course I never showed them to anyone."*

And I thought, *Yes, why not?*

No one would know it but me. I would never share it. It would stay here, locked in my desk drawer, away from prying eyes. It was just for play. Just an exercise. *What could it harm?*

My fingers flexed; I reached for the pen, for paper, and I began to write.

I lost track of time. I missed the afternoon excursion on the lake, and was not brought back to myself until Bayard opened my bedroom door and called in, "Do you mean to hold a grudge all day? Sylvie's about to serve dinner."

It was only then that I realized the sun had set. The words I'd written were splotchy and smeared where my hand had dragged across the pages.

I called back, "Start without me. I'll be there soon."

His sigh was heavy. "Vanni—"

"I'll be there."

He closed the door. I took the pages and locked them into the drawer. I couldn't deny that starting from Bayard's ending point had been a kind of liberation. It was not really mine, but at least I was writing instead of staring in frustration at a blank page. I was already in a better mood because of it.

Still, I had no real wish to face Estes or Louisa today. I had not forgiven them for last night. I toyed with the idea of pleading illness, but I knew Bayard would never allow it. No, I would have to join them, or be called a coward or worse.

The writing had distracted me from everything. I still wore only my drawers, and my hands were stained and spotted with ink. I took my time washing and dressing. When I went to meet them in the salon, Estes and Bayard were debating the existence of God.

Because, of course, they would know.

I sat down, getting a nod of acknowledgment from Bayard and Miss Wentworth, and poured myself a glass of wine. Estes ignored me. Louisa gave me a dismissive glance.

"But you believe that vampires and fairies exist," Bayard was saying. "You have no proof of either, and yet you require proof to believe in God."

Estes answered, "Because belief in God requires action, does it not? You don't ask me to worship a vampire, nor to believe that my fate is in his hands, but the very definition of God requires that I do both things. You're not asking just for belief, but faith."

"You believe you have a soul, yes?" Bayard persisted, though I knew his own belief was tenuous at best—he had once said to me that, like Byron, he denied nothing, but doubted everything. "Is that not proof of God's existence?"

"I had not realized they must be connected," Estes retorted. "How does one follow the other? I have a soul, therefore there must be a God? What logic is that?"

"The real mystery is what becomes of our souls," Louisa said. She was sitting on the floor, near Estes's feet. "Where do they go when our bodies are gone?"

"To heaven or hell. Or purgatory." I didn't realize I'd spoken until they turned to stare at me.

Estes said, "And there, my friends, is the kind of unsupported superstition that makes it impossible to engage in reasonable discourse."

"It's not unsupported. The Bible tells us—"

"The Bible? That tedious mishmash of myth and legend? It's second-rate writing by zealots determined to impose their will upon the world."

"Those 'legends' came to men through visions, Jules," Bayard argued. "How can you be so quick to disavow the truth of visions when you suffer from them yourself?"

"My visions tell me there is no God," Estes said. "What makes their visions truer than mine? The spirits I see know nothing of your mythological heaven or hell. They wait to be shown the way to the stars." He took a quick sip from his flask.

"I doubt those who wrote the Bible relied so heavily on laudanum," I said acidly.

Estes glared at me. "We have no idea what they relied on. Perhaps they were eating poisonous mushrooms. Perhaps they had dyspepsia. We make gospel what might have been indigestion."

Miss Wentworth had been rubbing her hand incessantly as she listened, and I saw—or thought I did—the same glimmer of pain I'd seen last night. "We cannot hope to know the truth."

Estes frowned at her.

"The spiritualists believe we can know," Bayard contradicted. "I was at a séance a few months ago. They were trying to call the spirit of a man who had been lost at sea."

"Did they contact him?" Estes asked.

"*Something* answered. His mother believed she was speaking to her son, and was quite relieved to hear he'd died peacefully."

"You sound as if you don't believe it," Estes said.

"Not that I didn't believe, but . . . he died when his ship went down in a storm. I should think that anything but peaceful. It was what she wanted to hear, but it was too prosaic for me. Why does no one ask the real questions?"

"What questions are those?" Louisa asked.

"What is the world like beyond? Are they still themselves, or something else? How securely are our souls connected to our bodies? When we lose one, does it change the other?"

"I think you might not like to hear the answers," Miss Wentworth murmured.

"Does Coleridge still keep his talent in death?" Bayard went on, musing. "Is he frustrated without the means to use it? Is Byron? What about Percy Shelley—he was an atheist too. Has he discovered God, or is his lack of belief proved?"

Louisa, who had been lounging, sat up straight. "We should try it."

"Try what?" Miss Wentworth asked.

"A séance. We could call Byron. He lived here—perhaps he would hear us."

I laughed. "Byron? He's long since been judged and sent to his eternal home. If he's with God, he won't answer."

"You mean only those in hell will speak with us?" Louisa asked.

"Why should any soul in heaven wish to return? They've been redeemed. They no longer care anything for this world. Only those jealous of this life would reply. How can their intentions be good? Séances are a trick of the devil. It will only bring spirits who mean us harm. If Byron is in hell, the last thing we should do is speak with him."

"Do you hear yourself?" Estes asked. "Do you not see how thoughtlessly you believe? If I told you the moon was made of cheese, you would probably believe that too."

"Only if you were a priest, Jules." Louisa laughed. "Then he would take your word for anything. What they say is quite sacrosanct."

"A man may study anything until he believes it," Bayard said. "I don't doubt your faith, Vanni, in fact, I admire the devotion it inspires, but in the end perhaps we are simply a mess of atoms with only our invented creeds to rule us. Why not ask questions? Perhaps we shall find an answer tonight."

The room seemed suddenly small and close and perilous. Father Ignatius, my confessor, rose before me like a wraith, and Father Sebastian, too, who had regaled us with such lurid warnings about the devil's ways that I'd had nightmares. "Then you'll have to do so without me," I said, rising.

Bayard said, "Sit down. You'll take part with the rest of us."

"You endanger your souls as you please. I won't endanger mine."

"We might have need of you, you know. You might be the only one among us who can spot evil when it's in the room. God knows I have no discernment, and Jules there only believes it as a concept invented to control us. Louisa likes too well to be frightened; she'd probably only think it a great joke if Satan tried to spirit her away, and . . . and what of you, Adelaide? Can you protect us from such harm?"

"We are well enough able to destroy ourselves," she answered. "There's no need to blame something otherworldly, if indeed such a thing as Satan exists."

"Well, it would be entertaining if nothing else." Bayard put his glass aside and rose. "We need a table. There's one in the gallery."

I was not going to go. I thought I could sneak away. I wanted nothing to do with this—I did not even want to be in the house while they did it. But Bayard saw my hesitation.

"Come, Vanni."

"Oh, let him go," Louisa chimed in. "He'd only ruin it anyway, with all his silly superstitions."

She went after her sister, who had not favored me with a backward glance. No "come" or "stay." Not a single indication that we'd had any conversation last night.

But Bayard gestured for me to follow as he and Estes walked off, joking with each other, laughing. How easily he'd insinuated himself, and in only a few weeks. I had not managed anything close to it after a year and a half.

I trailed after, jealous and stupid with it, knowing this must turn out badly—how could it not? Given Estes's contempt, and Louisa's obvious delight in making me a fool, it was not hard to guess who would pay the price when it did.

My apprehension grew as we went to the picture gallery, where there was a round table meant for card playing. The room had been mostly unused in the time we'd been here. The shutters were closed; it was pitch-dark. Bayard turned on the gas enough to illuminate the portraits lining the walls—all of them French kings, most of them glowering or looking disdainfully regal.

Estes gasped as the visages came into view, and I remembered him saying that he had a horror of portraits. To see him discomfited was at least one satisfaction.

Bayard seemed not to remember. He sat at the card table and looked about. "It seems suitably gloomy for a séance."

Estes shuddered. Louisa sat between him and Bayard. Then Miss Wentworth. Then me.

"Everyone take hands," Bayard instructed. When we were all linked, he looked pointedly at me. "I think we must relax."

"I'm supposed to be on the alert for evil—isn't that why I'm here?" I asked.

"No spirits will come if you're unpleasant," Louisa said.

"That is exactly the outcome I hope for."

Estes said, "Calina, try to put your bigoted papist beliefs aside for a time and enter into the spirit of the game."

"It doesn't feel much like a game to me."

"Vanni," Bayard said pointedly.

"Do you know what to do?" Miss Wentworth asked.

"I've been to a few of these," Bayard answered. "Close your eyes and concentrate with me. Put all your thoughts toward my words."

The room settled heavily about us, the pressing murk and those long-dead French kings stultifying. If there were a room in the Diodati meant for calling the dead, this was it. I felt as I had in the nave at the monastery, that there was something hovering, waiting. Miss Wentworth's hand flexed in mine. I glanced at her, surprised. She stared straight ahead, but she was as rigid as I. Was it evil she anticipated—or something else? What ghost was she expecting tonight?

Whatever it was, her sister seemed to have no such concerns. Across the table, Louisa beamed like a child waiting for Christmas candy.

"Spirits, hear us," Bayard intoned. "We are searching for the spirit of Lord Byron. If he be among you, send him to us."

Nothing but the sound of our breathing.

He quoted, "'The Lord is my shepherd . . .'"

I was grateful for the psalm's comfort, and also for the fact that this time Estes did not pervert it. I joined in while the others remained silent.

At the finish, Bayard said, "Oh spirits, we beseech you to send us Lord Byron. If you hear us, send a sign."

Nothing.

"Spirits, do you hear us?"

Silence.

Estes quoted Byron softly, "'To fly from, need not be to hate, mankind; All are not fit with them to stir and toil . . .'"

". . . 'Nor is it discontent to keep the mind, deep in its fountain,'" Louisa joined in a whisper.

Again, Miss Wentworth's hand flexed—more fiercely this time.

Bayard said, "Will you come to us, O spirit? Will you enlighten us? Tell us if you hear us."

Excruciating silence. Something gathering, waiting, wanting to push inside.

Tap.

I nearly started from my chair. Bayard's hand tightened to keep me in place. Miss Wentworth squeezed.

Bayard leaned forward eagerly. "Spirit? Byron, is that you? One tap for yes, two for no."

A screech, a scrape along the house from the outside, and then the pattering of what sounded like stones falling.

"He is here!" Louisa shouted.

Estes leaped to his feet with a scream. He backed away from the table, wide-eyed, putting up his hands to ward off an enemy, just as he had during his night terrors.

"Julian," Miss Wentworth said. "For God's sake—"

"What do you see?" Louisa pushed back her chair so hard it crashed to the floor, making us all jump. She ran to him. "Jules, what is it? Do you see him? What do you see?"

"The portrait," he whispered, pale with fear.

"What portrait?"

He held out a shaking finger. "Did you not see it? It disappeared and then returned. He *left the canvas!*"

We all looked toward the wall with the painted kings. None had changed.

"They're all just as they were, Jules," Bayard said.

"He was gone! He was gone and then he returned! Of *course* they look the same now! Don't you understand? He was gone!"

Louisa cried out, putting her face in her hands.

"Louisa, please," Miss Wentworth pleaded. "Louisa, don't—"

"It was an omen, don't you see?" Estes announced. "An omen of death! One of us is fated to die!"

Louisa let out a moan of horror. "Oh! Oh! Don't say it!"

Bayard said, "Come now, Jules."

"You don't see it! You don't see it! My God, I would tear it out!" Estes raced across the room, and we all watched in horror as he launched himself at the offending portrait and began to claw at it.

"Estes!" Bayard shouted, lurching to his feet. "Leave it! If you ruin it I shall run you through!"

Estes seemed not to hear him. Miss Wentworth sat utterly still, looking helpless and exhausted. Louisa backed into the wall, clutching her head, staring at the portraits as if they'd come to life before her.

I was done with all of it. Done with stupidity and mockery and blind ignorance. Done with conciliations that seemed to amount to nothing. I took the glass of wine I'd brought with me and strode over to Estes. I grabbed his shoulder and jerked him around, and then I threw the wine into his face.

"What the hell!" he sputtered. "What do you think you're doing?"

"Bringing you to your senses. Though I'm beginning to doubt you have any."

His hair dripped wine; it stained his pale skin, spotting his collar. He growled, "Damn you, Calina," and swung at me. Reflexively, I dodged, and his fist hit only open air.

Bayard was there before he could attempt it again, or before I could respond. He grabbed Estes's arm and pushed me so hard in the chest that I staggered and nearly fell. "Let's not turn this into a brawl."

Louisa hurried over, putting her arms around Estes as she glared at me. "Keep away from him!"

I clenched my fists and stepped back, stumbling into Miss Wentworth, who had come up behind me, and who was now scratching her chin so brutally and compulsively that I could not stop myself from drawing her hand from it.

"You'll make it bleed," I said.

She wrenched away. "Don't—"

From downstairs came the sound of breaking glass.

TWELVE

ADELAIDE

We all froze.

Mr. Calina said, "That came from downstairs." He ran to the door. "We'll need your pistols," he said to Bayard, who was right after him.

Bayard called back, "The women must stay here."

"Do as he says," Julian said to me. "Lock the door."

He followed them out, leaving Louisa and me alone. I went to close the door.

"No!" Louisa cried in panic. "We can't stay here."

"He told us to wait."

"We *can't stay here.*"

"Louisa, you have no idea what—"

"There are demons here!"

I took her shoulders, shaking her. "No, Loulou. No, there aren't."

"The picture moved!"

"It didn't. It was the laudanum—"

She wrenched free of me, pushing past to grab the door, and then flinging it open with such force it cracked against the wall.

"Louisa, no, you can't!"

But I was no match for her fear. She ran from the room.

I had known this would happen. I had known all of it from the moment Louisa had suggested the séance. I should have stopped it. Why hadn't I? What chance had there been that it would turn out any other way?

I went after my sister. "Louisa! Louisa, stop!"

Her skirts billowed about her as she ran. She stumbled down the stairs. I caught her arm, trying to pull her back, but she jerked free, tearing down the last few steps into the hall. A woman screamed. I heard racing footsteps; two figures flew past in a blur of motion. One of them pushed Louisa out of the way. She fell sprawling to the floor just as Bayard sped after the intruders. Then everything happened at once: the patio door crashed open; a shot rang out; Bayard veered to miss Louisa and then spun with a gasp and went down, a dead weight on top of her. She cried out in pain and surprise.

It was all so fast. I stood with my hand on the banister, staring blankly at my sister and an unmoving Bayard.

"Bayard?" Mr. Calina slid to a stop at the tangle of my sister and Bayard, and fell to his knees beside them. "Oh no. No, no."

"Louisa? Louisa, are you hurt?" Jules sounded panicked as he ran up. In his hand was a gun.

My sister said, "I'm fine. I'm not hurt."

"Bayard. Bayard!" Mr. Calina pulled Bayard from Louisa. He took Bayard's face between his hands, and when he brought one away, his fingers were smeared with blood. He turned to Julian. "What have you done?"

"He jumped into the way! I couldn't help it! He jumped right into the shot!" Julian's voice shook; he had gone pale.

"Why in God's name did you shoot?"

The maid appeared, looking horrified and fearful, kneading her skirt in her hands.

Louisa struggled to sit up. "He's not dead, is he? Oh, tell me he's not dead!"

"We told you to stay upstairs!" Mr. Calina said angrily. "Why did you come down?"

"There were demons in that room! Jules saw them too!"

I wanted to shake her. "You know there were no demons, Loulou. Both of you know it. There was nothing there but your own cursed imaginations."

Julian stiffened.

Louisa said, "You've never been able to see such things as we can, Addie. You can't—"

"Stop talking," Mr. Calina ground out. He had been examining Bayard, and now he looked up with relief. "He's breathing, thank God. I think it's only a graze. You could have killed him, Estes. Do you even know how to aim a gun? You could have killed any of us."

"He jumped in front of the bullet," Julian protested again. "I tell you I had them in my sights. If Bayard hadn't moved at just that moment . . ."

"But he's going to be all right, isn't he? Please tell me he's going to be all right." Louisa reached to touch him, and Mr. Calina shoved his elbow at her, pushing her away.

"Don't you think you've done enough harm?"

"This isn't my fault. How can you say it's my fault?"

"Who was screaming about demons? Who didn't stay where she was told?"

Bayard groaned.

Mr. Calina turned back to him, Louisa forgotten. "Bayard, for God's sake, talk to me."

Bayard's eyes flickered open. He blinked, and then frowned. "What the hell?" He put his hand to his head. "I feel like I've been hit with an anvil. What happened?"

"Estes shot you," Mr. Calina said.

"It was an accident!" Julian cried. "Damn you, Calina, you know that's not what happened. I was firing after the intruders."

Bayard struggled to sit up, groaning again.

Mr. Calina said, "Careful. You've just been grazed by a bullet."

The maid said something in French. Both Mr. Calina and Louisa looked at her.

"What is it? What did she say?" I asked.

"That it was our fault for calling the devil," Louisa said softly, and I saw again the start of that too-familiar fear.

I didn't know whether to cry or scream. "Tell the woman to be quiet."

Mr. Calina glared at me. "You should have stayed upstairs. None of this would have happened if Louisa hadn't been in the way."

"He's right. You were told to stay," Julian said.

Of course it was not Julian's fault. It never was. "You had Louisa overwrought with your foolish talk of devils and portraits disappearing. What did you expect would happen?"

Julian looked as if I'd struck him.

"He's not to blame," Louisa defended. "He can't help seeing those things, Addie. I saw them too."

"Your nonsense nearly caused a tragedy."

Julian stepped between us. "Loulou's sensibilities—"

"She is not a child," I said. "Nor are you."

"Then stop scolding as if we were," Louisa said angrily. "You're not my mother, or Julian's. You're no one's mother."

It was perfectly lobbed. She knew it would hurt me and it did.

Louisa's eyes glistened with tears. She showed her emotions in a way I never could. Julian pulled her to her feet and into his arms, soothing her, saying, "There's no need for any of this. It was an accident—"

"You were too quick with the gun." Mr. Calina's voice was sharp. "And the women should have stayed upstairs. There's plenty of blame to go around."

Bayard stumbled and fell heavily into his secretary as Mr. Calina helped him rise.

Louisa said plaintively, "Bay, you don't blame us for this, do you?"

He winced. "My head is about to explode. Hand me my walking stick, Vanni, will you?"

Mr. Calina glanced around. "Where is it?"

"Right there, on the chair. Beside my coat and hat," Bayard said.

"I don't see them."

Bayard winced again as he turned to look. "They were right there. I left them when we came in from the boat."

Mr. Calina asked something of the maid in French, and when she answered, he translated, "Sylvie saw them too, just before she went up to tend the fire in the salon. It seems that our intruders were thieves."

"Damn, that stick cost me a pretty penny. That lion's head was solid gold."

"As soon as you're situated, I'll go for the police," Mr. Calina said.

"But you'll have to go into Geneva, won't you? It's past midnight," I said.

"Wait for morning," Bayard agreed.

"I've done it before."

"Yes, but not on my order. Last night was worrisome enough. I won't have your drowning on my head. We're safe for now."

Louisa lifted her head from Julian's shoulder. "Are we? Are you certain? How did they get in? What if they come back?"

I said firmly, "They won't come back. Not after someone shot at them."

"We heard glass breaking. Probably they came in through a window," Mr. Calina said.

Julian said, "It seems I was right the other night after all. There were people outside. Perhaps the next time, you'll believe me."

"By all means, we should rely on your witness." Mr. Calina snorted. "Given that when there actually were people in the yard, you were too busy seeing Louis the Sixteenth vanish to notice."

Louisa pulled from Julian's embrace to go to Bayard. "Jules and I will help you upstairs." She gave Mr. Calina an annoyed look. "He'll need bandages. Fetch them, will you? And don't you think you should check the windows?"

Mr. Calina looked ready to protest, but then Bayard said, "Yes, do."

"We'll get you set right," Jules said, taking Bayard's arm over his shoulder. Louisa took Bayard's other side. Together they helped him up the stairs.

As they disappeared from sight, Mr. Calina said beneath his breath, "Yes indeed, go with those who nearly killed you tonight."

"She didn't mean it," I said wearily. "She never means it. Neither of them do. They just get so . . ."

"I liked it better when you were blaming them," he said. "You'd best go upstairs."

But I knew going upstairs would mean watching Julian and Louisa bending their heads together, conferring in whispers, conspiring, excusing, justifying. *Sometimes I envy you, Addie. You don't know how torturous it is to be possessed of such feeling. I would love to be so reasoned.*

She never suspected that sometimes I wanted to be the tempestuous storm that everyone else must tiptoe safely around, to scream as I had on the boat. What a relief it had been. How easy life must be when everyone else took responsibility, when they made the excuses, when all it took to win was charm and a whispered *I wish I could control myself better,* and that slip of fear in her eyes that told one it was true.

I was so tired. I did not think I could manage to look at my sister again tonight, and I did not want to hear Julian's rationalizations. So I said, "I'll stay and help you look around."

"I can't allow it. I don't know if someone is still inside. I can't guarantee your safety. And frankly, Miss Wentworth, I've had enough of being blamed for things I can't control." Mr. Calina gestured to the maid, who still looked half-terrified, her gaze bewildered and darting between us. He said something to her, and she came toward me. "Sylvie will escort you back to your room."

"I'd rather stay here."

"Do you not understand? I don't want you here. None of you. You and your cursed sister and Estes can all go to hell. Bayard could have been killed, thanks to the three of you."

"What a tragedy that would have been for you." His anger raised mine; I was tense and wounded and he was there, once again a convenient target. "Who would you be without Bayard? Just another would-be writer groveling for attention. Why, no one would notice you at all."

My barb stuck; his expression went stark with surprised hurt, and then grimly furious. "That's a pretty statement coming from you." He barked an order to the maid, and she scurried off, quick as a cockroach, disappearing into the gloom beyond the hall. "Do you ever say no to either of them? They're cavorting about like lunatics, and all you do is sit there and watch. Are you even in the world, Miss Wentworth? I begin to wonder if the reason you know ghosts so well is because you're one yourself."

My chin began to itch. "You don't understand anything—"

"Frankly, I never wish to. I don't know what Louisa told you when she dragged you all here, but I assure you it was some half-mad fantasy. Bayard didn't want her to follow us. He hoped to put her out of his life forever. We weren't expecting you. So do me a favor and take your sister and your lover and go back to London, or Concord, or wherever the hell you want. God knows I'm sick to death of the lot of you."

He slapped his hand against the railing post for emphasis, and then he strode off, disappearing into the darkness of the hall.

I rubbed my chin, but the itch only grew worse. Nothing would relieve it, nothing but my nails, nothing but pain, and so I stared out the still-open door, into a night soft with sound, the *shhusshh* of a breeze skimming the lake touched with the scent of snow from the mountains and the faint hint of lavender, ghosts and demons in the branches, regrets and sorrows, and I scratched, scratching and scratching until it no longer itched but burned, and when I finally forced myself to stop, my fingers were smeared with my own blood.

Julian did not come to bed until I was already there. I pretended to be asleep, but I wasn't, not then, and not later. Whenever I closed my eyes, I dreamed of the storm, lightning and curses, spirits trying to embrace the ones they had loved, and I would jerk awake again.

I must have slept eventually, because I woke to the sun climbing high into the sky and the sound of voices downstairs, Julian's among them. I dressed and went to join them on the terrace.

The day was beautiful, again with last night's snow-scented breeze, blending now with the perfumes of cows and budding grapes and sun-warmed stucco. Birds tweeted as they flew from branch to branch, fluttering the leaves, raising the objections of crows and squirrels. It was difficult to believe in last night's terrifying chaos, or it would have been, had Louisa not turned from the railing where she and Julian stood to say, "The police are here. Bayard and Mr. Calina are with them."

"Already?"

"Apparently Calina set off at dawn." Julian's eyes were mostly iris. His hand went reflexively to his pocket as if to reassure himself that his flask was there, but then he caught my dismay, and let his hand fall.

The muffled voices emerged from the first floor, growing louder as the men I assumed were police stepped onto the lawn. Mr. Calina followed, and then Bayard, who was nodding as he listened to one of the police officers. He wore a bandage at his temple.

Mr. Calina looked as if he hadn't slept. His hair was unbrushed, which was so unlike him that Julian asked, "Could he not find a comb this morning?" He still wore the clothes he'd had on yesterday. His watch chain dangled loose, and the red-and-black embroidered waistcoat was half-unbuttoned, the collar of his shirt removed, buttons gaping open.

Bayard's calculated dishevelment was intriguing and nonchalant and fashionable, even with the bandage. Mr. Calina only looked disheveled.

"You've barely searched," he accused the officers.

"What is there to find?" one of them replied. "We cannot help it if all the world wishes to stare at Monsieur Sonnier."

"This wasn't staring. It was trespassing."

He shrugged. "I suggest a guard dog."

"I suggest that you find the thieves and prosecute them so we have no repeats."

"How should we find them, monsieur?" asked the other officer. "You saw nothing to identify them. Only—what was it? Gray coats? Or they might have been brown or black? You have no idea how tall they were or what they looked like. You do not even know if they were men."

The other police officer said, "We will send someone around to the pawn shops. The cane, at least, should be easy to identify."

"I told you it wouldn't *be* in the pawnshops!" Mr. Calina exploded. "Whoever stole it took it because it belongs to Bayard. That's the only reason they broke in—to see him. It's a souvenir. They're not going to sell it."

"How do you suggest we find such a thing, then?" asked the officer reasonably. "Shall we search every house on the lake?"

"Bah!" Mr. Calina threw up his hands. "God forbid that you should do your job."

Even from where I stood, I saw how the officer bristled. He turned to Bayard. "We will watch for the missing items, Monsieur Sonnier."

The other officer looked at his notebook. "A herringbone coat, a straw hat, and a cane of . . . pine, was it? With a gold lion's head?"

"Ebony, you fool," Mr. Calina said.

Bayard put a restraining hand on his secretary's shoulder. "Ebony, yes."

"Do you intend to tell us how you mean to keep such a thing from happening again?" Mr. Calina asked.

The policemen exchanged a glance. One of them said, "Perhaps Geneva was not the best place for a holiday. Not for a man of Monsieur Sonnier's fame. We are beset by tourists most of the year, and many of them have come this season solely to see such a famous writer. You understand, we cannot control them all. There is no law against looking."

"But there is one against breaking and entering, isn't there?"

The man inclined his head in agreement. "If you discover who has the things that were stolen, we will certainly pursue the matter."

Mr. Calina made a sound of frustration and walked away. Bayard spoke to the policemen in quiet tones, and the three of them went across the yard toward the road.

Julian said quietly, "He should not have lost his temper. It will do no good."

"He doesn't want us here," I heard myself say.

Julian turned to me in surprise. "What?"

"He told me last night that we were unexpected and unwelcome. He said we should leave."

"Of course he would say that," Louisa said.

"Why?" I asked softly. "Why of course?"

A warning was in her eyes. "I've told you already, Addie. He wants to keep Bay all to himself. But Bayard asked me to visit him here."

"Did he?" I asked. "Did he really, Loulou?"

"Yes. I told him I would like to see Geneva and he said he would be angry if I traveled alone. What is that if not an invitation?"

I looked back to the yard, and beyond it to the rippling lake. "I think we may have overstayed our welcome last night."

"It was an accident," Julian stated again.

"He wasn't the least bit upset," Louisa said.

"Have you spoken to him this morning? Is he still so forgiving?"

"Why wouldn't he be? Really, Addie, you're making far too much of this."

To Julian, I said, "I think we should consider leaving."

"And go where? There's no money."

"Perhaps your father would see reason. Perhaps he could help—"

Julian laughed shortly. "You were standing there when he ordered me from the house. Did he look the least bit reasonable?"

No, not reasonable. In fact, he'd resembled my father on one of his worst days, with his hair on end as if he'd tried to pull it out, his cheeks red and bulging as Julian had protested, *"But it's Adelaide I love. Would you have me ignore my conscience?"*

"Your conscience? Your wife is expecting and you think to just pretend she doesn't exist? I warned you Emily was unsuitable, and now you've only replaced her with an even more unsuitable whore. I hope your conscience can live on love, because you shall have nothing more from me."

"No, but it's been months, Jules. It's possible. Things change."

"Really? Have your parents? I assure you my father has not. Besides, there's Bayard to consider. I need him. You know that."

"You've written almost nothing," I said. "How can he recommend what doesn't exist?"

"It sounds as if you no longer believe in me."

"No. No, but if things like last night keep happening, there will be more gossip, and it will be only a matter of time before someone realizes who we are, and it will all start again. We've caused him nothing but trouble since we've arrived."

Louisa said, "We aren't going anywhere."

"You and Bayard have become friends," I went on to Julian. "We should go before that's ruined."

He considered.

"Oh, please don't speak again of hiding in some small town," Louisa protested. "The talk is so old, Addie. Surely it's died out by now. They'll all be gossiping of something else."

There was a noise behind us.

It was Bayard and Mr. Calina, and now I could see what I hadn't at a distance. Spreading from beneath Bayard's bandage was a bright purple bruise, and one of his eyes was black. As handsome as he was, it only gave him a rakish look. In contrast, Mr. Calina had circles beneath his eyes, and he was unshaven, and swarthy enough that his beard shadow seemed to darken his entire countenance.

Bayard said as he approached, "Vanni thinks the thieves were looking for me, and the police agree. They suggest we disappear for a few days to discourage anyone who might be thinking about trying the same thing. For my own safety, of course." He made a face. "They'll put out the word that we've decided to take a house somewhere else and perhaps that will be enough."

I gave Julian a pointed look. It was a perfect opportunity, and suddenly going away was what I wanted most to do. We had stayed here long enough. Bayard had no real interest in Louisa; he'd told me that himself, and if he had not, Mr. Calina had made it very clear. We could leave. Surely Bayard and Julian were close enough now that Bayard would offer to help, even if we did.

But Louisa rushed in as if she knew what I was thinking, "Perhaps a tour? I have always wanted to see the Mer de Glace."

"They say it looks like a stormy sea frozen in place," Julian said dreamily.

"Oh yes!" Louisa said. "You've been there, haven't you, Bay? You would be a perfect guide."

Mr. Calina said, "He's nearly an invalid. I've been trying to convince him that what he needs is a quiet inn and solitude, but—"

"Oh, you can't mean it," Louisa said. "You would be so lonely without us."

I said, "Louisa, he is hurt. Perhaps it would be best."

She glared at me.

"Of course, Bay, if it's what you require, we'll understand," Julian said. "I feel guilty enough for shooting you. I would not do anything to delay your healing."

Bayard shook his head. "There's no need. But I fear I'm not quite up to climbing glaciers. I had thought perhaps the Castle of Chillon. We could stay at Villeneuve. From there it's an easy walk to the castle."

Julian smiled. "I should like that very much."

My own protests died. I glanced at Mr. Calina, who gave me a look that said better than words how much he wished we had all disappeared during the night.

"We could see for ourselves the dungeon where Bonivard was locked away," Bayard went on. "I could use the same kind of inspiration that caused Byron to write 'The Prisoner of Chillon.'"

"Your publisher would surely appreciate it," Mr. Calina commented.

I had not read Byron's poem in some time, but it was hard to forget the bleak loneliness and suffering he had captured in the story of the prior of St. Victor who'd been imprisoned for conspiring against the Duke of Savoy. I was not at all certain I wished to see the site of such misery. I had enough sorrows of my own.

"Indeed," Bayard said wryly. "Pack enough for two days, and bring anything you think valuable, just in case the police are wrong. We'll leave in the morning. Come with me, Jules, and distract me with your philosophies."

Julian hurried after him like a supplicant, and Mr. Calina followed more slowly after, and when they were inside, Louisa turned to me with a triumphant smile.

"Do you see, Addie? You were wrong. He cannot bear to have us go." She hurried after them, vibrant and happy.

I turned back to the lake just as the wind came up, and watched it whip the quiet ripples into white-crested waves.

THIRTEEN

VANNI

He had not listened to my argument, of course. When the police left, and Bayard told me that they'd suggested we leave for a few days, I'd laughed. "Yes, of course. Why don't they just admit that they're incompetent and be done with it? Besides, we can't just leave the way it is. The window's broken."

"The police said they would send a glazier over. It will be fixed before we return. We'll leave tomorrow."

"Tomorrow?" I could not hide my dismay. I was to have tea with Vera Brest tomorrow. *We'll have the garden to ourselves,* she'd said. Her full mouth and the kiss I'd hoped to turn into more. Not only that, but I was anxious to return Colburn's money and ask him to rip up the contract. Last night, I'd been so annoyed I'd nearly written in the journal again, and I wanted the temptation gone before some other incident—and there was no doubt there would be one—conquered my resistance. "But I've been invited to tea."

"For God's sake, you've been drawing out your seduction of that woman long enough that another two days won't matter. Send Sylvie back to her with a message that you'll see her soon." Bayard put his hand to his head. "Have we a headache powder somewhere?"

"I'll find one," I assured him. "So what do we do with our guests? They won't be happy to leave, but I suppose I can—"

"We'll bring them along."

"Bring them along? Why? You wanted to be rid of her, and now you've got reason. Thanks to her, Estes nearly killed you last night."

"I'm willing to forgive them this time. Jules is a bad shot, but that's hardly a crime."

"It could have ended as one," I noted. "We came here for quiet, remember, so you could write, and now—"

"Please don't nag at me today." He touched the bandage at his temple, wincing. "You're right, of course; last night was a fiasco, and if it were anyone else, I'd have them out the door, but I'm not done with him. If that means I have to bear Louisa for a while longer, then so be it. I can at least think of a use for her."

Nothing I said could change his mind. Finally, he said, "You're making my head worse. Stop talking. Let's tell them to pack."

And so, the next morning, we took the road to Geneva, each of us with little more than a small bag. The women insisted on carrying their own—"We are women, but we are not helpless, Mr. Calina," said Louisa tartly when I noted it. No doubt one more oddity of their Fourierian upbringing. I carried Bayard's bag, as he looked half ready to faint. Mine was not heavy, but I was too aware of what it held: Bayard's story, with my own addendum. I'd tried to leave it locked away with the journal, but at the last minute I'd fetched it again—I couldn't help but hope that—as Bayard said—I too might find inspiration in the place that had inspired Byron.

Bayard did not keep a carriage here; most of our travel was done via the lake, and so there was no need. The distance to the city was not great, and he claimed that the jarring and swaying of a carriage would only make his head worse, and the fresh air might help. I was dubious—he looked terrible—but he could not be persuaded otherwise, and so I watched him carefully, and we were all silent in deference to his obvious pain. Louisa darted anxious glances at him, as if afraid she had already lost his attention in the two days she'd had to sleep alone—I wished to hell it were true. Estes walked beside him, where I should have been, putting his free hand to Bayard's arm whenever he seemed to stumble. Miss Wentworth trailed behind, slowly enough that I had to keep waiting, and when I said, "It would be best if you caught up," she said, a bit nastily, "Forgive me for delaying you." She was obviously not the least bit happy to go to Chillon. I wondered why, but I was still angry with her for the other night, and so I didn't ask.

The morning was at least pleasant, if cool, with clear skies and a calm lake scattered with flocks of ducks floating lazily near the shore. There was no breeze to sweep away the scent of manure or the clouds of dust raised by passing carriages or wagons or a herd of goats, whose tinkling bells clashed discordantly with their bleating. When we reached Geneva, those bucolic smells gave way to those of the city—stone and fried fish, smoke and baking bread, tar and sewage. The pier clamored with the talk of other passengers, of which there were quite a few. As we walked to the ship, the boards creaked beneath our feet, and gulls jawed and swooped so low it seemed they meant to snatch the hats from our heads. Bayard pulled his brim down low to hide his face, and flipped up the collar of his coat, and left the arrangements to me. We passed the officers lined on either side of the pier without incident. I handed our passports to the soldier who stood at the entrance of the boarding plank, and he glanced over mine cursorily and handed it back. Then he opened Bayard's, hesitating at the name. I tensed as he glanced up.

"Are you really—"

"Yes, he is," I interrupted. "And I'll thank you to keep your voice down. We're not looking for attention."

He stared curiously at Bayard, but he handed the passport back without a word, and we boarded, Estes and the Wentworth sisters following.

"It's so chilly this morning," Louisa said with a delicate shudder. She smiled at Bayard. "Let's go inside."

I stopped her as she started toward the main salon. "Not there. It's too crowded."

"What do crowds matter to me?"

"It's not you I worry about." I indicated Bayard. "The small salon, please."

"But no one goes there."

I didn't bother to argue. While not many recognized Bayard on sight, I did not trust her to keep it quiet. The fewer people, the better. "This way."

Miss Wentworth said, "I think I'll watch the view for a while."

She started toward the railing. Louisa looked worried and touched Estes's arm. "You'd best go with her, Jules. She's been short with me all morning."

He nodded, looking equally worried, and went after her. Once Estes was gone, and Louisa no longer had to hide that she and Bayard were lovers—barely hiding, really. How much laudanum must a man drink to be so oblivious?—she claimed Bayard, clinging closely and insistently as we went to the small salon, which was intimate and well-appointed, with a few upholstered striped chairs near the unlit fireplace, two settees, and heavy burgundy drapes at the windows. The only thing to mar the illusion of an elegant parlor was the bare, scuffed floor. There were not many people there, but those had no wish for company, as I knew from experience. Most of them read or slept and ignored the others. As the ship started off, the clerk came around with his slate, asking us where we wished to go and taking money for the tickets, which I paid for us all from Bayard's purse.

Bayard slumped onto a settee and rested his head in his hand, looking both exhausted and in pain. Louisa sat beside him. When I came to join them, she complained, "There's nothing to do in here."

"You could take in the view with your sister," I suggested. "It really is beautiful."

"I've seen it nearly every day, haven't I? From the boat or from the terrace."

"You might find inspiration for your contest story." I had not seen her write a thing, and I didn't think she meant to try, but I couldn't help baiting her. "After all, the deadline gets closer every day."

"I think you're the one who needs inspiration, given what you showed us the other night."

"You've given up the contest already, haven't you?" I asked.

She gave me a dark look. "I haven't had time. Bay likes me to sit near him while he writes."

"Then you mustn't be too busy, given that he's written nothing the last few days."

Bayard said in warning, "Vanni."

I shrugged. "It's true, isn't it? Hanson is going to start haranguing you any day. You can't even bring yourself to finish your story for the contest, which is too bad, because it's fascinating." Which I should know, as much as I'd studied it.

"I am going to throw you overboard if you don't stop," Bayard groaned. "Or at least I'll try to."

Louisa said, "You've read his story? When you're competing as well? That hardly seems fair."

"I'm his secretary. Of course I've read it."

"It gives you an advantage over the rest of us. Why, you could even be stealing Bayard's ideas."

A bit too close.

Bayard lifted his face from his hand. "Do you really think I'd let someone steal something I wrote?"

155

Louisa's eyes sparkled with malice. "If I were you, my love, I wouldn't trust another writer to copy out my work. You need a secretary who harbors no ambitions of his own."

"I don't worry over Vanni's ambitions. Even if he were to take my ideas, what could he do with them that would make any difference to me?"

It sounded like disdain, and it wounded. *Say nothing,* I warned myself, and for once I listened, barely managing an "Excuse me" as I rose abruptly. I made my way out of the salon, to the railing, and let the view and the breeze raised by the ship's movement relax me by degrees. I had spent so long tending to my own ambitions and trying to be indispensable to Bayard that I'd let everything else in my life—friends, amusements, interests—drift away. I had only my father and his expectations, and Bayard, and here was Louisa Wentworth telling him to distrust me, and the worst of it was that she was right. He *should* distrust me. I was betraying him, not just with the contract I'd signed, but with the story I was stealing—

No, I wasn't stealing it. I wasn't. I was playing with it. I was experimenting and nothing more. I would never share it. It was only that Louisa Wentworth knew where I was most defenseless. Why shouldn't she? I had told her things I had never told another living soul. I'd been so exhilarated by her interest those six months ago—even knowing what must be the truth of it—that I'd shared my hopes, my obligations, my insecurities. This was her petty revenge for London—though she had been just as much to blame as I, equally blinded by wishful thinking.

But I made it so easy for her to malign me. I had to keep a better rein on my temper. I couldn't let these people affect the future I wanted for myself. My own actions made me vulnerable.

I should not have left the salon. She was probably criticizing me as I stood here. I should be beside him, defending myself.

I turned to go back. It was only then that I saw what I would have already heard, had I not been consumed by my thoughts. Chattering, a low and constant murmur, small screams of delight. A crowd had gathered at the door of the small salon, all of them trying to get inside. I'd seen it before. I knew immediately what it was.

Someone had recognized Bayard.

I hurried toward the salon. Before I could reach it, Estes and Miss Wentworth stopped me. I hadn't even noted they were near.

"Whatever is going on?" Miss Wentworth asked.

"Bayard," I said curtly.

"Look at them," Estes said in amazement. "You'd think they'd never seen a writer before."

"He's not just a writer. He's a god to some of them," I pointed out.

"What would that be like, I wonder?"

"Wretched, I should think," Miss Wentworth said.

"Would it?" Estes asked. "People clamoring for you? Hanging on your every word? Stealing your coat just to have something you touched?" A melancholy came over his face that I recognized, because I'd seen it in myself. Envy was in his every line. In this, we had something in common. It did not make me like him better.

"I've got to get in there," I said. "See if you can't find a steward or a clerk or someone."

"I will," Miss Wentworth volunteered. Then, to Estes, "You should help Mr. Calina."

I didn't wait to see if he followed as I rushed to the door, trying to get through. "Pardon me. Please let me through. Pardon me." People pushed me back. Some glared. Another elbowed me in the stomach.

"Wait your turn, sir! We all want to see him," said a woman in a lacy hat.

The salon was so full of people it was hard to move, but I forced my way through. Bayard was just where I'd left him, standing now, his hat pushed back, the bandage, the bruise, and his black eye only accenting his paleness. He smiled, but I recognized the pain in it, and how he anchored himself near the settee. At any moment, he might swoon.

I searched for Louisa—there, pressed to the side, looking upset and uncertain, separated from him by the crowd.

"Step back, please!" I demanded as I reached the front and turned to face them. "I must ask you to step back."

"Where the hell have you been?" Bayard asked in an undertone. He shook someone's hand. "Yes, thank you. Thank you so much. I appreciate that." And to someone else, "No, nothing to worry about. A hunting accident, that's all."

I gestured for them to move back. "I'm afraid I must ask you all to leave. Mr. Sonnier is here on holiday. I'm sure you understand."

The woman beside him ignored me, twittering over him as if he were the Second Coming. "Oh, Mr. Sonnier, I think you cannot know how much I admire and respect you. I would do anything for you—you have only to ask it."

I stepped between them. "Madam, if you will please move on." Gently I took her elbow, leading her away. I could not go far; only a few feet, but she obeyed tearfully, and the crowd swallowed her up.

Estes burst through, his already wild hair electrified with static. "Now, now, good people! I'll thank you all to return to your strolls about the deck and leave Mr. Sonnier in peace."

He said it so confidently that I wanted to laugh. They didn't listen to him any more than they had me. In fact, the crowd surged closer, as if afraid they would be repulsed before they could get to Bayard. Estes looked crestfallen when he realized it.

I turned back to the crowd, no longer patient. "Move back," I demanded. "No crowding. You'll have your turn."

Until help arrived, there was nothing else to do. Bayard's jaw clenched. I stood close to him, and once or twice he swayed, bracing himself against me. I looked toward the door, hoping for Miss Wentworth to arrive with help, but instead all I saw were more people pouring in. Bayard would never survive if this lasted the entire four hours. He would have my head.

"Now, now, we'll have none of this! The salon won't fit the lot of you—you must disperse!"

With relief, I saw the steward at the door, two crewmen behind him. He looked irritated and perplexed. He spoke again, in German, French, and English. His crewmen began not so politely forcing people out. Slowly but surely, they rid the small salon of the crowd, even through the protests.

When only a few people remained, the steward stepped up to Bayard. "So you're the trouble?"

"Apparently so," Bayard said, his voice heavy with relief, though he was charming as always. "Thank you for your help."

"All these people wanted to see a *writer*?" The steward was obviously confounded by the idea.

I said, "We're off at Villeneuve—is there someplace we can go until then? Out of the way? Otherwise he'll be mobbed the entire time now that they know he's here."

The steward still seemed bewildered, but he nodded. "Aye. Come with me. We can't have the boat listing because everyone's gathering in one place to stare at a man who scribbles."

To me, Bayard murmured, "Nothing like the hoi polloi to humble a man."

I was glad he was amused. He might just as well have been furious. And then I realized, as we all followed the steward, Bayard's hand on my arm for support, that he was.

"You should have been here to prevent it," he said to me tightly.

"How did they discover you?"

"She went to the window and called me over."

I winced.

"She said something about the view inspiring one of my novels."

"She wanted you to acknowledge her," I said. "I think she's upset about last night."

"She's a willful little fiend."

I couldn't tell if he spoke with admiration or annoyance, but I did hear a slip of impatience with our guests.

He went on, "It never would have happened if you had been here instead of stomping off in a pique."

"She insulted me," I said quietly.

"For God's sake, Vanni, do you think I care in the least about that? She's just a woman. Stop letting her get under your skin."

The steward took us belowdecks, to a small and somewhat desolate room used by the crew. It smelled of sweat and oilcloth and cheese—an unpleasant combination—and consisted of a row of narrow wooden lockers and some slatted benches. Two small portholes showed the sky, but the view didn't matter, as they were too high to look through. A chessboard littered with pieces was on one of the benches.

I said, "There's no private salon?"

"We've a great many passengers on this voyage, sir. This is the best I can do."

Bayard said, "It's fine, Vanni. Thank you, my good man. I'm grateful for your help."

The steward left us.

Estes gestured to the chess set. "Care for a game, Bay?"

The two of them sat to play. Bayard nearly fell onto the bench as Estes set up the board. Miss Wentworth stood to the side, watching, as quiet and distracted as she'd been when we'd first boarded.

With what I hoped was cold politeness, I said, "I haven't yet thanked you for fetching the steward so quickly, Miss Wentworth."

She answered, "He was already on his way. He'd seen the crowd. He was very surprised when I told him what caused it."

"Usually Vanni is quite brilliant at preventing such things," Bayard said. "Unfortunately this time he was too busy sulking."

Estes laughed.

I turned away. Once again, taking the blame, and though it was my fault for leaving, the real cause was at the far side of the room, wandering back and forth, dragging her hand along the back of the bench, obviously troubled and transparently trying to get someone's attention—probably Estes's, given that Bayard was constrained by his promise to keep their affair secret, and angry with her as well. They both ignored her. I knew Bayard would keep doing so, at least for a time—it was his favorite punishment to inflict on a woman. It was some comfort to know I was not the only persona non grata in the room, and I confess I was glad to see her distressed. The only thing I would have liked better was if she were gone.

Villeneuve stood at the head of the lake, keeping watch over the valley of the Rhône, which in one direction was filled with Lac Léman, the water reflecting the dark mountains of Savoy, and in the other was carpeted in bright green and fertile fields, with the ribbon of the river winding through.

The vine-covered hills around Villeneuve were beginning to feel redundant, as were the scents of cows and hay and grapes, but the village itself was pretty and neat, surrounded by an ancient wall, with heavy clouds of deep gray smoke rising from the train station at its back. A short distance away, near the shore, was the black shadow of the Castle of Chillon on its little island.

A hotel squatted at the foot of the pier, but Bayard had in mind the Hôtel Byron, given his obsession with the poet, though the inn had nothing to do with Byron beyond its name. It was a short walk, and toward Chillon, and we were all so tired of being cooped up in the steamer that we embraced it eagerly. The road along the lake was a popular walking tour. There were people everywhere, many carrying bags, others following carts drawn by donkeys or goats. Bayard did not hire one—I don't think it occurred to him, given that he was unburdened with luggage—and no one asked him.

The hotel was very grand, four stories with a squarely classical edifice that murmured a soothing gentility, nestled at the foot of hills of terraced vineyards backed by the imposing Savoy. A Swiss flag flew from its roof. The proprietors of the hotel understood that the lake and the view of the Dents du Midi were its main attraction, and a large parklike space stretched before it, lavishly landscaped with parterres, terraces, flower beds, and wide gravel walkways that sloped down to the shore. It was a charming place. It was also full.

"We've only two rooms," said the desk man apologetically, eyeing us. "I am sorry."

"I'm Bayard Sonnier," said Bayard, stepping forward. "Perhaps that makes a difference?"

The man nearly wrung his hands. "I'm afraid I could not make room for God himself, monsieur."

Estes said, "It will do, won't it? Adelaide and Louisa will take one, and the three of us shall take the other."

The man sighed. "There are only three beds total, monsieur. Two in one, one in the other."

"Well, then, Louisa and I will take the one, and the three of you must share the two," Adelaide said.

"It seems we have no choice," Bayard said.

"There are other hotels," I protested.

"None that suit me like this one." He gestured for me to pay. "It's only for two nights. We can adapt."

Obediently, I paid from his purse while we all wrote our names in the register.

"We'll meet for dinner in the garden in an hour," Bayard told the Wentworth sisters as they followed the porter through the magnificent hall to the stairs and their room on an upper floor. The three of us went down the spacious corridor to ours, with its window that seemed too large and lofty for the view—a terrace at the back of the hotel.

Estes let his bag fall to the floor with a thud. "You paid for the room, Bay. You should have a bed to yourself."

Bayard laughed. "And have you telling the story of how I played the prima donna at the next dinner we attend? I don't think so. We'll flip a coin. Whichever two draw the same face will share."

Which, as it turned out, were me and Estes. Bayard got the bed alone after all.

"At least you can't complain that it wasn't fair," Bayard said, throwing his bag onto the mattress and stepping to the window. "Not much scenery, is there?"

I sat on the bed, leaning against the headboard and wishing for a bottle of wine all to myself.

Estes said to Bayard, "How often does that happen? The scene on the steamer, I mean?"

"Often enough," Bayard said. "Especially since *The Temptation* came out."

"Everyone wants to get a look at the debauched and melancholy Gerard," I commented.

"How terrible, to be mistaken for one's own character."

"They say to write what you know," Bayard said with a tired smile. "Everyone believes that I did. I suppose there are parts that aren't far wrong."

"You enthralled both Louisa and Adelaide with it, you know," Estes said. "They read it in Concord. When we came to London, it was all they could talk about, that they might stumble upon the great Bayard Sonnier. When Louisa met you, she could hardly believe her luck."

"She made her own luck," I could not help saying.

Estes frowned at me. "What is that supposed to mean?"

Bayard admonished me with a look.

"Just that she's very determined, isn't she? It's not surprising that she found him."

"She found him? I'd thought they happened upon one another in a bookshop."

Bayard said, "I think Vanni only meant that she recognized me, which is what happened."

"I see." But Estes looked thoughtful. "What then? After she recognized you?"

"Hmmm. I hardly remember. I think"—Bayard looked at me as if I might somehow have divined whatever lie Louisa had told Estes about their meeting—"I think I invited her to accompany me to Lady Arris's salon."

"She said you took her to tea," Estes said.

"Is that it? Well, she would know. I have so many things. I can't keep them straight."

The lie was so labored I was certain Estes must feel it. What did it matter if he knew? Better if he did, if he grew angry with Bayard for seducing her and took her away. In fact, I could not conceive of a better outcome. I said bluntly, "You had dinner. She drank too much."

Estes jerked to attention.

Coldly Bayard said, "Ah yes. The conversation was so engaging I think we both lost track of how many bottles we'd had. I took her home directly after."

Yes, directly after taking her to bed—scarcely six hours after she'd knocked on the door looking for me and come upon him instead. Six hours, when it had taken me a café, tickets to a melodrama, and a walk in the park to manage a kiss. Well, it was what she'd always intended, wasn't it? She would not have settled for anything less than becoming Bayard Sonnier's lover. God knew she'd come close to it when she'd thought I was he, but I had been nervous at the lie I hadn't quite told her, and she had been impatient at my hesitation, unfastening my waistcoat, her hands hot through my shirt, breathing into my mouth: *Someplace quiet. Someplace private.* But I'd had no such place, and no money to procure a hotel room, and she would have wondered at that anyway, because she knew where I lived, and I had been afraid to take her there, afraid of what would happen, of what *had* happened . . .

Estes exhaled and took out his flask, taking a quick sip before he tucked it back into his pocket. "That sounds like Louisa. She is so fierce, so very passionate. She doesn't think, she acts. She and Adelaide are very unlike."

I was unsure which was a compliment, and which a condemnation, though who could find Louisa's temperament something to admire? And he wasn't even accurate, was he? I'd seen Adelaide Wentworth's temper enough to know there was indeed passion beneath her coolly untouchable exterior.

Estes was still talking. "Do you believe such a thing as a *donna ideale* exists?"

"An ideal woman?" Bayard made a face and then said thoughtfully, as if repeating something he'd heard, "One who possesses the soul of your soul? Perhaps. I have not seen it."

"I've searched for it all my life. I despair of finding it in a single body, but if I could marry Louisa's vivacity to Adelaide's tranquility . . . well, together they are the perfect woman."

I found myself bristling. "One woman is not enough for you, Estes? You must have two?"

"I am certain he meant no such thing," Bayard said.

"Does Miss Wentworth know you find her so lacking, Estes?"

"Lacking?" Estes looked confused. "She is my inspiration. I could not live without her."

"It sounds as if you could not live without both of them."

"Vanni, perhaps you should get us a table for dinner," Bayard ordered. It was more than an order. It was a warning.

I recognized that look, and I knew better than to argue. "Of course."

I grabbed up my hat again and went out. I had no idea why Estes's words had so vexed me. His relationship with the Wentworth sisters—whatever it was—was none of my concern. It was surely not worth maddening Bayard further, given that he hadn't yet forgiven me for the steamer. But my agitation didn't leave me as I went to the garden, where there were tables laid for dinner, and ordered a bottle of wine, and it wasn't until the second glass that the conversation in the hotel room faded into insignificance.

FOURTEEN

ADELAIDE

Louisa was unnaturally silent as the porter showed us to our room. It was small but lovely, the window overlooking a terraced garden filled with clusters of anemone and lavender, punctuated by roses, and a graveled and well-tended promenade that drew the eye to the lake, where the sky was reflected in vast swaths of pink and twilight satin, the tops of the mountains hidden by a band of sunset-colored clouds. The tables and chairs at the lakeside were emptying now, as people returned to their rooms to change for dinner.

My sister plopped onto the bed with a dramatic sigh.

"What did you do?" I asked.

"Why must you always assume I was the one who did something?"

"Because it was obvious Bayard was angry with you, and Mr. Calina seemed equally irritated."

"I only called Bayard to the window."

"You called him by name?"

"Yes, of course. What else was I to call him? How could I have known what would happen?"

"You saw the telescopes at the d'Angleterre and the boy who drowned just to get a closer look. If those things didn't tell you how people love him, the break-in certainly should have. Really, Loulou."

She slumped. "I only wanted him to talk to me. I wanted to know he forgave me for the séance and . . . everything. This will be our third night apart."

"Perhaps that's for the best."

"Why would you say such a thing?"

"Because I meant what I said yesterday. We've overstayed our welcome. We should leave—"

"Leave? And go where? Back to Concord? Or to your small fishing village or whatever it was you said? Why? So you can bury yourself, and Julian and me with you?"

"Louisa," I said patiently. "You will only end up being hurt if you stay."

"Bayard would never hurt me. He loves me—"

"He loved Marie Arsenault, and he's still grieving her."

"Don't be absurd. How could he be grieving? She made a fool of him."

I looked out the window, at the soft lapping waves against the shore, the way the pink of sunset tinted the landscape so the rocks looked blacker, the edges of everything more distinct.

She went on, "Who told you that he loved her? Vanni? Of course, it must have been him. Just as he told you that we were unwelcome. It's not true, Addie. He hates me. He would say anything to hurt me."

"That's the second time you've used his Christian name," I noted, looking at her over my shoulder. "And I don't know why Mr. Calina would hate you, given what you've said about how little you know him."

She looked down again, twisting the nubs on the chenille coverlet.

I came away from the window and sat on the bed next to her. "Why are you lying to me?"

"I'm not."

"You forget to whom you're speaking, I think. What happened between you and Mr. Calina?"

"Nothing at all."

"If you do not tell me the truth, I will tell Julian about Bayard. I will insist that we leave." It was a threat I didn't know if I would carry out.

She looked mulish; I thought she would keep insisting, and I readied myself to try another tack, but then she took a deep breath, surrendering. "Do you remember when we first came to the villa, and you thought he was Bayard when they came ashore?"

"Did I?" I hardly remembered.

"That's what happened to me too. I thought he was Bayard."

I said nothing, too startled by her words and what they must mean to respond.

She rushed on, "It was when Bay was publishing that serial, do you remember? There was a chapter every week, and so I went to his publishers' office and I waited for him to bring in the next one."

I should have known. She was prone to such compulsions, and she had wanted so to meet him, but I had not thought, I had not realized . . . She'd told me she was shopping and exploring the city, and I was just so grateful that she was gone, that I did not have to manage her shifting moods for even a few hours, though I was also afraid of what trouble she could cause without me. I'd started at every knock on the door.

"The only picture I'd seen of him was that etching on the flyleaf of *The Temptation*—you remember, don't you?"

I nodded.

"So hard to tell anything from that. I didn't know he had a secretary. I only saw a man with dark hair, and he was handsome, and he *could* have been the man in the etching. Not only that, but he dressed so well. I followed him to a café and he had bundles of papers—it was the next chapter, Addie, and Bayard's name was all over the pages, and . . .

and why shouldn't I have thought it was him? It was his fault too. He lied to me."

"He told you he was Bayard Sonnier?"

Louisa hesitated.

"The truth, Loulou."

She shook her head. "But he never denied it either. I told him I already knew who he was, you see. Well, at least I didn't do more than kiss him."

I only looked at her.

"I didn't," she insisted. "He's so careful and *slow*, but I thought he was falling in love with me, and so I went to his house. I meant to . . . well, yes, I meant to seduce him. Don't give me that look, Addie. Why shouldn't I? You did the same with Jules."

"I did *not*."

She shrugged. "When I got there and I asked for Bayard, it wasn't Vanni who came to the parlor, and I realized how he'd tricked me, and . . . you see."

"So he believes you threw him over for Bayard," I said.

"Oh, he believes no such thing," she said bitterly. "He knew that I thought he was Bayard. He meant to deceive me."

I could not say otherwise. I didn't know him. But I did know my sister, and I knew how capable she was of deceiving herself. I also finally understood that strange antagonism between them. It wasn't so strange now that I knew the truth.

"I ended it that night," she said. "He saw I was with Bayard. He has no reason to believe that I cared for him at all."

I said quietly, "Did he tell Bayard any of this?"

She looked horrified. "No! I don't think so. Bay has never said a word of it."

The things she had dared, but then, she had always been daring. We had been raised to believe that social customs didn't matter, that women should be as free as men, and it wasn't until I'd left my family that I realized the disservice that had been done to us. How could one live in a world that judged and condemned the slightest deviation from what was accepted? I had not thought it wrong to run off with Julian. I had assumed that everyone would forgive us because we were in love. I had dragged my sister along and never once considered how the world might view it.

But I had paid for it, and so had she. The difference was that I knew it, but, like Julian, Louisa believed that it was the world that had erred, that if she could only make it see reason, she would be forgiven and admired. I had wearied of the effort. I had wearied of how she took whatever she wanted without regard to anyone else. I wondered now if she'd hurt Giovanni Calina. I wondered what he might do about that, given the opportunity.

It was time to leave Geneva. It was time to disabuse her of the myth she persisted in believing. And if it was cruel as well, so be it. Perhaps it was the only way for her to understand.

My hand itched. I ignored it. "Louisa, I don't know if Mr. Calina meant to use you, but Bayard certainly does. He cares nothing for you. He told me so. He doesn't think of you as a muse. He doesn't love you, and he won't. He told me that he's never felt for a woman the way he felt for Marie, and that he never will again."

She looked at me as if my words made no sense. "You spoke to him of this?"

"I was worried for you." That was not quite true, but it made me feel better to think that I had been.

"When?"

"The night Mr. Calina read us his story."

"But I haven't been with Bayard since then." Her voice rose. "If I could just be with him, I could make him change his mind."

"I don't think so, Loulou. I'm so sorry, but perhaps—"

"No," she said, rising, shaking her head. "No. He doesn't know what he feels. He hasn't given me a chance. I've inspired him. The ghost story—that was my idea. He wouldn't have started writing it if not for me. I know I can make him fall in love with me. I can. We wouldn't have to worry then. He would keep us with him always, and even if he knew the gossip it wouldn't matter. I'll be his muse, and he'll do everything he can for Julian."

"Louisa, sit down. Please."

"You don't think I can do it. You don't think anyone could love me."

"That's not true. You know it's not true."

"Why shouldn't Bayard be the one?"

"I just don't believe you can change him."

"Why? Why shouldn't he love me? What's wrong with me?"

"Nothing. Nothing at all."

Her eyes narrowed. "Sometimes I truly hate you, Addie."

She wrenched open the door and stalked out, slamming it behind her.

I should follow. The darkness had been in her eyes. I knew that voice. *Follow. Take care of her. Watch your sister.* All the lessons of our childhood. *You're the responsible one.*

But I ignored it, and I let her go. And there was a part of me that thought how relieved I would be if she never returned.

She was not back when the time came to go to dinner, and so I went without her. The table d'hôte was set up in the dining room, and the rich smells of butter-sauced fish and roasted meat made my mouth water. I went out the open doors to the garden, where the dining room extended. There were already many people out there eating and drinking. Candles in hurricane glass flickered on the tables, and strategically placed oil lamps dangling from cast iron poles lent a soft illumination. The lake and the mountains were dark shadows beyond the sloped terraces, made darker and more mysterious by the glow of lamps set along the promenade. The soft slapping of waves on the shore played beneath the talk.

I glanced about for Julian and Bayard, but didn't see them. Then a man sitting alone at a table rose and beckoned, and I realized it was Mr. Calina. There was already a bottle of wine before him, and a half-full glass.

The last thing I wanted was to join him. His words from the other night still pricked, but it wasn't only that. It was now what I knew about him and Louisa. I had not quite come to terms with it yet, and so I would be nervous and uncomfortable. But I didn't see how to avoid sitting alone with him.

Then, with relief, I heard Julian and Bayard come laughing into the garden.

"There you are!" Julian took my arm, and we went to the table. "Where's Loulou?"

"On a promenade," I said.

"So late? Alone?"

"There are porters everywhere," Bayard pointed out as he sat. "She can't go twenty feet without one of them offering his help."

Reluctantly, Julian said, "I would feel better if—"

"She's in a temper," I told him.

He paused, but pulled out a chair for me. "Ah, only that."

"My head hurts," Bayard said. "I'm in no mood for tempers tonight. I hope she's calmed herself."

"You'll soon discover if she has," Mr. Calina said, nodding toward the far side of the garden.

Louisa flounced in. She had not gone back to the room to change, and her color was high. Or perhaps it was only the dim light that made it seem so. It was unfair how it flattered her, but perhaps it was less the light than her nature, which shaped her for attention wherever she went. She was in high spirits too, though I didn't know if it was anger that made her so, or something else.

The only chair unoccupied was the one between Mr. Calina and Julian, and she sent a quick and longing glance toward Bayard before she took it. "Oh good, you've already ordered the wine."

"We'll need glasses, and another bottle," Bayard said. The porter nearby sprang to attention, and the next thing we knew, the waiter was there, bringing wine and instructing us on the dishes included in the table d'hôte that night.

Julian and I had the buttered perch, a hotel specialty. Louisa waited until she saw Bayard take roast beef, and then she took the same. Mr. Calina took only bread and cheese, and not much of it.

"Aren't you hungry?" Bayard asked him.

"I'm drinking my dinner tonight," he said.

That did not sound as if it boded well.

Louisa took delicate bites of beef, constantly glancing at Bayard, who ignored her completely, and as the minutes went on, and we spoke of inconsequential things, all of us too hungry to converse but for Mr. Calina, who poured another glass of wine, I watched my sister's frustration grow.

"This is delicious," she said finally. "I think it the best table d'hôte I've had."

Bayard shrugged. "It's unremarkable."

Louisa scowled.

"Well, let me try it." Julian speared a bite from her plate. "It is delicious."

Bayard let out a heavy sigh. "Must we really discuss roast beef?"

Mr. Calina sank back in his chair, tearing broodingly at his bread.

"So we go to Chillon tomorrow?" I asked, changing the subject before Louisa could say something to further irritate Bayard.

"I want to see the oubliette particularly," she said. "What was it that Byron wrote of it? Bayard, do you remember?"

"I don't recall that he mentioned it," Bayard said.

Her face fell. "I don't remember where I read it then, but it was quite chilling. Such a horrifying thing, to fall to your death among—is it sharp stones or knives? Can you imagine it? Taking a step onto what you think is a stair and falling into nothing, and then being torn apart in darkness?"

"I *am* eating," Bayard said.

"You said you didn't want to discuss roast beef," Louisa said.

Bayard held up his fork pointedly, a bite of beef dangling from a prong, very rare, dripping blood. "Do you imagine talk of people being cut to ribbons any better?"

Mr. Calina laughed, swallowing it in a gulp of wine at Bayard's quick glance.

Louisa's expression set. I knew that face. Quickly, I said, "The fish is so fresh it reminds me of the trout we used to catch in Concord. It was in the pan almost before it stopped flopping."

Louisa said, "Bayard doesn't wish to speak of death or food, Addie."

"On the contrary," Bayard said, putting down his fork and turning to me with undivided attention. His eyes were a remarkable color in the candlelight, reflected flames dancing. Though I knew it was for Louisa's benefit, and not because I'd said anything especially fascinating, it was startling how strongly it affected me. I felt suddenly anxious to please, a little breathless. "You fished yourself?"

"They did everything themselves on the farm," Julian interjected. "I told you."

"I've never much cared for fishing," Bayard said. "I don't have the patience for it."

"It's very soothing," I said. "And meditative. I have often solved the world's problems while sitting on the shores of the pond."

Bayard smiled. "What solutions did you come to?"

"Ones that got lost in daydreams, mostly. Dragonflies can be very distracting."

"I should say so. Nothing should be able to fly like that, don't you think? They seem to defy the very laws of nature. One minute you're trying to figure out how they dart so quickly, and the next thing you know, you're counting how many different colors you see. Which is most common, do you think? Blue?"

"I used to capture them for Addie, as she liked them so," Louisa broke in. "Have you ever caught a dragonfly, Jules?" She leaned into him, clutching his arm, and threw me a look as if to say, *I will show you how jealous Bayard gets. You will have to take back everything you said.* Which was foolish, of course. If Bayard did grow jealous, Julian would discover the liaison Louisa wished so to keep secret.

But Bayard either ignored or was oblivious to her machinations, and Julian did not pull away. He gave her an affectionate look, one I felt to my center, and laughed. "Never. Though I've never tried."

"One must be very fast."

"I miss Concord sometimes," I said to Bayard, as if he and I were the only ones at the table, my own little attempt at punishment, not just for Louisa, but for Jules too. "I think you would like it. My father used to say that you could find God in everything." I tried not to think of him talking to the wheelbarrow. "Certainly it was true there."

"I think one can find Him here too, don't you?" Bayard asked. "The mountains, the lake. The storms . . ."

"Who would have thought Bayard Sonnier such a romantic?"

This flirtation meant nothing, we both knew it. But I understood how half the world had bowed before his smile. I understood why my sister craved it. "It's hardly a secret. Anyone who read *The Temptation* would know it."

"Have you not always said that your characters aren't you?"

"They aren't me, but they come from me," he said. "They are birthed from what I know. And I think we all play different roles, depending on the circumstance, don't you? 'My name is Legion: for we are many.'"

"I have another theory," I said, teasing. "I wonder if they are not a disguise. I think you like people to believe you are Gerard from *The Temptation*. Or Matthieu from *Lac du Bourget*, with all his bitterness and cynicism. It's your own way of confusing the world. No one can ever quite know you, if you are not yourself."

Bayard lifted a brow and smiled into his wine. "There may be something to that."

This was a game. I felt us playing, Bayard determined to teach Louisa a lesson, Louisa determined to deny it while at the same time admitting nothing, confessing nothing.

"I'm surprised to hear you say you miss Concord, Addie." Her tone was caustic. "Given that you could not wait to be away, especially after what happened with poor Mr. Tomlinson."

I froze. I could not believe she had mentioned it.

"Mr. Tomlinson?" Julian asked.

Mr. Calina's dark gaze slid to me. He reached for the wine and poured more into his glass, and then he sat back again as if he meant to savor whatever was about to happen next.

I disliked him for that, but not as much as I disliked my sister in that moment.

"Oh, now this is a funny story," she said. "I can't believe you never told it to Jules, Addie."

She knew I hadn't. She knew how it embarrassed me. I had thought it embarrassed her too. But the game had turned. I was to be punished now for Bayard's attention, and for everything I'd said to her in the hotel room, everything I now knew about her and Giovanni Calina.

"It was a long time ago," I said sharply. "I hardly remember it. It wasn't important."

"You hardly remember it? Oh, I don't believe that. It was the biggest thing to happen in Concord in months."

"Tell us, then," Julian said, his gaze coming to me, questioning. I could not meet it.

"Mr. Tomlinson came to spend the summer with Mr. Alcott—he was the son of a friend, I think. He was such a funny little man, wasn't he, Addie? He was crippled. One leg was shorter than the other, so he'd had a special boot made. A huge, clomping thing. Why, he was almost too frail to lift it."

I stared into my wine. My scabbing chin began to tingle. I curled my fingers into my palm to keep from scratching, but then the itch only traveled to my hand.

"I suppose he might have been handsome but for that, and he was really very nice. But quiet. He liked to read prayer books and religious tracts, and you know Addie is so quiet herself, well, she caught his eye."

Louisa had, at last, won Bayard's attention. Julian's was riveted to her.

"Anyone could see how in love he was with her. His eyes followed her everywhere. He was never invited to something where he didn't ask if she would be there as well. Do you remember what Jenny Caldicott called him, Addie?"

I shook my head.

"Of course you do. She called him Little Jack Horner, and said Addie was his Christmas pie. Because he kept to the corners so, just staring at her, at every entertainment."

"Louisa." My voice was barely a whisper.

"It was impossible to avoid him. He was so appreciative of every attention, wasn't he? He wanted so to please. He followed us on our walks, even when we tried to walk faster because he couldn't keep up. We were only protecting Addie, of course, because he embarrassed her."

The very thought of it was humiliating, his anxious hovering, his trembling hands and ardent glances. *What is your opinion, Miss Wentworth? Do you not find the evening sublime, Miss Wentworth? Where will you be this afternoon, Miss Wentworth? Shall I read you this prayer? It's really so lovely. It reminded me of the reverence I see in you.* My father smiling as if it were some great joke. Mama saying, *"Oh, but he's such a gentleman, Adelaide. Surely you can be kind."* Then, that lovely, moonlit evening, and Oliver Easterby's tease, *"Adelaide Wentworth, patron saint of cripples,"* and the others laughing, singing an obscene song on the shores of the pond: *"Addie's got a cripple, who goes where'er she goes, and someday soon she'll be the girl whom only cripples mow."*

"I once knew a woman like that," Bayard said thoughtfully. "She was unbearable. I can sympathize."

It was a kindness I appreciated, but before I could respond, Louisa said, "Unbearable is the perfect word. Well, finally Addie had had quite enough."

"Please, Louisa. I can't imagine anyone is interested in this."

"But Julian is interested in everything about you, aren't you, Jules?" Said so sweetly.

Julian looked uncertain. The question was still in his eyes, but now too was curiosity. Even if I managed to keep her from finishing the story tonight, Julian would demand it one way or another. He would have it from me, or, if I refused, from her. Some evening, when I'd gone to bed and they stayed up to make themselves giddy with ghost stories and creepiness, she would tell it.

It wasn't just her words that held them, either. She knew how to tell a story and always had. Presenting a mystery and solving it, bit by bit, always raising another question. How flawlessly she did it. And how animated she was! How she commanded the stage! I had to admire it, even as I found it intolerable. She gathered her audience and held them with that beguiling tilt of her chin, the trembling curls at her throat, the gaze that ensnared. She could have told them anything, because they were in thrall to that nature she wielded so heedlessly.

She repeated, "Yes, she'd had enough. The poor man simply would not take no for an answer, would he? We had to do something, else Addie would be his prisoner all summer long. Perhaps longer, because rumors were spreading—"

"Rumors?" Julian asked.

"Everyone assumed he would win her; he was just so persistent. Everyone thought Addie would be lucky to have him. He did have an inheritance, didn't he, Addie?"

"I don't remember."

Louisa rested her chin upon her hands. "She was desperate, anyway, and so we came up with a plan, Jenny and Addie and I. It was really very simple. It worked a little better than we'd hoped."

"What was it?" Julian asked.

"Jenny told Mr. Tomlinson that Addie wished him to meet her at the pond. Well, of course, he came. It was nearly dark by then, wasn't it, Addie?"

I glared at her.

"I was hiding in the bushes. Adelaide waited onshore. She pretended to be glad to see him, and then she flirted with him—oh, what a mess she made of him, and she hardly knows how to flirt! She convinced him to go swimming with her in the pond, and she stripped down to her chemise and went into the water—you should have seen his eyes!" Louisa laughed delightedly. "He undressed in a trice, and went in after her, and once he was in the water, Jenny and I raced out and stole his clothes, and Addie swam to the far shore and got out to join us. It was only a joke, you see, but it turned out badly."

Badly indeed. He'd flailed so in the water. *"Miss Wentworth? Miss Wentworth, where are you? Adelaide?"* The three of us had laughed in the bushes as he came limping out to find his clothes gone. He'd tried vainly to cover himself; frustrated and embarrassed and then . . . then he'd burst into tears . . .

How cruel we'd been. He'd called and called, and finally we had rushed off and left him there to find his way home. We were halfway to the house when it began to rain.

"There was a storm that night. He had to walk home in the dark and the rain without any clothes. We'd taken his spectacles too—they were in his pocket, you see. We didn't even know they were there. The poor man ended up getting lost. When he didn't come home that night, Mr. Alcott came over to ask if we'd seen him, and we all said no. By then, we were afraid of getting in trouble, and Addie made us promise not to tell. They sent men out the next morning to look for him."

I could not believe that I had done it, even now. But I'd been afraid that things would end the way the village predicted. There were so few men willing to take on our family, and by then the rumors about my father were increasing, his episodes of madness becoming more than episodes. I was the only one capable of tending him; my mother was ineffectual and debilitated by discouragement, particularly as Louisa's moods became more unstable. I alone was possessed of patience and a steady, implacable temperament. My parents' reliance on me, Louisa's reliance, became more pronounced with every passing hour. I was worried that I would spend my life caring for them all. I knew that my parents would never force me into marriage, not with their Free Love attitudes, but they favored Mr. Tomlinson, who seemed a perfect solution for all of us, because he would never ask me to abandon my family. He would marry me, and I would be stuck in Concord forever, stuck with the responsibilities that weekly grew more overwhelming, and in my head it became a fait accompli. I'd wanted Mr. Tomlinson gone with a fury that frightened me.

But then, after what I'd done to him, I became afraid of something else entirely: my capacity for cruelty. I was so embarrassed at what we'd done, at what I had put in motion. It had been my idea.

"What happened to him?" Julian asked.

"Oh, they found him cowering near some tree, I think. He had a fever from exposure, and he was in bed for two weeks. When it was over, they sent him home."

I had never visited him. I had not sent him a note. He had said nothing of what happened, no doubt as humiliated as I was.

I told myself it was only a youthful indiscretion.

You weren't that young. Sixteen. Old enough to know better.

Or that I hadn't realized really what would happen.

You knew exactly what you were doing.

The evidence of what I could be was something I could not look at. I could not bear to speak of it. I had not been able to tolerate Jenny Caldicott after, and I was glad when, in the fall, our family moved from Concord to Boston for a year. When we returned, she was gone. I had no idea where.

And now . . . I hated that I could still feel these things. I hated that they still had such power after so long. My chin burned, and my hand; it was all I could do not to rub them. Louisa looked the very picture of innocence.

"I was only sixteen," I managed.

Julian covered my hand with his. "Which one of us has not done a very stupid thing?"

I saw his compassionate concern, the Julian I loved. But it had not been just a stupid thing. It was a heartless thing, and I was so angry at Louisa for telling it, for reminding me of it, that I didn't know how I could forgive her.

Bayard said lightly, joking, "Ah, what cruelty lies in even the finest woman's heart. I vow, Adelaide, you make me frightened for the male gender. If even a soul as gentle as yours can hide a viper, there can be no hope for us."

Louisa laughed; it was false and high, still trying for his favor. "I fear that my fellow women would not applaud my telling the story. It's our great secret, you know. We never reveal to men how vindictive we can be. It's sometimes our only weapon."

"I am well enough acquainted with it, believe me," Bayard said wryly.

Mr. Calina reached for the wine. He said nothing, but his watchfulness condemned me, and I wanted to excuse myself and go to my room, away from his probing gaze, but I also knew that to leave now would betray how much the story troubled me, and so I sat there for an hour as the conversation turned to other things, seething at how my sister had once again sacrificed me to gain what she wanted. I kept forgetting that when it came to games, she was the best player of us all.

I glanced across the table at Giovanni Calina, and he lifted his glass in a mocking toast as if to ask again, *"Do you never say no to either of them? Are you even in the world, Miss Wentworth?"*

I rose so abruptly I knocked the table. Wineglasses rocked. Julian and Bayard looked up in surprise, their conversation halted. "I'm more tired than I'd thought," I said. "If you'll excuse me."

Louisa said, "I'm not ready to go yet, Addie."

"Then stay," I said with a strained smile that I hoped did not reveal how glad I was to leave her there.

"I'll see you to your room," Julian said.

"I don't want to interrupt your conversation. I'll see you in the morning."

The men rose. Bayard said good-night. Julian kissed my cheek. Mr. Calina watched me with that penetrating, uncomfortable gaze. I fled from it. I fled from them all, back to my room, and once I was there, in darkness illuminated only by the glow of the lights outside, a blooming, shadowed darkness, I tried to breathe again. My hand itched unbearably, my chin. I gripped the bedcover, the nubby chenille, and in my mind's eye I saw again the way Louisa had twisted those nubs between her fingers during her confession. I could not order my thoughts or find purchase within them. The ghosts of blame and regret were too hard; they would not let me go, as much as I wanted to release them.

But there were no weapons to defeat that, were there? There was no way now to ask for forgiveness from those I'd wronged, not from Mr. Tomlinson, nor Emily Estes. No way to atone for my selfishness or my cruelty. Affinities excused nothing, no matter how Julian or my parents or I wished it. Emily had stood on my doorstep in Venice, the water from a high tide lapping at her boots. Even in my surprise at her arrival and my wonder that a woman so heavily pregnant could manage the trip from London, I had noticed how fast the canal flowed behind her and thought that all she must do was take one step back. *"You know I was his muse once too. He left me for you—do you think he won't leave you too? He's tired of you already. He's in Paris with your sister, did you know that? You will never be happy with him."*

One step, or a small push, and those words, those terrible words, would fall into nothingness. She would be out of my life. Jules and I would not be so reviled. We could return to London and make a life together. One push.

For the first time, my chin began to itch. What I'd done then, the words I'd said, only made worse the curse she'd placed upon me, her curse that took my perfect skin, the remnants of my reputation, my own unborn child in payment for hers. Emily's fatal inspiration . . . *"I was his muse once too."*

A fatal muse. A man who'd betrayed his wife and child because he told himself he was building a more perfect world, a man who believed art should obey few limits, and that love should obey none.

"What would I write about?" I'd asked Giovanni Calina.

"Perhaps ghosts," he'd answered.

And there, at last before me, was the weapon I'd been searching for.

It wasn't until much later, when I was interrupted by a knock on the door and Louisa's tentative voice, "Addie? You've locked me out," that I paused and looked down at a pencil in my hand that I could not remember using, paper on the desk I could not remember fetching, and realized that I had a story more than half begun.

FIFTEEN

VANNI

I was so drunk when we returned to the room that the entire evening seemed like a very disorienting dream, which was just how I wanted it. The story Louisa had told about her sister didn't surprise me in the least—not that she told it nor the viciousness it revealed. I only wondered what Louisa meant to gain by it. That she had a reason was clear, though I was too befuddled to decipher it. She was truly the little fiend Bayard called her. Still, I'd found the tale fascinating, and what was even more fascinating was that Estes was as blind when it came to his mistress as he was to everything else. Tranquil, he'd called her. How had he missed that her tranquility was only a disguise? She was as much an imposter as I.

Not that it mattered. It had nothing to do with me. My own goal for the evening had been to keep quiet and drink enough for numbness, and I'd managed both admirably.

I ignored Bayard and Estes and let my coat and my hat drop wherever they landed—a twinge of remorse for the hat, though I could not remember exactly why I wanted to take such care of it. Once I had my boots off—a struggle I was wholly unequipped for—I collapsed upon the mattress, managing only to unbutton my waistcoat and my shirt and throw my tie to the floor. My watch chain slid from my pocket, dragged by its ornaments, and I fumbled with the clasp and let it fall too.

"Move over, you drunken sot," Estes said—was that disgust in his voice? I neither knew nor cared. "You're taking up the whole bed."

He shoved me, and I rolled obediently over.

"Christ," Bayard said. I was quite sure that was disgust. "What the hell got into you tonight?"

"Only wine," I mumbled.

The room spun. I squeezed my eyes shut. It helped only moderately.

The knock on the door made me open them again. Bayard stopped in the midst of pulling off his shirt. Estes moved, jiggling the mattress. My stomach pitched; I took a deep breath to settle it.

Bayard went to the door and called out, "Who is it?"

"Louisa." Her voice was muffled and teary. "Addie's locked me out." Bayard cursed and opened the door.

Louisa stood on the other side, teary indeed. "I'm sorry. I didn't know where else to go."

"Well, of course you must come here," Estes said, sitting up.

Bayard said to him, "Of course she can't. Are you mad? A woman in a room with three men? They already half think I'm Satan in disguise. I like this hotel. I'd like to return to it one day. Go talk to Adelaide. See if you can resolve things."

"He won't be able to," Louisa said. "It's not Jules she's angry with, it's me. It won't matter what he says, she won't let me in. She wouldn't even open the door."

I rubbed my eyes, trying to erase the fuzziness around everyone in the room that made the whole scene feel like a hallucination. I was not actually sure it wasn't. "You shouldn't've told that story." Even to my own ears, it sounded garbled. I could not form my tongue properly around the words.

"You're drunk," she sneered.

Bayard ignored us both and said to Estes. "Try anyway. Obviously Louisa can't stay here."

"Just have her share your bed," I suggested. "It'll be no different than any other night."

The room went quiet.

"What did you say?" Estes asked.

Bayard leveled me a threatening stare. I'd already forgotten what I'd said or why he should be annoyed.

"No one'll tell," I said, putting a finger to my lips, trying not to slur. "It's a secret, yes? Just like before."

"He's talking nonsense." Louisa looked dismayed in a way I liked. What had made her so? I wanted to know for future reference. "He's had too much wine."

"No." Estes was so tense that his skin stretched thinly over the bones of his skull. Skeletal. A bit frightening. "Calina, what did you mean?"

The room suddenly seemed far too bright. I put my hand to my eyes and groaned.

Louisa gestured dismissively. "Look at him—he's going to be sick. He doesn't know what he's saying."

Estes said to Bayard, "Are you at least going to be honest with me?"

Louisa said, "It's nothing, Jules. Of course it's nothing. You mustn't think—"

"Quiet," Estes ordered her. To Bayard, "Are you making love to Louisa?"

"O' course he is," I said, hearing my carefully cultivated accent give way to Bethnal Green and too drunk to care. "Why d'you think she

186

dragged you to Geneva? To look at the scenery? God knows she don't care about it."

Louisa paled, but her eyes fired so with fury I wondered that I didn't melt.

Estes got up. The bed shook. Again my stomach turned. I groaned.

"How long has this been going on? Since London?"

"Why should it trouble you? You're a Free Lover"—hard to manage those vowels—"or is all that only talk?"

"Oh stop!" Louisa turned to Estes, beseeching. "I didn't want you to be angry with him. I knew you would be great friends and I was afraid I would come between you. It was for you, Jules. I was only thinking of you."

Bayard said grimly, "I understand if you're angry, Julian. I can only say that Louisa thought it best, and as she knew you better, I didn't want to disagree."

"I don't think you do understand. Not really." Estes spoke with such deliberation that I looked more closely at him.

It wasn't just anger I saw, was it? What else was there? Jealousy? Yes. He was trembling with it. His face blurred; the room twitched.

Bayard said, "I know you feel responsible for her—"

"I thought you were my friend, and you've been lying to me, bedding her behind my back—"

"She made us all promise," I slurred. "A secret."

Louisa lunged at me with a stifled cry. Bayard grabbed her, pulling her back before she reached me, but I was already reacting, slow and clumsy, trying to scramble away. I fell off the bed, crashing hard to the floor with a jolt that jarred my skull painfully and made my stomach pitch.

Estes took up his coat and went to the door with a dignity that was spoiled by the wild mess of his hair. "I cannot bear to look at either of you just now. I'll join Adelaide."

He walked out, slamming the door. I covered my eyes with my arm. "Good. I'll have the bed to myself."

"You aren't staying," Bayard said. "Get out."

I let my arm drop, unsure that I'd heard him correctly. "What?"

"Get out. You can't stay here."

I was having trouble thinking. "Why not? There're two beds. She shares rooms with her sister and Estes all the time." Or at least, that's what I thought I said. Bayard seemed not to understand, so perhaps not. "Makes you wonder, don't it? His perfect woman—"

"Be quiet! You've ruined everything!" Louisa cried.

"Poor Loulou." I mangled the words completely. "Why so sad? Because Jules don't want you anymore?"

"Get out," Bayard said. "Now."

"Where am I to go?"

"The hall. The garden. The lobby. I'm certain you can find a place."

"You're joking."

"I assure you I'm not. Get out. Take a blanket if you like."

I staggered to my feet. Bayard threw me a blanket, and the next thing I knew I was in the hall.

I fell into the wall twice as I made my way down the stairs. In the lobby, there were only a few porters about. I meant to find a comfortable settee, but somehow I managed to walk right through the lobby, and then I couldn't find it again, and then I was in the garden, stumbling into a parterre, trampling some plant, and realizing painfully that I was barefoot. I was cursing that, when I took an unexpected step over the edge of a terrace and into the one below, my hands plunging through a bed of flowers. My stomach lurched; I vomited where I knelt, all over pansies or petunias and my hands, and it was a moment before I could gain my feet again, and then, another terrace, another fall—where was a porter when I needed one?

The lights had all been extinguished along the promenade, but I managed to find the gravel path. I wandered down it until I reached the shore. I bent to wash my hands in the lake, lost my balance again, and sat hard in cold water.

I froze at the shock of it. A seagull perched on a nearby bench cawed at me, stirring me through my stupefaction, and I rose, dripping, and tried to shoo him away. He only stared at me, spread his wings, and settled again as if to taunt me. I ran at him, waving my arms, shouting, and he considered me as one might a madman. Finally, I threw myself onto the hard, cold bench, which seemed the greatest affront I could offer. The gull flapped his wings and screeched in my face before he flew off, and I settled myself to sleep.

Somewhere, I had dropped the blanket.

SIXTEEN

ADELAIDE

The furious knock on my door made me start. "Let me in!" Julian shouted.

I had not really thought Louisa would simply accept that I'd locked her out, but neither had I expected Julian to sound so angry when he came to lobby for her.

I shoved the story I'd been writing into my portmanteau, hiding it away, not ready to share it. It was still too new; I was uncertain what I meant by it, or whether I meant anything at all. I unlocked the door. Julian stormed inside.

"Did you know Louisa was having an affair with Bay?"

I had thought him here to persuade me to forgive my sister, but it was obvious that he'd forgotten what had passed at dinner. Equally obvious was the jealousy and distress in his eyes that told me that all my suspicions were true.

The estrangement between us did not lessen the pain of that.

Julian paced. "I thought he was my friend, and all the time he was seducing her like a scoundrel."

I could not resist a jab. "Louisa is a grown woman. If they feel an affinity for one another, why should it upset you so?"

"You know what he is. You know his reputation."

"So does she. Just as she knew yours."

He stilled. "What are you saying?"

There, my courage died. If I accused him outright of making love to my sister, I could never unsay it. I was not certain I was ready for that. Louisa was with Bayard now. There were already so many things to overcome if I meant to love Julian again, as I hoped; why add one more? "Only that she ran away with us willingly, and she knew what it might mean. Just as I went with you, knowing about Emily."

I so rarely said her name that he stiffened, though he knew as well as I that she never left us.

"That was different," he argued. "I was honest with you from the start."

"What makes you think that Bayard wasn't honest with Louisa?"

"Because he's a charming rogue. He would have promised things . . . done things . . . Damn it, Adelaide, how can I keep her from harm if she lies to me? I'm her guardian."

How we tiptoed around it. "We were taught that love is no crime, Jules. You were quick enough to take advantage of that. You can hardly blame Bayard for doing the same."

"I can blame him, and I will."

"Then you will lose a friendship you already treasure."

"We will leave here. All of us."

"I would like nothing better," I said frankly. "But Louisa will not forgive you for it. She means to be his muse."

His perplexity was almost amusing. "His muse?"

"Have you not seen it? She's jealous of how I inspire you. She hopes to outdo me with Bayard. That's what she wants." It was true. Louisa's desperation for Bayard's love had never made sense; it was never part of the plan. We hadn't needed him to love her, we'd only needed to make him our friend. But now it was clear to me, once again, what my sister wanted: everything I had.

"This rivalry you feel with Louisa is ridiculous. I've told you that before."

I laughed shortly. "Sometimes I think you hardly know her. Do you not remember how anxious she was to go to London? She meant to search out Bayard even then, just so she could say that of the two of us, she had the greater man."

"The greater man?" He looked stricken. "Did she say that? Is that what you both think? That Bayard is greater?"

"No, of course not. He's the more famous—that's all I meant."

"That is hardly my fault." Julian's voice was clipped. "I've been maligned and reviled because people persist in clinging to ludicrous and outmoded beliefs. Bayard caters to them. He gives them what they want. I give them what they need. No one appreciates that."

His usual lament had taken on new colors with the addition of Bayard, but still I had heard it too many times before.

"I know," I said, trying not to sound jaded.

He sat on the edge of the bed. Then he said, "She meant to search him out? Truly? That's what Calina implied, but . . ."

I sat beside him. "She felt left out."

"You should have heeded me, Addie. You should have been kinder to her. She feels everything so intensely. It was difficult for her."

Always Louisa. Would it be so hard for him to acknowledge that I might have a reason for my resentment? I was always taking care of her, but when the time had come for her to do the same for me, she had failed miserably. *Why don't we invite someone for tea, Addie? I think you should hold a calling day. You're so dull! Come to the theater with me. There's a new play at the Malibran. You really can't just sit around mourning all hours. Julian, tell her. Tell her it's not the same as losing someone she knew . . .*

"I was grieving, Jules. I'd just lost a child I wanted very much. One I thought you wanted too."

"Of course I did. But there are reasons for such things other than curses. You said yourself that you were overwrought. One can hardly blame you. They should have seen—"

"Emily is a shadow over us. I don't understand why you don't see that."

"She had found another life. Why would she have cursed us?"

"You weren't there to see. You did not even read her letters."

"What would have been the point?" He sounded beyond fatigued. "Everything was done between us and had been for some time. Why should she have been forced to live with me when I was in love with you and she was in love with someone else?"

"Did she know it was done between you? Is it certain that she was in love with someone else?" I asked. "When she spoke to me—"

"Whatever she wanted, she did not come to Venice out of a desire to be with me again, I can promise you that. She understood. She agreed with me about marriage. We no longer felt anything for one another."

"That is not what she said."

He made a sound of frustration. "Who knew her best, Adelaide? Why should we let Emily's fate cripple us forever? It was terrible for you, I know, but it's all over now."

"It's not over, Jules. I fear it will never be."

"Such unnecessary guilt—can't you see what it's doing to you, Addie? To us? When I need you so much, and you turn from me"—he looked away as if the sight of me was too much to bear—"I need your help now more than ever, and yet your eyes hold nothing but disdain and that damnable grief. Don't you understand how it's affecting me? I can hardly write, and meanwhile Bayard is outdoing me with every stroke of his pen."

"That's not true," I said.

He raked his hand through his hair, standing it on end. "It is true. I feel it every day. And Louisa feels it too. I did not realize why she has had so little time for me, but now I do. She's decided that he is the better writer—why should she not go to him?"

This too, was familiar. That I should be in need of solace did not occur to Julian. But perhaps that was my fault; I was too used to taking on burdens without complaint, and hadn't I promised myself to support him in all things? He was meant to change the world; my certainty of that had never wavered. What was my own suffering in comparison?

I put my hand on his shoulder. "She doesn't feel that way. Nor do I. Bayard is more famous, that's all. But he's not a better writer, Jules, surely you see that? One day, the world will see it too, but in the meantime you must forgive him. You must not let Louisa's affair with him come between you—do you understand? You've insisted we stay, and you cannot lose sight of why. We have no other choice now. You cannot do anything to jeopardize your friendship with him."

He raised his head. I felt him settle beneath my hand. "Of course. Of course you are right. Bayard is what matters."

"Louisa knows that too," I assured him. "She is working all the time in your favor. She can influence him. We are both on your side. Don't forget that."

"No, I won't. I won't." He put his arm around me, pulling me close. "You are so wise, my love. What would I do without you?"

I said nothing, relieved at his acceptance. He could have just as easily decided to make Bayard his nemesis. I had seen him turn good things to bad before, with less reason. And though I wanted to leave before we caused Bayard more inconvenience, which seemed such a small word for what we'd brought him, there was no denying we needed him, and for more than Julian's career. We'd been living off Bayard since we'd arrived. I did not know what we would do without him.

Julian said quietly, "I will do as you suggest, but I wish you to take your own advice about Louisa. It pains me that you battle one another. She is not your enemy, Adelaide."

"Of course she is not," I said, and it was both true and terribly false, because my sister was my enemy, yet she was also the person in the world who loved me the most, just as I was those things for her in equal measure. Affinities, love . . . what were those compared to the bonds that secured my sister to me? But I did not say that to Julian, nor did I say what I feared: that those bonds were inescapable.

SEVENTEEN

VANNI

It was a miserable night. The crickets never ceased their cursed chirping. I was nauseated and wet and shivering into the bruising cast iron of the bench. At some point, I must have fallen asleep, because I jerked awake when I rolled off, disoriented and blinking into the light of early morning.

My whole body ached, and my trousers were unpleasantly damp. My shirt was mostly unbuttoned, my waistcoat wholly so—and both were streaked with something that looked disgustingly like the contents of my stomach. My bare feet were filthy. I could only imagine what the rest of me looked like: unbrushed hair, a day's growth of itchy beard, and no doubt I was as sallow as I felt. I would be lucky if I didn't get thrown out trying to return to the room.

I started back, through parterred gardens and terraces, benches and tables, a labyrinth of prettiness. I had no idea how I'd managed this last night. At one terrace, a gardener was already hard at work bolstering trampled petunias and . . . well. He glared at me as I passed, and I tried to smile nonchalantly and pretend that I was only taking a morning stroll half-dressed and barefoot.

Beyond some contemptuous looks, and porters who were rather obviously and obsequiously blind, I managed to get to our room relatively unscathed. The door was locked. I swore loudly enough to make some woman down the hall start and hurry away. I knocked, but no one answered. Either Bayard was ignoring me, or they were already in the dining room for breakfast. The realization of the humiliation I was going to have to endure now almost made me want to throw myself in the lake. There was no help for it. I buttoned my shirt and my waistcoat, swept my hands through my hair in an attempt to tame it, and trudged reluctantly to the dining room.

Bayard and Louisa were at a table in the garden, as we'd been for dinner, and the moment I saw them, I remembered the secret I'd revealed, Estes leaving, Bayard's anger.

I should have stayed on the bench.

It was too late; they saw me. Louisa went rigid. Bayard scraped me with his gaze, even worse than usual given the lividity of his bruised face.

"Christ. Have you looked at yourself?"

"The room is locked."

"You know, some men look elegantly louche after drinking all night," Louisa said. "You are not one of those men."

I didn't have the energy to take offense. "Go ahead—mock all you like. But can you be quick about it? I need to sit down."

"Before you fall down, no doubt."

"So Bayard has forgiven you," I said sarcastically. No doubt her "perfect" breasts had something to do with it. "Is all right with the world again?"

Bayard said, "No. If you've lost me a friend, I won't forgive you."

"Nor shall I," Louisa told me. "Not if you beg me for a thousand lifetimes."

"I'm devastated. Truly."

Bayard pushed out a chair with his foot. "Shall I order you some raw eggs? I've heard that's a certain cure."

My gorge rose. I forced it down. "God, no."

Bayard turned back to his plate, cutting into fried fish, taking a bite, chewing. "People are starting to stare, Vanni. Sit down."

Reluctantly, I did as he ordered.

Bayard broke off a piece of the fish and waved it beneath my nose. "This is delicious. Care for some?"

I glared at him. "I'm sorry. I apologize. Would you like me to get on my knees?"

"That might be a start." Louisa brightened. "I should like to see you beg like the little dog you are."

I put my head in my hands, massaging my temples. "I feel like the very devil."

"We had eight bottles of wine last night. You drank at least half of them," Bayard said. "You may have to throw away that waistcoat."

"Please, yes," Louisa said, wrinkling her nose and edging away. "I can smell it from here."

"Estes would have found out eventually." I tried to excuse myself. "Everyone else knew. All he had to do was actually open his eyes. Frankly, I'm surprised the other Miss Wentworth hadn't told him already."

"Adelaide would never betray me," Louisa said.

"A pity you don't give her the same consideration. That story you told last night . . ."

She actually seemed ashamed. And guilty. "I hadn't thought it a secret."

Bayard choked a laugh. "She asked you to stop a half-dozen times."

"I thought it would amuse you." She caressed his arm. "Did you not find it entertaining?"

He drew his arm away. "Why don't you fetch Vanni some tea and toast? He looks ready to swoon."

Had I asked it, she would have laughed in my face, but now she only pouted and obeyed.

When she was gone, he said to me, "I should let you go for last night."

"I'm sorry," I said, a bit more desperately than felt good. "I'm sorry. But since she's been here, it's been impossible. You've hardly been writing. You don't get paid until the novel's turned in, remember, and—"

"I'm not an automaton, whatever Hanson wants to believe. And if you blame anyone for that, it shouldn't be her, it should be Julian. His conversation is fascinating. It makes me forget sometimes that I should be working. I haven't had such an amiable companion for some time."

Because I could not be as scintillating as a laudanum-drunk atheist poet.

"As to the rest: You've been rude to Louisa and just as rude to her sister. You've allowed your petty irritations with them to distract you from doing your job. What happened last night was insupportable. These are my *guests*, Vanni. You will apologize to Louisa for telling Julian about us. If he deigns to stay after this, which I doubt, you will be cordial and pleasant—to all of them. Or I will send you on your way without a reference. Am I understood?"

I nodded, feeling sick. "Completely."

"Good." He glanced past me. "Here she comes now. I want to see it done prettily."

Louisa returned, bearing tea and toast spread with half-congealed lumps of butter. I had no doubt she'd meant for it to be deliberately disgusting. She had also brought a pot of grape jam, which was the only thing that looked good. And a small glass of something bright green.

"Absinthe," she said wickedly. "I've heard it is an excellent cure for overindulging."

The thought of alcohol roiled my stomach. And absinthe, straight, with no sugar and water . . .

"A superb idea," Bayard said, equally malicious. "Best to do it in one gulp, I think. Go on. Restore your pleasant self to us, Vanni."

He gave me a pointed look. I scratched at my unshaven jaw and took up the glass, assailed by the herbal, licoricey scent, debating it.

"Don't tell me you're afraid," Louisa chided.

I swallowed it in a gulp, choking on its bitterness, my stomach protesting and then . . . I felt marginally better.

"You see?" A smile that told me she was waiting for me to throw it back up. "I was right."

Bayard said, "I believe Vanni has something to say to you."

"Do you?" She twisted to me. "Oh, please tell me. I'm dying to hear."

"I . . . I wanted to apologize to you for last night. I should not have told Estes." They may have been the hardest words I'd ever said.

Louisa looked surprised. Bayard lifted a brow, and I read his message clearly. *Not pretty enough.*

I cleared my throat and tried again. "I'm really very sorry. Perhaps there is nothing I can do to make it up to you, but I would like to try."

She considered me. I had no doubt her mind was leaping to find some truly miserable way for me to redeem myself.

"Well," she said finally, with another self-satisfied smile. "I accept your apology. As to how to make it up to me—I don't know yet. I haven't seen Jules. Perhaps he will challenge Bayard to a duel for my honor. If he does, you can be Bayard's proxy."

"I don't need anyone to take on my battles for me," Bayard said irritably.

"Oh, but my darling, I would rather he killed Mr. Calina than you."

I laughed. "Given how bad a shot he is, I think I might survive him."

Bayard stared at me, and belatedly I remembered his threat.

"Forgive me," I said.

Louisa said, "I should dearly love to see you humbled, Mr. Calina."

Except that was what she'd already been doing, wasn't it? Humbling me. Every moment since we'd met.

Bayard reached into his coat pocket and drew out some papers, handing them to me. "Here. Some work for you. As you can see, you're quite wrong about my being too distracted to write."

Incredulously, I said, "You did this last night?"

"This morning," Louisa put in. "When I woke, he was scribbling away." She gave him an affectionate smile.

"Is it the end of the story?" Even as I said it, I realized I hoped not. I'd looked forward to it. Madame Brest waited. But the pages I'd written, my own leap into his imagination . . . I was not ready for that to be over. I did not want to see how well his vision surpassed mine.

"The story? No, who cares about that? It's the next chapter of the novel."

I glanced down at the pages. The writing squiggled before my eyes, dancing across the paper. I groaned. "Be merciful, Bayard. Let me do these tomorrow."

"Let me see." Louisa plucked them from my fingers.

"You won't be able to read it," I said.

She furrowed her brow, concentrating. "'. . . but then daylight broke, and'—my, you do have terrible handwriting—'Juan . . .'—it's Juan, isn't it? 'Juan strode purposefully to the . . . window.'" She looked up in triumph. "There. It's not impossible, is it?"

Bayard looked stunned at the ease with which she'd read. I was equally so. I snatched back the pages, shoving them inside my waistcoat and saying to Bayard, "I'll put them in my bag and change. If you'd let me have the key . . ."

"I've half a mind to let you suffer all day, but you do stink." He handed me the key. "Meet us in the lobby, and we'll walk over to the castle."

"I wonder if he can walk so far in his state," Louisa said. "Perhaps you should think about staying behind, Mr. Calina."

Bayard ignored her. "Don't take too long."

I hurried to the room and put away the pages, cursing myself for getting so drunk last night. My instincts told me it would be best to stay out of sight for a while. There wasn't a person in our party who wasn't annoyed with me for something. I could use the time to make a fair copy of Bayard's work—he would expect it by the end of the day. But it was clear that Bayard intended the walk to Chillon to be part of my punishment, and I was too ill to read the pages without nausea anyway, even with the absinthe, which, despite its reputation, was no miracle worker.

I washed and shaved and dressed and went to meet them.

As I came into the lobby, Bayard said, "Ah, returned to your sartorial splendor, I see."

I had half hoped Estes and Miss Wentworth would decide not to go, but no, there they were. Estes hovered restlessly behind the settee—how had I not seen there was a settee last night?—while she sat at the end farthest from him, and the tension between them was palpable. Then I remembered, as if through a dream, the look on Estes's face when he'd realized the truth about Louisa and Bayard. Jealousy. I'd seen jealousy, hadn't I?

He was watching Louisa, who, now that her secret was known, had neatly attached herself to Bayard's arm. That would not last long—he disliked public displays of affection—but Estes seemed distressed by it.

Confusing, and yet familiar too. It reminded me of something. What had I heard about him in London? There was always so much gossip, so many names, and as I had not known him then, there was no point in noting it. Whatever it was, I simply did not remember.

Miss Wentworth rose—a bit too fast, too rigid. There was a slight flush in her pale cheeks, the point of her chin was red and forming a new scab, and she had sleepless circles beneath her eyes. "Good morning, Mr. Calina. I confess I'm surprised to see you walking among us this morning."

"It was a near thing," I told her.

Estes only gave me a cold look, made colder by his laudanum-constricted pupils. So I was not forgiven there, either. Well, messengers of bad tidings were never welcome, but other than the fact that I'd told him something he didn't want to hear, I'd done nothing wrong. It was Bayard he should be angry with. And Louisa. But clearly I'd missed Bayard's apology, and Julian's acceptance of it, as there was no talk of duels, and he was here, walking with us to Chillon.

Bayard said, "Let's be off."

Estes marched ahead—not completely appeased, then—and Miss Wentworth sighed. Bayard caught my gaze and jerked his head at her. Already I was growing tired of this, but obediently I went to her and offered my arm.

She eyed me. "I suspect that of the two of us, you're the more likely to stumble."

"I can't deny that."

Her gaze went beyond me, to Bayard and Louisa, who were following Estes. "I'm to be your punishment, is that it?"

I was taken aback.

She went on with a small laugh, "What a group we are. But it looks as if Bayard has forgiven my sister for the steamer. As usual, Louisa gets exactly what she wants."

"Yes," I said quietly. "But he's good at grudges. He won't let her forget it."

"No one has forgotten anything, it seems. Louisa least of all."

She looked pointedly at me, but I didn't understand.

Miss Wentworth did not elaborate. "Go on, Mr. Calina. You can have no wish to walk with me, and I would rather walk alone."

There was no disdain in her voice; there was no emotion at all. Still, it chafed. She strode off without another word, and I wanted nothing more than to return to the room and sleep.

The walk was lovely and mostly quiet but for Louisa's inane chatter. "How beautiful it is this morning! Look at all the boats!" "Oh, such butterflies!" "Does it not seem to you that the mountains are crowding the road? Why, those cliffs seem right above our heads!" As if she were unaware that she was the exact center of everyone's displeasure. Or perhaps she was aware, and this was her way of annoying us all into stupor. It was hard to tell.

We were crowded at every small grouping of cottages by beggar children who cajoled and held out their dirty hands for alms. Many of them bore large goiters—as did their parents—and one or two were clearly imbecilic. It was thanks to some mineral deficiency on this side of the lake, I'd read, but what that was, and what anyone meant to do about it, was a mystery to me. The sight of them was disturbing, but they seemed to unduly distress Estes. "My God, look at them!" he murmured as he dragged his flask from his pocket, drinking deeply.

Bayard gestured for me to attend to them, and so I found myself surrounded as I doled out coins from his purse—coins which were disappearing rather too rapidly for my taste.

Julian gave Bayard a small smile. "Thank you."

Ah yes, Bayard was well on his way to redemption.

We walked on.

"We're at the most poetical part of the lake," Bayard observed at one point, stopping to take in the view. "Made famous by both Rousseau and Byron."

It was easy to see why. Lac Léman was the purest dazzling blue, dotted with sailboats and steamers, and here the mountains were close and steep and imposing, inspiring and menacing at the same time. It seemed one could be on their slopes in a mile, though the mile passed, and they were still no closer, a chimera one kept moving toward but never reached. Snow fields shone on their upper slopes, clouds hovered, pink and blue and white, near their tops, all of it reflected in detailed purity in the lake below. The air smelled of wildflowers and dust. The green trees of Chillon's oval island seemed to grow straight out of the water, and the castle walls glowed a pale beige in the sun, its many-headed towers roofed in red.

The island was on the margin of the lake, only a hundred feet distant, connected to the shore by a narrow, enclosed bridge. I paid the visitors' fees, and we went inside. A soldier stood just past the entrance, beyond him a table spread with engravings of the castle and its grounds, pamphlets about its history, and copies of Byron's "The Prisoner of Chillon," held down with paperweights made of round, palm-size stones painted with the castle and its environs, all of it for sale. Beyond that were the great castle gates, and a paved courtyard, with the towers of the castle and battlements rising all around.

Chillon had been built in the twelfth century, and owned by the Duke of Savoy, but now it served as an armory, and the main floor, with its pillars stretching into dark ceilings patterned with wooden squares, was huge, with a massive fireplace at one side and the coats of arms of the Swiss cantons of every governor painted on the walls. Benches and tables lined the room, and there was weaponry of all kinds, but even with all of it, the large room felt empty. We did not linger there, all of us wanting to see the dungeons that had so inspired Byron. Down stone stairs, through a chamber with sloping slabs of stone where the condemned had slept awaiting their execution, beneath a huge blackened beam from which they'd been hung, and then into the main chamber, which surpassed my expectations.

It was awe inspiring, actually, dizzying, with its seven stone columns reaching into vaulted ceilings like those of a cathedral. *In Chillon's dungeons . . . massy and gray / Dim with a dull imprison'd ray . . .* Byron's words were so present they might as well have been carved into the stone. The rock from which the castle had been hewn served as rough, tumbling walls on two sides. Some of the pillars still had their iron rings, where prisoners had been chained. The only light came from small apertures cut into the stone; the only view was the sky. *A sunbeam which hath lost its way . . .*

There were few other visitors today; we were the only ones in the dungeon, and our footsteps and breaths were loud in the emptiness, flung into the shadows of stone. I could hear the rippling of the lake against its outer walls, and could not help thinking of Byron's prisoner, Bonivard, listening to that ceaseless sound.

"Look! Here is his signature!" Louisa exclaimed, and we all went over to see where Byron had chiseled his name into a pillar. Miss Wentworth traced it lingeringly with her finger, as if she found something wondrous in it. I noticed the way her action drew Bayard's gaze. He seemed transfixed by her, and I remembered returning the night they'd mocked me to find them together and companionable in the kitchen. I remembered thinking I'd stumbled upon a clandestine meeting. I thought: *Louisa has little time left.*

It wasn't as if I hadn't known that—he'd been ready to give her up in London, and it was only because she was here and available that he kept her now. But for him to be interested in her sister . . . Suddenly, Estes's jealousy took on another hue. Perhaps I'd been wrong. Perhaps it wasn't over Louisa and Bayard, but Bayard and Miss Wentworth.

Estes wasn't watching now. He walked a shallow rut in the stone floor around a pillar—the tread worn by Bonivard's pacing at the end of his chain, or so the legend went. Estes paused, looking up at the apertures, at sun that barely reached into the dimness. In fact, I had the strange impression that the apertures weren't illuminating so much as providing escape for what little light existed in the dungeon, as if it too were desperate to flee the dank chill.

"How Bonivard must have wanted to fly," he said softly. The sun chose just then to grow stronger, to gild him, turning his hair into spun sugar, and he looked so plaintive and sorrowful that I almost forgot I disliked him.

I heard a small gasp—Louisa. She clasped her hands before her. "Oh, Jules, you look like an angel!"

The moment fled. He did not answer, but only turned away, and reached for his flask, and to my surprise, Louisa's dark eyes filled with tears.

Her sister's expression grew more forbidding.

My head pounded, the absinthe I'd drunk turning traitor; this was too complicated for me. I forced myself to look up into the vaulted ceilings. *Oh God! it is a fearful thing / To see the human soul take wing* . . . The dungeon was both oppressive and beautiful—odd that two such opposite things should not just coexist, but do so in such harmony. The press of its history, of dread and fear, seemed to have seeped into the walls.

"Is there a name for that?" I wondered aloud.

Miss Wentworth asked, "A name for what?"

"For a place that holds the memory of suffering. When its history lingers so one can feel it."

"No," Bayard said thoughtfully. "I have often wished for one."

"You should invent it," Miss Wentworth told him.

Bayard smiled. "If I tried, Hanson would say: 'This isn't a word, Sonnier, you must change it.' I would fight to keep it, and Hanson would fight to be rid of it, and in the end I would let him have his way. Editors are very literal beings. They don't appreciate it when you make up words. Readers don't either, for that matter. They love to find a mistake, and they love to tell you about it. I'd probably get two or three hundred letters about it."

Estes looked startled. "Do you really get that many letters? Two or three hundred?"

"I don't know." Bayard shrugged. "It was an exaggeration. I don't keep count."

He did get that many, and we both knew it. But he threw me a glance, and I said nothing.

We went to view the other rooms. Several people milled about, staring at brass cannons and painted shields. I tensed, as I always did when in public with Bayard. The chances that he would be recognized were small, but I noticed how often Louisa tried to take his arm. After the incident on the steamer, whatever trust I'd had in her—which had never been much—was gone.

I whispered to her, "Not here. Or do you want him angry with you again?"

"Why shouldn't they know he belongs to me?" she asked.

"Because he doesn't. Don't mistake it, Louisa."

She lifted her chin. "You're the one who mistakes it." Still, she obeyed me, albeit petulantly.

We wandered through the many rooms, but none were as interesting as the dungeon, and I was growing bored until we got to the Torture Chamber.

A large post that reached from floor to ceiling stood in the center. It was blackened, and there were many hooks and pulleys embedded into it. Estes stared at it in drunken horror. Louisa touched one of the iron rings with a tentative finger.

"Can you imagine?" she asked quietly. "Look here—you can see where it was burned by a hot iron. And here too. Oh . . . the whole thing is marked. How those prisoners must have suffered."

Estes put a trembling hand to the post, looking stricken. "They're all around us."

"Their spirits?" Now Louisa looked horrified.

"Just above our heads." Estes's voice was almost too quiet to hear. "They can't escape. They fill all the space."

His hysteria at the Diodati, and Louisa's, had started just this way. I saw the same signs. That this was happening here, now, was impossible. People were close enough to hear; a few began to tender us curious glances.

I turned to a nearby guide. "Do you think you could empty the room?"

He looked confused. "Empty it, monsieur? How should I empty it?"

"Get everyone out of here."

"Why would I do that, monsieur?"

Bayard took hold of Estes's arm. "Not here, Jules. Not now."

Estes turned to him with wide, unseeing eyes. He shook off Bayard's hand and shouted, "They're all talking at once!" He grabbed his head with a cry of terror, and then the post with both hands, looking up into the vaulted ceiling.

The curious glances turned to outright stares.

Miss Wentworth stepped back, uncertain and helpless, just as she'd been the night of his terrors, the night of the portrait, and I was sick of that too. I left the useless guide and went to her. "Stop this. You must stop this."

"You think I can?"

I did not expect her bitterness.

"Look," she said, gesturing. "You see? He has no need of me. Louisa is already managing it."

Louisa had pulled one of Estes's hands from the post. She stepped between him and the pillar, forcing him to look at her. "Jules—Julian."

"They cannot find the way out," Estes said hoarsely, loudly.

"We can show them." She looked up, spreading her hands, calling, "Follow us! Follow us!"

Bayard looked astonished. Miss Wentworth watched with narrowed eyes. The other visitors in this room regarded us like freaks at a museum, which I was beginning to think we were.

Louisa dodged from beneath Estes's hands, her skirts spinning around her ankles as she swirled to the door like Titania biding Oberon to come, to dance. "Follow me! Follow me! Julian, you must help! Are they following?"

He seemed entranced as he looked to the ceiling, and in wonder, he said, "Yes. Yes, they're following! This way! This way!" He too began to wave his arms. People backed warily away, whispering. The guide rushed nervously out the door, where Louisa had stopped, waiting for Estes, and when he got there, the two of them turned their eyes to the ceiling, watching an invisible host swarm to freedom. Everyone else, me included, stood dumbfounded.

"They're gone!" Estes said at last. He swooped on Louisa, embracing her in his relief. Too long. Too ardent. She looked exultant when he released her. She looked at us all as if to say, *You see? I fixed everything.*

Miss Wentworth turned coldly—who knew that it was possible to move with such frozen deliberation?—and went into the small room just beyond where I stood, where there was an opening in the floor with a railing built around it.

The oubliette, where hapless prisoners had fallen to their deaths. Three steps, four, and then only darkness, and a pit filled with ragged rocks and sharp blades.

I would not have approached her there for any amount of money.

But Louisa did. She was either a fool or oblivious. I didn't know which. I did not hear what she said to her sister, but I saw Miss Wentworth's chilly stare in answer. Louisa ignored it. She put her hands on the railing and looked down with a shudder.

The flash of hatred in Miss Wentworth's expression was so vicious that I thought for a moment she might push her sister. The railing would not keep Louisa from falling; it was merely a warning to the unwary tourist.

But then, just as quickly, it was gone. "Be careful, Loulou." She grasped Louisa's skirt, jerking her back from the rail, and Louisa spun with a frightened wail, throwing herself into her sister's arms. Miss Wentworth gripped her hard, pulling her away from the oubliette, not releasing her hold, clutching Louisa desperately, as if afraid someone might try to pull them apart.

"I'm sorry," Louisa sobbed loudly. "Addie, I'm so sorry." Miss Wentworth's gaze pinned me where I stood. She was stroking Louisa's hair, murmuring comfort—last night, everything, obviously forgiven—and in her dark brown eyes I saw such a profound love and sorrow that the hatred I'd seen before felt impossible. But no, I hadn't mistaken it.

I could only stare back, stunned and confused at the contradiction, and suddenly I was thinking of Bayard's story, my own additions. The witches. *Something wicked this way comes . . .*

The idea struck unerringly and completely. Sisters. Jealousies and competitions and enduring love. Doppelgängers, opposites. Together, the *donna ideale*. The characters leaped to me; the story grew so solid I could hold it in my hand; words tumbled into place.

Suddenly I was burning for pen, for paper, and before I knew it, I was racing out of the Torture Chamber and into the courtyard of Chillon, not waiting for any of the others—I had forgotten they existed—as I made my way alone back to the Hôtel Byron.

EIGHTEEN

ADELAIDE

L ouisa sobbed in my arms, overwhelmed by my forgiveness.

Forgiveness. What an illusory conceit. I forgave her the story she'd told last night, but how could I forgive all her small betrayals, which I doubted she even realized she'd committed, so many things interwoven, things that were her fault, mine, our parents' . . . where did one charge begin and another end? How was I to tell the difference?

I stared blankly at the niche above the oubliette with its image of the Virgin Mary, to whom prisoners offered a final prayer before making their fatal descent, and waited for Louisa to calm herself. Finally, she drew away. She said in a low voice, "I know Jules must have told you."

"That he discovered your affair with Bayard? Yes."

"It was Mr. Calina's fault," Louisa said.

"No doubt he felt justified."

"Justified? For what? How have I harmed him?"

"Is what you did to him in London not a good enough reason?"

"I told you, I did nothing!"

I glanced into the Torture Chamber, where Julian leaned against a wall, swaying with the laudanum he'd been drinking all morning. He looked barely able to stand. The crowd was gathering, whispering, pointing. It was too much attention. It was time to go.

"We can speak of it later," I said. "For now we must get Jules out of here."

But it was already too late; guards came into the room; the guide directed them to Julian.

Louisa followed my gaze. "Oh no."

We hurried over just as the guards took hold of Julian, who laughed. The exhilaration of his spirit rescue was still in his eyes. "We saved them!"

"Is there a problem, gentlemen?" I asked.

One of the guards said, "We've orders to take him, and her too."

The other guard reached for Louisa.

She jerked her arm away before he could touch her. "I'm not going anywhere with you."

"They're with me," Bayard said, stepping up. "What's the complaint?"

His tone was short. I did not think I was imagining his displeasure. The bruise on his pale face only reminded me that he had reason not to find Julian's visions as fascinating today as he had in the past. How many more disturbances could we cause him before he was no longer amused? I was very much afraid today would prove to be the end.

"Public drunkenness," said one of the guards.

Louisa said haughtily, "I am not drunk."

Bayard said, "Please. I'm Bayard Sonnier. There needn't be any trouble." He spoke quietly, but people had moved close to listen. One woman exclaimed, "Bayard Sonnier!" and clapped her hand to her mouth. There were titters of excitement. His name wafted through the crowd on a murmur.

This was even worse. My hand tingled. I gripped it hard, digging my gloved fingers into the itch, hoping to stop it.

The guard said, "Bayard Sonnier? The writer?"

"The very same," Louisa said haughtily. "Wouldn't the newspapers like to hear how inhospitable you were to such a great man?"

The guard drew back, looking at his partner. Both considered the crowd. I thought of the mob on the steamer. This could turn so very quickly.

"We'll leave immediately," Bayard promised them.

The other guard said reluctantly, "We'll escort you to the door."

"Thank you." Bayard frowned and looked around. "Where's Vanni?"

"I saw him hurry out earlier," I told him.

"Why? Where would he go?"

Julian reached into his pocket for that damnable flask. I stayed him with a hand, and shook my head.

"Mr. Calina knows the way back to the hotel," Louisa said. "He'll no doubt meet us there. Or he's gone forever, which would hardly be a bad thing."

"Well, there's no help for it, I suppose." Bayard gestured to the guards, who were waiting impatiently. "Lead on."

We only gathered more attention as we left, guards on either side. Bayard wore a long-suffering expression. How unbearable this must be for him. The only saving grace was that none in the crowd knew our names, at least not yet.

We had grown a tail, people following, whispering, gossiping. The guards took us to the door, and then stood watching as we crossed the covered bridge to the road.

"Quickly," Bayard said in a low voice. "Where the hell is Vanni? Why is he always disappearing when I most need him?"

The way back was silent and tense. I waited for Bayard to tell us that it was time we departed, but he said nothing. I was aware every moment of our trailing followers, though none dared to approach us. Perhaps it was due to Bayard's forbidding expression. Even Louisa seemed to understand he was not to be trifled with. She came up beside me and held out her hand. In her palm was an oval stone, dark gray speckle with a white quartz stripe down its middle.

"For you," she offered. "I found it before dinner last night, at the shore."

Before dinner, when she'd been angry enough to leave me. Her walk along the shore had not calmed her, either, or she would not have told the story of Mr. Tomlinson. Yet she had paused for a moment in between those things to pick up a rock she knew would please me.

I took the stone, which gleamed in the sunlight as if it had been polished. "It's lovely. Thank you."

It had never been easy to stay angry with Louisa; she was always eager to atone, desperately sorry for her transgressions, frightened by her lack of control. She made one feel ungracious for holding a grudge.

"I thought you would like it," she said simply.

When we reached the hotel, it was late in the afternoon, and the grounds were bustling. Couples strolled along the lakeshore while children dashed in and out of the water. Others lounged at the tables and benches in the gardens, delighting in the sunshine, and it seemed every flower celebrated the warmth by releasing its fragrance. Talk was a constant buzz punctuated by laughter and splashing, and now and then a shout.

As we approached the garden, gazes turned to our growing entourage. Such a crowd was a curiosity. It would be only a matter of moments before Bayard was discovered.

He knew it too. He paused and said quietly, "We'll return to the way things were when we checked in. Louisa, you'll stay with your sister tonight. Jules and Vanni and I will share the other room."

Louisa looked disappointed. "Oh, but why should we? No one found out last night."

Annoyance crossed Bayard's face. "I'm going to see if Vanni's in the room. If he is, I may throttle him."

"That should be something to see," Julian said. "I'll go with you."

"Oh no, let's all sit in the garden for a bit first," Louisa said. "It's such a lovely afternoon."

"Louisa, can't you see that he must go now? He'll be nothing but harassed in the garden," I said. As he and Julian hurried off, I went on, "I only hope the two of you haven't ruined everything."

"How have we done that?" she asked.

That she did not understand was exhausting. "You caused his maid to leave so he had to find another. Julian shot him, and you caused a scene on the steamer. And now, if that wasn't enough, Bayard had to announce himself to rescue you and Jules from the guards. We'll be lucky if he doesn't set us out. Even if he doesn't, don't you think people will wonder about his friends shouting at spirits at Chillon? What do you think will happen when they find out who we are?"

"Why do you keep going on about that? This isn't London. The gossip couldn't have followed us here." But she looked uncertain. The crowd was dispersing now; Bayard Sonnier was their interest, not the women he'd left behind.

We were passing a rosebush with heavy pink blooms, and she stopped, wistfully touching the petals. "Do you remember Mama's pink roses, Addie?"

I was troubled both by her obliviousness to our situation, and her sudden sad thoughtfulness. "Of course I remember."

"I wonder if she ever thinks of us?"

"I don't know. If she does, she's never written to say."

I knew it was a mistake the moment I said it. Had I not been so distracted by Bayard and the crowd, I never would have.

Louisa's gaze sharpened. "Does she even know where to write? We've moved about so often."

Reluctantly, I said, "I've sent her a letter with our address each time."

"You did? I had no idea."

"I didn't want to distress you."

She went ominously quiet. It was too familiar, and I wished I'd said nothing. I wished I were alone, back in the room, lost in my story. How lovely those hours when I had, for once, not thought of my sister, when I'd forgotten my constant, pressing worry.

Calmly, I said, "It's the past, Loulou. Did we not decide to put it behind us?"

"Yes." Her voice was nearly a whisper. I felt her fight herself, and then gain hold. "All their talk of Free Love and affinity, and how woman shouldn't be just chattel—they are such hypocrites."

"Julian was married," I reminded her.

"What should it matter? 'Marriage is a set of chains.' How often did they say that to us?" She aped our parents' aphorisms bitterly. "Jules was a prisoner, was he not? Emily was a vindictive witch—"

"Louisa!"

"She was. Coming to our house that way, blaming you. Causing all that trouble. It was all her fault! She made Jules unhappy from the start. Should he have sacrificed his life to her? Why should she have expected that?"

"Why should she not? Julian did marry her. He made a commitment; she had a right to expect him to keep it."

"What? You cannot tell me that you suddenly believe in such a binding marriage."

"No, but we don't know what Jules said to her, or what he promised."

"We do know. He told us. I don't understand why you believe her, Addie. She had every reason to lie to you. It only proves that she was not worthy of him." Louisa parroted Julian's words unthinkingly, ever his acolyte.

"It doesn't matter now. We can't go back."

We walked in silence for a moment.

"It was a good thing we left, Addie, wasn't it?" Her voice was almost pleading. "We're happier now, aren't we? I'm better than I was."

I heard her hope, as well as her fear that she was not, that she would never be. "Yes. We're happier. You're better."

She seemed relieved. "You don't regret Jules, do you? He needs you so."

In that too, I heard hope and fear. With no money or family to support us, our choices had dwindled to nothing, and Louisa was as aware of it as I. Admitting my errors would not change that.

"No," I said. "I don't regret it in the least."

The others did not meet us again until dinnertime. I had found a table in the corner of the dining room, half hidden in the shadows, though Louisa had disagreed vehemently at the location.

"No one can see us here."

"That is exactly the point," I told her. "The scene at Chillon was quite enough, don't you think? Bayard will thank us for privacy."

Which, it turned out, was more than true. He and Julian looked harried as they came to the table.

"Thank God," Bayard said, gesturing to the waiter to bring wine. "Someplace quiet at last. I've been nothing but harassed all afternoon."

"They've asked us to leave," Julian said.

"To leave? But why?" Louisa asked.

Bayard looked grim. "It appears that my secretary made rather a mess of the garden last night."

"I knew it must have something to do with him," Louisa said.

"And then there's the small matter of 'Bayard Sonnier and the Spirits at Chillon,'" he went on cuttingly. "Apparently there were several other hotel guests in the Torture Chamber this afternoon. No one's talked of anything else since it happened. We are currently unwelcome at the Hôtel Byron. They're half afraid we'll see ghosts in the walls and start chanting spiritualist hymns."

Julian looked chastened. "I am sorry, Bay."

Bayard nodded curtly. "I've sent Vanni to handle it. I don't think they'll put us on the street before dinner. But if he manages to appease them, it might be a good idea to spend the rest of the evening quietly reading in our rooms."

"Should we perhaps look for another hotel tonight?" I asked.

"I don't think that necessary. In fact, I expect they'll thank me for this later, when they become famous for it. I promise you that next year, you'll see the story of it printed on advertisements. 'Here is where Bayard Sonnier saw ghosts,' or some such thing."

"But it wasn't you who saw them," Louisa protested. "Jules and I should be the ones they mention."

"I'd prefer that, believe me. It's a pity you aren't famous."

"But Jules is quite famous. Why, 'Cain in the Garden' was banned!"

"That's infamous," Julian said wryly. "I think it not quite the same thing."

Stubbornly, Louisa said, "It is beautiful and inspiring. I will never understand why people cannot see that."

I tried to think of some way to steer the conversation to less dangerous ground, but I didn't need to, because just then Mr. Calina came into the dining room, looking as besieged as had Julian and Bayard before him.

"They've agreed to let us stay," he said, taking a seat. "But we must be gone before noon tomorrow, and we're not to come down to breakfast, nor stay at dinner past nine. We're not to speak to ghosts, have fits, or get drunk. We're to go to our rooms and stay in them. No sleeping in the garden."

"That sounds reasonable enough," Bayard said. "I suppose the only question is whether you can bring yourself to obey."

Mr. Calina looked sheepish. "I think I can manage—at least, the drunkenness and the sleeping-in-the-garden part. The ghosts aren't within my power."

"There are no spirits here," Julian said seriously.

"Really? Why? Have you no more laudanum?"

"Because no one has died here," Julian snapped back. "At least not recently."

"Something to be thankful for," Bayard said with a shudder.

I said, "Where did you go when you left Chillon, Mr. Calina? The way you went racing out, I half expected to see the police chasing you."

At my question, he looked startled, and then annoyed. "I'd forgotten some letters Bayard wanted me to write."

"Yes, he was madly scribbling when we returned," Bayard said. "The next time, Vanni, it might be a good idea not to leave your employer wondering if you've jumped off the bridge or fallen into the oubliette."

"It wasn't Mr. Calina who nearly fell, but me," Louisa said. "Would you be sorry, Bay, if I were nothing but broken and bloody ribbons at the bottom of a pit?"

He sipped at his wine. "I dislike seeing pretty things ruined."

She smiled, her dimples deepening. "Are you saying that you think I'm pretty?"

That she hadn't heard what he didn't say was typical.

"Now you're only fishing," he said.

"Women like to hear compliments sometimes, you know."

"I compliment you, don't I? Why, just last night I—"

"Oh stop!" Louisa said, blushing. "That's not what I meant."

"And truly not what any of the rest of us wish to hear." Julian's voice was strained. "Didn't you say they wanted us done with dinner by nine, Calina? It's nearly eight now."

Julian's obvious discomfort only added to my own. I was relieved when we all set to the task of eating, and the conversation turned to other things. When it became clear that Bayard wasn't going to ask us to leave, I pushed aside my worry and let my mind wander to the story I'd started last night. I wanted only to return to it, but there would be no chance to write tonight, not with Louisa there. I had no wish to tell her of it.

I was lost enough in my thoughts that it surprised me when Bayard rose, saying, "I think it's time we retire. The porters are beginning to give me the evil eye."

Julian threw his napkin to the table, and Louisa scrambled to her feet.

I looked up from my stewed rabbit, only half eaten. "Oh, will they mind very much if I finish?"

"As long as it's not me, I don't see why not," Bayard said. "Vanni will stay and see you to your room."

"Oh, he needn't. I can find my way well enough."

"I'd feel better if he did." Bayard looked at his secretary. "No wine."

Mr. Calina raised his glass, which held only water. "Not a drop, my liege."

Julian leaned to kiss the top of my head, saying, "Good night, my dear," and then the three of them were gone, and I was surprised at the extent of my relief.

I had meant to ignore Mr. Calina and finish the rabbit, but instead I found myself turning to him, asking, "Why did you really rush off today?"

He leaned back in his chair. "I'm flattered to think you so interested in anything I do."

"You needn't be unpleasant."

"Why not? It's something we have in common, don't you think? Unpleasantness."

"I wish Louisa had not told that story," I said.

"It wasn't flattering. I'm not surprised that you hate her for it."

"Oh, but I don't," I said. "How could I? She's my sister."

He said nothing, but only gave me a look that reminded me of how our gazes had met when Louisa and I were at the oubliette. How much I'd hated her in that moment, both for calling attention to us and for comforting Julian, but Mr. Calina could not have seen that, could he?

"We've had our difficulties, but she's—"

"She's a bitch," he said bluntly. "I'm sorry, but I should think you'd know it better than anyone."

His vulgarity surprised. "Be careful how you speak of her, Mr. Calina. I will not have her maligned."

"She doesn't need me to malign her. She does so very well herself." He reached for the wine bottle.

"I thought you promised Bayard not to drink tonight."

"Talking about your sister brings out the worst in me."

"I imagine it would. Did she hurt you when she chose Bayard instead?"

He paused, the bottle forgotten. "She told you?"

"She said you lied to her, that you let her believe you were Bayard."

He looked torn.

"You did," I said.

"I didn't lie," he told me. "I simply said nothing, and she assumed . . ."

"Dear God. Please tell me that did not go on for long. She said the two of you only shared a kiss. Is that true?"

"I am a gentleman, despite what you may think."

So Louisa had been honest about that, thankfully. "No gentleman lets a young woman believe he is something he is not."

"I'm not denying responsibility. I should have said something. But she's to blame too, for not wanting to hear it. There were a hundred things to tell her otherwise, if she'd wanted to see them."

"That's very convenient for you to say."

"Louisa wants to believe what she wants to believe. You know it as well as I. Estes swallows enough laudanum to turn a horse into a mystic and tells her there are spirits flying about and evil things in the shadows, and she's suddenly in hysterics and seeing them too. Tell me: Do you think Louisa really sees such things? Or is it just that she craves attention?"

"I don't know."

"Come now."

"I don't," I said again. "You don't understand. His visions can be so sublime. Louisa wants to believe in them just as I do."

"You're no better than your sister then."

"Do you not believe there are things in this world we can't see?"

"Yes. I just don't think they're flying around the salon at the Diodati. Maybe at Chillon. There was a feeling about that place . . ."

"A history of despair," I remembered.

He nodded. "So I suppose I can't deny it might be true. Perhaps it's only that I dislike them both, and I'm being unfair."

"I understand about Louisa. But why should you dislike Julian?"

His smile was small. "I've been uncharitable enough tonight. I'd rather not add to it. Besides, I think Bayard was wrong about them not minding our lingering. The porter is glaring at us. We should probably go."

I had not eaten any more of my rabbit, but my appetite was gone. He rose and offered his hand, and I took it, and heard myself say, unbidden, unthought-of, "I've started writing story," and the release I felt at the admission brought the same thrill of excitement I'd felt writing it.

He seemed impressed. "You have? For the contest?"

"I don't know," I said honestly. "I don't know what it's for. But I felt I should take your advice."

"My advice?"

"To write about ghosts."

"Oh. Well, that's good, isn't it? Perhaps putting them on paper will take them from your eyes."

I wondered if he had any idea how much I hoped that could be true.

NINETEEN

VANNI

She seemed lost in silence as I escorted her to her room. "Good night, Miss Wentworth," I said, and she answered me with a distracted nod before she opened the door and disappeared inside without another word. I stood there, discomfited, feeling like a nonentity—not a feeling I liked, but one with which I was left almost every time I had any dealings with one of the Wentworth sisters. Damn them both.

But cursing did not dismiss them—no, how could it, when they'd been dancing in my head all afternoon? Not as themselves, but as the witch sisters Aurora and Leila, churning spells and wreaking havoc in a mountain forest while they cursed the fates that had tied them together. I'd come rushing from Chillon in a fevered sweat and ensconced myself in the hotel room without taking off my coat, losing myself in words until Bayard and Estes came through the door, and then blathering something about letters that Bayard didn't remember asking me to write. It wasn't that I thought he would mind my writing a story, but I had no doubt he would mind very much when he learned I'd appropriated his. Fortunately he was too distracted over the proprietor's request that we leave the hotel to question me.

I'd managed that as well as I could, which hadn't been easy, especially given the owner's fear that the spirits might have followed us from Chillon—who knew that an otherwise rational Swiss could be so superstitious? My headache, which had been lost in the elation of inspiration, returned. I had really wanted nothing more than to eat and fall into bed, but then . . . Adelaide Wentworth.

It troubled me that Louisa had told her of our—what did one call it? An aborted possibility of an affair? A badly conceived attempt at seduction? A fortunate near escape? It bothered me that I had not been able to defend myself. Miss Wentworth threw around the epithet of *no gentleman* so assiduously. Ridiculous that it should wound me every time, yet it did. I had escaped poverty and anonymity by such thin margins—well, I supposed I had not yet escaped, had I?

What made it worse was that I was genuinely curious about her now. There was much more to Adelaide Wentworth than I'd suspected. Surely it wouldn't hurt to probe a bit more, especially as my witchy sisters wanted understanding and complexity. The Wentworths had inspired them; now they could provide the insight I needed. Whether I could gain that and emerge unscathed was another question.

When I got back to the room, Bayard was writing and Estes was reading. It was quiet but for the faint song of crickets and frogs beyond the window, and the rapid and unhesitating scratch of Bayard's pen across the paper—which made me both glad and depressed. Estes asked, "Is Adelaide in her room?"—no *hello*, or *thank you for attending to her*. I nodded, and he turned back to his book.

Bayard glanced up from his work. "Did you get those pages copied? They're more important than letters I don't remember."

"I'll start on them now," I said.

I was grateful for the distraction of the task, even through the throbbing of my head, and grateful too that I at last had something to send to his publisher. I would post these in Geneva on our return, so I set to it. The night, for once, was peaceful and uncomplicated, and we retired early. I fell into dreams of half-garbed witches gamboling about rocky alpine meadows, one with dark and flying hair, and another with Vera Brest's face, and when I woke, it was with an uncomfortable mix of unsatisfied desire and a fervent yearning to work on my manuscript. I managed to attend to neither.

Instead, I played Bayard's faithful servant and organized the return to Geneva. This time, I'd learned my lesson, and I procured a private salon. Bayard did not thank me, but his relief was obvious. Once everyone was ensconced, I said, "If you don't need me, I think I'll get some air."

Bayard waved me out. I went up to the deck and stood at the rail, staring unseeingly at the scenery as the steamer started off. I was glad to be returning. At least at the Diodati I had the privacy of my own room, and the peace of the lake in early morning. Not only that, but I was anxious to see Colburn and be rid of the nagging disquiet I felt over his contract. I had managed to put it from my mind these last two days. Leaving the journal in my desk had helped—there had surely been enough fodder to write about, and enough temptation too, but fortunately, my witches had distracted me. I also wanted to turn my hauntingly erotic dreams about Vera Brest into reality. She would not be happy that I meant to cancel the contract, nor that Bayard had written no more of his story, but perhaps I could distract her with kisses—

"How beautiful." Adelaide Wentworth came up beside me, curling her gloved fingers about the railing. "The mountains seem so close, they make one feel small."

That she'd sought me out eased some of my lingering resentment over how easily she'd put me aside last night. "Yes. Majestic, I think."

"A perfect word. I've never felt God's presence so much as I feel it here."

I glanced at her in surprise. "You haven't embraced Estes's atheism?"

"I don't know," she said with a small shrug. "I was raised to Transcendentalism, but I have never been wholly accepting. Sometimes I think I believe as Julian does, and then other times . . . it feels there must be something, don't you think? Even if it's not a biblical God."

I thought of the monastery. The camaraderie of the boys I shared rooms and lessons with. The day portioned into its precise parts, every moment accounted for. I'd taken pleasure in ritual and prayer and the comforting reassurance that I was not alone. "I've never been much of a philosopher. I've never doubted His existence."

"I suppose that's what comes of being told what to believe at a young age. One never thinks to question."

How long had it taken her to offend me this time? Two minutes? Three? I stepped back. "Just so. I'll leave you to your contemplation."

She grabbed my arm. "No, please . . . I'm sorry. That's not really what I meant. Please don't go."

"Why? What can we have to say to one another? You've made it quite clear that you consider me hardly fit for conversation—"

"Have I? How have I done so?"

"Just now, you accused me of being uncritical and ignorant."

She flushed, making the bright scab on her chin more conspicuous. "I also said I didn't mean it the way it sounded. I wasn't thinking of you in particular, but of everyone."

"Everyone."

She nodded and turned back to the view, looking perplexed. "And I don't mean just when it comes to religion, or philosophy. We are taught to be what we are. Do you think it possible that we can ever find our way clear of that?"

I had the feeling she was speaking on another plane completely, following a conversation that had nothing to do with me, and that made me think again of my story, the witch sisters, my curiosity. So I came back to the rail, and she turned to me with a quiet, sad smile that I found strangely engrossing.

Another disconcerting moment with Adelaide Wentworth. They were beginning to seem the rule.

I heard myself saying, "When my father sent me to the monastery, it was because he wanted me to be clear, as you say."

"You mean he wanted you to be a priest?"

I shook my head. "He sent me there to learn. It was a boarding school. He hoped I could be something other than what he was, or what I would have been had I stayed at home."

"What would you have been?"

"Nobody. A cobbler, just as he was. Or perhaps a pickpocket, or something worse. It was always a possibility." At her questioning look, I explained, "We lived in Bethnal Green. Perhaps you know it."

She shook her head. "In London? I've spent so little time there."

That seemed odd, given that it was Estes's home. "It wasn't the best part of town. My mother died soon after I was born. My father did his best to keep me out of trouble, but I was clever. I think—I know—he worried over what I might do with that cleverness. So, away to the good Benedictines, to turn me into a scholar and a gentleman. But as you noted last night, I sometimes forget how a gentleman should behave. I fear it's the thinnest of veneers."

She winced. "I'm sorry. I can be cruel sometimes. I don't like it in myself. I wish it wasn't there."

I said wryly, "We were all given a special talent."

She laughed, short and sudden, startling a gull that was swooping low, sending it soaring away. "You were supposed to deny it. I am certain you must have learned that in gentleman school."

"It would just have been compounding one lie with another."

She laughed again. It ended on a sigh. "Oh, I feel I have not laughed in a hundred years."

I felt as if I'd done something remarkable, something to note at last.

"There you are!" Estes came marching over, the cloud of his hair bouncing with every step. He looked worried as he took her arm. A brief and distracted nod at me.

"Mr. Calina has been regaling me with stories of his youth," she said.

"I see." But that was distracted too. "You've been gone so long that Louisa was concerned."

"Oh, yes, I did say I'd be only a moment . . ." The rest of her sentence was lost as he led her off. Neither of them looked again at me. She did not say good-bye. The interlude—if that's what it had been—was over. My sense of accomplishment slid away, that familiar insignificance taking its place. What did it matter? It wasn't as if I cared about any of them but Bayard. It was a blessing that she'd gone, in fact. I could return to my fantasies of Vera Brest, and mull over my witches, and perhaps add another dimension to them now that I knew something more of Adelaide Wentworth.

Except that I did not, I realized. She had told me nothing of her history. I had talked only of my own.

We returned to a quiet, empty villa with, blessedly, no boats bobbing in the harbor, no one lingering on the road. While I knew it was only a matter of time before word reached the village that Bayard had returned, I was thankful. The window had been fixed—one thing, at least, that didn't prove police incompetence—but I'd sent Sylvie back to Vera Brest for the interim, and there was no maid, and so no welcoming fires, and no dinner.

"Perhaps the famous Estes eggs?" Bayard suggested, but Estes, who was bent over the tea table, furiously scratching things out on the pages before him—a constant scritching that made me want to shout at him to get a new pen nib before he sent us all insane—seemed not to hear.

Bayard turned hopefully to me. "Vanni, can't you make macaroni or something?"

Miss Wentworth rose. "I'll see what's in the pantry."

"I'll go with you," Louisa said.

The two of them disappeared. Estes seemed not to notice that, either.

Bayard said to me, "You'll have to go to Orsini's tomorrow to fetch Sylvie back."

"I had been thinking to go tonight," I said.

He glanced out the window at the sunset, the snow on the mountains slowly turning a golden-tinged rose, as if the caressing light were reluctant to leave the peaks, the rest lavender and blue. "Will she have missed you?"

"I have reason to think so."

"Take advantage of it. You'd best go before she retires. Unless you plan to meet her in her bedroom." He lifted a brow. "Do you?"

"I doubt she'll be abed. Orsini's salon is tonight."

"You could try it, you know. I've had some success that way. Taking her by surprise, so to speak. Easier to manage a dressing gown than the armor of a corset and petticoats."

Estes laughed beneath his breath.

"I'll take that under advisement," I said.

Bayard leaned back, sprawling, on the settee. "Don't make me despair of you, Vanni."

I went to my room to get my coat and hat, and unlocked my desk drawer. I tucked the five hundred pounds into my pocket, and then I went downstairs, pausing when I heard talk coming from the kitchen. I told myself to ignore it and go. Instead, I went quietly down the hall, just in time to hear Miss Wentworth say, ". . . you didn't tell him, did you?"

"I didn't, but why shouldn't I, Addie? What should be so secret about it?"

"It should be enough that I want it to be."

"He said he was thinking of going there after he left Geneva. What if he does? What will I do?"

"Go with him, if you like. If he invites you."

"But how could I leave you? What of our plans? Jules must stay with him, you know he must, but he won't without you."

Silence. The sound of something popping in a skillet. The smell of onions and butter.

This was none of my concern. But despite myself, I crept closer, just outside the doorway, against the wall.

"You would not consider it?" Louisa asked in a voice so quiet I had to strain to hear. "Not even for me?"

Silence again. Then the almost violent scrape of a spoon against the skillet. Over and over again, as compulsive as scratching, and below that Miss Wentworth's beleaguered voice. "How can you ask me?"

"It wouldn't be the same," Louisa said. "Venice is *not* cursed, whatever you think—"

"I won't return there."

Louisa let out a near howl of exasperation. "Sometimes, Addie, you do frustrate me so."

"Then go. But you'll have to do so without me."

A slap of hands on a wooden surface that made me jump. I hurried away, worried that Louisa might come out to find me hovering.

I went to the rowboat and tried to lose myself in the exertion, in the anticipation of flirting eyes and a heart-shaped face, full red lips, but I kept thinking of Venice, a cursed city, a city of ghosts, the Wentworth sisters within it and mysterious plans. What plans? The words sounded nefarious, but perhaps that was just because I was used to the shady underbelly of Bethnal Green, and so suspected the worst of everyone—a habit the monks had not quite managed to quell. My thoughts were so full of their talk, spinning theories a hundred different directions, that I was surprised to discover I'd reached the shore before the Orsini château. Twilight was gone, night on full. Lights from the mansion flickered in rippling reflections across the water. There were carriages, music floating on the air, blending with that of crickets and the nickering of waiting horses, the ruffling lake. I had to call myself back, to remember why I'd come. Vera Brest. Distracting her with kisses.

The butler was polite as always, ushering me inside, and I'd no sooner gone two steps than I saw her, coming from the salon, holding a glass of champagne. She started at the sight of me. A vaguely disconcerting expression crossed her face, gone before I could say what it was. Her smile the next moment made me forget it completely.

I had been in the midst of taking off my coat, but she flew at me, shaking her head, saying, "Browne, fetch my shawl, please. Mr. Calina and I are going to the garden."

I didn't protest; the garden had been the place of our greatest intimacies. She drank the rest of her champagne in a gulp and put the glass on a nearby table. "When did you return?"

"Just now," I said. "I couldn't wait to see you."

"I have missed you as well."

The butler returned; she wrapped herself in her paisley shawl, fringe shimmying over her bare arms, and we went outside, around the corner of the house to the garden. We were not quite alone; the doors were open to the salon, and the music and talk floated out, now and then another couple. She led me to a bench nearly hidden beneath an arbor draped with pale climbing roses smelling of honey on the cool night air.

She said, "How was Villeneuve? And the castle? Did you see the dungeon?"

"It was beyond my expectations. You should allow me to take you there some time."

"Sylvie told me why you left," she said. "Was it all most frightening? You must tell me every detail."

I could not resist the order, not when her warm hand was already slipping into the opening of my coat. Even as I told the story, all I could hear was Bayard's voice in my ear, *"Don't make me despair of you,*

Vanni . . . *Take her by surprise . . .*" It seemed an imperative, and when I got to the part when we'd heard the window break, it became too hard to ignore. I managed ". . . and Sylvie screamed," before I kissed her.

She allowed me almost nothing; her lips parted only slightly, only the barest touch of her tongue, the faintest taste of her champagne-sweetened breath. She pushed me away with a tiny laugh, alluringly breathless. "You are very impatient, Mr. Calina."

I tried to pull her back. "My name is Giovanni. I would like to hear you say it. I've thought of nothing but this for days."

"Giovanni, I was not expecting you."

"What does that matter?"

"My husband is here," she said.

I drew away. Her hand fell from my coat. "Your husband? I thought he was in Portugal."

"He was. But he is on his way to Paris, and stopped to see to me first."

I could not keep my disappointment from my voice. "When will he be gone?"

"Soon." She leaned close again, brushing my cheek with a kiss. "Waiting will make it all the sweeter."

But I'd already been waiting for what felt like forever. I untangled myself from her and got to my feet. "What will happen if he finds me here? Should I expect a challenge?"

"A challenge? Whatever for? He knows nothing about you."

Which should not have surprised me. Why should he? She wouldn't tell him, of course, but we had been seen together often enough. Rumors might have reached her husband, and I half wanted that. I wanted to know that I was not an irrelevant passing fancy, that people had noted me. She would declare her love. He would challenge me to a duel. The world would speak my name as I lay dying with a bullet wound to the chest . . . or no, he would lay dying, and we would be exiled . . .

That embarrassing romantic streak of mine again. Practically, of course, it was far better this way. Better that he had no idea who I was. Still . . .

She gripped my hand. "You're angry. I'm sorry, but what is to be done? I did not know you had returned, or that you meant to come tonight, or I would have sent a note."

"Of course. I understand. I should not have come unannounced. Where's Colburn? Is he inside?"

"He was in the small salon when I last saw him," she said. "I will take you there."

"You needn't trouble yourself. I'll find him. But would you mind fetching Sylvie for me? I'm to bring her back."

"Sylvie refuses to return to the Villa Diodati," she told me sorrowfully. "She is too afraid."

"Afraid?"

Vera Brest shrugged. "Spirits, thieves, and of course, Mr. Sonnier's reputation. Can you blame her?"

I couldn't, but I was not sure which would be more exhausting, searching again for a maid, or having to play her role myself.

Together, we went back into the house. I was still reeling with disappointment and thwarted hopes—nothing new, why did I not expect it?—as I left her to hunt down Edward Colburn. I found him in the small salon, just as she'd said, playing cards.

When I came up to him, he nearly leaped to his feet. "Calina!" and then, in a lowered voice, "Have you something for me?"

"I'd like a word, if you don't mind."

He excused himself and followed me to a relatively quiet corner. "What is it? All of Geneva heard of the break-in. I do hope you've written it in some detail—"

"I haven't written it at all." I reached into my pocket, taking out the money. "I'm not going to. I've changed my mind. If you would be so good as to tear up the contract and take this back—"

"Take it back? I shall do no such thing." He looked affronted at the very idea.

"It's all there. Every penny. I was wrong to think I could do this. The dishonor—"

"What about the dishonor of reneging on an agreement? You've made a deal, and now you must uphold your end of it."

"Look, you can hire someone else. I haven't spent the money."

"Then you're a fool. I'm not taking it back. Who else would I hire? Who else knows him as you do?"

"I won't do this. I can't."

"Then I'll see you in court." He shoved my hand, still holding the money, back at me. "You signed a contract, Calina. Not only will I sue you for breaking it, but I will make certain every paper in London hears of it. No one will ever sign you to another. You will never publish another word. The next time I see you, you had best have something to show me. I expect the journal by the end of the summer, as we agreed. Or you'll hear from my lawyers."

He strode away while I stood stunned and disbelieving that he'd refused me so vehemently. I might have stood there all night, but then Vera Brest came up to me, taking the money from my hands, tucking it back into my pocket. I realized she had followed me. She had seen everything.

"Come now," she cooed, taking my arm, leading me to the door. "You should have said what you meant to do, my love. I would have warned you that there was no point. Edward will not change his mind. All the plans have already been made. It is to be printed in the winter."

"But I don't want to do it," I said stupidly.

"Why would you throw this opportunity away, Giovanni, my love?"

My name, *my love*. She came suddenly into focus; I realized we were outside.

"Go home." She twisted my watch chain, pulling me close as if to belie her words. "Think of how famous you will be, and how well you deserve it."

"I'd only be admitting that I'm not good enough to publish on my own merit." I was babbling, trying to make her understand the fears I couldn't myself unravel—that I was merely pretending to be an artist, compromising before I'd even really begun, denying everyone who'd had faith in me. My father. Bayard. Myself. "I'd just be taking advantage of Bayard's name."

"Do you not do that now?" she asked. "When we met, you mentioned him right away, hoping to impress. You already use him, my love. Why not be paid for it?"

She was so short that the top of her head came only to my collarbone. She opened my coat and stepped inside, all of her against me, her breasts, her hips . . . She pressed her mouth to my jaw, and I felt myself crumble.

"Now, you must go, but I will send for you when my husband is gone. And you will bring Mr. Sonnier's story—it must be finished by now, yes?"

I could not bear to think of that. "Not yet."

"No?" How disappointed she looked. "You cannot make him finish it?"

"I cannot make him do anything."

"Make him finish it for me," she whispered, tantalizing, an almost kiss. When I bent to make it more, she slid away. "Not here. Not now. Someone will see. Now, do you promise?"

I was so full of her I could only nod. My entire body heard the bargain. Bayard's story in exchange for her, but I was willing to be used. Once I was in her bed, I could make her forget she'd ever wanted anything but me.

It wasn't until I was on the opposite shore again, climbing to the shadowed gloom of the Diodati, that my desire faded to nothing, and

I realized that convincing Bayard to finish his story—assuming that I could—meant that it would no longer be mine. It meant giving up my witchy sisters, and in my befuddled, desire-racked brain, that meant giving up Adelaide Wentworth too, and her secrets. Venice and curses and mysterious plans. The sadness in her eyes—what had caused those things? Vera Brest and Colburn faded in the rush of my curiosity. Once again I had the sense that I needed the answers only Adelaide Wentworth could provide, and I was uncertain that I could give that up, even for Vera Brest.

TWENTY

ADELAIDE

Over the next two weeks, I wrote, or I thought about writing. The contest deadline now began to weigh, because I had decided that I did want this to be my entry. I wondered how it would fare against the others, even as I wasn't entirely certain it would have any competition. Bayard only said, "I'll get to it," when asked, which sent Jules into greater, more frustrated fervor. Louisa was not even trying, and Mr. Calina was ominously silent. I didn't know if he was still working on the story we'd mocked or not writing at all.

Although I'd decided to compete, I said nothing of it to Julian, writing only when I was alone, grabbing whatever moments I could. I didn't know why I kept it so secret, or why the only person I'd told was Mr. Calina. I suppose it was only that I wanted someone else to know, and he felt safely outside the others, removed enough to make no judgments, belonging only to himself.

It was difficult to find the time to work on it without anyone else noting. No other maid had been found, and so we shared her duties, fending for ourselves for breakfast and lunch, but taking turns cooking dinner. I did more than my share, hoping to alleviate the subtle but persistent dissatisfaction I'd felt from Bayard since Chillon, but even if I could not physically set down words, I was writing them in my head, developing my story of a fatal muse, full of furies and retributions from beyond the grave, my own *Frankenstein.*

Yet the story seemed full of pitfalls and terrors, every decision costing another, every choice narrowing the scope, so I was confused over how to proceed. I wanted advice, and so, one evening, as I watched Julian struggle, I resolved to ask for it.

I waited until he put down the pen and sat back in his chair. "Yesterday I thought it was all coming right again, but today I'm back where I started. Nothing seems to work—not the rhyme, not the words. I hardly know what I mean to do."

"I've written something," I burst out.

"What?"

"I've been writing a story."

He turned to me. "You? But you've never written anything before."

"I have. In fact, I used to write a great deal," I admitted. "But not for a very long time."

He looked thoroughly confused. "What made you decide to take it up again now?"

"I don't know. The contest, perhaps, and then Mr. Calina said I should write about ghosts—"

"Calina?" Julian's voice sharpened.

"I've written about twenty pages, but I don't know if it's good, or if I should continue with it. It's more difficult than I remembered."

He laughed shortly. "I should say so. Have you not seen me here every day tearing my hair out?"

"Do you think . . . do you think you could look at it?"

239

His gaze was measuring. "Are you certain you wish me to? What if I don't like it?"

"Then I shall stop," I said with more certainty than I felt. "That's all I want to know. Is it worth pursuing?"

Julian held out his hand. "Very well. Let me see it."

I nearly raced to my bag and pulled out my notebook. My fingers trembled as I handed it to him. How had Mr. Calina managed it with such calm the night he'd read his work to us? How had he borne the criticism? Now that I was in the same position, the memory of our cruelty was excruciating. Julian had been the second to speak that night, I remembered. He had delivered the blow with such unerring precision, as if he knew which words would do the most damage. Surely he would not be so cruel with me.

I whispered, "Be kind."

"Do you want kind or true?" he asked.

"I don't know."

While he read, I stared at the ashes of the fire, which we had let die because the evening was so warm. Soon, Louisa, whose turn it was to cook tonight, would call us for dinner.

"Stop scratching," Julian said.

I had not realized I'd been rubbing my hand, which felt on fire. I gripped it hard, willing myself to ignore it, and waited for him to finish reading. The clock ticked doggedly, each click a hundred hours. Beyond that, only the trill of an evening bird on the tree outside, Julian's breathing, and mine, the turning of the pages.

Finally, he turned the last one. He put the pages on the desk.

"Addie! Jules! Dinner is ready!" Louisa called.

"Well?" I asked, unable to bear Julian's silence another moment. "What do you think?"

"It has something," he said, and there was an edge to his voice I didn't recognize; me, who knew all his moods so intimately. "Yes, there's something."

"Is that good or bad?"

He was strange, too thoughtful.

"Jules, please—"

"I should have seen that you would have talent, given how well you inspire me."

It was so what I wished to hear that I thought I must be dreaming. Excitedly, I said, "Should I continue it, then? Do you think the ghosts of the wife and child too angry? I did not know which would be better—should they be icy or furious, do you think?"

He let out his breath, a quiet sound of despair. "Oh, Adelaide. A curse. A murder. A drowned wife and child . . . This is us, isn't it? You're writing us."

I had expected praise or reluctant dismay, or even disdain. But not distress.

"The only reason you feel we live beneath Emily's shadow is because you make it so." He leaned forward, urgent. "Writing this will only make things worse. Don't you see how this hurts us? Your refusal to forget? Your unending grief? You wallow in it. It's long past time that you put it all behind you. Don't write any more on this." He snatched the notebook from the desk and tossed it into the fireplace, and I sat there numbly, falling back in time, to Mr. Calina losing his temper, paper curling among the flames. But now the fire was dead. My story only scattered the cold gray ashes.

Julian came to me and took my hands, which would not unclench because I was trying so very, very hard not to scratch. He peeled them apart. His were so warm. "Don't you see how sad this makes you? It cannot help you to relive it this way."

"Perhaps putting them on paper will take them from your eyes."

"I thought it would help."

Julian shook his head sorrowfully. "To think about it all the time? To write it down? How can it? I want you to forget this, Adelaide. Be again the woman you used to be. Can you do that for me?"

My chin and my hand itched unbearably.

"Is it not enough for you to be my muse?" he asked softly. "Is it not enough to love me?"

I blinked away my tears and nodded, the habit of concession, and he kissed me gently, my lips, my cheeks, the corners of my eyes.

"So you'll put it away?"

"Yes. I'll put it away."

He smiled; I saw relief in it. He lifted me to my feet and wiped my tears with his thumb. "It's what's best, my love. Now, shall we go to dinner? I'm sure Louisa's slaved away."

As we went out, I glanced at the pages in the hearth and felt both relief that they were undamaged and a desperate urge to set them afire. I was glad not to look at them anymore.

I followed Julian to the kitchen, where we'd taken to eating these last few days because none of us wished the effort of carrying food and dishes to the dining room and then down again.

The others were already gathered. Louisa looked flushed and dewy and lovely. Bayard was pouring wine. Mr. Calina sat at the far end, leaning against the wall, and when we stepped inside, his gaze came to me and he frowned. I wondered what he saw that made him look so.

The food was already on the table, fried potatoes beneath a layer of melted Gruyère, and plump sausages splitting with their juices. Louisa was a better cook than I, and it was all perfectly done, but it was tasteless in my mouth. I had only a few bites before I could no longer stomach it. Only the wine seemed to go down easily.

"This is delicious," Julian said to Louisa.

"I thought Mr. Calina's stew last night far better," Louisa said coyly. "I think he's the best cook of all of us, don't you agree, Addie? Perhaps he should fix all our meals. It can just be another part of his job."

"Leave him be, Louisa," I said, too sharply.

It was as if I'd set a spell to freeze them in time. Louisa looked stunned, Bayard surprised; and Julian frowned. Only Mr. Calina did not look at me. He was studiously focused on his plate.

I said, "I'm not feeling very well, I'm afraid. If you'll excuse me . . ."

Julian caught my hand as I rose. "Adelaide—"

"I'll be fine." I attempted a smile, which seemed to comfort him. "I'm just going outside for a bit. I think some air might help."

He looked worried, but he let me go out into the darkness, which held a growing chill but was otherwise welcoming. The crickets were so loud I felt comfortably surrounded. I went to the bench, but I didn't sit on it. Instead I sat on the grass, and then lay back to stare up at the sprinkled stars. Spirits who had made their way out of purgatory, or confusion, or wherever, to climb into the sky.

I expected Julian or Louisa to come for me, but neither did, and I was glad; I wanted to be alone, to sort through my thoughts. But when I heard the muffled footsteps on the grass perhaps half an hour later, I felt a surprising relief.

"Am I intruding?" Mr. Calina asked as he came to a stop beside me. The glow from the house limned him; he was a near shadow.

I closed my eyes and let out my breath. "No. I'm looking at the stars."

"With your eyes closed? That's quite a trick."

"They are so blindingly bright."

"It's the mountain air. They look close enough to touch too."

"You're tall," I said, opening my eyes again. "They're right above your head. I think you could reach one if you tried."

He reached up, on his tiptoes, fingers scrabbling at nothing. "Still too far."

"Julian's spirits," I mused. "I suppose it would be a shame to pluck one from the sky, when they've worked so hard to get there."

He sat on the bench, forearms on his knees, his hands dangling between them. An owl hooted, low and rhythmic, from a nearby tree. Neither of us said anything for a long moment, but it was oddly comfortable.

I said, "Where are the others?"

"Julian's washing dishes and Bayard is reading Tennyson aloud. Louisa is listening like a penitent."

"Did they see you come out here?"

A pause. "Yes. I told them I meant to see to you."

"Jules didn't mind?"

"Well, I don't think he liked it, but he was elbow deep." Silence again. Then he said, "I don't wish to overstep, but—"

"Nothing's wrong."

"No, of course not. I didn't think there was. Especially not when you defended me to your sister."

The surprise of it made me laugh. "Yes. You must have thought that strange."

"More like earth shattering. I thought I must be dreaming."

"Come, it can't have been that rare."

"I assure you it was. Since you've been here, you've berated and mocked me—"

"You are not very kind to remind me of it."

"No, I'm not."

The grass was prickly beneath me, tickling at the back of my neck. It should have felt wrong to lie there while we talked. It did not. "Julian wants me to stop writing my story."

"Why?"

"He is afraid that—" I paused. Should I tell him this? Should I tell him anything at all? "He is afraid the things I'm writing about will make me sad."

"You're already sad, aren't you?"

The tears came unbidden to my eyes. I closed them tightly again.

"What's your story about?" he asked.

I took a deep breath. "There's an artist—or no, it's really not about him. It's about his wife and child, only they're dead. She committed suicide, and the child dies of neglect, but the artist is too busy with his art. It's all he cares about, you see. Nothing else matters so much as that, and he longs for recognition, but he's ignored and dismissed and no one knows his name. The child and the wife become ghosts, and come back to haunt him, and they become his muses—in death, they inspire him more than anyone alive, and he creates in a frenzy, but the real torment is that they strip his originality from him, and so all he can do is create what has already been done, yet he can't stop, and the ghosts drive him to madness and suicide, only really it's murder, because they've made him do it . . . it gets a bit complicated."

"Perhaps you might simplify it a bit."

"That's the problem. I don't know how. I'd thought once that I might like to be a writer, but it's been forever since I wrote anything, and even then it was mostly poetry. Very romantic and horrible. I was trying to be like Byron without one-tenth of his skill."

"That does sound horrible."

"Our father made us keep journals so he could read them and correct our notions of the world, but . . ."

"But?"

Our world, the world, grew more unreal for him, day by day. "He stopped asking for them, and we stopped keeping them. This is a much different thing."

"You take what you know and apply it to the things you don't."

"What I know," I repeated. "That is just what Julian wishes me not to do."

"Well, I'm afraid I can't help you with that." He rose. "I'll leave you to your thoughts. I wanted to be sure that you weren't trying to drown yourself or—"

"Did you really think I might?"

"You seem better than when you came into the kitchen."

I said, "Mr. Calina."

He stopped, looking at me over his shoulder.

"Would you read it?" I had not known I was going to say it, but once I had, I realized I'd wanted to ask him since he'd appeared in the yard. "I would like to know what you think."

"Why?" he asked. "Why not Bayard?"

"I couldn't. He must be besieged with amateur writers wishing for his opinion. I could not be one of them. Perhaps later, if you thought it showed promise . . ."

"What makes you think I would know?"

"Because I've seen your work." I sat up, feeling more confident now. "You have a talent—"

"For hackneyed characters, you said."

"I also said they spoke with feeling."

I saw his apprehension.

"Please. But I would require that you be honest with me. No allowing mediocre work because I'm a woman, or because you . . . because you feel sorry for me. Do you think you could do that?"

"I don't know. I've never tried."

"An experiment then. But it must be a secret. Julian can't know. He won't understand. I've already promised him I would stop working on it."

"Then why don't you?" he asked.

"Because I don't think I can. I think I would regret it if I did. I should, I know. He's probably right. It will just remind me of too many things I'd rather forget, but . . . oh I know it makes no sense . . ."

"No," he said. "It makes perfect sense."

There was a fervency in his words that made me look at him more closely. I heard a mystery there, which was intriguing, because I had never seen mystery in him before. I had never thought to wonder what secrets he might keep. It startled me to see something new. It startled me to wonder, when I had not truly wondered about another person for a very long time.

But he was already turning to go.

I said, "Thank you, Mr. Calina. I don't think you can know how much this means to me."

"I have a good idea, believe me."

I blushed at the tacit reference to the night of his reading. "I hope . . . I deserve retribution, I know, but . . ."

"I may be many things," he said, a tease in his voice. "But I prefer to leave cruelty to those for whom it's a talent."

"One I wish I didn't have," I reminded him.

"Just so," he said with a smile, and walked back to the villa.

TWENTY-ONE

VANNI

When Miss Wentworth came back inside, and we all adjourned to the salon for wine and talk; she was quiet and thoughtful, and Estes kept looking at her as if he expected her to burst into flame. But then again, so did Bayard, while Louisa flirted and teased and tried vainly to get his attention. *Not much longer,* I thought again, just as I had when he'd stared at Miss Wentworth in the dungeons of Chillon. The undercurrents were exhausting. I excused myself early and went to my room, undressing to my shirtsleeves before I sat at my desk and unlocked the drawer.

The story was on top. I thought of Adelaide Wentworth on the grass. *"He is afraid the things I'm writing about will make me sad . . . it will just remind me of too many things I'd rather forget."*

What things? Why had Estes and Louisa ignored her mood tonight? What was it I'd heard in the kitchen about Venice and their plans? Was it something to do with why they'd come here? The mystery of her deepened; I hungered to draw it out, to delineate it. I lifted out the pages, anxious to return to them—and there, beneath, the leather-covered journal, the thick fold of banknotes reminding me that everyone believed I could make a name for myself only by gossiping about another writer, and that even this story I loved was not my own. Everything in this drawer was evidence of my paucity of talent. I did not think it possible to hate myself more than I did at that moment.

But it turned out that I could indeed reach greater depths of self-loathing. As I tried to shove the drawer closed—a definitive damn-you shove just to make myself feel better—it was stopped by a letter from my father that had wadded itself into the corner. One more mockery. My father's faith, his pride that I had made myself into something, that I was an educated man, an artist, a gentleman—he would be so ashamed if I betrayed Bayard, and equally ashamed that I had entered into a contract I had no intention of fulfilling. There was no way to keep it from him. Whether I finished the journal or Colburn sued me, the world would know of my perfidy. Bad judgment all the way round. All because of a temper tantrum—well, what else was new? No way to win.

I didn't want to think about any of it. But there was my story— Bayard's story—staring back at me, begging me to lose myself in it. Nothing could be done with it, but it was a relief to feel something other than despair when I took up a pen, and a relief to forget my father and my obligations, and so I began again to write.

I was well into it—truly, I had never been so consumed by anything I'd written—when a knock on my door made me start. I flung my arms over the story, knocking over the bottle of ink in the process. "Dammit!"

Then I realized that the door wasn't opening, and Bayard wasn't striding in, and it hadn't been one of Bayard's perfunctory knocks anyway.

"Mr. Calina?" The voice was soft through the door. Miss Wentworth.

I glanced about for a rag—nothing, of course—and ended throwing some blank paper over the spill—a brutal waste—and went to the door without considering my state of undress. Really, I should simply consign myself to the dogs.

I opened the door. Whatever she saw on my face made her step back. "Oh. I'm sorry. I didn't mean to interrupt."

I heard the muffled talk from the salon down the hall, and I wondered what the hell she was doing here. "It's all right."

"I brought this."

It was only then that I realized she had a notebook in her hand. She thrust it at me. It felt gritty. Gray dust stuck to the damp ink blackening my fingers.

"Just"—a quick glance over her shoulder—"remember, please keep this to yourself."

I nodded. Her gaze swept me, and I could only guess what she was seeing, untucked shirt trailing to my thighs, half-unbuttoned, fingers covered with ink. I expected to see disgust in her eyes. Instead, she only said, "You're writing?"

I tried to flick away the dust clinging to my fingers. "Where were you keeping this? The hearth?"

"Yes," she answered simply. "Are you always so messy? Or is it that you're throwing your pens in a temper? Your desk is covered with ink."

Surprise made me blunt. "How do you know that?"

"I saw it when I brought your pages back the other night," she said.

"Well, it is surely covered now. You startled me and I knocked over the bottle."

"Oh." She tried to look past me into the room. "Would you like some help cleaning it up?"

"No!" Too much. I said again, more quietly, "No, thank you."

She stood uncertainly, as if there were something else she wanted to say, but didn't know how. "Are you working on Bayard's pages or your own?"

"What does it matter?"

"I had hoped that we hadn't dissuaded you from writing a story."

"Because it would trouble you to know you'd crushed a dream?"

"Because you have talent, as I said. I had thought . . . if you were . . . as you're looking at mine . . . I should be happy to do the same for you, if you wish." She said the last in a nervous rush.

But, of course, the only thing I was working on was the story I'd stolen from Bayard, an exercise only. I'd promised myself never to show it to another living soul.

Then again . . . how would she know? She hadn't seen Bayard's story; only I had. He hadn't even spoken of what it was about. And I'd changed it so much. I'd rewritten the beginning; I didn't think it contained any of his original words. I'd been working away on it, but I had no idea if it had any merit. Perhaps it was just more unoriginal clichés, hackneyed characters piled one on top of the other, and how would I know it if no one else read it? I was writing about sisters, but I had none. No brothers, either. I remembered that I wanted her insight. I wanted her history. What better way to get it than to let her read it?

Cautiously, I said, "I do have something I've been working on."

Sudden interest. "For the contest?"

"An exercise, really. I hadn't meant to share it. I don't know if it's any good."

"I don't know if mine is good either. We will be discovering together."

I hesitated. *Don't do this.* But the desire to know if it was worthwhile overcame me. "Wait a moment." I hurried into the other room, to my desk. I set her notebook down and grabbed my pages. The ink had seeped onto the very edges, marking them, wicking deeper into the margins. One last chance to say no, which I should do. *Yes, I should absolutely do it.* I could not fully claim this. I had not meant to.

I tightened my hold on them and returned to her. *Put them back. Change your mind.* But I handed them over. "You won't say anything of this to the others?"

She clasped the pages against her breast. "I'll say nothing. I promise."

We stared at each other mutely. Nervousness—mine, hers—jumped between us. I felt so sure that this was a terrible idea that I could not think of another thing to say.

"Good night, Mr. Calina."

She retreated down the hallway, my pages with her, one step, two, gone and gone, and I swallowed the urge to call her back and closed my door, resting my forehead against it—what the bloody hell had I done? *She won't know,* I reassured myself. How could she? There was nothing to worry about.

I went back to my desk. Her pages were covered in handwriting that looked like that of every well-to-do woman I'd ever met—broad loops, flourishes, perfect penmanship for those who had nothing more to fill the hours than practicing—but here and there it declined, becoming rushed, slanting precipitously. It had not one-tenth of the difficulty of Bayard's handwriting. I picked up the notebook, that gritty feel again. When I shook it, dust—ash—fluttered to the floor. In the hearth. I remembered what she'd said about ghostly muses. A madman who could only imitate others. A bit too familiar, wasn't it? She couldn't know—could she?—that my story had not been mine to start with, or of my fears that I would never have an original idea, that I too was only a counterfeit. I glanced over the first paragraph.

No one noticed her as she boarded the train for Geneva, except to note that she was a woman alone, but once viewers saw that she was well dressed, buttoned up, hat secured into hair tightly bound with pins, nothing untoward, then gazes politely turned to other things. But later, the passengers on that

train would say, "Yes, I remember. I saw her that morning,
just before it happened. I had not thought anything of it."

I sat down and read until the end.

She was waiting in the kitchen when I woke before dawn to take my usual row upon the lake. "You're awake," I said in surprise.

"I know you go out on the lake in the morning, and I thought—of course, it's ridiculous to think you might have read it already. I don't expect it—"

"I've read it."

She let out her breath, and then tensed. "After Jules fell asleep, I read yours as well."

Now it was my turn for that nauseating mix of relief and anxiety.

"This might be the only chance we have for privacy," she said. "I don't wish to take your boating from you, but perhaps you would not mind so much to give it up for today."

"Come with me," I said, wondering that I offered it. I treasured my hour or so alone on the lake; I had never wanted to share it. "Then no one will interrupt us. Sometimes Bayard writes early. He might come down if he hears us."

She didn't hesitate; I had the sense that she'd been waiting for me to suggest it. "Very well. You don't mind?"

That she understood my need for those hours, that she didn't wish to intrude, removed any lingering feeling that she would. "We should go now, or we'll miss the sunrise."

I grabbed an oil lamp, and together we went outside. The air was cool and blue; in the grove of trees at the far end of the yard, birds had begun to sing good morning. She wore boots that slipped on the path, so I took her arm to steady her, and she pressed into my side, catching her balance, and I felt a little stir at her softness—like Louisa, she wore no corset, and her dress was one I'd seen her wear often before, blue to match the morning, and flowing, with a sash of deep purple about her waist. We said little on the way down to the shore. Once we were there, I bade her climb inside the boat and I pushed it out into the water. The sunrise was just beginning to hint at the margin of the world, and as I rowed us out, I nodded toward it, so she twisted around to watch.

It started with a ribbon of gold, a bright stripe that silhouetted the mountains bordering the lake, growing wider and wider, turning the lake into gold leaf, and then rising, pink and orange now, a bit of red, and then light spreading slowly slowly slowly, turning gray rock rosy, and then a race of light to the snow, and quickly gone, leaving a sky the color of periwinkles, studded with clouds that had been slate and were now white.

I stopped rowing, letting us float, and we watched it in silence. She twisted around again and said softly, in a voice full of awe, "Is this what it's like every morning?"

"Better sometimes. Every day's different."

"I should not like sleeping so much." She smiled, but it was melancholy. "I admire your ability to leap forward to greet the day."

"I'm hardly leaping," I said. "It's habit mostly. When I was at school, we had to be up with the dawn. I never unlearned it."

She gazed off toward the shore. "Sometimes I feel I could sleep my life away."

Everything about her was so sad. "That would be a pity, given your talent."

She jerked back to me. "My talent?"

"You have more than a little."

"You like the story, then?"

"So far. It's really just beginning, though, isn't it? I think you must be looking at a novel."

She leaned forward eagerly. "I had thought that as well, but I wasn't certain. I was afraid that would be making it too long."

"You're trying to do too much in the first few pages. It's confusing. Draw it out, and then . . . you know, you're best at the supernatural. The ghosts and their fury are chilling." When I'd been reading it, I'd been struck at how well she managed the horror. So much better than I had. I was envious of her skill, as unformed as it was. "Your description of Caroline's drowning was harrowing. Did you take it from that boy's death when you arrived here?"

"No." Distractedly, she rubbed at her hand.

I grabbed it, unable to keep from stopping that compulsive scratching. She jumped at my touch, but then settled when I looked at the red, scaly skin and said, "Have you no salve for this?"

She drew her hand away. "It's all right. I've grown used to it. It comes and it goes."

"I don't think you should grow used to it," I said. "Does nothing help?"

"It's fine. It's not more than I can bear. I deserve it."

The boat drifted in circles now, drawn here and there by the current in a rising breeze. "You deserve it? Why?"

She drew into herself like a cockle in a shell.

"How have I offended?" I asked.

"You haven't."

"Clearly I have. You're glaring at me as if you'd like to turn me to stone."

"I am?"

"You might as well have venomous snakes for hair."

That brought a laugh.

It was a rare enough thing to hear that I wanted it to stay. "In any case, I think with some changes your story could be very good. I hope you'll let me keep reading it."

"Do you think the curse works? Julian felt that it was absurd, but then, he doesn't believe in curses."

"Yet he believes in demons and moving portraits," I said sarcastically.

She pinked. "Julian's cosmology is complex."

"It seems the world moves to whatever rules he wishes to set."

"There is a pattern to it."

"One only he sees, I'll warrant."

She made no answer to that. Her gaze was disconcerting; I could not read it. "Do you believe in curses, Mr. Calina?"

"I'm Italian. My father stopped buying carrots from a woman at the market because she gave him the evil eye."

"Yes, but do you *believe* in them? Truly? Do you believe someone can have that kind of power?"

Did I? I wasn't sure how to answer.

She went on when I said nothing, "Your witches cast curses and spells, but that's not what's real in it. What's real are the two sisters, and how they both love and hate one another. You've captured it so well—do you have sisters of your own?"

I shook my head.

"Or brothers?"

Again, "No."

"Then how do you know these things? How do you write them so convincingly?"

"I didn't know I had."

"How do you understand?"

"You and your sister," I dared to say. "Watching you."

"Oh, I see."

"The two of you seem so woven together. Like doppelgängers. I hadn't known that about siblings before now."

"Yes. I suppose that is the problem." Her voice was so soft it was almost impossible to hear, and then she gave it strength. "Your story isn't about spells and magic. It's about sisters. When you focus on them, you are quite brilliant. Curses don't belong to you, Mr. Calina. You should take them out of the story."

"And leave them to you," I said.

A nod. "I understand them better."

"Why is that?"

"I'm under one," she said, meeting my gaze. "Can't you tell?"

She'd liked my story; she'd thought it good, and I told myself that was enough; that was all I wanted. But the truth was that I wanted suddenly a great deal more, and I could not even explain to myself what that was. Who was Adelaide Wentworth? What had happened to her? Was the curse she spoke of something to do with Venice? With those ominous-sounding plans? Why did she affect me the way she did?

They were questions I couldn't answer.

We came inside, and she went to the kitchen without another word to me, and I went upstairs. I was passing the salon when I heard a noise and caught a motion from the corner of my eye. I stepped back into the doorway to see.

There, clasped in one another's arms before the window, were Estes and Louisa.

Almost before the sight registered, they noted me and sprang apart. Louisa twisting up her loosened hair, smoothing her dress, Estes buttoning his waistcoat. "There you are!" he said—too boisterously, given how he disliked me—and came toward me. "Louisa said you were out in the boat."

I waited for his point. When it didn't come, and he only stood there looking foolish, I asked politely, "You were looking for me?"

Now Louisa, rushing up, smiling in that breathless way that was too familiar. "Have you seen Addie this morning? She's quite disappeared."

"I took her out with me. To watch the sunrise."

Estes looked confused. "In the boat?"

"She was up when I was."

"Oh. I see." He was completely nonplussed.

Louisa was equally so. "She wanted to go out with you?"

"Well, I didn't drag her." I turned to go. "She's in the kitchen now."

Estes eased past me as if he could not wait to be gone. "I'll see to her."

I kept walking. Louisa raced up beside me. "Vanni."

"What do you want?"

"It wasn't what you think. He was only comforting me. I was worried about Addie—"

"Were you?"

"She didn't leave a note. She wasn't in the yard. We had no idea where she'd gone."

"Last night she looked ready to hang herself, and neither of you seemed troubled."

"That is why I was worried this morning," she said softly. "It's unlike her to disappear."

I stopped. "He belongs to your sister, Louisa."

"What business is it of yours? And I told you, it wasn't what you thought."

"Is this why you wanted to keep your affair with Bayard a secret from him?"

"No! No, I told you why. Jules thinks of me as his sister—"

"I had no idea that brothers were usually so passionate with their sisters. But then, I've never had either, so you must forgive my ignorance."

"It was not what it seemed," she insisted.

"I'm having no trouble with my eyesight."

"Perhaps not, but you are the most blind man I've ever met." She nearly spat the words. "You don't understand anything, and you never have. You dislike Julian, and you hate me, when I did nothing at all to lead you to believe . . ." At my incredulous look, she trailed off. She licked her lips and glanced away. "I know you can have no reason to wish me well, but if you said something of this to Bayard, or Addie—"

"Say something of what?" I goaded. "You've just told me it's not what I think."

"It isn't." So quickly.

"Then what are you afraid of?"

She grasped my arm. "Please, Vanni. If you ever cared for me even a little, you must say nothing of this now. It would only make things worse between Adelaide and Julian, and she mustn't stop trying."

"Trying what?"

She went on as if she didn't hear. "And Bayard is more irritable with me every day. If he were to think . . . he would throw me off, and it would be over nothing. It wouldn't be true. Even you can't dislike me so much as to tell him such a lie."

"Don't be too certain."

"You are impossible."

"Who would know that better than you?" I shook off her arm.

"Julian will say the same, and you know Bayard would believe him over you."

I could not argue that. I started walking again. She did not follow, but she said, "We could destroy you, you know. Julian and I. Bayard would never trust you again."

"Then why do you worry?"

I was relieved when she said nothing more. I went to my room and found Bayard's latest pages there, piled upon the others I hadn't yet got to because I'd been too busy working on the story. He'd placed a blotter over the stain of ink—Bayard tending to me, again these small but generous gestures that made up for his sometimes casual cruelty, that told me he cared for me when I was least prepared to believe it—and I felt sick with guilt over the secrets I was keeping from him: the story I'd stolen, Colburn's contract, and now what I'd seen between Louisa and Estes. Adelaide was right; the press of regret and shame were the most unbearable of ghosts.

TWENTY-TWO

ADELAIDE

Y ou went on the boat with him?" Julian asked when I returned.
"I couldn't sleep. Mr. Calina offered to show me the sunrise."

"I see." But it was clear he did not.

"Am I not allowed to see a sunrise?" I asked.

"Of course you are. I'm certain it was lovely. I've envied it myself—that he goes out, I mean. I imagine he finds a great deal of peace in it."

Carefully, I said, "You would have to ask him."

"I hadn't thought you cared much for him, and yet this morning . . . and he went to you last night—"

"You could have done so instead."

He glanced away. "You didn't want me."

"Why would you say that?"

"There's a way you have . . . you would have told me to go back inside, that you wanted to be by yourself."

I could not deny the probable truth of that.

"It seems I cannot comfort you anymore."

"That's not true," I said quietly. "But sometimes it's better that I'm alone."

"Calina is not being alone, Adelaide. What does he say to you that I cannot say?"

"He knows nothing of me. He's only being kind. He doesn't understand."

"You mean that when you look at him you don't see everything I failed to do in Venice, is that it?"

My chin itched. I curled my fingers into my palm. "No, of course not."

"How was I to stay when my father demanded that I come to London to see him? What is it that you think I should have done?"

"Perhaps you should have left Louisa with me," I offered.

"You didn't want her there. You'd been nagging me to find a place to send her for months. You wanted her gone. You said it a hundred times."

Another thing I could not deny.

"She was suffering. She was not herself, and I thought the trip to London would do her good. I thought it would help you as well, given how poorly you were feeling. You said her melancholy only worsened yours. We were gone only two weeks, and she was better when we returned. Even you must admit that."

She had been better. But it hadn't been just London. There had been Paris too, which had not been part of the plan, and which I had not known about until Emily Estes informed me. I had not wanted to believe her. How would she have known such a thing? It had to be a lie, and I'd been so angry with her, but two telegrams to Julian in London had gone unreceived, and I'd known then that Emily had told me the truth, and that she kept better watch on Julian than did I. When Julian and my sister had returned, it had been with a new kind of intimacy, which only strengthened my growing suspicions, and confused my anger and grief.

He went on, "I didn't know Emily would come to Venice or that she would seek you out. I certainly didn't know what would happen. I hadn't heard from her in months. How could I know? You cannot blame me for not being prescient."

The way he turned things around, the way he absolved himself. It was so difficult to fight with him, because he refashioned the argument so that only an unreasonable person would see the fault in his words. I was befuddled now, trying to remember how this conversation had started, what I had accused him of. He had so neatly explained it so many times before; why was I still debating?

"Emily and I weren't compatible. I saved her by leaving her. Now she has the chance to look for someone who might love her as she deserves."

"Louisa needs distraction—you're her sister, can you not see that? She's lost weight. She isn't sleeping. I'm afraid she'll grow worse if I don't take her away for a week or so. You should not be burdened with such things in your condition."

"My father called for me. How could I refuse to see him? We were living on polenta."

Julian took my arms. "You're looking for reasons to hate me."

"No! I'm not. Truly I'm not. I love you."

"As I love you. But don't you see how you must reach an accommodation with the past? I have. Louisa has." He released me. "Tell me what would comfort you now, Adelaide. Should I send for Calina, as he seems to have a magic touch?"

"Don't be jealous. It doesn't become you."

"I'm not jealous. How could I be jealous of him?" Julian stepped away. "He's a grubby leech of a papist. Has he told you where he grew up?"

I shrugged. "In London. I can't remember."

"Bethnal Green. The slums. What do you suppose he learned there but thievery and dishonesty? I expect one day we'll discover he's been defrauding Bayard."

"Now you're the one being unfair," I said.

His pale gaze narrowed. "I don't trust him to take you out in the rowboat. He has hardly any skill. If something happened to you out there, I would not be able to bear it. It would be the end of me."

"Jules." I reached for his arm.

He jerked back. "Don't go in the boat with him again."

He marched from the kitchen. When he left, I felt, as I always did after such arguments, stupid and ridiculous. He was right; I must get past these things. But thus far, all that had made me feel better was my story, and I wanted to work on it now, despite my promises to Julian. He would understand eventually. He would see how I needed it. And the deadline was approaching. If I meant to present my story as a fait accompli, there was still so much to do.

Mr. Calina's opinion had been so encouraging that even Julian's anger could not banish my joy. His suggestions also held a touch of brilliance. I yearned to return to it, but how to do so without Jules knowing?

"Adelaide," Bayard said from the doorway. "How are you this morning?"

I heard worry in his words. The impatience I'd been noting in him was not in evidence today, nor had it been last night, when he'd been solicitous, asking my opinion, bringing me into the conversation whenever I fell away. When I'd returned from giving Mr. Calina my manuscript, Bayard had said, "She's returned!" as if there were something triumphant in it. He was as observant as his secretary, but then again, anyone who had read his work knew that he saw more deeply than most.

"Very well, thank you," I returned. "I went out to see the sunrise with Mr. Calina this morning."

He raised a brow. "Really? Did he behave himself? Have I any reason to shoot him?"

I smiled. "He was a gentleman."

"Well then, I suppose my efforts are paying off. Though I'm annoyed with him." He reached into his pocket and flipped out a letter. "My publisher is complaining about the 'recent slowness of the mail.'"

"Has it been slow?"

"I think it more that he's received no pages lately. I don't know why. I've given Vanni enough that he should have sent at least two packets."

I thought of Mr. Calina's story. "I'm certain he has a good explanation."

"A good explanation for what?" My sister walked into the room. She touched Bayard's shoulder lingeringly, and I saw that impatience cross his face. So it was not gone, as I'd hoped.

"For why my secretary has failed to send new pages to my publisher," he said, sitting at the table.

"Why hasn't he?" she asked. "You've been writing every morning for two weeks, since Villeneuve."

"Precisely."

She sat beside him, and he eased away, just slightly. Louisa frowned. "He's in his room all afternoon. What can he be doing if not making your fair copies?"

"Writing letters, perhaps?" I suggested, feeling guilty that I knew exactly why he had fallen behind, unable to reveal it. "Going over accounts?"

"Perhaps," Bayard said. "But he's always done those things, and they've never impacted his work before. I shall have to talk to him."

Louisa said, "Oh, but you've given him so many pages. However will he catch up?"

There was a deliberation in her voice I recognized. I gave her a sharp look, and she widened her eyes guilelessly.

"He'll have no choice," Bayard said.

"I could help," she said, then, when he shook his head, "I could. Do you remember at the hotel, when I read the pages you gave him? Even Mr. Calina was surprised at how easily I did it. I have excellent handwriting, too. I would so much love to help you. It would be my own little contribution to genius."

Bayard looked uncertain.

I had no idea what she meant to do, but her tiny, catlike smile made me nervous. "Perhaps you should talk to Mr. Calina first," I suggested to Bayard. "Then, if he claims to need help . . ."

"He won't," Louisa protested. "You know how he is, Bay. He's so selfish when it comes to you, and so prickly. He'll only give you some excuse about why it can't be done and lose his temper as well. He'll never admit to being lazy or . . . or overwhelmed, or that he's doing something he shouldn't be doing. Please. I would like to, and you'll need to send something to your publisher right away, won't you?"

"Only to make him happy," Bayard said dryly. "Which is hardly required."

"I've nothing else to do this afternoon. I could get right to it. You wouldn't have to pay me either, or perhaps a kiss?" She curled her fingers around his arm and said softly against his ear, "Think how much money you could save."

This was not simply her discomfort with Mr. Calina and their past, but a new vindictiveness. What new thing had happened between him and my sister? The thought troubled me. I could not dismiss my sense that she was, once again, courting secrets. I had never known a time that it wasn't true, and I was exhausted with it. I wanted straightforward. I wanted things in the open. I wanted to look at something and know with certainty that it was ever and only what I saw.

"Loulou, Mr. Calina depends on his job," I said.

Louisa said sharply, "Then he should do it. Otherwise, he can hardly be surprised when Bayard decides to find someone who can. Adelaide, why do you defend him? What did he do this morning, bewitch you? You've never pretended to like him before."

"I've never disliked him."

"Really? Then I was only imagining that you scolded and belittled him? Or that you made fun of him with the rest of us?"

I was acutely aware of Bayard's silence, of how he watched us.

"I have never disliked him," I insisted again.

"What did he do, Addie? Make love to you?" She turned to Bayard, laughing, teasing, flicking her finger at the curl of hair behind his ear. He ignored her; his gaze came to me, uncomfortably scrutinizing. "Addie's always been so susceptible to flirtation. I think a man could make her do almost anything if he declared an interest!"

"That is not true," I said quietly, ignoring a surge of anger, cautioning myself to pay attention. I knew her well enough to know this had nothing to do with me.

"Now please, Bay. Please? Give me a pen and some paper, and I will transcribe away."

Bayard seemed to rouse. He batted at her hand. "Very well. If it will keep you from distracting me for a few hours."

She did not seem to hear the criticism in his words. She threw me a triumphant smile. "You'll see how well I do it. I won't need to ask you a single question."

"That is just what I want," he said with a thin smile.

Beyond came the hard clatter of the knocker on the front door, loud enough to echo downstairs.

Bayard tensed. "Don't tell me they've discovered I'm back already. Where's Vanni?"

We heard the quick footsteps on the floor above, the answer, and Bayard relaxed until Mr. Calina appeared in the kitchen a few moments later with a letter in his hand. He gave it to Bayard, who opened it with a resigned sigh.

Louisa and Mr. Calina studiously avoided looking at each other. It was so obvious and so curious that I could not help but watch him as he went to the sideboard. He tore off a piece of bread and buttered it liberally, all the while saying nothing. Louisa darted him a single venomous glance before she dedicated herself again to Bayard.

Bayard dropped the letter to the table. "Oliver Dodsworth is in town."

I asked, "Who is that?"

"A poet. Well, really a philosopher. I think Jules should meet him. They'd probably like each other."

Mr. Calina paused in the midst of taking a bite. "You mean to take Estes to Orsini's?"

"Why not? Dodsworth will certainly be there. Colburn's visiting too, and there's a matter I'd like to discuss with him."

"What matter?" Mr. Calina sounded alarmed.

"A letter he published recently—nothing to concern you. Besides, I wouldn't mind getting out for a night. Wouldn't you?"

"Oh yes!" Louisa said. "I should love to!"

"Louisa, we haven't been invited." Even had we been, how could we go? She could not be so unaware.

She ignored me, turning excitedly to Bayard. "Oh, but you won't leave us behind, will you? Not if you're taking Jules. I vow I have been away from society for so long I could burst. Will there be music? Dancing?"

"Louisa," I said.

Bayard exhaled. "Yes, why not?"

"You want us all to go?" I hoped he didn't hear my horror at the idea.

"Of course. It will be something different to do."

My chin tingled. "Who will be there?"

"Mostly English travelers. Some French. A German or two probably, and Vanni's little Portuguese with her no doubt idiotic husband. I warn you, there will be nothing but gossip and stupidity, but I should like to introduce Jules to Dodsworth, who is at least interested in something other than what count seduced which prima donna."

We could not go. Of course we could not go. But how to demur, how to say thank you but no. I wanted to shoot Louisa for suggesting it. All I could hope was that Julian would find a graceful way to refuse.

Mr. Calina said, "I'll stay behind, if you don't mind."

"I do mind," Bayard said, giving him a very pointed glance, one that Mr. Calina obviously understood. "I'm certain you and the lovely Brest can keep your hands off each other for an evening, given what you've managed so far. I want you there. And by the way, give half of those pages I put on your desk to Louisa, will you?"

Mr. Calina stiffened. "Why?"

"Because I got a letter from Hanson yesterday. You haven't sent a packet in days. I assume you're overwhelmed. Fortunately, Louisa has agreed to ease your burden by copying some pages for me."

"I'm not overwhelmed."

"Then why haven't you sent a packet?"

"You weren't working—"

"That hasn't been true for some time. I saw the pile on your desk this morning. There must be fifty pages there or more. I don't know what's been distracting you, but it can't continue. Let Louisa help until you catch up."

"I don't need her help."

"I think you do. Bring the pages down, Vanni. Now."

Mr. Calina opened his mouth to protest, but then Bayard said, "No more arguments."

"As you wish," Mr. Calina answered curtly.

Bayard said to me and Louisa as he left the kitchen, "We'll leave for Orsini's about five. I'll find Jules and let him know."

Louisa laughed in delight.

Mr. Calina looked ready to explode. To my sister, he said, "I suppose this is your doing."

Louisa flounced to the door. "It's hardly my fault that you've failed to do your job. I'll be on the terrace. Please bring Bayard's pages there immediately. I'll need paper too, and a pen. I assume you have spares?"

She was so imperious that I flinched. When she went out, he threw the rest of his bread and butter to the sideboard. "She will ruin me." It was said beneath his breath. I think he hardly remembered I was in the room.

"Why would she want to do that?" I asked, and when he started, I knew I was right; he had forgotten me. The brightness of the morning with him in the boat tarnished slightly.

He started to say something, but then obviously decided against it. "There's no reason. I didn't mean it. I was only angry."

"You're not telling me the truth."

"It seems to be endemic, doesn't it?" He went to the door. "I'd best fetch things before she decides to whistle for me."

"Don't let her do this," I said, surprising myself. "Stop her."

"How am I to do that, Adelaide?" he asked with disconcerting wretchedness. "Tell me how. Do you know? Have you ever tried? God knows I've seen no evidence of it."

It was true; I could not deny it. He'd said it before, I remembered, that night of the break-in, when he'd accused me of letting Julian and Louisa run roughshod.

Now, I could only say what I knew. "It's easier to let her do as she wants and hope that she eventually loses interest."

"What if she never does?" he asked.

"What else am I to do?" Julian paced before the window. "He wants me to meet this Dodsworth. The more I protested, the more he set his heels."

"We cannot go," I said in a low voice.

"And if we don't?" he stopped, turning to look at me. "They must already know we're here. That maid saw it all, didn't she? It's quite a story. Chasing demons, séances, break-ins. All she has to do is mention my name, and if only one person there knows our history—British travelers, isn't that what he said? They're no doubt gossiping about it even now. Do you think it would be good to let him just walk into it alone? Without any of us there to explain?"

"I think we would only make it worse," I said.

"Of course you would think that." He was angry now. "Poor Adelaide, who dislikes a quarrel and would rather run and hide."

"That's an unkind thing to say."

He let out his breath. "I'm sorry. We have no choice, Addie. It was inevitable that he would find out. It's time we accepted that. We will go and try to mitigate it as best we can. Perhaps it won't be as bad as we think."

"We've done nothing since we arrived but create problems for him. Now he'll be dragged into our scandal as well."

"Perhaps it will amuse him." But I could see Julian didn't believe that. "One never knows with him."

No, one never did. But I'd seen Bayard on the streamer, and at Chillon. I'd seen his growing exasperation with Louisa only this morning. Julian reached for the laudanum on the night table and pulled his flask from his pocket.

"Is there any money left?" I asked. "Or have you drunk it all away? If Bayard asks us to leave, what will we do?"

Julian ignored my accusation. Deliberately, he filled his flask and capped it. "We have a few pounds. Enough to get us out of Geneva. Perhaps as far as Lausanne. We will do the best we can. I will do what I must to win Bayard's forgiveness, and Louisa can help with that."

"He's growing tired of her."

"Then you must help me persuade him. He admires you." Julian came to me, taking my hand. He stared at the eczema there.

Uncertainly, I said, "Do you mean that—"

"You can be charming when you wish it," he said with a feeble smile. "You charmed me, certainly."

I stared at him.

He glanced away uncomfortably. "Help me remind him why he loves us."

"Yes, of course." I couldn't keep the chill from my voice.

"You mistake me. I only mean that we must be together in this, Adelaide. Louisa too." He released me and went again to the window. "Perhaps it would be best if he set us out."

"Why would you say that?"

"All this invigorating beauty, and what have I to show for it? Half a page, perhaps less? I'll never meet the deadline. He's made me feel how inferior I am."

"You aren't inferior, Jules. You're the better writer. You know that."

"Am I? I begin to wonder. It's not only that. It's . . . I need you here with me, Adelaide. I rely on you. Now, more than ever. I need you to help me through this slump, whatever is causing it."

"I'm right here."

"Yes, but you've been distracted. I don't know if it's Calina or something else, but I feel it."

It was on my tongue to explain, to tell him about my story, but I could not say the words. I wasn't ready. I wasn't confident enough to resist him. He wanted me to belong to him alone. I tried to remember that it had been what I wanted too.

So I went to him. I put my arms around his waist and rested my head against his back and tried not to feel resentment.

He clasped my hands in his own. "This will be all right. If nothing else, we have each other. You and Louisa and I will brave the world together. We don't need Bayard Sonnier."

"No, of course not," I said, pulling gently away, and we said nothing more as we dressed for Orsini's.

TWENTY-THREE

VANNI

Louisa's vengeance had been so well executed that it caught me unawares. She had a mad genius of her own—but then, hadn't I already known that? In the month or so she'd been with Bayard in London, and the days before with me, her manipulations had been many and varied, and so I should have known to expect more of the same. But this time, I had no way to fight her. This time, I had fallen so neatly into her machinations it was as if I had directed them.

I'd left Bayard's pages waiting too long, absorbed in my story—stolen from him, *what a fool you are*. Even Adelaide Wentworth's praise did not ease my apprehension. All I could hope was that Louisa lost her hold on Bayard, which, frankly, it seemed she might do at any moment.

We met in the salon when it came time to go to Orsini's. Bayard eyed me. "How long did it take you to get your hair that way? I think I shall call you Vainy from now on."

I should never have neglected those pages. I had not thought he would care. He was so nonchalant when it came to publisher demands. *"Let the parasites eat themselves. What will they do, Vanni, refuse to publish me? There are a dozen others who will be happy to take their place."* It was always I who insisted, who pushed, who nagged.

My already bad mood grew worse. The last thing I wanted was to go to this damned salon, especially with Colburn there, expecting pages. I had nothing, of course. I still hoped to convince him to release me, but given our last encounter, I doubted I could. The only saving grace was that he was unlikely to confront me before Bayard, as the whole thing depended on my employer being unaware of my duplicity.

Estes looked nervous, fingering his unadorned watch fob as if he wished to check the time, though he never pulled his watch. Louisa was vibrant in sprigged green, a scooped neck, lace, a skirt festooned with ruffles. Quite honestly, it was rational dress at its most beautiful—the shock it would cause at Orsini's was at least one entertainment to look forward to. Her sister's gown was more sedate, puffed sleeves at the shoulder narrowing to the wrist, a simple gold and black brocade, but the overall effect was regal. I had not seen these before—obviously their best, and meant for balls and suppers we hadn't attended. Adelaide looked polished and self-possessed—or she would have, had it not been for the scab on her chin, had she not been pushing at her glove to reach the red skin on her hand that trailed to her wrist beneath her sleeve.

"Well, shall we go?" Bayard asked. "Come along, Vainy."

It was already not amusing. If he kept this up all night, I would want to strangle him.

The rowboat was too small for us all on a journey across the lake, and so we took the sailboat, mooring it at a dock a few villas down and walking the rest of the way to the Orsini château. Louisa twittered with excitement. Her sister and Estes drew back; I heard them arguing quietly behind us, then Estes pulled away, clearly frustrated, and walked on ahead, toward Louisa.

I slowed until Adelaide caught up with me. "Is everything all right?"

"I did not want to come," she said.

"You don't like salons?"

"I don't like society." Her tension only added to that rigid, queenly dignity. Again, she rubbed her hand.

"Why not?" I asked.

We reached the Orsini yard. She stopped short, pulling me to a stop with her. "If I come to you tonight and say we must leave immediately, will you make Bayard do so?"

I was puzzled. "You must know I can't force him to do anything."

"But you will try this time. For me."

She didn't wait for my answer. My puzzlement only grew as I watched her join Estes. Something was wrong. I had no idea what. Something to do with the plans she'd spoken of with Louisa? It put a further pall on my mood as we went to the door. I didn't see Colburn—thank God—but neither did I see the one person who could have saved the evening for me. It had been days since I'd laid eyes on Vera Brest, and she had not sent so much as a note. I tormented myself by wondering why, if she would be here tonight, or her husband, what I would say if we encountered one another.

The same tepid champagne and soggy anchovy toast were making the rounds, but the crowd seemed larger than usual tonight. Perhaps Dodsworth's arrival had tempted others. I had met him a few times in London, and so had no need of an introduction. I would say hello later; for now I left Bayard and the others to fend for themselves, and went looking for Vera Brest. I searched every room for her, keeping well on watch for Colburn. I spotted him in the gallery—and unfortunately, he spotted me too. A lifted brow and a jerk of his head to summon me, but I pretended not to see it, and dodged out again quickly, wanting more than ever to find Vera and spirit her away to some dark part of the garden. Was that her jowly, portly husband in the corner? Or that dour-faced man over there? He must be older, of course. Fat. Balding. As opposite from me as was possible. A man I could save her from.

Finally, I had to admit that she was not here, or at least, not in the salon or anywhere else on this floor. Perhaps she was in her apartments upstairs, ensconced with her husband—the thought made me sick—or in the gardens with him, walking arm in arm—I could not bear to see it. I ended my search in the small salon, also crowded, mostly with tables of men playing cards. I stood near a whatnot filled with knickknacks from the Orsinis' travels and hoped Colburn would not think to look for me here, as I rarely frequented the card tables. My father—not to mention the monks—abhorred gambling.

A woman nibbling contemplatively on anchovy toast swept me with her gaze; there was an interest I didn't mistake. She set aside the toast and fingered the pearls dangling from a very large topaz. "I do not think we have met, Monsieur—"

"Calina," I said politely. "Giovanni Calina, at your service."

"Renée Chaubert," she offered in return. She gave me a coy look beneath lowered lashes. "It is a lovely gathering, don't you think? Monsieur Orsini has a beautiful home."

I could not keep from glancing to the door for Colburn. A group had gathered there. A woman raced in from the hallway, flushed, her eyes flashing. She pushed her way into the group, urgent whispers, relaying some bit of gossip, obviously salacious, given the hush that followed, and then the titters, the shocked exclamations.

I forced myself back to small talk. "Yes, it is beautiful. Have you seen the murals in the dining room?"

Renée Chaubert said, "The murals? Why, no. I confess this is the first time I've been here. Have you known Monsieur Orsini long?"

"A few months."

More people came in—not Colburn, thankfully. The gossipers grew in number, bobbing their heads like congregating birds, the bit of scandal repeated, the horrified delight, the gasps. I wondered how someone had transgressed.

"Really? You must be an artist, then? Or a scientist? A philosopher? You have the look of an actor about you. Yes, I could imagine you on a stage."

"None of those. I'm a writer."

"Ah, a writer." Again that tilt of the head, the slanted glance beneath half-lowered lids. Bedroom eyes. She put her hand on my arm, distracting me from the flurry on the other side of the room. "You must forgive me. I'm not much of a reader. Should I recognize your name?"

More talk. More snickering. A woman's aborted cry of shock. I struggled to attend to my conversation.

"I haven't published anything yet." This was my least favorite admission to make. And next to it—"I've been very lucky to come under Bayard Sonnier's patronage, however."

"Bayard Sonnier?" Her hand tightened on my arm. So she was enough of a reader to recognize his name. "You know him?"

"I came here with him tonight. He's about somewhere—"

"*The Temptation* changed my life." She clasped her other hand to her breast in an expression of rapture.

I wished I hadn't mentioned him. "Did it?"

"In ways you cannot imagine. And he has taken you under his wing! What a lucky man you are, monsieur." She gestured wildly to a man who had just come into the room. He was tall, dark haired, with an aristocratic visage—long nose, high forehead, an elegant way of moving. A gentleman in every sense of the word.

He came over. "There you are, Renée. My wife sent me to find you."

"Mathias, have you met Monsieur Calina?" she introduced. "Monsieur, this is my good friend Mathias Brest, from Portugal."

The husband. The room seemed to narrow to his elegance, the wealth he exuded, and I felt myself shrivel in comparison. He barely glanced at me. "A pleasure. I hope you will pardon me for taking her away."

"Of course."

Renée Chaubert tendered me a smile. "Good-bye, monsieur. It was indeed a pleasure."

Mathias Brest's farewell smile was preoccupied; he had already forgotten me, if he had really ever noticed to begin with. I felt myself disappearing, fading into nothingness, and I was struck with the urge to find Vera, to prove to her—and myself—that I existed.

I forgot Colburn. The tenor of the night had changed; I was aware that every room buzzed—the gossip was something big—but I was no longer interested. I wanted to take Vera into an empty room and show her I would not be easily dismissed or ignored. I would give her a reason to pay attention. I would give her a reason.

I hurried past the salon, the dining room, the ballroom, and then . . . there she was, standing at the stairs just beyond the ballroom, talking to a group of women, whispering intently, obviously those salacious rumors again, sneers. I cared about none of that. I remembered far too well the taste of her, perfumed champagne, and I wanted it again.

When she saw me, her eyes widened. I saw a kind of horror in them—horror? She made no move to come to me, and so I went to her. I brushed up to her, touched her bare arm above her glove, smiled. "Madame Brest, what a pleasure to see you again."

The women with her went silent. Vera Brest looked at me desperately, begging me with her eyes to walk away.

"Monsieur Calina." Her voice was brittle with strain, and then her gaze leaped beyond me. "I believe someone is looking for you."

I looked over my shoulder to see Adelaide standing alone, people drawing away as if she were diseased. Her expression was as desperate as Vera Brest's. Her chin was bleeding; she had lost her self-possession—in fact, she looked lost completely, and her gaze fastened upon me as if I were her redemption.

I was hardly aware of moving away from Vera. I hurried to Adelaide, drawn irrevocably by whatever invisible leash she'd attached to me.

Her eyes filled with tears. "Please. Tell Bayard we have to go."

"What is it? What's wrong?"

"Just do it. Quickly, Vanni. Please."

That she spoke my name both unsettled and warmed me. I glanced back. Mathias Brest had joined his wife, and the women she'd been talking with gathered in a tight knot to stare at me and Adelaide Wentworth.

In fact, everyone was staring at us.

I realized suddenly that the gossip I'd noticed had something to do with her.

"Where's Bayard?" I asked quietly.

"I don't know. But you must find him, and Louisa too. Jules and I will meet you in the garden. Hurry. Please."

She left me, but the stares didn't abate when she was gone. I heard whispering as I passed—whatever this was, I was now part of it. I was halfway down the hall when I felt a hand on my arm, and turned to see Colburn, excitement in his eyes.

"I cannot believe Sonnier dared to bring Julian Estes and that woman," he said in a low voice.

Again, that flutter of recognition, a feeling that there was something about Estes I should have known. I pulled away. "Not now. I'm in a hurry—"

"Of course. But if you don't write of them, I shall have your head." He gave me a triumphant smile and disappeared into the crowd, and urgently I pressed on, thinking only of the tears in Adelaide Wentworth's eyes.

I found Bayard in the ballroom, talking to Dodsworth. There too, was Louisa, but Louisa as I had not seen her before. Reduced, abandoned. She stood near the curtains, half hiding within their rose-colored richness. No one spoke to her. When she caught sight of me, her relief was so unexpected that I stumbled. I gestured toward the open French doors leading to the garden, the smoke in the room misting the lamplit darkness beyond. Louisa and I had never understood one another, but she understood me now. She nodded, and crossed the room with an uncharacteristic furtiveness.

I hurried over to Bayard and Dodsworth. I felt oddly in a dream, people staring, talking behind their hands. I tapped Bayard, and he turned with an anger that took me aback.

Dodsworth drew his pipe from his mouth, exhaling smoke. "Calina. Bayard told me you had not abandoned him. I'm glad to see it. Loyalty is a rarity in these times."

I was too distracted to do more than nod. In Bayard's ear, I said, "We must go."

"Did she send you to fetch me?" he asked bitterly.

Louisa or Adelaide? I had the feeling that using the wrong name would be a mistake. "She?"

"I don't want to go." He gestured to Dodsworth. "I'm in the midst of a conversation."

"And I shall not thank you for taking him away," Dodsworth said. "I've looked forward to his company for months."

The stares were piercing. Again, quietly, "They're in the garden, waiting."

"Let them wait."

"I don't know what has happened," I said carefully, "but she's in a state."

His gaze sharpened. "She can bear it well enough. She insisted on coming. Now she gets what she deserves."

I shook my head. "Not Louisa."

Bayard glanced toward the garden doors. Half to himself, he said, "She knew what would happen. So did Jules."

I was more confused than ever, but I said more quietly still, not for Dodsworth, "She's going to fall apart if we don't get out of here. Louisa looked half ready to do so as well. Do you really want a scene?"

He said nothing at first, and then, a smile to Dodsworth, an offered hand. "I fear I've been called away, Doddy, but you'll come to the Diodati, won't you? We'll sit around the fire and drink until the early hours."

"I'd like nothing better," Dodsworth said, and then he too glanced about the room. "Why, there does seem to be quite a fuss, doesn't there?"

I said good-bye and ushered Bayard into the garden. There were other people, congregating mostly near the doors and the windows, but although their glances were curious, they weren't excoriating. I could not find the others in the shadows at the edge of the garden, but then I saw them—the arbor where Vera Brest had kissed me. Hiding.

Estes rose from the bench to meet us. "When you asked me to come, I did warn you that perhaps we wouldn't be welcome."

"It's all so stupid." Louisa ran to Bayard, who made no move to take her into his arms. "You don't believe it, do you, Bay?"

Bayard said nothing to either of them. He walked quickly from the garden to the road, and we followed, chastened, nervous. I said, "I'm afraid I don't understand."

"Then you're an idiot," Bayard snapped.

For once, I listened to my instincts and bit back an angry retort. No doubt the others felt his temper as well; no one said anything more as we walked the short distance to the boat, and nothing as we boarded her.

There was no moon; the stars that glittered the sky ended abruptly at a band of darkness above the mountains. From them came a muffled thunder that made me think of that day on the boat during the storm, Adelaide's howl of pain and rage. I glanced at her, but she stared down at her hands, clasped in her lap, fingers clenched and rigid. Louisa sat beside her, darting glances at Bayard, her full mouth so pinched that her upper lip disappeared. One could see that the urge to speak was nearly impossible for her to contain. Estes sat beside me, hanging his head, his mane of hair falling into his face, a pale shadow, his weariness evident in the slump of his shoulders, his silence.

I would not ask, not again. We were off, moving slowly into the lake, the sail luffing, not much breeze, though more thunder at the mountain-tops, a flash of lightning glowing on the undersides of the clouds above the peaks. Adelaide looked up at that, and I caught her eye at last. She only mouthed *Thank you*, and looked down again.

"Is it true?" Bayard asked.

Louisa rushed to answer. "Of course it's not—"

"Not you. Him." Bayard jerked his head at Estes. "Is it true?"

Slowly, Estes raised his head. "Which part?"

"Any of it. All of it."

"There is no ménage," Louisa put in impatiently. "Not as they say."

Ménage à trois. Estes and Louisa breaking from one another as I walked by the salon.

"No?" Bayard's voice was icy. "Why shouldn't it be true? You're Free Lovers, are you not?"

"It is not as they understand it," she said. "I'm as Julian's sister—is that not right, Jules?"

Bayard said sharply, "That only means they're calling it incest. In the eyes of the law, you are his sister in truth. It's illegal to make love to the sister of your wife."

Estes seemed to rally at that. "That's ridiculous. Not only is it a foolish law, but Addie and I are not married."

Adelaide watched quietly, intent. She said nothing. Why did she say nothing?

Bayard obviously noticed it as well, but he said acidly to Estes, "That makes it worse. You're Free Lovers and you left your wife for two sisters—that's what they see. Why should they not think it a ménage à trois? Or see it as anything but immoral?"

That was the rumor I'd heard about him. I remembered now. Estes had left his pregnant wife for another woman in America. It had meant nothing to me then. I'd heard no rumors of incest—surely that I would have remembered—but now I understood what had happened at Orsini's.

Estes said, "Bayard—"

"Is it true? Are you making love to Louisa too? Perhaps you don't mind sharing. But I do."

Unless it was because he wished to share, of course. The list unspooled neatly in my head. Marie Arsenault and her stepdaughter; a dinner party that turned into an orgy I'd had to listen to through the walls all night long; Bayard's artist friend Debarge—not his friend any longer—and some grisette in the parlor, where I'd come upon them unawares and backed out so hastily I'd tripped over the carpet and sprawled heedlessly on the floor. All the things Colburn had paid me five hundred pounds to document. I heard again what I'd been too distracted to heed. *If you don't write of them, I shall have your head.*

Through my guilt, or perhaps because of it, I thought, *Tell Bayard.* A word planted in his ear about what I'd seen in the salon—or not seen; what did it matter? One word, and Louisa would be gone, Estes gone. Adelaide gone.

Adelaide.

Then Estes said, half angrily, "They are making a mockery of us. You must know that, Bay. They're only jealous gossips. Adelaide is the soul of my soul."

I don't know if anyone else saw the way Louisa stiffened.

Estes's last words were patinated, as if he'd said them often before. Adelaide closed her eyes, and I knew then that I would say nothing—not because of Louisa's threats, but because I didn't want to hurt Adelaide.

The sail flapped, the breeze shifting. Bayard adjusted the rudder, and we were moving again, the water black silk all about us, the stars above like dust motes in sunlight, seeming to float heedlessly in space, so many they were a glowing fog.

"I have not had many real friends in my life," Bayard said. "I had hoped that you would be one of them."

"I am your friend," Estes insisted. "I'll tell you whatever you wish to know. Just ask it."

"Your wife . . ." Bayard prompted.

"Yes. Emily. We married when we were very young. It turned out we were not meant for each other. The best thing I could do was to free her to choose someone else."

"The way they talk of us . . . one would think we had rousted Satan from hell instead of simply following our consciences." Louisa's voice shivered with disdain. "Why should any man or woman be unhappily bound? Why shouldn't women be allowed to have lives of their own instead of being forced to marry? We have no other resource but men. No wonder Emily—"

"Louisa!" Adelaide said sharply.

Estes's face was solemn. "No, it's all right, Addie. I imagine he's heard that tonight as well. Emily took her own life. She did not have a strong mind. My father disliked her. He felt she was below us, and I'm afraid he belittled her at every opportunity. I had not expected to be in America so long, or I would have asked her to leave the estate and visit her family. I was trying to be kind, you understand. Things had deteriorated so between us . . ."

"They say she was expecting," Bayard said.

A nod. "The child could not have been mine, though she tried to pretend it was when her lover proved untrustworthy. I had not laid eyes on her for months! But she was desperate; I see that now. When we returned to find London so inhospitable, we went to Venice. Emily followed us. She threw herself into a canal."

A canal. Venice. The conversation between Louisa and Adelaide in the kitchen. A cursed city. *I won't go back there.* This was the curse she'd spoken of, I realized. This was her sorrow. It was all in her novel.

"She threw herself into a canal," Bayard repeated. He looked at Adelaide. "I heard something else tonight."

"It's not true," she whispered. "I swear to you it's not."

Bewildered, I asked, "Of what are you accusing her?"

Bayard said. "It's not my accusation. Everyone in that room tonight called her a murderess."

"Murderess!" I blurted my shock.

"No charges were ever brought," Estes rushed in. "Adelaide was a suspect, yes, because she was the last person to see Emily alive, and they felt she might have reason to do such a terrible thing. Of course she did not. She was completely absolved. But it was unfortunately in the papers, and so now here we are, with lies masquerading as truths, damnable gossip—and never was there a more innocent victim."

I'd seen cruelty in her. I'd seen hatred. I remembered thinking she would push her sister into the oubliette. But she had not, of course she had not, and this . . . murder . . . the accusation felt nebulous and indistinct. I could not imagine it of her, and I knew by Bayard's expression that he felt the same.

"How did I not know of any of this before now?" Bayard glared at Louisa. "You kept all of this from me."

"Please, Bay . . . it was all in the past. It was only rumors—why should I have mentioned it? There was no reason. We never went anywhere. I did not think you would hear it."

She was right about that. He'd still been smarting over Marie, and he'd holed himself up in his rooms and hardly stepped foot out of them. The last place he'd wanted to be was in society, where the rumors—mostly true—of his shocking behavior dogged him. He had gone to no parties, no dinners, and because of that, neither had I.

"We went to Italy to escape the gossip," Julian said miserably. "And then, after Emily's death, it was best to leave Italy too. It took some time for it all to reach London. When it did . . . we came here."

"To foist it all upon me," Bayard said. "Are you mad? How can you possibly think I could help you? Me? Rumors attend everything I do. I have enough to manage my own indiscretions without managing yours as well."

"My father cut me off," Julian said bitterly—as if he could have expected something different. "The rest of society followed his lead. They whisper of murder and immorality everywhere we go. We have been pariahs, living like animals, all because of prejudice and ignorance. We have nowhere else. We had hoped you would be more enlightened."

"I might have been, had you told me the truth," Bayard said. "God knows I understand rumors better than most men. But now I've been dragged into a scandal that is for once not of my making. They think you're insane, you know, and me with you. Seeing spirits, shootings, and somehow they've discovered my liaison with Louisa on top of it. How do you think they learned of that?"

"The telescopes?" I suggested. "Or no . . . Sylvie."

Bayard gave me a grim look. "I had rather thought something else. Are you sure you said nothing of it to a certain dark lady?"

I went cold as I remembered that day in the garden, my babbling, trying to please Vera Brest, speaking out of turn. She'd promised to say nothing. She'd promised to keep it secret. But she'd turned away from me tonight, and I had not mistaken the horror in her eyes.

"It isn't Mr. Calina's fault." Adelaide's voice was so quiet I half mistook it for the burble of water against the hull. "We should never have gone tonight. We should have told you the truth."

That she defended me was gratifying, but she was not looking at me as she said it. She was staring at Estes, who shifted beneath her gaze.

Louisa said, "Oh, Addie, how were we to know they would still care? It's been months."

"Some things people never forget," Adelaide said.

No one said anything more. The breeze had mostly died. The journey back home, in restless, joyless silence, seemed to take a hundred years.

TWENTY-FOUR

ADELAIDE

I could not stop reliving the walk into the château, with Bayard joking before me and Louisa smiling as if she'd just opened the grandest gift imaginable and Julian taut with strain, and then people noting, wondering, and then knowing, their whispers and their condemning stares. Even Vanni had not been unaffected, as separate from us as he was. I'd watched that woman turn from him. She was his lover, I assumed, petite, dark eyed and dark haired, burning with a vivacity that reminded me of my sister. He had seemed so stunned by her rejection that I'd felt sorry for him, or I would have, had I been thinking of anything but my own need of him, and the impulse to run from those horrified faces and those ceaseless whispers that even now filled the bedroom, pulsed from the walls, shushed when my head hit the pillow.

I woke before the dawn and pulled on my dressing gown, stepping between the curtains and the window, hiding in chintz. Julian's even breathing was comforting and familiar. The night was lightening. I heard the faint sound of the front door. The glow of gaslight lit the yard and then was shut away again, but now I saw him moving across the lawn, his head bowed, his step quick, as if he could not wait to be gone.

I wanted to fly after him. But Julian had said no, and I was exhausted by the thought of arguing with him. At the edge of the yard, at the start of the steep path that wound through the vineyard to the shore, Vanni looked back and up. I knew by the way he paused that he saw me at the window. I pressed my hand to the glass, a flex of my fingers, a refusal to a question he had not asked. He turned away, disappearing over the crest.

I slipped from my hiding place and went quietly and carefully to my bag, taking out his pages, my notebook. As soundlessly as I could, I left the bedroom. Louisa's door was closed; I knew she was within. Bayard had said not another word last night, and had stalked to his room alone when we'd returned. Louisa had stood there with a trembling mouth, and I waited for her distraught tears and her growing anger to turn to something more, to be made manifest in solid things, heavy things, things that crashed easily into walls or broke apart on the floor, satisfying ruins. *Sometimes that's all I want, Addie. It's all I can think about. Tearing apart the world, smashing it to pieces.*

Even Julian saw her storm gathering. "Loulou, it will be all right. I'll work things out with him in the morning."

She ignored him, saying to Vanni, "It's all your fault."

"My fault?"

"You told that woman about Bayard and me—"

"He's had affairs with dozens of women since I've known him. That's hardly what they care about. I knew nothing about the rest. It's your own behavior that hurts you." He dismissed her with a gesture. I knew how she would take it. I knew what she would do.

She flew at him; Julian was on her before she got two steps, pulling her back.

"You'll only make things worse," he said. "Don't be a fool. Go to bed."

His admonishments to her were rare, and always had the same effect. She sagged, and suddenly she was sobbing. Julian held her tightly, whispering, stroking her hair.

Vanni laughed in soft disbelief, then caught my glance, and his laughter died. He went into his bedroom, slamming the door.

I'd told Julian I would take Louisa to her room, and he released my sister to me. Once we were there, I undressed her; I brushed her hair. She was like a child beneath my ministrations, my obedient little sister. When I finally made to leave her, she turned from the mirror, saying miserably, "I try to be good. I do. I try to be better. There's something wrong with me, Addie, isn't there? I am like Father."

"Of course not."

"I'm afraid . . . do you think Bay hates me?"

"It took him by surprise. Give him some time to reach an accommodation." Though I wondered if he would, or could. An accused murderer, a ménage à trois, a pregnant wife committing suicide. It seemed far too much, especially when coupled with everything that had happened since we'd arrived. "We should have told him what to expect."

She had fingered the ribbons on the dressing table. "He wants me to leave."

"Don't be silly, Loulou," I reassured her. "You inspire him, just as you wished."

"I do, don't I?" Hope touched her uncertainty and then gained purchase. "The contest story was my idea. And he's been writing every morning. It's impossible what he does . . . so many pages. His pen just flies!"

"You see? Tomorrow, be contrite. He won't be able to resist you."

"You're right," she said. "Of course you're right. What would I do without you, Addie? No one understands me as you do."

I had been glad to leave her to herself. I remembered the expression on Bayard's face when he'd come into the garden, which was anger, yes, but also something more. On the boat, I'd heard that he felt betrayed. He had trusted us, and we had made him look foolish. We had imposed upon him and brought him only trouble, yet he'd excused all of it, and we had repaid him by letting him go into that ballroom unarmed, unprepared. Perhaps Louisa would not be able to charm him into good graces again this morning, nor Julian. Perhaps today would be our last at the Villa Diodati. I imagined being on the train with nowhere to go and no money to go there, a threesome again, and my despair grew so I had to stop on the stairs. I clutched Vanni's pages and my notebook more forcibly, concentrating on the stiffness of the cover, the thick warp of his paper where it had absorbed spilled ink. The night had given way to dawn beyond the window. I knew that on the boat, Vanni watched the faint line of sunrise etch itself against the horizon.

I went to his room, which was quiet, dimly lit by the window in the adjoining room, but feeling small and cramped with shadow. His bed was unmade; the room smelled of sleep. I went into the next room, and set his papers, scrawled with my notes, on his desk. The window over-looked the trees and flowering shrubs on the hillside. His room was just where the villa abutted the slope, where the three stories at the lakeside rear became two at the front, and the rosebushes beyond the balcony grew nearly to the railing. Without thinking, I opened the window, and the clean stone-and-water scent of the lakeside in the morning swept into the room, along with a chorus of frogs. It was too chill yet to bring with it the perfume of roses.

I meant to return his story and then go. I meant to find a quiet, hidden place to write. The kitchen, for an hour or so, or the empty maid's room downstairs, where no one would think to look for me, and I would release all the tension and dismay of last night into words. But instead, I pulled out his chair and sat down. I picked up his pen, mea-suring the heft of it, the smoothness in my hand, and then I uncapped the ink. It did not feel strange at all to sit here; it felt as if the room welcomed me, as if it might be offended if I left.

I opened my notebook, and my story unfolded as if my mind knew exactly what must be written.

That was how he found me.

The click of the door brought me to myself. I heard him pause. "Bayard?" and then he was in the doorway between the rooms, staring at me.

"I hope you don't mind," I said, embarrassed, not knowing how to explain. "I brought back your story and then . . . then I just sat down."

"You just sat down." He spoke the words as if they were foreign.

My hand tingled. My chin. He frowned when I started to scratch, and I lowered my hand again.

"I don't mind," he said. "I'm just curious as to why."

"I wanted to find someplace where Julian wouldn't find me. To write." I gestured to my notebook. "I didn't think he would look here."

"You should have come out on the boat with me."

"Jules doesn't want me to."

"Why not?"

"He's afraid you might drown me."

He looked astonished. "You mean deliberately?"

I laughed. "Oh no. No, no. But he doesn't trust your skill."

"He trusts nothing about me. I suppose Louisa has been regaling him with stories of my faults."

"I doubt she's spoken to him of you at all."

I did not mistake the quick hurt that crossed his face, that flash of wounded pride. "Of course not. Why should she? I'm hardly worth noting."

"If she told Julian that she knows you well enough to know your faults, she would have to tell him the truth of how she'd mistaken you for Bayard. He is already reeling from the discovery that Louisa and

Bayard are together. I don't think he could reconcile that too, and she would never risk his good opinion."

He accepted that without question and glanced at the notebook, asking, "Did you write anything new?"

I nodded. "It's easy to write here. The view from your window is calming, don't you think? Not like the lake."

"I thought you found the lake beautiful."

"Oh yes, beautiful. But it's always so wild. Even at its most placid, it feels—I don't know, threatening. As if it's biding its time before it overtakes us all."

"I think you must have been too affected by that drowned boy. Or . . ." He paused, measuring. "Or perhaps the death of Julian's wife."

"Is that your way of asking me if I murdered her? What are you imagining—that I pushed her into the canal? That's what the police thought." *One step back was all it would take, a small shove.*

"I don't think you murdered her," he said simply.

"No?" I bit off a laugh. "Then you are an anomaly, I assure you."

"I think her death affected you deeply," he said. "I think you blame yourself."

"Why would you think that? I hardly knew her."

I don't know what he heard in my voice. I had thought it very even. I was so used to telling lies, to pretending all was well, that it was second nature.

He shrugged. "I see it in your story."

"Stories have nothing to do with their authors. Bayard said it—didn't you hear? 'My name is Legion: for we are many.'"

"That's not true for every writer. Besides, that's the reason you're writing it, isn't it? To exorcise your ghosts?"

Uncomfortably, I said, "It's only a story."

"It's why Estes doesn't want you to work on it. It's not because he fears it will make you more sad. It's because he fears the truth in it." He waited as if he expected me to say something. I wasn't certain what he wanted, and in my silence, he said, "Well . . . I'll leave you to it. Stay here as long as you like. I won't tell anyone." Disappointment colored his words. He started toward the door.

"Don't go," I heard myself say. "You're always walking off. Why do you do that?"

He stopped, looking over his shoulder. "I'd thought to give you privacy."

"I don't want privacy."

He turned back, uncertain, wary.

"Write with me," I said. "Will you do that? Stay and we'll write together."

Now he looked bemused. "There's no other chair."

"Sit on the bed," I suggested. "Or I will. Or I'll sit on the floor. I don't care. Whatever you suggest, only, just stay."

He looked about helplessly.

"You want to go," I said, disconsolate. "You're afraid of me now. Or you think I'm mad. I don't blame you."

"No." He folded himself up, those long legs, sinking to the floor, his back against the door frame, leaning his head on the wall. "I could use some paper. I'm messy enough with the pen as it is. It would only be disaster without a desk. But there's a pencil there if you'll hand it to me."

The room was so small that he was only inches away. I had to move the chair to keep from stepping on his feet. But he said nothing of discomfort and neither did I. I didn't want to give him a reason to change his mind. I handed him the pencil and the paper, and he smiled at me, and the sun went bright, filling the room with the spicy scent of roses.

We wrote that way, quietly, companionably, until I heard the sound of footsteps overhead. "Julian," I said, glancing up at the ceiling. "Or Louisa."

"Hmmm." He didn't look up from his writing.

I blew on the ink to dry it, and closed my notebook. "Could I come back here? If we're allowed to stay, I mean. Perhaps it's no use even asking, but would you mind?"

Now he did look up. "You should tell Estes."

"Then he'll make me stop."

"Say no."

I sighed. "How easy that sounds."

"Isn't it?"

I shook my head. "Jules is very insistent. He would make us both miserable. He likes things to be the way he wants them to be."

"But the world isn't his to rule, is it?" Vanni asked. "You aren't his to rule."

In that, he was wrong. I couldn't blame him for thinking it. I had thought it once myself. I had been brought up believing it, but now I knew better. I *was* Julian's to rule, as long as this world remained as it was. What did it grant a woman with no husband or family to support her but disapproval and disgrace and poverty? Not only that, but I loved Julian still. Yes, I did, in some way I was having trouble fathoming. Out of habit perhaps, or in hope.

"Say no, Adelaide," Vanni urged. "I would like just once to see them not run you over."

There were so many things I could not say. "I'm his muse."

"Why would telling him you wish to write change that?"

"Oh, I think muses are very delicate creatures, don't you? Inspiration is very particular. I imagine you would not like your own muse to change colors."

He glanced down at the papers propped against his knees. "I don't have a muse."

"No? Not the woman I saw you with last night?"

His gaze darkened, but he only said, "Perhaps that's my problem. Perhaps I should find one."

"Perhaps you should." Upstairs, the moving about grew louder. "I should go. I don't know how I'll hide this if Jules is awake."

"Leave it here," Vanni said. "I'll lock it away if you like."

"But then I would have to find you to get the key."

"Just leave it on the desk, then. No one ever comes in here. Well, except Bayard. But he'll just think it's mine, and he won't be interested."

I remembered the night that Bayard and I had waited for Vanni to return from the lake. "I don't think that's true. He believes you have talent. He told me so."

"Did he? Was he drunk?"

"You could learn from him, you know." I had said the wrong thing. Vanni's smile died.

"Just so. You should go, unless you want to be caught here. God knows how we would explain it, given that neither of us wants to say the real reason."

The room felt small again, and confined; he seemed to take up too much room. I did not know how to regain the ease of it. So I rose, and started to step past him.

"Did you know he had a wife?"

I stopped.

"When you ran off with Estes, did you know he had a wife? Or did he lie to you about it?"

"I knew," I said. "Julian does not believe in lying."

"You're telling me that he doesn't lie?" How sharp was his skepticism, and what was that I saw in his eyes? Pity?

The answer was more complicated than he could know. Like Louisa, Jules saw himself the hero of his own life. I suppose we all did, but Julian's heroism was writ large; in his mind, those who could not understand his motives were ignorant or afraid or willfully blind, and therefore not worthy of placating. "Jules sometimes has trouble understanding why other men won't follow his precepts."

"You mean Free Love?"

"That, and other things. He is, in his own way, the most moral man I've ever known. He told me he had a wife almost the moment we met."

It was the second thing he'd said to me that day on the porch. My hand had gone to his as if it could not imagine anyplace else to be. Julian had clasped it. *What a pleasure to meet you, Miss Wentworth. I left my wife in London.*

It had shocked my father, such a non sequitur it seemed, and Louisa had laughed as if she meant to make fun, but Julian was oblivious to both of them, and not the least embarrassed, and I had thought only *I have waited for you.*

"So you knew," Vanni said, "And you ran off with him anyway?"

I heard his judgment, and could not help flushing. "I loved him. There was an affinity between us—"

"Which he must have also felt once with his wife."

"Were you not listening last night? They made each other miserable."

"Still, it's not quite the honorable thing, is it? Leaving a wife in a delicate condition—"

"He wasn't the father," I defended, though I did not know for certain, could not know. He'd spent three months in Concord. There was the time it took to travel there and back, and when I saw her she was nearly to term. *"I hadn't touched her for months before that,"* Julian had said. *"She loves me as little as I love her. She's found someone else, I'm certain."*

"Did the immorality of it never trouble you?"

"Does it trouble you to be cuckolding your lady's husband?"

I was gratified when he blinked in surprise.

"You see?" I went on. "If I were a man, would you ask me this question? Would you think it so wrong? You with your pretty little love, Bayard with Marie Arsenault—how is what you're doing different than what I did? You have no answer, I see, because there isn't one. Women must depend on men. Most of us have no money or standing on our own, and no way to gain either. But when you're done with whatever her name is, you will simply walk away. You will think nothing of how you leave her, or what would happen to her if her husband threw her into the street. What would she have? Where could she go? Who would not be sanctimonious or judgmental about her fate? Women risk so much more than a man will ever risk, so do not speak to me of morality." I prepared myself for his censure and his scorn.

"You're right," he admitted finally, looking as amazed by his words as was I. "You're right. You've risked a great deal. Is that why you won't risk more?"

I frowned at him, not understanding.

"Is that the real reason you're afraid to tell him you want to be a writer? Are you afraid he'll leave you if you become something different than he imagines?"

"Yes," I said, jolted into honesty.

"It would be dishonorable for him to do so," he said.

"But that's what I've been saying, Vanni, don't you understand? In Julian's eyes, it would be dishonorable for him to stay if he no longer cared for me."

"What about guilt?" he asked, his voice so casual it raised alarms. "I would say guilt was equally binding. Perhaps more so. Wouldn't you?"

Upstairs, a door closed.

Vanni said, "Someone's coming down."

This time, I did not linger, and he said nothing to make me stay.

TWENTY-FIVE

VANNI

I had not expected her, or my gratification at finding her sitting in my chair. I had not expected how easy it was to write with her there.

But mostly I had not expected the way she'd looked up and smiled, acknowledging me, acknowledging us, before she turned again to her story.

How does one fall, you might ask? How did I?

Like this. With her quiet smile that told me I was seen.

The shock of it kept me sitting long after she'd gone and I had no more reason to be on the floor. I could not believe that I hadn't seen it coming, that I'd been so hapless. She had sneaked up on me so subtly, enchanting me before I knew to be wary. I knew I was a fool—she belonged to Estes, though given what she'd told me this morning, perhaps not as firmly as I'd thought. Or perhaps more so—how would I know? She was troubled, and confusing, and I should stay well away from her for the remainder of their visit, which I suspected would not last much longer. Those plans she and her sister had spoken of had gained some clarity last night. Not such a mystery as I'd thought. That they'd come here meaning to use Bayard was obvious—they had no money or refuge—but now, how could he keep them? They'd plunged him into another scandal, and one he would not soon be free of. The news of their visit—no doubt with plenty of invented details about murders and Free Love and incestuous orgies—would be in London before the week was out.

No, they would be gone soon, on a train, heading back to their exile and their poverty. But even knowing that, I could not banish what I felt. Finally, I could not stay in my room with it. It seemed to permeate everything. I couldn't write. I could not even think. All I could smell was roses.

By then, it was afternoon, and they were all on the terrace. Adelaide was at the railing, staring at the lake. Bayard was there too. The wound at his temple was now a shiny pink, the bruise only the faintest hint of yellow. Everyone looked tense but for Louisa.

"He had eleven pages for me!" Louisa exclaimed to me with a triumphantly malicious expression—how did the others not note that? She was at the little cast iron table, busily transcribing. I wanted to put my hands around her slender throat.

"Shouldn't you be packing?" I asked.

"Packing? Whatever for?"

I looked at Bayard, who said curtly, "Julian begged. They've nowhere else to go, so I've allowed them to stay until the contest deadline. A few more weeks. That way he can send a few letters and find another savior."

I stared at him in surprise. I hadn't thought he cared about the deadline. He surely wasn't bothering to meet it.

How was I to bear a few more weeks?

"I hope you managed to get the other half of those pages done," he continued. "Louisa's already finished hers."

"By this afternoon."

"Remind me again: What do I pay you for?"

I realized two things: One, Bayard was not the least sanguine about their scandal. And two, while he was angry with everyone, it was me he intended to punish.

Adelaide twisted slightly to look at me. She mouthed, "I'm sorry."

Estes stood close to her, his arm brushing hers, his hip—how did he dare to touch her that way? Did the man feel no guilt at all? He said, "A messenger brought a letter for you, Calina. I put it on the chair."

I recognized the handwriting from here.

"I hope you managed something with the good Madame Brest last night before all hell broke loose. At least then the evening wouldn't be a complete loss." Bayard's voice was icy. Louisa flushed. She was not so unaffected as I'd thought.

Adelaide's gaze went to the letter. I did not miss how deliberately she turned away. Even through my dread I felt a flicker of hope that she might be jealous, but then I remembered our conversation about morality, and I felt guilty before I picked the missive up. I wished Vera Brest hadn't written. What could she have to say? *Please do not return. Keep away from me. How dared you bring those people to this house?*

I turned to go into the salon, to read the letter in private, but Bayard forestalled me.

"No, don't go, Vanni. Tell us what the dear lady has to say about last night."

So this was how it was going to be. The others went very quiet, Estes and Adelaide turning to watch, Louisa raising her head. Bayard's gaze challenged. I wanted to tell him to leave me the bloody hell alone. I was tired of this. Done with this.

But I wasn't done, was I? In my own way, I was no better than the others. What else did I have but Bayard Sonnier?

I gritted my teeth and opened the letter, scanning it.

"Go on," Bayard urged.

"She's sorry to have run off last night."

"Run off? Did she run off? And you did not run after? Tsk tsk. Have I not taught you that courting is very like hunting? But I imagine the whole predator/prey aspect eludes you."

Steady, I warned myself. *Steady.*

"I hope she tells you to return," Bayard went on, raising a brow, waiting for my answer.

I could not look at Adelaide. "She asks me to wait until the gossip dies."

"Ah, of course! Does she approximate when that might be? Two months from now? Six? A year?"

I shook my head.

"What else? Go on, Vanni, don't be shy. We're all waiting to hear."

I folded the letter. "That's all."

"Why, that can't be all." He extended his hand. Flexing his fingers. *Come.* "Here, give it to me."

"It's private," I said rigidly.

"Private? Did you just tell me it was private?"

"Bayard." *Stay calm.* "Please."

"Hand it over. Or have you something to hide?"

Adelaide, venturing where no one else would go, "Bayard, perhaps not . . . a love letter—"

He swiveled to her so abruptly she faltered. "He is my employee, Adelaide. Are you telling me I can't demand that my employee answer my question?"

She reddened.

I couldn't stand it. "Here. Take it. Take it." I threw the letter at him; it fluttered to the terrace.

He stared at it. He might have let it lay. There was a chance. But Louisa—damn her, groveling for favor—scrambled from her chair to retrieve it, to hand it to him. He took it and glanced it over. That thin smile I'd learned to dread.

"'*My darling Giovanni,*'" he read, then, to me, "Well, you've got farther than I thought. Christian names! And 'my darling.' She must not be too distraught over last night, surely?" Back to the letter. "'*I believe I told you to stay away until I wrote to you, and so you cannot be upset with me for my surprise and it is unfair for you to come and search me out when you know I cannot acknowledge you—did you mean to destroy everything? I could not help it as you know and then to bring those people! I will do all I can to convince Orsini to have you back, but it will be a hard task, I fear, for he has declared that neither you nor Mr. Sonnier will ever set foot in his house again. Of course, he is prone to such tempers, and they will fade with time.*'"

Another glance up. "You see? All is well! We shall be able to go back eventually. Fear not! Ah, what else have we . . . '*I cannot be seen with you now you must understand, but I will miss you terribly!*' Of course she will. Such an intrepid lover; who would not miss you?"

I could not look at any of them.

"'*I will write you the moment we can be together again, and you can bring the story to me—it is finished, yes?—and we will read it in the garden, as we did before. I beg you, do not forget! It will be soon. Until then, I kiss you and dream of you. Affectionately, Vera.*'"

That the letter was done was no relief.

"I suppose imaginary kisses are the best she can hope for, eh, Vanni? What story is she talking about? Your ghost story? You must have changed it considerably if she's actually looking forward to reading it. Is that what you've been spending your hours on? Am I *paying* you to write your own story?"

"Of course not." It was all I could do to say it.

"What is that? I'm afraid I didn't hear you. Louder, please."

I glared at him. "No."

"No? Well then, all I can suppose is that she's reading the mess as it was. She is Portuguese, so perhaps she's unused to reading English.

Or perhaps it's only that she adores you. Ah, I can imagine it. Staring into one another's eyes, chastely holding hands and calling it a grand love affair—"

I dived at him before I knew I was moving.

Estes lunged between us. "No, Calina!" His hands on my shoulders, pushing me back.

I struggled to get past him. "Let go of me!"

Bayard threw the letter to the ground. "Go ahead, Jules, release him. Let him do his worst."

Estes pushed me harder. I pushed back. His hold on me tightened. Bayard was smiling now, laughing, delighting in how well he'd managed me, taking pleasure in my rage.

"Why don't you let me go if I'm such a disappointment to you?!" I shouted at him—damn Estes's arms, damn his hands. I could not get free.

"Don't tempt me," Bayard threatened.

I twisted in Estes's hold, half-strangled. "You think you're such a wonder, but you're not nearly so good as you think!"

"Enough." Adelaide stepped between Bayard and me, coldly forbidding. "That's enough from both of you. Jules, let him go."

"You must be mad—"

"Let him go." She was imperious, commanding, and to my surprise, my anger drained away and my good sense—such as it was—returned, and I realized what I was doing, what was at stake, what an idiot I was.

Estes released me with a "Go after him again and I'll throw you in the lake myself." I pushed him hard and stepped away. Adelaide put up her hand, stopping him from retaliating.

I took a deep breath, straightening my waistcoat, my watch fob. Louisa had returned to the table, and now she watched intently, not delighted at my humiliation, as I'd expected, but looking perplexed.

"Forgive me," I said stiffly—too little, not helpful.

Estes put his hand on Bayard's shoulder, a show of friendly support that I would never have presumed to make, and especially after last night.

Bayard stepped away. The evidence that he was still irritated with Estes did nothing to make me feel better, because then Bayard turned to Adelaide and said, "I'm going for a walk. Would you care to accompany me, Adelaide?"

It was clear that he meant her alone. I heard Louisa's pained gasp. Estes frowned.

I should have anticipated this. I'd seen it already at Chillon, hadn't I? I'd known it was only a matter of time before he pursued Adelaide. That he chose now to do so was meant as a punishment for both Estes and Louisa—that it punished me as well he could not have known. I hadn't known it until this morning.

Bayard did not acknowledge any of us, but waited for Adelaide, who said, "Oh," in a small voice, all her imperiousness gone, replaced by uncertainty. She looked at Estes, then Louisa, then me. Then, for Bayard, a tentative smile. "I would be delighted."

Bayard said to me, "I think it would be best if you removed yourself from my sight for a time."

Louisa picked up the letter, and held it out to me. She was red cheeked, obviously angry at Bayard's attention to her sister. "Don't forget your letter, Mr. Calina."

Everything narrowed to that piece of paper dangling from her fingers. I didn't take it, and I didn't wait to see Adelaide take Bayard's arm. I brushed by Louisa roughly, and fled to my room, where I wrote a letter to my father about my very promising future, and waited for Bayard to decide what he would do with me.

TWENTY-SIX

ADELAIDE

We walked down the path in silence, but once we reached the stony beach, Bayard said, "My temper's quite passed. You needn't worry."

"Are you certain?"

He was quiet. Then, "No, I suppose you're right. I am still angry. The three of you made me look a fool."

"I'm sorry. But in my defense, I did say we should not go."

"But not why. How was I to know?"

"I was more worried for you than for ourselves. If anything, I'm—"

"Ashamed?"

Vanni had thought the same thing. "No, not that."

"That's what I will never understand. What kind of freedom is there in being reviled? You were sick at what happened at Orsini's—no, don't bother to deny it. I should think it more difficult for a woman. You are such social creatures."

His words cut deeply. "I have Julian. And Louisa."

"Yes, Louisa."

Was that distaste I heard?

"None of this was her fault, you must understand," I said quickly. "Julian and I brought her with us. I had not thought to make her a pariah. She is not to blame—"

"Really? What of the talk is true?"

I stumbled at his brusqueness. He caught my elbow to steady me. "Jules told you everything last night."

"I want to hear it from you."

"I was a suspect in Emily Estes's death. I cannot deny that. Nor can I escape it."

I could not read his gaze. "Yet you said nothing of it."

"What should I have said? 'I'm sorry, Bayard, but you should know I've been accused of murder'?"

"For a start. You had to know it was only a matter of time before I discovered it."

"Yes. But I was afraid you would turn us out if you knew. If I had told you then, you would never have let us stay."

"Undoubtedly," he admitted.

"It's true we have nowhere else, but that's not the only reason we came. It's not the most important reason. I had hoped . . . we had hoped you might help Julian professionally. He needs you so much."

He said nothing to that. We had lost him completely, just as I'd feared. All of this had been for nothing.

I said quietly, "You told Julian we could stay until the deadline. Do you mean to rescind that?"

He shook his head. "No. But I warn you that I have no more patience. And I expect the truth from this point on. Do you understand?"

I could not keep the relief from my voice. "Yes, of course."

"Is Julian bedding both you and your sister?"

I should be used to the accusation; I'd certainly heard it enough. But I wasn't. It still disconcerted.

"If you tell me he's not, I'll believe you," he went on.

"But you didn't believe either Julian or Louisa when they denied it," I said.

He glanced away. "I don't trust Louisa. She's . . . unstable. I'm telling you nothing you don't already know."

"She is trying very hard." The same excuse I'd always made. What would it be like, I wondered, never to have to say it again?

He snorted. "Do you know what she did to my study when I told her we were leaving London? She tore it apart. Literally. It took the maid two days to clean it up."

"She was very sorry for it, you know."

"Sorry doesn't replace ten rare books and an expensive globe."

"She has always struggled with her temper."

"A perfect match for Vanni," he noted. "The two of them could level cities together. But you're right; she was very contrite after. As Vanni will be, when we return. Contrite and miserable. I hate that in both of them."

"Well, you have no one to blame but yourself for Mr. Calina today." I offered it cautiously, girding myself for his scorn.

He lifted his face to the breeze, which blew back his hair to show more of the wound Julian had inflicted. It would most assuredly be a scar, and a constant reminder of that night, but it did not mar Bayard's profile, which was distinct and striking. "Yes, I suppose that's true. But I am all admiration for how you managed him. I would have bloodied him. God knows I wanted to. Until you rose up like a Valkyrie, which was much more interesting than fisticuffs."

"A Valkyrie? I'm afraid I don't know what that is."

"It's Norse. A mythical warrior maiden. Very intimidating. What's interesting to me is that you seem to calm Louisa as well. You have a steadying hand. Beauty transforming the savage beast, just like in the fairy tale."

The compliment only exhausted me further.

He said, "You didn't answer my question."

"Julian loves me," I said, lying by omission. "I was the one who insisted on bringing Louisa when we ran off together. My father was difficult. I couldn't leave her behind."

Bayard's gaze sharpened as if he sensed there was more to ask, but those were the questions I was not prepared to answer. They held every uncertainty in my life: my fear that my sister had inherited my father's madness, that Julian would love her better or abandon us both or bind me ever tighter, that my future would be no different than the present, the past never loosening its hold. And so I said quickly, changing the subject, "What will you do about Mr. Calina? Will you let him go?"

"Julian says I should. Louisa has said it all along. Even when we were in London."

I had known they both thought it, but not that they had lobbied for it. I had asked them not to meddle in Bayard's affairs; I did not know what angered me more, that they were working against Vanni or that they had ignored me. I wondered if it was a plan they'd come up with together, one more collusion, one more thing that kept me firmly out.

This, at least, I could fight.

"They don't know him as you do," I said. "You should not listen to anyone else's opinion."

"Even yours?" He laughed lightly. "No, I can see that you wish me to consider yours. Do you have a liking for my secretary, Adelaide? He took you out on the boat; this morning I heard you talking together. What do you talk about?"

I thought of the notebook on Vanni's desk, the story ghosting beneath everything I said and all I thought, distracting, insistent, and I wanted to tell him *we talk of writing*. I wished I could tell everyone. "Many things. I suppose you could say we are becoming friends."

Bayard considered. "How singular."

"Why do you say that?"

"I never hear him speak of any friends. He never asks for a day off to visit anyone but his father or a brothel." He said it baldly, completely unapologetic of my sensibilities. "He's thin-skinned. He's vain. He's proud. But he does his work—or at least, he did until recently. He's amusing and intelligent, and I admire what he's made of himself, given where he comes from. Still, he was indiscreet, which I will not tolerate, and that temper . . . I'm growing tired of it. When we were in Lausanne, he went storming off one night and got into a fight with a pianist at a brothel. I had to pay for the repairs. He took offense with a man at Orsini's, and it was only my intervention that kept it from escalating badly. He's been on his best behavior since, but he's also insulted Julian and he's been a problem with Louisa—"

"I don't think you can blame him completely for that. What happened in London was at least partly Louisa's fault."

Bayard stopped. "In London? What happened in London?"

I had assumed he knew. But then, no, of course not. It painted Louisa in such a bad light; of course she would never have told him. I scrambled for something to say, some suitable excuse, an unexceptional reason.

"Adelaide, what happened in London?"

"She was upset with him for managing your schedule so well," I said finally, lamely, the same lie I'd told Julian, though Julian wanted to believe well of her and so accepted things much more easily. I feared Bayard would not be so compliant. "You know how she is—had she been able to see you every moment of the day, she would have. He kept her from interrupting you too often. Very admirable, really. It would have been difficult to say no to her. Anyway, of course she dislikes him for it. She saw him as a . . . an obstacle."

"I see," he said slowly.

He didn't believe me; I sensed it, and I was surprised at how desperately I wished he would challenge me. I wanted him to demand the truth; what a relief it would be to tell him something that was not an excuse or a lie, to protect no one for once. To let consequence fall where it may. *Let it be over.*

I was both disappointed and grateful when he only said, "Well then, I suppose I won't let him go. Just yet."

"You're very generous."

"I am not generous," he said. "But I don't mind you thinking so."

After that, we talked of other things: the view, the city, when the fanatics who revered his every move might return to plague us. Bayard added his wry commentary as we laughed at gulls fighting over some bit of food, flapping and cawing raucously until whatever it was dropped into the lake and sank. He was an entertaining companion, and I liked being with him, and understood what it was that had so charmed multitudes. Yet when we returned to the villa, I was relieved. I wanted nothing more than to be back in Vanni's room, bathed in his quiet understanding and his friendship that demanded nothing of me, listening to his pencil racing across the page while I wrote the story that gave me the solace I had so wished for.

But Louisa was waiting for me with that set expression that made me want to sigh.

"What did he say to you?" she blurted. "Why did he ask you to walk with him?"

"I told you we should not interfere, but you could not leave well enough alone, could you?" I said.

"I don't know what you're talking about. What have I done?"

"You've been nagging Bayard to let Mr. Calina go."

"Vanni?" Louisa's expression went blank in surprise, and then she took my arm, pulling me into her bedroom and closing the door. The room was a mess, evidence of Louisa's temper last night, and her fear over losing Bayard, clothes strewn everywhere, blankets and pillows and books thrown heedlessly about.

"You will ruin that dress, leaving it on the floor that way."

"Why did you defend Vanni?" she demanded. "Why do you keep defending him?"

"Because it would be unfair for Bayard to let him go, when he's only reacting to the way you and Julian bait him."

"I was not the one baiting him this morning. Neither was Julian. Bayard doesn't like him—it has nothing to do with us."

"That's not true. He does like him. He finds him difficult, yes, but he's willing to keep trying to sort him out."

She frowned. "I don't understand. Why do you care what happens to Vanni? What are you about, Addie?"

"Is it a crime to want to help someone?"

"No, if that's all it is."

"Of course that's all it is."

"I don't like the way you look at him lately. Neither does Julian."

"How do I look at him, Loulou?"

"As if you share secrets."

Immediately I thought of my story. But no, she knew nothing about it. She couldn't know. Julian would not have told her, would he? There was no need for panic. No need for my chin to start itching or my fingers to twitch. This was only Louisa, trying to manipulate and unsettle me.

"He has a lovely mouth, don't you think? No man should have such perfect lips. I have always thought it. Do you know what they feel like, Addie? Has he kissed you the way he kissed me?"

She was probing, hoping to find a weakness, and suddenly I was finished with it. Again, I thought, *let it be over.* I grabbed her wrist hard, yanking her toward me. "You had best be careful about the things you say, Loulou. The gossip last night made Bayard suspicious. What would he say if he knew about London, hmmm? Do you think you would still be his muse if he discovered you'd been kissing his secretary's 'perfect lips'?"

She paled and pulled away, rubbing her wrist, looking frightened and somehow reduced, and I didn't know if I was glad for that or sorry.

I forced a calm I didn't feel and went to the shoes thrown haphazardly on the floor. "I'll help you clean up this mess, but really, Louisa, you must learn to control yourself. Bayard is still upset about his study. It's astonishing that he wants anything to do with you at all."

She sagged. "I know. I try, but . . . I didn't mean to."

"Come now, fold that dress and put it away."

"Adelaide," she said softly. "I just don't understand. He's only a secretary. He's not one of us."

How could I say that it was that very separateness that appealed? "Let's get this all back into your trunk."

She came to me. "Promise me you won't have anything more to do with him."

The habit of managing Louisa, a lifetime of saying whatever would keep her calm and even tempered, cajoled.

I fought it.

"I can't promise that," I said.

"Why not? Why can't you?"

I drew away, picking up the shoe, setting it beside its mate beneath the window.

"Julian will not like it," she said.

"That's between me and Julian." I picked up a flat gray box I hadn't seen before. "What's this?"

She tensed. "Oh, that. It's nothing."

"Really?" I lifted the lid. Inside were several paper lanterns made of frail rice paper, folded. I took one out and opened it into a ballooning cube. Red strings looped to a little gondola at the bottom, meant to hold a candle. "Where did these come from?"

But I already knew, because just then I saw the receipt inside.

"They're nothing, Addie."

"From Paris? When you and Jules were there?" I rocked the paper balloon gently, sending the gondola swaying.

Louisa nodded reluctantly. "We thought . . . we thought they would look like spirits rising into heaven."

"Of course." I could so well imagine it, Louisa and Julian looking over the display, heads bent close together, Louisa's delight and his joy in her pleasure as they laughed and played in the streets of Paris and spent francs we did not have. What else had they done together while I shivered in a cold room in the Venice police station, already ill with a difficult pregnancy and trying to ignore contractions that were far too early as they peppered me with questions in a language I couldn't understand? What other delights had they indulged in while I had been miserable and afraid, haunted by the sight of Emily's bloated body, her words *"You will never be happy with him,"* and desperate to locate Julian? The telegrams had taken the last of the coins he'd left me. It had fallen to a police officer to comfort me, his halting English making me cry, his stranger's chest I'd sobbed into after I lost the baby.

"Addie, please. Please don't look that way."

"Shall we set them off tonight? What do you think?"

"I was saving them."

"For what?"

"For Julian's birthday."

"Oh, that's months away. Let's use them to show Bayard how grateful we are for his friendship instead. Don't you think he would like it?" Before she could answer, I was out the door with them, and she had no choice but to follow behind. The hall smelled of burning potatoes and singed bacon. I opened my bedroom door. Jules was bent over his poem, looking frustrated and unhappy.

"Jules, look what we found in Louisa's trunk! The paper lanterns—do you remember? The ones you bought in Paris?"

His gaze dodged to Louisa behind me, which only infuriated me further, this memory they shared, and one that held none of my suffering. They were in Paris, buying frivolous paper lanterns.

"We're going to set them off tonight," I went on, hearing my words skitter and fall, too fast, breathless, unable to stop them. I felt that my sister's mania had come upon me, and I embraced it as a welcome change. "Come—it's twilight already. It will be dark soon."

He set aside his pen. "Adelaide—"

"Hurry, hurry." I dashed from the door, down the stairs. Bayard had obviously forgiven his secretary, and vice versa. He and Vanni were in the salon, drinking wine and spreading bread with a soft and fragrant vacherin.

"Vanni burned dinner," Bayard informed us.

I plunked the gray box of lanterns on the settee. "Look what Louisa squirreled away—paper lanterns!" I tore the lid off the box, taking out the one I'd unfolded and putting it in Vanni's hands. "We've decided that we should go down to the lake to light them."

He held it gingerly, as if afraid it might crumble.

Bayard drained his glass. "Why not? That will give those telescopes at the d'Angleterre something to see."

Louisa watched me uncertainly. Julian trailed into the room. "I'd thought Louisa meant to save them for a special occasion."

They exchanged a glance. Louisa said, "Yes, I—"

"What can be more special than today?" I insisted. "With all of us together, and a beautiful evening? We'll show the world how little we care for their gossip. We will be exactly who we wish to be."

Bayard grabbed the two bottles of wine from the tea table. "Vanni, bring some candles and the matches."

Vanni eyed me, but he said nothing, still cradling the lantern in his hand.

I took up the box again and went after Bayard, scarcely heeding whether anyone followed. Outside, crickets sang; the air was softly scented with fruit. Twilight was deepening: blue lake, blue sky, dark blue trees and blue slate mountains, blue world. The first stars started to appear.

Bayard balanced one of the bottles on the upturned rowboat resting onshore. The other he brought to his lips, gulping deeply of it before he handed it to me, and with a grin, I set the box of lanterns on the boat and followed suit.

"A woman after my own heart," he said, then turned to look at the lake. "Here should be good, don't you think? We'll set them off from that rock there." He pointed to a half-submerged flat boulder.

Julian and Louisa reached the shore. Both looked wary and worried. I said, "It's the perfect night for it, don't you think? Jules, it will look just like your souls ascending to heaven." Louisa's words, Louisa's image.

Julian said, "The souls look like mist, not flame."

"Then we'll just imagine that they're falling instead. Stars falling back to earth to resume their ghostly shapes."

"That would be a tragedy," he said softly.

"Oh, but perhaps it's really where they wish to be. Not in the cold, dark sky, but here, with us, among the living and the breathing."

In his look was everything that had ever passed between us, and suddenly I was thinking of my story again, of a ghostly muse turning her lover insane, with a little thrill of vindictiveness.

Vanni took the last few steps down the path, juggling a box of candles and another of matches, the lantern I'd given him hanging by the strings wrapped about his wrist. With barely a glance at me, he went to Bayard, who was going through the box and taking out the lanterns, one by one, laying them on the hull, ready to be set afloat. Vanni untangled the lantern from his arm and put down the candles and the matches. "This one," he said, giving Bayard the lantern. "This one first."

The candles were too long; Julian took the knife from his pocket and cut them down to size while Louisa stood by nervously, darting glances to him, to me. It was the first time I'd ever seen her neglect Bayard. He did not seem to notice. He and Vanni lit one of the lanterns, and Bayard went to the rock he'd pointed out before. He stood on the very edge of it and gave the lantern a gentle toss. It floated, for a moment, and then sank like a stone, plunging into the water. The candle sputtered and went out. Louisa made a small, panicked sound.

"One's done," I said cheerfully. "Now another!"

"I think the candles need to be smaller," Bayard said to Julian. He grabbed the wine, drank, passed it again to me. I noted Julian's displeasure as I drank, how he reached for his flask.

I handed the bottle to Vanni, who whispered, "What's wrong?"

"Why, only a betrayal or two," I told him, stepping away before he could respond. I picked up a lantern, unfolding it, blowing gently into the balloon to inflate it, then took the lit candle from Bayard and set it gently into the gondola. This time, when it was sent aloft, it lingered a bit longer before it too plunged into the lake.

"This isn't how I imagined it at all!" Louisa cried.

"No? How did you imagine it?" I asked. "Tell me, Loulou. Something romantic, no doubt? A dozen lanterns rising into the sky until they disappeared into the heavens? A violin playing in the background? Someone declaring their undying love?"

I said it to her, but I was looking at Julian. He did not meet my gaze but studiously cut the candles, his jaw clenching.

"Perhaps, if we set them all off at once, that's what you'll have," I said to my sister. "Come, let's light every one of them, so Louisa shall have her wish! We've no violin, but I could sing, I suppose. Now all we need is someone to vow their love."

No one said anything. Louisa stared at me.

"Or perhaps," I went on slowly, "we could think holy thoughts instead. Something less romantic, more . . . funereal."

"Adelaide," Julian said in dismay.

"Perhaps a tribute to those who have died."

Louisa edged closer to Julian.

"Well, what are we waiting for? Come, Bayard, you take these. Mr. Calina, take those over there." I gathered the lanterns as I spoke, shoving them into Bayard's hands, and Vanni's. I took a handful of candle stubs, of matches, and went to the rock. I set the lanterns in a line on the boulder, setting candles into each gondola, and then I lit the match.

Vanni said, "Perhaps not all at once."

I glared at him. The match flickered out. "Are you taking my sister's side?"

Vanni shook his head. "No, of course not. It's only . . . you seem distraught."

"You hardly know me well enough to say. Hand me the matches."

"Let me." Bayard knelt beside me. He struck another, and then lit each of the candles. They sputtered gamely, growing stronger with each breath.

"Now," I said, taking one up, as did Bayard. Vanni hesitated until I gave him a pointed look, and then he did too.

One by one, we sent them into the air.

One by one, they plummeted down again to become sodden lumps of paper floating in the harbor, all but the last, which caught fire, burning to ash with a glorious, ravaging flame, a shooting spirit-star, plunging to the earth to drown.

"Well," I said with satisfaction, "that was a disappointment, wasn't it?"

Julian and Louisa stood motionless by the upturned rowboat. In the faint glow of the candle we'd set there to light our way, I could not see their expressions, but I felt my sister's regret and pain, and Julian's too.

"Who's for wine?" Bayard asked. He passed around the bottle. Louisa shook her head when he offered, and went to sit alone. It was all very calculated, of course, and obvious that she meant for one of the men to follow. At this point I was not certain who she wished for more, Bayard or Julian. Neither obliged. Bayard sat on the hull and drank. Julian took a not so surreptitious gulp of his laudanum. Vanni grabbed a handful of the remaining candles from the box and followed the shoreline some distance away, out of earshot, a deliberate exile. We all watched him settle the candles and light them before he sat to stare out at the lake, every inch the brooding poetic hero.

We were silent; the mood had turned as funereal as I'd wished, every little tension between us splintering. Finally, Bayard tossed the empty bottle onto the ground and said, "I'll get another."

He went off. He was to the base of the path before Louisa scurried to her feet and hurried after. "Bay! Bay, wait for me!"

Julian glanced toward the shore, to the winking, blinking candles and Vanni, a shadow against the stardust glow of the lake, and asked gently, "What was that about, Adelaide?"

"There was no money for anything. I couldn't pay a bribe or hire a lawyer or even buy coal or food. I was being questioned about your wife's murder and I had no idea where you were. I was alone and afraid and upset. But you were buying fripperies in Paris."

"It was just after my meeting with my father," he said. "We were celebrating. He'd promised me the monthly allowance."

The monthly allowance was another one of his father's special little punishments. It would have been enough money for Julian to live on, barely, but could certainly not support the two women who lived with him.

"We've already talked of all this," he went on. "Must we revisit it again?"

I looked at the wavering, tiny flames along the shore. Even at a distance, even removed, Vanni was somehow more solid and present than Julian, who sat on the rowboat's hull beside me.

I said, "Do you ever wonder what she would be like now?"

Julian's sigh was long-suffering. "There was no *she*, Adelaide. We don't know whether it was a girl or a boy."

"I know," I said. "I always knew."

He paused, then said, "No, I don't wonder." There was a soft brutality in his words, a pointed *move forward, stop grieving*, which made me want to hurt him.

"What of Emily's unborn child? Do you ever wonder about him?"

"Why should I? It wasn't mine. Stop this, Addie. It's not me or Louisa you want to punish. It's yourself."

"No. I am quite certain it's you and Louisa."

He put his hand on mine. It was warm, his fingers long and slender as the rest of him, unworked, uncalloused, the hands of a poet, the hands of a man whose engine was his brain, whose work was the realm of the spirit. Those fingers had touched me in ways I had not been able to imagine before I'd met him. They had brought me such pleasure. But that pleasure was gone now, and I wondered what it would require to bring it back. What words would be good? Which would prove the spark?

"We can have another child, you know. If that's what you want. We'll try again." He curled his fingers around my hand. "We'll go upstairs now, if you like. We'll conceive one here, in Geneva, where there are good memories."

"Are there? Whose memories are the good ones, Jules? Yours? Louisa's?"

"I'd hoped yours. We can be as we were before. The poet and his muse. To know you love me is the purest inspiration. I doubt you can understand. I don't think that anyone but another writer could, but that's what I feel."

Once, the words would have thrilled me, but now all I could think about was my story; now, all I heard was *I doubt you can understand.* I wanted to shout *Yes, I do understand. I know.* Perhaps it would make things better to tell him I meant to be a writer too. To see admiration in his eyes might prove the spark I needed to want him again.

"You're a gift I've been given," he went on. "I don't know what I did to deserve you, but if anything ever happened to take you away . . . I don't want to imagine it."

Then I realized the truth: there would be no admiration. I'd already tried to show him, and he had only thrown my notebook into a dead fire. What made me believe it would be any different now? He wanted me to forget my pain and disappointment. Such messy things they were, so hard to manage. They only reminded him that I was a flesh-and-blood woman, and not what he imagined me to be: the purest and most transcendent of inspirations, his fantastical muse, who could exist only in his realm of poets.

But I was not that, and I could no longer pretend to be.

TWENTY-SEVEN

VANNI

I was in bed, awake and staring at the ceiling. I'd been thinking about her, of course, and so it seemed no surprise when I heard her tap on the door. Like Bayard, she didn't wait—of course not, why should anyone?—but cracked it open and peeked around the edge, bringing the glow of a candle with her.

"Oh! You're still abed." Disappointment. Restlessness. "Don't you mean to go out this morning?"

"You mean in the boat?"

"What else would I mean? Might I go with you?"

"I thought Estes didn't want you to go out with me anymore."

"No, he doesn't. But I don't care about that."

The elation I felt at that faded the next moment, when I recognized that strange exhilaration that had gripped her last night—but it had subtly changed. There was no rage or desperation today. It was still disquieting, but better than her sadness, at least, though that had not really disappeared.

I sat up, forgetting that I wore only drawers, and her gaze dipped shyly from my chest.

"Give me a minute to dress. I'll meet you downstairs."

She stepped back and closed the door, leaving me again in darkness.

I washed and dressed quickly, not taking the time to shave, as it took too long and I was impatient, though I did brush my hair until it shone—yes, very well, it was the vanity Bayard had called it—and then I hurried downstairs. She waited near the door.

"We're going to miss the sunrise," she complained as I lit the oil lamp and ushered her outside.

"We've plenty of time."

The ground was wet, the path slippery in places—clouds had moved in overnight; the air held a damp promise. I took her arm in several spots to help her, and she didn't pull away—which I found encouraging, though I knew I shouldn't. A few birds twittered from the branches overhead, but the lake felt quieter than usual this morning, heavier.

"I suppose it might not be the best morning for it," she said, looking up at the sky. "Do you mind the rain?"

I might have braved a storm to sit with her in that boat this morning. "Not the least bit. It's not raining anyway. Not yet."

I flipped the boat and pushed it into the water, holding it for her. The only sign of last night's destroyed lanterns was a candle stub lodged between the rocks, which she didn't seem to notice. She settled into the bow like a queen, and I rowed us out—not much conversation, given my back was to her—and when we reached my favorite spot, I banked the oars and let us float, turning in the seat to face her. She had leaned back, her arms resting languidly on the sides, staring up at the sky and looking like that Millais painting of Ophelia, though there was no vacancy in her eyes, and no helpless toss of her pale hands. In fact, she looked so alive it was a wonder that I'd compared her in any way to a dead woman—then I realized that there was a reason I had, that there had been something dead in Adelaide Wentworth until this morning, but it was gone now, and the difference was startling.

It had to do with last night, perhaps, where she'd been overexcited and a bit untethered. Something—or someone—had changed her. I remembered with a pang that Bayard had returned from their stroll whistling.

"What is it?" she asked, her gaze returning to me.

I nodded toward the horizon. "The sunrise."

She sat up, twisting to see the glow, not a blazing light as it had been last time I'd taken her out, and not spreading golden, but instead only a dark gray sky lightening. The blue of the mountainsides was broken by foggy wisps, gray fog, white streaks of snow. The water was slate. The scene was beautiful but lonely, and I felt again as I had last night, staring into darkness, as if I were some minor character in a story not my own. A fiction.

Again, I thought of Bayard asking her to walk with him. I told myself to say nothing of it. Instead, I blurted, "I suppose I have to thank you."

She turned again to look at me. "For what?"

"For convincing Bayard to keep me. He said you'd asked him very prettily." I could not keep the jealousy from my voice, because what he'd also said was that we'd all tried his patience beyond endurance, and he had half a mind to put us on a train and send us out of his life—except possibly for Adelaide. *Do you suppose it's much different making love to a murderess?* And then, to my strained reply that she'd never been charged, *"Yes, but it makes her more interesting, and they owe me something for putting up with them, don't you think?"*

I never knew how serious he was about anything, but that he was capable of returning their many embarrassments by cuckolding Julian, whom he'd made his friend, I had no doubt. He'd never failed to seduce a woman he'd set out to woo, and I'd seen Adelaide's admiration for him and remembered the way they'd smiled at each other at the hotel in Villeneuve before Louisa had told that terrible story.

"How did you meet Bayard?" Adelaide asked.

I'd heard this before. This oh-so-casual interest that was really meant to discover something of him. Resentfully, I said, "I'd heard he was looking for a secretary, and I wrote for an interview. He wrote back to say that my qualifications intrigued him. We met and he hired me."

"That's an odd thing to say, don't you think? That your qualifications intrigue. How so?"

"I had languages—French and Italian—which he said he needed, as he planned to travel as soon as he got his affairs in order. He liked the idea that I'd been schooled in a monastery. He said the Catholics either raised brilliant minds or destroyed them completely, and he was curious as to which mine was."

"Did he discover which?"

It was a moment before I realized she was teasing. "Well, I'm assuming he didn't think it destroyed, though I'm not entirely sure. He likes the idea of his own generosity. I suppose it just as possible that he thought to repair me."

She smiled, and I forgot my resentment in the impulse to tell her everything I'd ever thought or wished for.

"In any case, I also told him that I wanted to be a writer, and I hoped to learn from him. I suppose that was the most important thing. Again . . . appealing to his generosity. I'd gone to his publisher with a collection of my stories. That's where I saw Bayard's notice for a secretary. I hadn't been able to get an appointment so I slept on the stoop to be there before anyone else the next morning, and Hanson told Bayard that I had initiative—actually, what he said was that it might also be blind, stupid obstinance—but that my work showed some talent, and so . . ."

"You really stayed there overnight?"

I nodded. "In the rain. But I was desperate by then. I must have looked like a derelict. I think he only let me in because he was afraid I would die on his stoop—not good for business."

"Why were you desperate?"

The litany wound through my head. Three lost jobs over my temper and no references forthcoming; poetry rejected, stories not good enough; my father's cheerful hopes and unfathomable faith, and every day moving closer to admitting that I could not be what he expected me to be, nor what I wanted myself. Unable to face the humiliation of returning home to meet a bleak future, of admitting failure and seeing my father's disappointment as I took up my childhood jobs of cutting leather, sewing, hammering, fingers bleeding, and now and again a visit upstairs to Mrs. Leporello and her sad eyes as she took me to bed. *"Oh, Gio-Gio, to see you like this . . ."* No, I could not do it.

But it turned out that the uncomfortable, wretched night in the rain had been the best thing I could have done. Otherwise, someone else would have come before me and taken the job, and Hanson's reluctant admiration for my persistence would not have bought me anything. I would not have met Bayard or seen him laughing at Hanson's words. *"Obstinate, eh? Well, I could use a secretary with some obstinance."*

I was fairly sure he regretted that now.

Adelaide waited for my answer; it took me a moment to remember what she'd asked. "I was going to have to return home to my father. I couldn't face the fact that I'd failed. I can't . . . I can't fail again."

"You are very proud," she said plainly, *it is as it is.* Not the way Bayard said it, as if it were a terrible fault.

"I don't like to disappoint."

"Yes, I can see that. I know what that feels like." She gazed out over the water. Her skin was dewy from the mist; it silvered her hair like a veil. "But perhaps you should not care so much about disappointing,

Vanni. I can see it in your writing, you know. You want to please every-one, but you can't. You should please only yourself."

"Is that what you were doing last night?" I asked. "Pleasing your-self? Is that what the paper lanterns were?"

A frown of surprise. "Was it that obvious?"

"Didn't you mean for it to be?"

"Yes, I suppose I did." She sighed. "Do you think as the gossips do? That we are a . . . ménage à trois?"

I felt the danger in her words. "Why do you ask?"

"Don't tell me what you think will please me. Tell me what you really think."

"I think the gossip holds some truth," I said.

She nodded shortly—not an admission, only an acknowledgment. "Bayard has no more patience for us. Does he mean to throw Louisa over?"

"He throws over everyone eventually." It was the most warning I could bring myself to make, and it wasn't just about Louisa.

"Do you ever wonder what life could be if you simply did what you wanted and cared nothing for anyone else?"

"No. Or at least not since I was a child." What I wanted was too tied up with what everyone else wanted for me. Success. Recognition. I could not say, *if not for my father, I would do that.* There was nothing in his hopes for me that I did not hope myself.

"How lucky you are." It was spoken on a whisper. "There are days when I want nothing more than to be away. To just fly to someplace no one could find me."

"Why don't you?" I asked. "Leave Louisa and Estes behind and do what you wish?"

"I can't." It was so starkly said that it jarred me.

"You can't say something like that and expect me just to ignore it."

She seemed to glow in the opalescence. Her eyes were darker than her sister's, deeper and more silent.

"Why can't you leave, Adelaide?" I probed.

She sighed again, deeply, and let it fall into nothing, where I thought it would stay. I had been wrong to think that she might trust me enough to share. Suddenly I did not want to be out here another moment. I reached for the oars. "Well—"

"My father expected Louisa and me to win suffrage for women, write the novel that would prove American superiority in literature, establish Fourierian phalanxes throughout the world, and be shining examples of the perfect unions made possible by Free Love. That was when he was sane."

I laughed. I thought she was joking.

She did not even smile. "It was only the start of what he wanted from us. He believed we were goddesses who had been sent to earth to save humanity. Of course, he was quite mad when he believed that, but he wasn't so all the time. Julian never saw him that way. Father was in one of his calmer periods during Julian's visit. But two weeks before Jules arrived, Father had been convinced we could fly and he tried to throw Louisa out the second-story window to prove it." She spoke matter-of-factly. "Julian thinks we have mistaken everything. It could not have been what we thought."

I did not know how to react.

She went on. "My father was brilliant once. You would have found him fascinating. Everyone did. When I met Jules, he seemed to embody all my father's ideals. He too thinks a better world is possible, and he means to make it happen. When he said I inspired him, and he couldn't write without me, how could I have walked away?"

"But what has he achieved, really?" I asked. "He's gone about it all wrong. You know you'll never be anything but pariahs. The world's not ready for him. Perhaps it never will be."

"You couldn't possibly understand."

That stung. "No, of course not."

"It's only that it's very complicated. Even I don't see it fully. You see, I believed as Julian did, and I loved him. I thought our love could endure anything. But it seems it cannot withstand hypocrisy."

"Whose hypocrisy?" I asked.

"Everyone's. That's what I didn't expect. My father was furious when we ran off, in spite of all his talk. Julian refused to admit his responsibility for his wife. Even I am not so pure of heart as I wish to be. Life in the world is harder than it was in Concord, and ideals don't pay the bills, do they? But still I don't regret leaving. What I regret is bringing Louisa with us." The words came out in a rush, as if by saying them quickly enough she could pretend they hadn't been said. "But how could I leave her behind with a father who meant to teach her to fly?"

"She wasn't a child," I suggested quietly. "I rather think Louisa could have managed it."

"You don't know her as I do," she said. "She needs me. She can't manage anything."

That was not the Louisa Wentworth I knew. She managed this household, didn't she? She corralled us all and made us dance: Adelaide, Estes, even Bayard. And me. Especially me.

Adelaide went on, "It would have been better for both of us if I had. But I couldn't bear that she might be imprisoned the way I had been, and yet she was my prison. I just didn't see it then."

"She hasn't got you locked in a cell, Adelaide," I said. "Just walk away."

"Julian would never permit it, and it's too late now. She can't go back to Concord; our family has disowned us both. Julian hasn't enough money to support her separately."

"Marry her off," I suggested.

"Are you offering?"

I recoiled.

327

"You see?" she said. "I expect Bayard would find the idea just as appealing. Louisa would never chain herself anyway. She would think it a betrayal of principle, and Julian would agree. She listens to everything he says."

The despair I saw in her surprised me; it seemed too much for this, but even so, I sensed it was only the start of something else, a darker shadow that perhaps I did not want to peer into. Like standing on a city street, hearing shouts, a crash, on the next block. The choice: Do I run toward it? Or away?

I leaned closer, unable to keep my distance. "Listen, Adelaide, Estes is your solution then, isn't he? Leave her with him." Given what I'd seen, I doubted he would be devastated. "Leave them both."

"I've told you—there's not enough money. We had bailiffs coming after us in London. There's nowhere to go, and Julian needs me so much. He—"

"Bayard will help. I know he will. I will too."

"You?" Her smile was faintly condescending. "How can you help?"

I couldn't, of course. I had nothing. "However I can."

"You're very kind."

"I only wish for you to be happy."

"Well," she said. "We have another few weeks. It's more than I'd thought to have. I hope it's enough time to finish my story. I should hate to miss the deadline."

I said nothing to that, afraid of myself, of how intensely I felt, of what I might reveal if we continued the conversation. Quiet surrounded us. The clouds had descended—or perhaps it was just that the mist had grown heavier—and their weight tamped everything into peacefulness: the lake, the boat, even the mountains were easy and calm, their wild and untamed peaks hidden from view.

She said, "Just now it seems that there could be nothing in the world to hurt, doesn't it?"

I was surprised at how well she'd read my thoughts. "Yes. That's exactly how it seems."

Her sigh seemed to settle in the mist, in my chest. "If only it were true."

When we arrived back at the Diodati, Estes was waiting. We'd no sooner come up the stairs—both of us wet and bedraggled, because the mist had eventually turned to drizzle—than he was upon us.

"I thought I forbade you to go out in that boat with him."

Adelaide's hand went to her chin. I had not seen her scratch a single time on the boat, nor last night, either, I realized.

The thought of her doing so now enraged me. "What right have you to forbid her anything? You're not her father, nor her husband."

"This is between Adelaide and me," he snarled.

"Then perhaps you should not be assaulting her on the stairs, in my company." I took two steps toward him. "She has a right to go where she wants."

"Not when going where she wants puts her in danger."

"In danger? How is she in danger?"

"The boat could tip over, or get caught in the current. You haven't the skill to save her. You would drown her with your own incompetence. If she wants to go out, I'll take her."

"You? I could row circles around you."

"I grew up on a lake." Estes pushed his face into mine. "I know boats. Were there any on the streets in Bethnal Green? I suppose you might have needed one, given how full the gutters are with sewage."

I would have thrown myself at him if she hadn't grabbed my arm, holding me back. "This is not Mr. Calina's fault. I asked him to take me out this morning."

Estes's anger changed to disbelief. "You did what? Did you not remember our conversation?"

"I remembered it perfectly. But I wanted to go out on the lake, and as you can see, I'm fine."

"You're soaking wet. You'll catch pneumonia."

"Oh, now you decide to worry over her," I said.

Estes went rigid.

Her fingers bit into my arm so hard that I hissed at the pain.

"Perhaps you should see if Bayard has need of you this morning," she suggested.

When I resisted, she gave me a little push.

"Go," she said.

I acquiesced.

Estes said, "You can be her pretty servant all you like, Calina, but it will do you no good. She'll never love you."

"Jules!" she gasped. "That's enough!"

His sneering laugh followed me down the hall. "She'll never love you, because it's me she loves, and she always will."

She had seen a messiah in Estes. She had loved him, and she claimed he needed her inspiration still. Lunatic, divine poet, changer of worlds—and what was I? A secretary. Nothing. My temper was appalling. I had failed at everything I'd tried. I was too proud—she'd said it, hadn't she? It had not been a compliment. Whatever brilliance she saw in my story was not my own, but only borrowed, a pastiche. Why should she look to me for anything? What did I have to offer?

It had been a mistake to fall in love with her, but I didn't have to surrender to it. I would focus instead on my ambitions. Bayard's respect. A successful writing career. My father's pride. What was love compared to all that? Desire was easy enough to appease—there was still Vera

Brest, wasn't there? She had said she was waiting for me. Longing for me—*for Bayard's story.* She would write to me soon and tell me to come to her, and I would go, and this time there would be no hesitations. This time, I would take what I wanted and forget Adelaide.

As if on cue, the next morning's knock on my door came not from her or Bayard, but Louisa, who handed me a letter. "From your *love.* Though really, I can't see why you like her. She's so old."

"I prefer older women," I said. "They're less trouble."

"You mean they're desperate," she said.

I tried to close the door.

She put her foot in the way and pushed it open again, stepping inside. She looked around. "A maid's room. How appropriate."

"If you're only here to torment me—"

"Adelaide left our family—she left everything—for Julian. They were going to have a child—what, didn't she tell you? Well, you mustn't feel bad. She hardly tells anyone. It nearly destroyed her when she lost it. She wanted—wants—Julian's baby more than anything."

The sadness I'd seen in her. All her talk of death last night. Of spirits searching for those they'd left behind. Of the regrets I'd seen in her story and things I "couldn't possibly understand."

Louisa stepped to the door again—thank God—pausing with her hand on the knob. "She's just playing at you, Vanni, don't you see? To her you're like some . . . some faultless imaginary friend. She doesn't think of you as real, and when we leave Geneva, she won't think of you again."

She slipped out, leaving the door open behind her. I shut it quietly, leaning back against it, the letter from Vera Brest still in my hand.

Louisa's taunt had hit its mark, as usual. It only made it more imperative that I forget about Adelaide and the things I shouldn't want and couldn't have.

I looked down at the letter. I willed myself to be curious as to what it said, to remember Vera Brest's kiss. The taste of champagne, the feel of her breasts pressing to my chest—yes, I could do this. I could put Adelaide behind me—call it a temporary madness, a brief lapse in judgment, as had been her sister. I could turn the Wentworth sisters into near misses, thankfully in the past.

Reassured, I broke the seal and unfolded the letter.

> *My darling Giovanni,*
> *Today my husband announced that he will be leaving next week. I am to stay, as Madame Orsini is still in need of my comfort. I do hope Mr. Sonnier's story is done. Patience, my darling. We will be together again very soon. I wish so to kiss you.*
> *Your Vera*

I felt . . . nothing. It seemed the words reordered themselves in my head; I recognized them for what they were—a tantalizing promise meant to ensnare me. I was only an added bonus to what she really wanted: Bayard Sonnier's story. There would be no turning to Vera Brest for forgetfulness. There would be no turning to anyone. My resolutions were a mockery. Any hope of salvation had passed before I'd known to reach for it.

TWENTY-EIGHT

ADELAIDE

Louisa brought me a bouquet of lilies made of paper, petals delicately arched from scraping the paper over a darning ball. It had taken her hours, but what else had she to do? She wasn't writing, and while Bayard had taken her back into his bed, it was with an infrequency and lack of enthusiasm that left her often wandering aimlessly about the villa. *Do you still love me?* her gift asked, proffered with a trembling hand and a gaze that searched mine for reassurance.

"I wish I had paints. I would have colored them for you," she said as I took them. My acceptance was usually enough to relieve her guilt, but this time, she still seemed troubled. "I feel I hardly know you lately. It reminds me of . . ."

"Of what?"

"Of when you fell in love with Jules," she said. "You haven't . . . nothing's changed, has it, Addie?"

"Of course not," I told her.

But I wasn't going to tell her that something had. I said nothing of my story. Our history had taught me to be guarded.

When I was ten, my father had taken me with him to Boston, where he was lecturing, and I'd seen a dollhouse in a store window. I'd fallen in love with its gabled roof made of perfect, tiny shingles, its square bay window and fanlights of colored glass. I dreamed of furnishing it with miniature sideboards and armoires, of knitting bedcovers for little beds, embroidering carpets for its floors.

Unbeknownst to me, my father spent weeks building a copy of it. At Christmas, it was sitting at the hearth, tied with a satin bow, with a tag that read: *To my beloved daughters.* Not *daughter.* Not me alone. Louisa had clapped her hands and exclaimed, *"Oh, how we shall decorate it, Addie!"* but my disappointment at having to share it was crushing. I saw my father's hurt when I disdained it, but I could not make myself do otherwise. The dollhouse was relegated to a storeroom. Louisa lost interest in it the moment she saw I had none.

At fourteen, I'd found Byron. I'd fallen in love the way only a romantic girl can, carrying a book of his poems with me everywhere, dreaming of him. And then, one day, Louisa came upon me where I sat by the pond reading, and said dreamily, *"I do think* Childe Harold *the best poem ever written, don't you? It is so unbearably lovely!"*

And then, at twenty, there had been Julian.

If I were honest, I would say I'd known what would happen before we left Concord. One afternoon, I went to meet Julian in the yard, and Louisa was already there. They were laughing, and they looked so lovely there in the filtered sunlight, which shone through Louisa's skirts and turned Julian's hair into floss, that I'd stood in a daze to watch them. Louisa's eyes had been luminous. She had looked at Julian with such affection, and when he turned to her, I saw the flash of desire.

There was nothing vicious in it, I knew. It was only that she loved me so completely, and needed me so desperately, that she could not bear that any part of my life might be separate from hers. Louisa's mind was so untrammeled and variable. I knew it was only that she wanted to attach herself to the steadiness of mine.

But it was also why I kept the fact of my story to myself.

She was not the only one who noticed something in me had changed. Over the next days, Julian watched me and worried. He was cautiously affectionate. I felt him measuring everything, wondering if he should touch me, or kiss me, peppering the hours with little things to call me back. *"Do you remember when we laughed over that bullfrog at the lake?"* *"I was thinking of the dance at Gansevoort's when we sneaked out to look at the stars."* *"I know the moment I fell in love with you—we were sitting on the porch, do you remember? You laughed at how many gnats were in the lemonade."*

A hundred years ago, a past that was so far in the past, so colored by everything that had happened since that it seemed I saw it through a scrim, blurred and indistinct. It was my story, but it flitted in and out of my grasp; I could not quite make the memory settle enough to see it clearly.

But I said none of this to Julian. I crept out every morning before he woke. I went to my story, to Vanni, and we either went out on the boat or stayed in his room. I wrote feverishly and so did he, but we no longer spoke of the deadline. It was fraught with too much else, not just the competition now, but the day we were to leave, and to acknowledge it meant to answer the questions *Where will we go? What will we do?* I no longer believed I would finish in time, but it didn't matter. With every day I worked, I felt I was taking form, becoming more solid, no longer an extension of my father, or Louisa, or Julian. I was becoming separate, writing myself into being with every word.

"It's going away," Vanni said one morning, tapping his chin in explanation. "Your skin. It's healing."

"I told you it comes and goes." It was not quite true. I'd never had the condition as a child, and I'd been scratching constantly since Emily and Venice. It startled me to realize how used to it I'd become; I hadn't noticed that it had abated.

"I think it might be gone for good this time."

"When did you become a fortune-teller?"

"I don't need to be a fortune-teller to see that you're happier," he said.

"I feel I can breathe," I told him. "In this room, there's plenty of space."

"It's the smallest room in the house," he objected with a laugh.

I smiled back at him. "But it feels so much bigger when we're here together." Because it wasn't just Vanni and me in the room, it was our stories too, not just the ones we were writing, but the ones that existed still for us to write. The room felt like entire worlds. It felt like possibility. I felt also its fragility. It was of the purest color, even the hint of another would spoil it.

"Yes," he said. "I know just what you mean."

How strange to feel such an affinity with him, and one that was so untainted and easy. I had never known anything like it.

Julian never asked where I'd been. When I returned in the late morning, he was usually bent over his manuscript, his frustration evident, or he was at the window, clasping his flask. He no longer made any attempt to excuse it. I hated that he relied on it, and wondered that it had not caused more night terrors, though his sleep had become so restless I expected them. He had obviously purchased more of the drug; he would have no trouble finding it. Cologny was only over the hill, and Geneva not far. But as for the cost . . .

"We'll have to go soon," I said to him. "Will there be any money left when we do?"

He gave me a glassy stare. "If we're very frugal, and my father doesn't cut off my allowance."

I could not help thinking of those last months in London, when that meager allowance had not been enough to keep us from bailiffs or beggary.

"I will always take care of you, Adelaide. You should not doubt that."

But he had not taken care of Emily, had he?

"It will all come right," Louisa assured me the next morning as she looked to where he stood at the edge of the lawn, staring out at the clouds gathering over the mountains. "He's been blocked before, and you have always brought him round."

But I felt her anxious scrutiny too, and that night, as we all sat talking and drinking wine in the salon, it became unbearable. I wandered out onto the terrace. Bayard's gaze followed me, and I thought he might call me back, but then he only reached for the wine and let me go without comment. I felt Vanni watching me as well, and Julian. All of them, noting. Louisa, noting.

The day had been overcast, and a snow-scented wind had swept from the mountains to blow the clouds about, so that the dark of the sky split now and again to reveal a deeper blue spangled with stars, a tease. *Here is a gift for you, ah no! Not yet!*

When I heard the footsteps behind me, I turned eagerly, thinking it was Vanni.

But it wasn't Vanni, it was Bayard.

He came up to the railing beside me. "Is something wrong?"

"What could be wrong?"

"I don't know. You've seemed anxious all night." He took a sip of his wine as he contemplated the view. "You've been spending a great deal of time with Vanni."

I wasn't certain what I heard in his words. "So I have."

"Julian seems . . . troubled by it."

"Julian makes whatever friends he likes whenever he wants. He has no right to be upset if I do the same." It came out more bitterly than I'd intended. I saw the quick flare of interest in Bayard's eyes.

Louisa came onto the terrace, looking uncertain, trying to smile. "What are the two of you doing out here? Bay? Come back inside. I miss you."

He waved her away. "In a moment."

"Then I shall come and join you."

He said nothing, but even I felt the iciness of his unspoken *go away*. My sister faltered; her smile fell. She spun on her heel without another word, but I felt her hurt and her rage from where I stood, and I knew she wanted me to follow her, to give Bayard no reason to stay out here, to bring him back to her. I didn't move. Instead I said, "She cannot like that."

"I don't give a damn what she likes or doesn't like."

"You must be counting the days until we leave you in peace."

He only said, "Hmmm." Then, "Julian once said to me that he thought you and Louisa together the perfect woman."

It was not what I'd expected him to say, and it took a moment to understand. His words should not have hurt. That Julian felt so was certainly no surprise.

"I think he's wrong," Bayard said quietly. "Louisa makes the world believe she's the interesting one, but I've come to realize that it's really you. You're the fascination."

"I'm hardly—"

"You are." His hand edged closer to mine on the railing until our fingers brushed. Again, I felt the breathless thrill of his attention. Bayard Sonnier, looking at me, talking to me, saying these things. I realized with a little shock that he was offering me a chance to stay, that he was offering himself. But for how long, and what would it cost me in the end with Julian and Louisa? While my sister might be able to betray me this way, I could not do the same.

I drew gently away. "How flattering."

His eyes were very intent; I could not see their color, only the glint of them in the reflected light. "You're extraordinary, Adelaide. I would never take you for granted."

His implication was clear. *As Julian does.*

"Even the extraordinary becomes ordinary in time."

"Not always," he argued. "Some things never cease to amaze. Like a sunset."

I laughed. "I am no sunset. You would grow tired of me. You know you would. You're too easily bored. You're always searching for distraction."

"Like a magpie." He laughed shortly. "Ah, I fear you know me too well. Or perhaps I've lost my touch at seduction."

"You haven't lost your touch."

"But you are immune to it."

"Not immune. Just, there's Julian. And Louisa. I cannot forget about them. Nor should you."

He sighed, and then held out his arm for me to take. "Should we go back inside? I think we should not leave the three of them alone together for long. They might join forces, and then God knows what would happen."

I laughed again. But there were only two now in the salon. Vanni was nowhere to be seen. Julian and Louisa were on the settee, and she was clinging to him, weeping prettily into his chest. Julian looked up, his pale eyes flashing.

"What the hell did you say to her?" he demanded of Bayard, who stiffened.

Louisa always got what she wanted, after all.

I asked, "Where is Mr. Calina?"

"What does he matter, when your sister is so upset?"

"Louisa is always upset." I sat in the chair across and poured a glass of wine.

"What required such privacy that you would tell her to leave?" Julian's voice held the ugly twist of jealousy.

"I wanted a moment away from her, that's all," Bayard said bluntly. "Must she be in my company every moment?"

Louisa lifted her tear-stained face. "How can you say such things to me?"

"I've told you before that I'm no prancing monkey for your entertainment."

"Do you see that?" she asked Julian. "Now do you understand? Do you see how cruel he can be to one who loves him?"

"Christ. I only wanted a moment to myself."

"You weren't by yourself! You were with Adelaide!"

Bayard made a sound of frustration and strode from the room. Louisa wrenched herself from Julian's arms to race after him. "Bayard! Bayard, do not walk away from me!"

I sipped my wine.

Julian said, "What did he say to her?"

"Nothing."

"She said he wanted to be alone with you."

"If he did, I had nothing to do with it, Jules," I said wearily. "The man only wants some peace. Can you blame him?"

Down the hall, the bedroom door slammed shut, opened again, slammed again. Louisa shouted, and then Bayard, words I tried not to hear.

"No doubt he thinks to find it with you," Julian said. "He and his cursed secretary both."

"A rather different ménage than you're used to." I wasn't certain why I said it, but once I did, I didn't apologize or take it back. I could placate no more tonight. I wondered if I ever could again.

Julian's expression turned thunderous. "So you don't deny it?"

"What would you like me to deny, Julian?"

"That you're having an affair with Calina. And with Bayard."

"Both at once? How brave you think me!"

"What's wrong with you, Adelaide? Why are you behaving this way?" His bewilderment nearly made me laugh.

"You have made a foul accusation. How else should I be?"

"You're not denying it."

"Because you're absurd to suggest it." I put my wineglass on the tea table and rose. "We'll be leaving soon. You won't have to worry about Bayard when we're starving in some ratty boardinghouse."

He got to his feet as well, grabbing my arm before I could pass him. "It is Calina, isn't it? He wants you. I see it when he looks at you."

I jerked my arm free. "You will destroy everything with your selfishness and your blindness, Jules. Perhaps you might think of that."

He stepped back, stunned and speechless, diminished; all those honorable, beautiful things I'd once seen in him shrinking, and I felt both remorse that I should see him thus and guilt for my part in it. I fled downstairs, which was dark, the only light coming from the kitchen, and I followed the beacon of it.

Vanni was there, sitting at the table with another bottle of wine, his head in his hands, so his face was hidden, his shoulders slumped. It was as if he'd been conjured just for me, as if whatever played at being God *(God in the table, God in the lamp oil, God in the wine)* had heard my thoughts and set him there.

He looked up. I saw the leap of joy in his eyes, then it shuttered. What started as a smile slipped away. He glanced past me. "Where's Bayard?"

"Can't you hear him? He and Louisa are fighting."

"What about Estes?"

"Jealous. Brooding." I sat across from him and took his glass and a sip of his wine. "No one, it seems, was happy that Bayard and I were alone on the terrace."

He laughed shortly and rather bitterly. "No."

"I have come in search of a reasonable man." I took another sip before I pushed the glass back to him.

"And you think you've found him in me? I have been accused of many things, but never of being reasonable."

"I suppose that at some point we all become something we're not. Believe me, compared to those upstairs, you are the very picture of rationality."

He pulled the glass toward him, and stared into the wine. "Bayard finds you intriguing."

"It's only that he's bored."

"Most women find him irresistible."

"As do I, I'm afraid."

Vanni reached for the bottle.

"He's Bayard Sonnier, after all. I've never met anyone who was so exactly as gossip describes."

"I suppose there's something to be said for becoming the muse to a genius."

"That's what he would make me," I agreed. "It's funny, how essential that used to feel. His work is so important, and Julian's too, and when one measures things, perhaps that's what matters. I've no illusions that my own work is so worthy. Perhaps I'm only being selfish."

Vanni splashed wine into the glass. He was clumsy with tension. I wondered why, and then I wondered why he'd come down here to the kitchen. Certainly not for my pleasure, regardless of my imaginings. Something troubled him. Before I could ask, he said, "Perhaps you are. But how do we know? By whose ruler do we measure?"

"Anyone's, I suppose. One can't deny that Julian's poems are significant. Or that Bayard's stories are popular, and moving. When Louisa and I read *The Temptation*, our lives seemed so paltry next to it. It made us both want to be something more. Just as Julian's poems did."

"When I was young, my closest friend was Anthony Leporello. He lived upstairs, and one day we were in his kitchen and there was a *Bentley's Miscellany* on the table. Even now I can remember how fascinating I found it. Why, I don't know. I was only five or six. I couldn't read it. When his mother saw my interest, she read us one of the stories in it, about a girl dressing as a boy and fighting bandits . . . I don't remember the name of it, or really anything else. But I knew that I wanted to do that."

"Dress as a boy and fight bandits?" I teased.

He smiled. "Write stories. But really, my point is this: Mrs. Leporello told my father about it, and he decided to send me to school. That story changed my life. I don't think we can truly know the impact we might have on anyone."

"But it didn't change the world the way Julian's poems will change it. It only changed you."

"Yes, well, I suppose it's a matter of perspective. Perhaps one day I will be worth the paper it was printed on. Or perhaps not." He raised his glass in a mock toast. "As I said, we can't know."

I said quietly, "You're worth far more than that to me. If not for you, I wouldn't have written my story at all. I'd still be happy as Julian's muse."

"I would argue that you weren't happy," he said. "And frankly, I don't think you were that good a muse."

"I inspired 'Cain in the Garden.'"

"A poem that's been banned or reviled by nearly everyone who's read it."

"Eventually, they'll understand. They'll see the truth in it."

"Or not." His smile now was thoughtful. "But if you've come down here to ask me if I think you should be Bayard's inspiration, I'm going to say no. I don't think you should be anyone's muse but your own."

"It's good to know there's at least one person in the world who only thinks of what's best for me, and not how I can avail them."

His smile died. "You shouldn't be so sure."

"Why shouldn't I?"

"Perhaps I have my own motives. Perhaps I want something from you too."

"What would that be? My hairbrush? A bracelet to drape from your watch chain?"

He laughed, but it was rueful. "I suppose I deserve that."

"Don't try to pretend you're selfish. I know you're not." I took his glass again, drinking deeply. "Why are you here in the kitchen, anyway? I hope it wasn't because you wanted to be alone."

"I did want to be alone. I was angry."

"Why? Did Jules say something? Or Louisa?"

A shake of his head.

"Then what?"

"Nothing," he said. "It turns out it was nothing."

"So you're not annoyed that I found you?"

"No." He glanced away as if struck by an emotion he could not hold. "Not at all."

"I'm glad. You're the closest friend I have, Vanni. More than that, really. You're almost, well, like a brother, I suppose."

"A brother?" he repeated.

"Yes, and I hope you feel I'm a sister to you."

He let out a breath. "Perhaps not that. Sisters seem to be problematic in your family."

He seemed troubled still; I did not want him to be. His hand was half curled, and I touched his knuckles, urging it flat, pressing mine over. "Very well, not a sister. But a friend."

He stared down at our hands for a long moment. "Yes," he said. "A friend."

TWENTY-NINE

VANNI

She thought of me as a brother, and I was so in love with her I did not know how she did not feel it too, or how my burning longing when we sat so closely in my room, my foot nudging hers, her skirts brushing my ankle, did not set her aflame. Our intimacy in the boat—which seemed not only to defy the vast expanse of the mountains, but to contain them—was only friendship to her. I alone was helpless with love and yearning, desperate with jealousy. Compared to Bayard and Estes, I was nothing; I hardly existed. What had Louisa said? That I was Adelaide's imaginary friend. This idea that she might love me was as big an illusion as my dreams of fame and recognition.

I went to my room—the shouting between Louisa and Bayard had stopped, but now there were other sounds, even more unbearable given my frustration. There were Bayard's pages on my desk, half-copied—I'd been working diligently since he'd shared my job with Louisa. But instead, I unlocked my desk drawer, taking out my story. As I did every day, I considered the banknotes and the journal with most, but not all, of its pages still blank, and fought guilt and shame and the press of obligation. As every day, I closed the drawer and tried to forget about them. I would have to manage the problem of Colburn eventually, but for now, I was looking for solace, and so I tried to lose myself in the story, but I kept thinking about Bayard following Adelaide onto the balcony, Estes's obvious simmering, Louisa's piquant tears when she returned that I could not stay to watch—what had she seen? What had Bayard said? And what was happening upstairs now? Was Adelaide in bed with Estes? Had his jealousy made him passionate? Apologetic? Was he kissing her? Was he—? I jabbed my pen so hard into the paper that I tore a hole in the page.

I didn't sleep well, which wasn't unusual lately, and when I did, my dreams were erotic, tangled with Adelaide, and sometimes with Louisa and even Bayard, my guilt and yearning and ambition manifest—the mind is a truly torturous thing. When I woke to the sound of shouting and crashing, I thought at first that Estes was having night terrors again. Then I realized that Bayard and Louisa were still fighting.

Something crashed against the wall between our rooms so hard it shuddered. Louisa screamed—a sound I'd heard before, curdled, aborted rage—and shouted, "I will leave here and forget you! I will never think of you again!"

"Go then!" he shouted back. "But you can't forget me. I've branded you—just as I have all the others. You won't forget me, and no one will ever let you forget!"

Another scream, a thudding crash against the wall that made me flinch.

I got out of bed and pulled on my shirt, knowing that Adelaide would not come down to me this morning. Everyone in the house must hear this. Her notebook was on my desk, and I put it aside with regret and again pulled out the pages of my story—*yes, mine now*. How often must I say it before I believed it? While I had no intention of presenting it for the contest—how could I?—the deadline had prodded and pushed me so that it was nearing an end; it required only another scene or two and then the tragic close.

But the deadline now was a double-edged sword. I could not forget that it signaled her departure—unless, of course, Bayard succeeded in seducing her. It seemed too great a cost for the privilege of keeping her here, but would I rather she was gone from my life forever?

I could not bear thinking of it. I bent again to my story, and soon I was in my fever dream of a world, my alpine wood, my sisters whose fates were intertwined with the man who had climbed to the Mer de Glace expecting to find the sublimity of nature and found instead a mysterious shack filled with herbs and dried things and doppelgängers who both loved and hated one another, and his stumbling upon them would lead to his luckless ruin.

I wrote until the quiet roused me—too quiet; had Bayard and Louisa finally killed each other? I supposed I should face the morning and find out—and yes, I could not deny that Adelaide was the real draw, my pathetic wish to see her smile and my ridiculously fatal hope that I might somehow prevail, because, of course, how could I not win a contest where the main competition was two men she was convinced could change the world—*and no mention of you on that list, was there?*

I stepped cautiously into the hall. No one. The house felt silent and still, but I heard a noise in the salon, and instead of ignoring it, as I should, I stopped to look. It was Louisa, sitting listlessly on the settee, fully dressed, but her hair hastily and messily put up, her eyes red and her face swollen from crying.

"Forgive me," I said, dodging away as quickly as I could. "I didn't mean to disturb—"

"You do disturb me," she said bitterly. "Everything about you disturbs me."

"Then I won't torment you further."

"You told him, didn't you?" Her words stopped me before I got a step. "You told Bay what you saw."

Her calm enmity felt somehow more dangerous than her screaming, but I didn't pretend to misunderstand. "I've said nothing to him."

"You're a liar."

"I wish I had. I wanted to. But I didn't want to hurt your sister."

"Oh no, no one must hurt Adelaide. She's perfect, isn't she? Why, everyone thinks so."

I said nothing.

"She's not perfect at all, you know. If Julian's wife were alive, she would tell you."

"What does that mean?"

Louisa's smile was thin and knowing. "Adelaide's immoveable. Like . . . like the mountains. You should remember that, Vanni, for your own good. You can't get over or through or around once she decides something. And she does it in such a quiet way that you don't see it until it's too late. Why, she's so *reasonable*. She's so *amenable*. Everyone loves her."

"Well, you're always throwing things."

She glowered at me. "There's ink all over the wall. It will be a pretty mess for you to clean, *Mr. Secretary*."

I winced.

"There's nothing that belongs only to me. Even Bayard wants her, and Julian always has, and . . . they see a life with her and all anyone wants from me are days here and there and I can't write poetry or do anything, and I'm afraid . . . I know what people think when they look at me—I'm not stupid." Her face crumpled. "Everything's ruined now. I wish we'd never come here."

I had seen Louisa Wentworth screaming and furious, radiant with joy, shaking with hysteria. But I had never before seen this in her, this quiet desperation that seemed more properly to belong to her sister, and the resemblance between them grew so strong it was as if Adelaide had superimposed herself onto Louisa, or vice versa. Again, as I had in the Torture Chamber at Chillon, I felt how inextricably they belonged to one another. Louisa wanted to be free of her sister, as Adelaide wished to be done with Louisa, but it was as if the future unwound itself before my eyes, and I saw their dependency as a curse that would prove eternal . . . no, never apart. *Never apart.*

I stood helplessly, uncertain what to say or what to do, and then—how to describe it?—horror came into Louisa's eyes, followed by anger, and then a searing contempt, one after another, *this, this, this,* and last was a cunning that filled me with apprehension.

And then . . . pain.

"Go away," she said. "Go away before I do something we will both regret."

I did not question her. I left.

I spent all afternoon trying to clean the ink from the wall. Bayard's bedroom was a mess, blankets and clothes thrown everywhere, wineglasses shattered, bottles spilling, papers and books scattered heedlessly on the floor, the pervasive stale, musky scent of sex. It looked like nothing so much as a sybarite's den, and Bayard lounged satyr-like on the settee and watched me with narrowed eyes as I scrubbed the wallpaper. I'd been doing so for what seemed like hours, staining my shirtsleeves and feeling like a servant boy, when it became clear that I'd made almost no difference and couldn't, and Bayard said, "You've only made it worse. You might as well be done with it."

"Gladly," I bit off. "Next time you might consider a more temperate lover."

"She says the same about you," he said nastily. "About your lack of temperance, I mean. She wants me to dismiss you. You dislike her, she dislikes you . . . I wonder who will win?"

I picked up my waistcoat from where I'd laid it over the back of the chair to keep from spoiling its green-and-blue embroidered splendor, and put it on again, arranging my watch chain.

Bayard said, "That's an expensive waistcoat for a cobbler's son. And how many jeweled things are on that fob?"

"If you have more pages—"

"Why don't you go out in the boat or something?" His voice rang with irritability and displeasure. "I'm tired of looking at you. But leave Adelaide behind."

"Why?" I asked, although of course I knew.

"Why do you think?"

"What of Estes?"

"You heard him that day at the hotel. The sisters together are the perfect woman. I'd like to see if it's true before they leave."

"Louisa will gut you."

"Gut me? Ah, there you go now, sounding like a street Arab. Who says things like that? Besides, who cares what Louisa thinks? In fact, perhaps I'll have them both at the same time."

"You should ask Estes how he does it. Though I suppose you managed Marie and her stepdaughter together, and that went so very well, didn't it?" *Well* as in "end of the world, civilizations collapsing."

Bayard leaped from the settee, stumbling in his rage. "Get out."

It wasn't until I was in the hall, the door safely closed behind me, that I remembered I was running out of chances with Bayard, and he was all I had.

I wrote like a madman. I buried my dreams and my longings in words. The story came together at a fevered pace, my own looming disaster becoming the hero's, my own tragic end presaged. When Adelaide came to my room, I knew I should tell her to go. Estes was angry. Bayard was angry. Louisa too. We were all tense as the deadline drew closer. What they would do, where they would go, who they would beg from next—no one spoke of the time passing, but the awareness of it, and their uncertainty, colored everything. Adelaide would be gone soon, and my love for her—and my desire—meant that I would do something stupid at the least provocation. Brother or not, sister or not, I yearned to touch her. My wanting seemed to permeate everything. I could taste it. I could smell it. *"You're worth far more to me . . ."* Hadn't she said that? What if she was afraid of hurting Estes? What if she was uncertain, and a word from me might make up her mind? I gathered my *what if*s like wildflowers; I held them in a loose bouquet, tearing off daisy petals—*she loves me, she loves me not.*

"Estes's grown suspicious," I told her—one last grab at self-preservation. "Louisa too."

"Of what?"

"Of the time we spend together. Perhaps . . ."

"Perhaps what?" She had been writing as she spoke, and now she looked up, her brown eyes frankly assessing. "I will not have my life dictated by irrational suspicion."

"Yes, but—"

"Do you want me to go?" she asked. "Do you want me to stop coming here?"

Say yes. "No."

A relieved sigh. "I am only myself when I'm with you, Vanni. If that's all that worries you, please don't let it. I don't want to stop."

How was I to take that, I ask you? How was I to pretend it was nothing? *Brotherly?* Was she so oblivious that she didn't see how it wrapped me about? Was she waiting for me to do something? Was she hinting that I should do so? Why wasn't I acting upon it? What was wrong with me that I didn't, no matter how I wanted it? Was I destined always to be the man who had hesitated to kiss Louisa Wentworth? Who had not been able to move at more than a snail's pace with Vera

Brest? Who had not recognized Mrs. Leporello's seduction for what it was until she stood naked before me?

I stayed up until two or three each night, writing, more like Bayard than I had ever been, understanding for the first time the pure flush of inspiration, the inability to stop despite exhaustion and pain, fingers cramping around the pen, my neck sore, eyes stinging and head pounding from the gathering stink of burning lamp oil. I finally finished the story at four o'clock in the morning, two days before the deadline. I'd made it, and I knew the story was good. The best thing I'd ever done, or perhaps might ever do. Such a feeling—tingling, sweating, joy and fear and hope all woven together, the urge to reread it, to assure myself that it was as good as I thought, to linger in the words again. I had never known anything like this. It got tied up in my love for Adelaide, the two things intricately linked, and in my excitement—unshaven, barely dressed—I paced, waiting for her. The hours before dawn, and then, yes, there, her footstep in the hall, soft and barely audible, but I'd grown used to waiting for it. A lover's clandestine step, soft as a hushed breath. The knock—no knock, only a clicking of fingernails, and she was through the door, inside, looking breathless and lovely, and I wanted to take hold of her, to profess my love and open her mouth with mine and kiss her until there was no thought left to have in the world.

Instead, I thrust my pages at her, grinning like a cretin. "I've finished."

Her eyes lit. "You have? Oh, I'll read it straightaway."

"Your own work—"

"That will wait. This is far more exciting." She settled herself in the chair and gave me a look of such expectation I had to look away. Then she read the first words. "Oh! You've dedicated it to me."

"It would not have been written without you." *Or Bayard*, but of course I didn't say that.

"It's such a lovely sentiment. I'm so very honored." Her hand to her breast, her brilliant smile, and I wondered if she'd seen the truth that lay beneath what I'd written. The urge to confess what I felt was nearly irresistible.

"I'll fetch us some tea." For the first time, I was glad that we had no maid, and I had an excuse to leave that room. There was too much, everything I wanted in those pages, in her. I hurried downstairs, barefoot on the cool parquet, the house breathing softly of the summer dawn. I took my time in the kitchen, trying to calm myself as I fired the stove and put the water on, pacing instead, to the door, to the window, back to the stove. I felt I could wait an eternity for her opinion; I felt I would perish if she didn't offer it *now*.

When the tea was done, I took it upstairs, spilling some on the floor, swiping it with my bare foot. She didn't look up when I came into the room, her head still bent over my pages, a long strand of hair coming loose from her pins to make a dark, sweeping S against the back of her creamy neck, leading my gaze over the stepping stones of her vertebrae, a kiss here and there and there . . . I tore my gaze away. I picked up my tea and sipped it, too hot, too sweet—when the hell had I put sugar in it?

I was trembling—what was I, a child? I could not breathe. The tea didn't suit; I put it down again. I wanted only to stare at that curl, that bended neck, her white skin above her scooped collar, really so chaste. Nothing vulgar in her, nothing coarse.

She turned the page. I glanced over her shoulder. The last. Everything in me gripped and tightened. Where was she now? The first paragraph? The end?

Then, her exhalation. A pause that held the whole of my soul in it. "Oh, Vanni." She put the pages on the desk and rose. There were tears in her eyes. "Oh, it is so very, very good."

Unbelievable, to feel this way, as if the world had burst into sudden bloom. I saw a brightness I had never known to look for. "You think so?"

A nod. She smiled as if she could not keep herself from doing so, and reached again for the pages, her bent neck, that long curl sweeping, dangling, trembling. "Let me see. When they are at Le Jardin. Oh, let me find it. It was so brilliant . . ." Shuffling through the pages. The curl quivering with her movement, tickling. She swiped back at it impatiently. It was as if she gave me permission.

"Let me," I whispered. She searched, turning one page after another. I twisted the curl about my finger, and then I tucked it into a pin, and then—

Don't.

—I bent, driven by need, by hunger, by joy and love . . . too many things to deny. I kissed the spot where her neck met her shoulder, lingering, the warmth of her skin, so very smooth. I traced the steps of her vertebra with my finger, the faintest brush of a touch. I felt her stiffen, and still I didn't stop, though I knew. *I knew.*

"You must know . . ." I managed; I could barely hear myself. "You must know how much I admire—"

"Vanni," she said, twisting to look at me, panic in her eyes. "Vanni, no, please—"

But I could not stop. My own disaster, so perfectly, neatly laid. No one's fault but mine.

THIRTY

ADELAIDE

I realized far too late what I should have already seen, what Louisa had told me was there, and Julian, but I had been so confident in my feelings for him that I had not really considered that his might be different.

I hardly knew what to say. "Vanni . . ."

"You don't love him. I know you don't." His earnestness hurt. There was such desperation in his eyes. "You'd be happier without him. With me."

"No, I—"

He took my hand, pressing my palm to his skin, because his shirt was gaping open. I felt his warmth, the hair on his chest, the race of his heart. I tried to draw away, but he held me fast. "You said I was worth something to you. You smile and laugh when you're with me. You never do that with him."

"This has nothing to do with Julian. I don't—"

"No." He shook his head, insistent. "No. You must feel something for me. I know you do."

"You are my very good friend," I said carefully.

"Friends can become more."

Now, it was me shaking my head, me saying, "No. No, Vanni, I'm sorry."

His fingers tightened on mine. Hoarsely, he said, "I don't believe you."

"Don't force me to say it," I warned him. "I can't bear to hurt you."

"It's too late for that, isn't it?" There was such stark yearning in his voice, such reckless urgency. "Adelaide, please. God . . . please. I love you."

"I don't feel the same way." I spoke the words I did not want to say with steady precision, and I looked into his eyes when I said them so he would not mistake me, and wanted to cry at what I saw there. My own desperation mirrored his when I said, "But that doesn't mean we can't remain friends. I don't want to lose you—"

He dropped my hand as if it burned, stumbling blindly from the room, barefoot, disheveled. I heard him bang into something, and then curse, and then the door opened and he was gone, leaving me alone to wonder how this had all gone so wrong, and desolate at the thought of what must change now, of what his confession had done.

I started after him. I wasn't certain what I meant to do, only that I must somehow save what was between us, but when I stepped into the hall, there was Louisa, wearing her dressing gown, her hair loosely braided, fresh from sleep. "I heard voices." I remembered with dull regret that her room was just above; she had no doubt listened before. "Why are you coming from Vanni's bedroom, Addie?"

I tried to push past her. "I have to go—"

Before I could stop her, she went into his room. "Where is he?"

"Not here," I said impatiently. "And I must go after him—"

"Why? Why must you?" She went more fully inside, and I followed, afraid of her now, of what she might find, of what she might see. She glanced at the unmade bed, his boots, his coat over the chair. "What is this? Were you in *bed* with him, Addie?"

"Louisa, please. I really must go."

She wandered into the adjoining room. "Why, how companionable. Tea. It looks very like a lovers' tête-à-tête." She peeked around the doorway. "Is that what it is?"

Miserably, I said, "Of course not." My notebook was on the desk, Vanni's story. I could not bear for her to touch either, to taint them. I hurried to stop her, but she already had his pages in her hand.

"What is this?"

His papers had covered my notebook, but now it was exposed, and I knew she must recognize it. She had been with me when I bought it in Venice. She had chosen the color. *"Green for spring. That's what you must think of, Addie. Spring."* I wanted to dodge for it, cover it, hide it, but that would only draw her attention, and—

"Isn't this yours?" She put aside his papers and tapped the cover. She didn't wait for my answer, and my words were stuck in my throat anyway. She glanced at me shrewdly and picked it up, flipping it open. "And this is your writing. What's it doing here?"

There was no point in lying. "I've been working on a story."

"A story?" Louisa's expression went blank.

"Vanni's been . . . helping me with it."

"Helping? How?"

I should have recognized that tone. I'd heard it all my life. But I was bereft over Vanni's distress, and fearful of losing what I wanted so to keep. "He's been encouraging me. He doesn't see me the way you and Jules do, and he helps me understand what I could be, and—"

"What you could be?" she repeated. "What do you mean, what you could be? What about what you are? You're Julian's muse."

"That isn't enough for me anymore."

"Is that what Vanni's told you? That it isn't enough? But, Addie, it's *everything*!" She dropped the notebook; it hit the edge of the desk and fell to the floor, splaying open, pages bending.

I cried out in dismay and went to retrieve it. Louisa stepped in front of me. "This is what you've been doing all this time—writing your own story. I thought . . . well, I thought it was only all this about Julian's stupid wife—"

"All this?" I echoed.

"And Venice and the baby, but no, it's been this. Oh, Addie, do you not see what you've done?"

I had no idea what she was talking about.

She stepped closer as if she meant to shake me. "How can you be so selfish? Everything we've planned for—Julian's work, you and me and . . . if you leave us—you're supposed to be his muse!"

"I'm not that person any longer, Louisa. I can't help it."

"Yes you are!" she insisted. "You can't just change everything because some . . . some secretary—some *slum boy*—thinks he understands you. How can he? I'm the one who understands you. You belong to me, not him."

"I don't belong to anyone."

"You do! You belong to Julian too. To us."

"Perhaps you could take my place as Julian's muse," I said coldly. "Certainly it's what you've wished to do."

"I would if I could," she said, and I heard panic and despair. "But it's not me who inspires him. It's you. I wish it was me—I'd be much better at it. I wouldn't be running off at all hours to work on some silly story."

"It's not silly. It's helped me understand."

"Julian needs you. How are you to inspire him when you're out writing with . . . with *Vanni*? Julian's ideas are what matters. We're nothing without him. Everything we wanted, everything we're meant to be, don't you remember? You can't just change your mind now! What about me? Don't you care about me? You promised to be his muse."

"I didn't realize that it meant giving up myself."

"You should be glad to make the sacrifice! I would be."

"I wonder if you really know what that means."

She clenched her fists at her sides. "How condescending you are! You're a martyr to your suffering—just because you were home that day Emily came. It had nothing to do with fate. It could have been me or Julian just as easily, have you thought of that?"

"It couldn't have been either of you, because you were in Paris, buying paper lanterns."

Guilt crossed her face, and then became anger. "Women miscarry all the time. Emily wasn't punishing you, Addie—how could she? She's dead, and you're only sad, not cursed. It's nothing special. Everyone's been sad."

"Had you been there with me, I might have been able to bear it better."

Louisa flushed. "You wanted me gone. You could hardly stand the sight of me."

The same accusation Julian had lodged. The thing I could not deny. But I was tired of the way the two of them used it. "It's over and done, Louisa. Now I know what I want."

"Who cares what you want?" She kicked my notebook, sending it thudding into the wall. "You'll give up all this now. I'll have Bayard send Vanni away. You'll be yourself again."

I knew that expression, that lurking hysteria that demanded my obedience. I was done yielding. Why should I save her again? "No."

"You can't do this, Addie. You can't. It's not supposed to be this way!"

"The world isn't always what you want it to be. It's time you realized it."

She slammed her hands onto the desk. She swept Vanni's papers to the floor; the ink bottle went sliding. I grabbed it before it could upend. Then, viciously, she knocked over the penwipe, the pencils, a box full of pen nibs, all of it spilling to the floor. She jerked on the drawer, which didn't budge. "Why is this locked? What else is in here? What have you hidden away?"

"Nothing. Louisa, leave it be. It's not my desk—"

"He's ruined everything. You've ruined everything!" She jerked again on the drawer.

"Leave it alone." I tried to pull her away.

She twisted from my grasp. "Everything you did . . . Oh, how could this have got so far? You'll destroy Jules. He'll leave us, and then you'll leave me. I know you will." She had been jerking on the drawer, and now she stopped, gripping the bottom edge with white fingers. She stared at the floor, her shoulders rigid beneath the fine lawn of her dressing gown. Her voice became a whisper. "I won't let you ruin everything."

She bent, picking up a key where it had fallen among the pen nibs, and gave me a triumphant look.

I sighed. "There's nothing of mine in there, Louisa. You should not invade his privacy."

"Why not, when he's done everything he can to hurt me?"

"I think you've done your share as well, haven't you? Why not call this an end, Loulou? All you've done for months is tell me I must get better. I am. Isn't that what you wanted?"

"I wanted you to get better because of Jules and me." The key gleamed between her fingers. "I wanted you to see how important you are. Not because of some stupid story that makes you want to be something else. I wanted everything to be the way it was."

"I wasn't happy, even then." I echoed Vanni's words.

"Of course you were. We all were." She set the key in the lock and turned it. The catch clicked. She slipped open the drawer, rifling through its contents without compunction: a leather-bound journal, letters, a wad of folded banknotes that surprised us both. Louisa laughed softly. "Oh, look at this. Wherever did he get so much money? Do you suppose he's been stealing from Bay?"

360

"Of course not! How could you think that?"

"He's dishonest. He's a thief—does that change how you think of him now, Addie? And these." She shoved the letters into my face. "From Madame Brest. What about her, Addie?"

"I don't care about her. Vanni and I are only friends. How often must I say it?"

She pursed her lips, leafing through the others. I noted the name on them all. *Gaspare Calina. London.* His father, no doubt. "Will you please put them away now? You can see none of it has to do with me."

She let the letters fall, a cascade to the desktop. Then she grabbed up my notebook, closing it without regard for the bent pages. "We'll burn it, that's what we'll do—"

"No!" Furiously, desperately, I tried to grab it from her; she clutched it more tightly to her chest. "How dare you! For once can't I have something of my own? Give it back to me!"

"What's all this noise about?"

It was Julian. I stepped back into the bedroom to see him standing at the door. He held his flask. He looked as if he were struggling to focus. "Adelaide? What are you doing in Calina's room?"

Louisa stepped out too.

Julian's brow furrowed in confusion. "Louisa?"

She had the notebook, and stealthily she dropped it behind her, out of sight. "He asked us to fetch something for him," she lied. "A . . . a special pen."

"No," I said.

"Of course he did." Her eyes begged me to say nothing, to keep my story a secret, to return to those halcyon days when I was Julian's muse, and she was the one he looked at with desire, because I had been only a sort of symbol, inchoate, not quite real.

She went on. "But we haven't been able to find it, have we—"

"This is nonsense," I said.

"Addie, no—"

"I've been working on my story," I said firmly, turning away from her to meet Julian's gaze, "Vanni's been helping me."

Julian stared as if he didn't quite understand. "Vanni? You mean Mr. Calina, don't you?"

"Julian—"

"What story? You mean the one I burned?"

"I rescued it. I think it's going to be a novel."

"But you promised not to write it. You said you no longer wanted to."

"That's what you wanted to be true, but it wasn't. It was never true, Jules. I couldn't stop, and . . . and Vanni's made me understand that I need to write it."

"But he's no one. What does he know of anything?"

"He has talent. You said it too. More than a little, and—"

"Are you in love with him?"

"Why does everyone assume that?"

Julian's expression froze. He walked out.

Louisa said, "Now look what you've done."

I caught up with him as he was passing the gallery. I grabbed his arm, yanking away the flask at his lips so that laudanum splashed onto his chin. "Julian, wait. You must let me explain—"

"Explain what?" he demanded, wiping at the drops. "Why you lied to me? Why you've been sneaking out with him every morning? Do you think I don't see what's really going on?"

"We're friends. He's the one who told me I would find solace in writing, and I have."

He brushed at the air around his head as if to shoo away a gnat. "Yes indeed. No doubt he's provided ample *consolation*."

"He has, but not the way you think," I insisted.

"No? He looks as if he'd like to crawl inside you. Don't tell me he doesn't speak to you of love every morning, or that Bayard hasn't, for that matter." He swatted again at the insect, but there was no insect there, and my heart began to sink.

"It doesn't matter if they have. I'm not interested in them."

He snorted. "It's all my fault, isn't it? That's what you're going to say." Another swat. "You blame me for taking you from your family and your country. You blame me for Emily. You blame me for losing our child. Ahh! Keep your distance! I've no wish to tend to you now!"

The last was not to me, but to the air. He swiped again, batting something away, then dodged into the gallery, trailing something invisible, and I went after him.

He stopped short in the middle of the room, setting his flask on the gaming table, going rigid in an all-too-familiar way. "Do you see her?" His irritation with the spirit died; now he looked puzzled, then entranced. He stared up at the ceiling and pointed to the far corner. "There! There she is!"

"Who?" I asked.

"Our child," he said. "Why, it's our child."

"No, Julian. No. No."

"It is!" His light eyes burned. "She is there, and she says . . . she says . . . 'dear Mother, dear Father . . .'"

"Julian, please." He was blurring before me. "Please do not do this."

"'Dear Father, please tell my mother she must not be sad.'"

I closed my eyes. I felt I was collapsing in on myself, slowly and slowly, folding in half and then half again, folding and folding into a tiny box.

"'Tell her the story is not her destiny. Tell her that her future is with you. The world awaits what you will do together . . .'"

I opened my eyes again. Julian was no longer staring at the ceiling, but at me.

I said, "This is the cruelest thing you have ever done to me."

This time, I was the one who fled.

THIRTY-ONE

VANNI

I went outside, hoping the chill morning air with its misting rain would soothe my anger and mortification—a dismal combination, worse so because I did not know who to be more angry with, her or myself. I stared at the white-tipped waves rumpling gray Lac Léman and wanted nothing so much as to throw myself into it.

The grass was wet beneath my bare feet; the relentless drizzle slowly soaked through my shirt, and my hair was lank and starting to drip down my neck. I was cold and utterly miserable, and I waited for her to come after me, to say, *I was wrong. I realize it now. I love you,* or if not that, anything. Anything. I wanted her to call me back. I wanted her to show me that she cared what I thought or what I wished for. I would have welcomed any touch, no matter how humiliating—a depth of sinking to which I could not have imagined before now. I laughed ruefully at myself. I waited. She did not come, and that was the worst thing of all, realizing how fully I'd misread her, discovering that I mattered so little to her that she did not care to offer me the least comfort now.

Friends. A brother. What a fool I was.

I did not want to go back, but I was shivering. I would probably catch pneumonia if I stayed—what did it matter? No one in that house would worry over me. Still, I trudged across the patio and into the villa, going upstairs quietly, hoping to meet no one. The house was silent, the door to my bedroom closed. I paused. What if she was still there? Could I even bear to look at her? Could I bear not to? My heart pounded as I twisted the knob and stepped inside.

Louisa was sitting on my bed.

I groaned aloud. "For God's sake, what are you doing here? You're the last person I want to see."

"You look like a bedraggled rat."

"What do you want?" I went past her, noting the mess of the adjoining room, my papers on the floor, pen nibs spilled everywhere, the drawer to my desk gaping open and my letters strewn about the desk, banknotes scattered. I went cold, and then hot with sudden fear. "Bloody hell!"

"I wanted to see if Adelaide was hiding anything else from me." Louisa was behind me. Then, when I turned to face her, "Yes, I know all about it. The story you're helping her write, what good *friends* you are."

"I think you should go."

She didn't budge. "I want you to leave her alone."

"She's her own woman. She can decide well enough what she wants."

"You're only hurting her. And Jules."

"What can he have to complain about? He has the best of both worlds, doesn't he? Your sister in his bed and you . . . well . . . in his bed."

Her eyes narrowed. "You think you're so clever. You don't know anything."

"Perhaps not." I was exhausted, hurt, angry—really it seemed that God was finding more ways than usual to torment me this morning. "But do you know, I don't give a damn about Estes. He can go drown for all I care."

"Adelaide loves him."

She could not have aimed truer.

"And she doesn't love you."

Or yes, I supposed she could.

"And so . . . I want you to leave her alone. I want you to stop talking to her about stories, and being a writer. She is Julian's muse. We need her."

"Doesn't it matter what she wants?"

"It is what she wants. She has always wanted it. She might not see it now, but she'll regret this. She'll regret you. Promise me you'll leave her alone."

Cruelly, I said, "Why does it matter? You're leaving, aren't you? Only two more days, unless you can convince Bayard otherwise, which I doubt. He's done with you, you know. When he sends you off, Adelaide will go with you. And Estes too, thank God."

Her jaw clenched. "Promise me."

"No. Whatever is between me and your sister is none of your concern."

"Oh, it very much is," she said, those pretty lips thinning.

"I've had a trying morning. I want you to leave."

"Oh? Did you and Addie have a little tiff?"

"Get out."

I took Louisa's arm roughly, propelling her to the door. She stumbled over her skirts, tripping on the bedstead, taking me with her. I tried to catch myself against the wall, but she kept falling, onto the mattress, curving her arm around my neck so I had no choice but to fall with her. Perhaps that was what she intended. What was deliberate, what accidental . . . I don't know. Only that I was suddenly firmly on top of her, her hips to mine, her breasts pressed into my chest, a position I'd not been in with a woman in some time, and despite everything—*everything*—I went immediately and completely hard.

She felt it too. She murmured, "Isn't this what you want?" or perhaps it was *"Do what you want,"* or *"This is what I want,"* or something . . . I had no idea, only that she was looking at me, and my anger and disappointment and pain conspired against me, all that hot temper freezing into numbness, my heart and my head dulling, deadening. It was the most coldly deliberate decision I'd ever made to kiss her.

She responded as if she'd been waiting for it, her mouth opening, her tongue wrapping around mine, dodging, teasing, tasting. Her hands pulled at my shirt, jerking it over my head, and I nearly tore open her dressing gown, shoving it down her soft arms. She rose to help me, and then her chemise was gone too, thrown to the floor, and her perfect breasts—God, yes—were in my hands, and then in my mouth.

Her eyes were dark, as dark as her sister's. She tugged down my trousers, fingers wrapping around me, stroking, and I groaned and she spread her legs. She was Louisa—I knew she was Louisa—but then, somehow she was not. That superimposition again, she and her sister blending, entangled, one forcing the other to action. I loved Adelaide, and so I would have Louisa—of course, what else made sense? I thrust into her—her tiny yelp, her legs crossing over my back, holding me in place, drawing me deeper and deeper—*Adelaide*—biting my shoulder, pulling my chest hair so it hurt, and there was nothing I wanted so much as that pain. Pain to assuage pain, bitterness to assuage humiliation, sex as a form of vengeance, as punishment . . . hating myself even as I could not stop, wanting her and wanting her sister more and somehow that made it right.

We coupled like animals, desperate and clawing. Her breath was in my mouth, her moans, and then she cried out, clutching me tighter, throwing her head back, raising her hips hard and fast, her fingers digging into me, and I came—furiously, painfully, drowning, gasping for breath—as she twisted beneath me, her voice staccato and soft *ah ah ah* and then drawn-out *ahhhhhh*. She was throbbing; I was throbbing. I collapsed upon her. Her heart raced, or perhaps that was my own. She went lax, a deep breath that I recognized as one of satisfaction, and I closed my eyes and told myself it was not Louisa I held. Not Louisa whose wet warmth enveloped me. Not Louisa's breast still in my hand. Trying to ignore the voice in my head, the despair—*What have you done?*—and at the same time grateful that I'd done it. Relieved. Now it was only a matter of time before it all fell away. One minute, or perhaps the next, but it was over; it was done, and that was what I wanted most of all.

Her hand traced down my spine; I shuddered as much with revulsion as pleasure and could not bring myself to look at her, to acknowledge her in any way, but even as I slipped from her I stayed cradled against her hips and could not move.

It all happened at once—the half knock at the door, the creak of it opening, Bayard saying, "Vanni, I—," Louisa's scream and then her gasp and jerk, trying to throw me off, and I looked up wearily to see Bayard standing there, staring at us in disbelief and dawning anger.

Louisa scrambled from beneath me, yanking to free her dressing gown, which was anchored by my knee. "Oh, Bay! Oh . . . it's not what it seems!" Nearly crying as she tried vainly to cover herself with the bare bit of muslin she'd been able to pull loose—why did she care? He'd already seen every inch of her. Her hair fell over her shoulder, mostly loosened from its braid. A lovebite—I'd obviously done that, though I didn't remember—glowing brightly red on her throat, already turning blue at its center.

He was as furious as I'd ever seen him. Coldly, murderously so, but I felt it with a curious distance. I sat up, making no effort to cover myself, releasing the last bit of Louisa's dressing gown. She pulled it loose, draping herself in it, climbing from the bed. She was still talking. "It wasn't my fault! He forced me! I didn't want it! You must believe me!"

But Bayard wasn't looking at her. He was looking at me.

"Get out," he said, his voice low and even. "Before I strangle you."

I pulled up my trousers, but before I could grab my shirt, he jerked his head to the door—*now*—and so I went into the hall, where I sagged against the wall and waited like the stupid dog she'd once called me. My shoulder stung—a bite; she had nearly broken the bloody skin—as well as my chest. It felt in places as if she'd tried to rip out my hair.

They were yelling. Bayard sounding threatening and Louisa breathless, weeping piteously now, and then, of course—wasn't this what I was waiting for, after all?—I heard rapid steps, Estes appearing in the hall.

"What's that noise? Don't tell me they're fighting ag—" He stopped short, frowning at the sight of me standing there, shirtless, barefoot. "What's going on?"

Then Adelaide, coming down the hall behind him—dear God, *Adelaide*—and everything in me seemed to give way, the truth of what I'd done and what it meant impossible to accept, the destruction I'd wished for ill thought and devastating. She would never love me now.

She frowned at me, confused, yes—I was not usually standing half naked outside my own bedroom—then looked at my door, the voices coming from behind it, Louisa crying, and I saw it settle into her. I saw when she knew. "No," she whispered.

There was despair in that, wasn't there? A pain to match mine, which had swelled to swallow me, a similar anger.

"I'm sorry," I whispered back. Not enough, I knew.

Estes demanded again, "What's going on?"

I nodded toward Adelaide. "Ask her."

Estes looked at her in bewilderment.

The bedroom door crashed open. Bayard exploded from it—a bit dramatic, wasn't it? He was throwing Louisa over anyway; I'd only precipitated it. "Calina!"

He hadn't called me that for a very long time. Then I saw what he held. A journal clothed in oxblood leather, and I remembered my fear at seeing the drawer unlocked, opened, Louisa looking for secrets. A tidal wave of guilt and shame, and then overwhelming relief when I saw it was only the journal and not the story. That betrayal, at least, I could escape.

"Who asked you to write this?" he demanded.

There was not a single thing I could say in my defense. "Colburn."

He strode down the hall. Estes, still looking puzzled, and a bit shaken, followed. Louisa crept from my bedroom, blowsy, hair falling, pulling her dressing gown tight about her, though she wore nothing underneath; her chemise was still on the floor. She glared at me as if she hadn't participated fully, and then she looked at Adelaide.

"I had to," she said softly—a curious mix of regret and self-righteousness. "Don't you see?"

Adelaide's gaze hardened. The look she leveled at us—me—might have eviscerated had I been able to feel anything at all.

She said, "You could do this. After everything."

I didn't know to whom she spoke, me or Louisa. Neither of us answered.

My relief faded. I felt dull and nauseated as I went with them into the salon. Bayard stood at the hearth. The fire was dead, no maid to light it, and I had not thought to do it this morning. He took the box of matches from the mantel, and then he opened the journal and ripped out the pages I'd written, and one by one he set them afire and threw them onto the grate, where they curled and burned, a memory of a night of mockery and my ghost story turning to ash, too many things turning to ash.

"What is it?" Estes asked.

"A record of my exploits," Bayard explained grimly. "Written by my own personal Judas. What does thirty pieces of silver translate to these days, Vanni?"

"Five hundred pounds," I told him.

The papers flickered blue, smoking with the linen weft. It had been an expensive book, and very good paper. We all watched as if held by a spell. He burned even the blank pages—many more of those, not that he noticed—and then he threw in the cover.

He said to me, "Well, it looks as if Colburn is out five hundred pounds. He'll come after you for it, you know, but you won't write this again. You'll give him nothing, do you understand? If I hear a single rumor—a single word—of anything that I think has come from you, I will not only beat you within an inch of your life, I'll go to your father. I'm certain he would like to know just how dishonorably his beloved son has behaved."

The thought of it . . . of my father's face, and how his eyes had shined when I'd told him of my new position with the famous Bayard Sonnier. Splitting a bottle of wine I'd bought for the occasion, and the oysters I could afford for the first time. *"How proud I am of you, Gio-Gio"*—reverting to my childhood nickname, the one the whole neighborhood used before I returned from school and insisted on Vanni, as my schoolmates called me, because Gio-Gio was a baby name, and I'd become a man. His clever son.

Just so.

Bayard knew me very well, after all.

"You'll pack your things and leave in the morning," he continued. "I'll pay your wages through today. Be grateful for that. And as for you"—to Louisa—"I want you out of my sight for the rest of the time you're here."

"Bay, please." Louisa was sobbing again, this time in earnest. "Please."

"Oh for God's sake, Louisa. You are embarrassing yourself." Adelaide's voice was icy with disgust. She turned abruptly and left the salon.

"Or Vanni can take you," Bayard went on, ruthless, to Louisa. "Given that he already has. You deserve one another."

Louisa's sobs grew louder.

"What are you saying?" Estes's voice was flat. It was impossible that he hadn't put it together, but then again, perhaps not. For such a visionary, he was so remarkably blind.

"I caught them fucking," Bayard said brutally. "As you know, I don't like to share."

Estes looked stunned. Then furious. He looked at me as if he wanted to run me through. "I should call you out for this."

I could accept Bayard's anger, and Adelaide's. I deserved both. But Estes's . . . I was sick of his hypocrisy. "I'm happy to oblige. But I think your outrage is misplaced, don't you? It's not as if she's an innocent. Why not just admit you're jealous?"

Bayard's gaze sharpened. "Jealous?"

Louisa looked up from her hands, startled from her crying. "Vanni, no."

"All that Free Love talk, and in the end you're no different than any man with an unfaithful lover."

Estes flew at me, his fist connecting with my jaw. Pain exploded through my skull. I staggered; my own temper erupted, and I attacked; lovely pain as I hit him. I wanted to pound his face into oblivion, to stamp out his hypocrisy and his neglect of Adelaide, and how the hell had I lost her to him? How could that be possible?

We grappled; he pushed me into the wall, and I pushed him back, hitting his shoulder, and then his blow to my stomach—he was stronger than he looked—and my return, and we were tumbling against the settee, scraping it along the floor, and Bayard was stepping between us.

"Enough!" He shoved us apart, holding on to Estes's arm as he said to me, "Get out of here."

"He's a liar, you realize that?" I breathed. "He's been with her too. I saw them in the salon—"

"Get out." Bayard spoke through clenched teeth. Another choice made, not in my favor. He and Adelaide had both chosen Estes, and I didn't know why. What hadn't they found in me? What was missing?

There was no point in arguing; I walked out of the salon. As I passed the gallery, something caught my eye, a glint of light on metal—Estes's flask on the gaming table, abandoned, as it never was. Spite is a nasty thing, but I gave in to it. I took the flask and tucked it into my trouser pocket.

I went to my bedroom. I shut the door and I locked it—*a good idea to have done that long before now.* Louisa's chemise was still crumpled on the floor; the smell of her lingered in my sheets. I kicked the chemise beneath the bed, but it didn't disappear completely, the very edge of it trailing out, curling around the leg, and it was that, in the end—I could not even make a silly chemise do what I wanted—that broke me. Only a bit of lace-edged hem . . . and suddenly I was crying as I had not since I was a child.

I suppose I was waiting for her. I spent the afternoon lying on my bed, not packing, not thinking, numb to the pain of my jaw—which bore a rapidly growing bruise—as well as my ribs. Footsteps went back and forth in the hall. I'd heard a low voice now and again, but no woman's. When the knock finally came, my heart leaped so violently I felt almost dizzy. I pounced on the door, fumbling with the key, twisting it open.

Louisa.

My disappointment made me mean. "Back for more?"

She was nothing but contempt, but her hand trembled when she held out a letter. "This came for you."

I stared, for the moment not comprehending. A letter. For me. Everything had fallen so completely apart that it was hard to remember that outside these walls something still existed.

"Go on, take it." She shoved it at me until I had no choice. "I don't want to look at you any longer than I have to. I'm certain the feeling is mutual."

"Pretend to hate me all you want, but you liked it. I know you did."

Her animus faded. She sighed. "You do have a lovely mouth. But it doesn't matter, Vanni, don't you see? That wasn't why."

"Then what was?"

"I love my sister, and you're not what's best for her."

"How do you know?"

She didn't answer that, but stepped back from the doorway. "I suppose this is good-bye. I don't expect I'll see you again."

"Not if we're lucky," I said, half a joke.

I got half a smile in return. She started to go and then she paused. "She won't come to say good-bye, Vanni. I've spoiled you for her. You should try to forget her."

"I don't think I can," I said. "I'm in love with her."

"If that's so, then I really am not sorry."

She left, and I closed the door, locking it again, only then realizing that I still held the letter. It was from Vera Brest, which seemed now to be a name from another time and place and nothing to do with me.

> *My darling Giovanni,*
> *The best news! My husband is leaving tomorrow with the early train. You may come to me tomorrow afternoon. Edward hopes you will have something for him, and I hope you will bring Mr. Sonnier's story—he must by this time have written a great deal—and I will cover you with kisses.*
>
> *Tomorrow at 3:00—do not be late, or I shall be very cross with you. I have missed you so very much.*
> *Your Vera*

I would have laughed had I any sense of humor left. I would be well along the road to Italy by tomorrow at three. I planned to leave at dawn. I had saved some of my wages, and with that and my final pay, I meant to take the long way back to London. Weeks, hopefully months—as long as my money held out—before I returned to my father's disappointment, to ignominy and failure and debt collectors. If I could disappear for a year, it would not be long enough.

And as for the story . . . I went to my desk and gathered up the papers. How long ago it seemed that Adelaide had knocked upon my door and I had heard with joy her praise. Praise for a story I could do nothing with, of course, given its beginning—one more thing to add to the growing list of my impostures. A gentleman, a writer, an honorable man, a successful son. Bayard's friend. Vera Brest's lover. Every role a lie. In any case, the story had become the locus of my pain. I could not look at it without hearing Adelaide say, *"Oh, you've dedicated it to me!"* Bending over the pages, searching for the phrase that epitomized my pilfered brilliance. Her white, white neck, and that foolish tempting strand, my kiss . . .

Well, if nothing else, I'd made the deadline. It was a triumph of a kind, even if there was no one to share it with. I put the whole into a packet, tied and sealed. I addressed it to Vera Brest and set it on the pile to be posted. Let her have it. Let her read it and think kindly of me for sending her the gift of Bayard's genius. I would not arrive at three, or any time thereafter. But this . . . she would have this, and it was all she really wanted from me anyway. It was a relief to know that I had the ability to make at least one person happy, and the only other option was to burn it, which I could not quite bring myself to do. It had held all of my happiness once. Even in my misery, I could not forget that.

By then I knew that Louisa was right: Adelaide would not come to say good-bye.

I took out Colburn's five hundred pounds and scrawled a note, leaving it all on the desk. Then I packed my things for the morning.

THIRTY-TWO

ADELAIDE

I was furious with all of them. Julian, for his thoughtless selfishness, Vanni for making love to my sister after he'd told me he loved me, and Louisa . . . Louisa most of all, always Louisa.

I had locked myself in the spare bedroom, away, and in the morning, I was up with the dawn, standing at the window. When I saw Vanni cross the front courtyard, I didn't know which I felt more: sorrow or anger. I found myself pressing my hand to the window, but I didn't make a sound, I did nothing to tell him I was watching. I wanted him to go. I wanted him out of my life. I hated what he'd done and how traitorous it felt. All those things I'd told him about Louisa and me, all those things I thought he'd understood.

He had his bag over his shoulder. His hat and his coat were frosted with the fine mist of the overcast morning, his dark hair gleaming where it waved over his collar, too long, too thick. I remembered how smooth it had felt against my skin when he bent to kiss my neck, and the soft press of his mouth, and even just the memory embarrassed me. Even now I felt *no. No, please don't ruin this.*

Yet it wasn't really his confession that had ruined things. His love for me had been salvageable. But Louisa in his arms, Louisa with such intimate knowledge of him, that I could not forgive. How much like Julian was Vanni? How entwined was I with Louisa in that love he'd claimed to feel for me? He had known her first. He had wanted her first. In the end, had we been one and the same to him? Had we together been the perfect woman, as Julian wanted us to be?

I had thought that Vanni saw me truly as myself, singular and separate. For the first time in my life, not a "Wentworth Sister." I had believed that he belonged to me in a way that no one ever had, but she had found a way to make him hers, and so I could not bear to look at him again.

I watched him until he disappeared, and then I watched as morning came on, the clouds parting, sun hazing the mist and then sending it fleeing.

This time, when Julian knocked, I let him in. He was nervous, apologetic, beautifully remorseful. He was a man who looked more lovely in sorrow and sacrifice, like the angel Louisa had called him in the dungeons at Chillon, born for redemption.

"Have you seen my flask?" he asked a bit nervously. "I'd thought I left it in the gallery, but I can't seem to find it."

"I haven't," I said, and then waited for the real reason he had come to me.

"I . . . I thought it would be a good morning to go out in the boat."

"The boat?"

"The rowboat. You like to watch the dawn, you said. I thought perhaps you would miss it when he left, and so . . . go out with me."

"It's past dawn," I said. "You've missed the sunrise."

Julian paused, uncertain, then exhaled deeply. "Louisa and Calina—"

"I don't want to speak of it."

"Just tell me how."

"How what?" I asked sharply. "How did it happen? I don't know. I wasn't there. Ask Louisa."

Julian looked pained. "That's not what I meant. He's not worthy of either of you. What did you see in him? How did he seduce you both?"

I laughed. "I should think you of all people would understand, as you managed it yourself so well."

"Adelaide—"

"His only seduction was in letting me be who I wanted to be. He never told me I couldn't do something, or that I shouldn't. He was . . . he was perfect. For a time."

"Did you . . . did he . . . ?" When I gave him a chiding look, he glanced away in shame. "I love you, Adelaide. You know I do."

"So does he. But love isn't what I want."

Julian started. "He told you he loved you?"

"Oh, Jules. Trust you to see the wrong thing. I just told you it wasn't important."

"It is to me."

"You will have to come to terms with that on your own."

He considered, then said again, "Adelaide, come out on the boat with me. There won't be another time. It will be our good-bye, if you like. We can be as we were. Like those days in Concord under the willow . . . do you remember them?"

"Of course."

"We'll go out. We'll look at the mountains. We'll talk of whatever you want. Philosophies. Writing. You can tell me about your story."

I said quietly, "You can't just appropriate him, Jules. You can't just substitute yourself. It doesn't work that way."

"Why not? Why couldn't it? If you still love me?"

"I don't want to go out on the boat. Don't you understand? I'm grieving. I'm sad. I'm angry. I feel as if something's been stolen from me, and you can't make it right. You'll have to give me time."

"I have given you nothing but time. When will it be enough?"

"Go out by yourself," I urged. "Be alone—I don't think you know how to be. Think about what you really want from me."

"I already know what I want," he insisted. "Haven't I said it a hundred times? I want you to be my muse. As you were. As you will always be."

I didn't answer him. What could I say? It had always been an illusion. I had stopped being real for him months ago. I was already a ghost.

I looked out the window and thought of Vanni hurrying away.

Julian left in a flurry of confusion and hurt, a wounded boy, but this time I would not comfort him, or feel guilty. I went to my notebook, and I did what I had been accustomed lately to do: I wrote out my grief and my pain and my anger in my story, and it was afternoon when I finally looked up from the pages, and realized that I hadn't been disturbed for hours.

I closed the book and put aside the pen and went downstairs. Bayard was on the terrace; Louisa was nowhere to be seen, yet he had asked her to stay away from him, and so I wasn't surprised. But I was surprised that Jules was not with him.

Bayard looked up as I stepped out. He had been writing; pages dotted with black blobs, scratched out words. His fingers were stained with ink.

"What a mess," I said.

He gave me a rueful look. "I need a secretary."

I glanced away.

"I'm sorry, Adelaide. I know you liked him."

"Please. I don't want to talk about him." The lake was dark blue, the sky mostly so, though there was a band of heavy clouds that hid the mountaintops, and branches shifted with a strong breeze that chopped the water and sent the perfume of lavender and roses fleeing.

Bayard reached into his pocket. "He left this for you." In his hand were the banknotes I'd seen in Vanni's drawer, along with a folded piece of paper.

"I don't want it."

Bayard frowned. "Why not? Did he . . . was there something between you two? I'd thought he harbored a tendre for you, but you never seemed—"

"Where's Jules?"

"He went out on the rowboat. Hours ago now. I should think he'd be back shortly."

I searched for him on the lake. Vanni had always been easy to find, drifting as he had just beyond the mouth of the harbor, but I saw no sign of a boat or Jules. I sat down with a sigh, and Bayard said, "You don't have to tell me if you don't wish, but . . ."

"I'm writing a story." The words tumbled out. "Julian asked me to stop, but Vanni told me I should write it anyway. He was working on a story too—it was very good, by the way—and we were helping one another. That's all it was. We were partners, I suppose. And friends."

"Ah. What's yours about?"

He could have asked a hundred things. He could have asked about Vanni's story, or he could have been dismissive about women scribblers. He could have asked why Jules had told me to stop writing. Instead, he treated me as a fellow writer. "Curses," I told him. "A spirit muse set to destroy her maker."

"Well, that explains this." He tapped the banknotes, pushing them toward me.

This time, I took the folded paper on top, though not without apprehension.

Adelaide,
Please take this. It is one thing I can do for you.
Be your own muse.
—V.

"Five hundred pounds," Bayard said. "No doubt Colburn's money."

"I don't want it." I let the note fall unheeded, pushing the money away. "I don't want his guilt money or anything else from him."

Bayard's gaze was thoughtful. "I'll hold on to it for you. You may change your mind."

I knew I would not. Determinedly, I changed the subject back to writing. "I think it may end up a novel, but perhaps it would be best not."

"Write until you feel the story is told" was his advice. "Let it say for itself what it wants to be."

We talked like this for some time. The wind grabbed the clouds that had hidden the mountaintops and tossed them to cover the sun, and it grew chill and gray.

"Where is Jules?" It was Louisa, at the open doors, meek and cowering as if she expected a blow at any moment, and I did not know who made her most leery, me or Bayard.

Bayard tensed. He didn't answer her, but he looked up at the sky with a frown. I went to the railing. The water was as gray as the sky, and as turbulent. I did not see the rowboat or Jules.

"Could he have gone to Geneva?" I asked.

"He said nothing of it," Bayard said. "But perhaps, if the water grew too rough . . ." He capped the ink and gathered his papers, and together we scanned the horizon.

The rain began; still no Jules. We retired to the salon, but all three of us stood guard at the windows, watching and waiting. I began to feel a certain, terrible dread, but I told myself *no*. Julian was raised on a lake. He knew how to manage a boat.

"Why can't he swim?" Louisa asked me abruptly, as if she'd read my thoughts. Her arms were crossed over her breasts, worry bracketing her mouth. "How is it that he never learned?"

I'd thought he shared all his stories with her too. There was no joy in realizing this one was mine alone. "There was a sturgeon—or some kind of big fish—in the lake. His grandfather told him a story when he was a boy about how it had eaten his missing toes. Julian believed him. He wouldn't go in, not past his knees, unless he was in the boat. When he was older, he discovered it was frostbite that had taken his grandfather's toes, but by then it was habit, and he went away to school and had no need."

"I hope his grandfather is happy for the lie now." Louisa's voice was harsh. "If Julian drowns—"

"He's not going to drown," Bayard said sharply. "He's put in at Geneva, or one of the châteaus. He'll show up when the rain stops."

But he didn't. Not when the rain stopped that evening, and not later, after it grew dark. My dread grew into something monstrous; none of us slept. Bayard turned every gaslight up full in the rooms facing the lake, on every story. "It will give him something to navigate by."

When morning came, Louisa said, "We should go to Geneva to see if he's there."

Bayard shoved his feet into his boots and grabbed his coat. "I'll go. I should be back in a few hours."

"He'll return before you do," I said.

Bayard was grim. "I hope so."

He left, and Louisa and I held vigil, pacing from the salon to the terrace and back again. My chin and my hand tingled, and I curled my fingers about the railing so hard my knuckles turned white, and realized that Julian had not seemed to notice that the eczema was nearly healed. Only Vanni had commented upon it. I wanted his prediction that it would be gone one day to be true; it would mean that Venice was truly in the past, and I wanted to be strong enough to make it so.

Hours passed; the day was clear and bright now, the water smooth. As it moved into afternoon, boats sailed into the harbor carrying men who stirred the lake with long poles. Bayard had obviously alerted them that Jules was missing, and suddenly it was the day we'd arrived again, and they were searching for the boy who had come to see Bayard and drowned, and Jules and Louisa and I were standing on the shore as Julian's eyes grew distant and Louisa searched for Bayard, and I'd mistaken Vanni for him, just as Louisa had once done.

I turned to my sister, who had become more restless than ever with the boats. "Do you see him? Do you see his spirit?"

She turned to me, horrified. "Why would you say that? He's perfectly well. Bayard will bring him back, and we'll all laugh at our worry."

"But could you? If he were there?" I prodded, unable to stop, needing to know. What was pretense, what was truth? Did Louisa even know herself? "Could you see his spirit? Julian saw that boy's the day we came here. Did you see it too? Rising to the stars?"

"What is wrong with you, Addie? Why are you saying these things? Stop it. You're distressing me."

"God forbid you should be distressed."

"I don't understand why you're not. Julian might be . . . he might be . . . and you're standing there as if it doesn't matter to you in the least."

She stared determinedly out the window, eyes shining with fear or grief or whatever it was she imagined a woman might feel as she watched for a doomed lover. I felt the bonds between us knot ever tighter, and was overtaken by such a profound weariness that I could stand there no longer, waiting for them to drag Julian's body from the depths.

I left Louisa to keep her worried vigil alone and went to the bedroom I shared with Jules. I pulled a shirt from his trunk and buried my face in it, breathing deep his scent and thinking of yesterday morning. The way I'd watched Vanni go and said nothing, done nothing. Julian's desperate plea that I had refused to consider, because I wanted to punish him for not understanding what I'd lost: my faith in him, our child, Vanni. *"Come out on the boat with me."*

And if I had? What then? What had he intended? *"It will be our good-bye."* What had he meant by that? Had he meant to drown us both? Was this a suicide or an accident? I saw him standing before me, uncertain, beautiful, sad, just as his wife had once stood before me on the water steps of our house, her heels at the very edge, the canal coursing dark and relentless behind. The words I'd thrown at her. *"You mean nothing to him—or to me. He doesn't want you and never will again. Understand me. He will never belong to you again."*

He could not do this. He could not leave me this way. He could not just go with everything unresolved between us, with no way for me to atone, no way to find absolution. He could not leave me with only regret and guilt.

Yet far worse than those things was my relief. If he was gone, I need no longer try to love him. There was no need to find my way through the rubble of the past, to forge a clear path when there could not be one. The relief was in itself a grieving, because it meant that the love we'd once shared in the dappled sun of the willow could only be a memory, a nostalgia. So much undone, so much possibility unrealized. I did not know how I was supposed to feel now, without him. Julian had meant to change the world, and if he was gone and the world was not changed, what responsibility did I bear for refusing to play my part? What debt did I now owe and to whom?

I heard voices, and a step on the stair. The knock was loud and purposeful, and I did not want to answer it. I wanted another moment, another hour, a day. Let the truth remain unspoken, just for a little while longer, because to speak it meant I had to find a way to live with myself.

"Adelaide," Bayard said in a heavy, tired voice.

I opened the door. His arm was braced on the frame, his head bowed. He looked stark and pale and more exhausted than I'd ever seen him. His eyes were the only color in his face.

"They found the boat. It was overturned. Half-sunken. They haven't found him."

He watched me as if he feared I might collapse.

He said, "He could still be alive, but—"

"No," I said. "He's gone."

Bayard nodded slowly. "Probably."

Now I heard my sister, downstairs, sobbing piteously, the grieving widow.

Let her have him. Let her have this too, and then it will be done.

I said, "Ask her if she sees his spirit."

Then I closed the door.

It was a week before his body washed ashore near the Orsini château, which was a bit too ironic. He was bloated and picked at by fish, nearly unrecognizable, Bayard said, but I didn't know that for myself because Bayard would not let me or Louisa look upon him. I saw only Julian's trouser-covered legs and a single booted foot, but I recognized him by both things.

It was Bayard's idea to have a funeral pyre on the beach, and his charm and celebrity won permission from the authorities in Geneva, but when the pyre was lit, Bayard became so distraught that he plunged into the lake and swam for two hours. He had not gone swimming since the boy's drowning, and now it only called attention to the fact that our visit here had been bookended by drownings. If there was meaning in that, given that it was also how Emily had died, I did not want to know it.

Louisa and I served as witnesses until it was over, but the pyre was not very efficient; it was as if heaven did not want to take Julian, though why should it? He had not believed in any heaven, or any god. I hoped his spirit had not become one of the lost and struggling that he'd seen at Chillon, but instead had found its way to the stars.

Afterward, I did not know what to do. Julian's father had made it clear that he wanted nothing to do with us, and as I was not Julian's wife and had borne him no child, I could make no demands. To go back to Concord was impossible, even had I wanted to. Bayard, who obviously felt pity, or even responsibility, paid me to transcribe his novel, and said we could stay until we had someplace to go, as long as Louisa kept her distance. And so, six weeks later, we were still at the Villa Diodati, but not for much longer. Bayard had rented the house only for the summer; soon, he would be moving on. He did not offer to take us with him, and I didn't ask. What we would do weighed upon me, and the only thing I could think of to help us was my story. Bayard had said he would send it to his publisher when it was finished, and I had dreams of grandeur, I suppose. Julian had died on the day of the contest deadline, though I didn't want to look for meaning in that, either. Of us, only Vanni had met it, even if I was the only other one who knew. But that I'd written anything at all seemed significant and encouraging. Why should I not make my living as a writer? If Bayard could do it, and Julian, why not me?

I spent hours every day working on it, speeding through it, and I was only pages from the end on the day that Louisa and I were walking back from the Cologny market. We were silent, when once we might have been chattering away. We were not so easy with one another as we'd been.

She looked out toward the lake and murmured, "It was all such a waste."

I had been thinking of Julian, and I knew she spoke of him too. It seemed, as it often did, that she was somehow privy to my deepest thoughts. "Not a waste. He left 'Cain in the Garden.' One day they'll come to appreciate what he wrote."

"That's not what I meant," she said. "Everything he was to be and to do, and . . . and our promises to each other and leaving Concord, and Emily's death. We'd been through so much, and I couldn't bear it, you see. I was so afraid of how he was changing you, and I didn't know what else to do and now I've ruined us. I've ruined you and me."

I stopped short on the road.

She stopped too, but she kept speaking without looking at me. "I wanted to be important. I wanted Jules to look at me the way he looked at you . . . the way they all looked at you. I had them first. Bayard and Vanni, but they didn't want me, they wanted you, and you are so much stronger than I am, Addie, and I need you so much, and I hated that too."

"What are you saying, Louisa?"

She looked pale. "I wanted Vanni to leave you alone. I wanted him to go. I knew if I . . . it was easy enough. He always wanted me"—she lifted her chin with a trembling pride—"and I thought if I went to bed with him, everything would go back to the way it was. I didn't know Jules would be so upset, and I thought you would be happy again, and now he's dead and you're unhappy and Bayard hates me too, and—and it was all a waste."

Vanni. Grief swept me, that terrible *missing* that I pretended I did not feel. That *missing* when I struggled with a passage in my book and could not think of the right word or how to phrase it, and I half turned to ask him, knowing even as I did that he would not be there to answer, and his face would come into my mind: those dark, dark eyes, the way he bit his lip when he wrote, and that half-amused smile. He felt like something unfinished, a piece of me I could not quite throw away but that didn't fit anywhere else. He was not part of my life, and yet somehow he was the most important part of it, because without him, I would not be myself.

Louisa's eyes were glassy. I remembered Vanni standing in the hall, arms crossed over his bare chest, unshaven, sadness drawing down his features as he said, *"I'm sorry."* Julian's desperation as he pleaded for me to come out on the boat with him. My refusal that had either saved me or condemned him. All of it due to Louisa, the architect of my unhappiness . . . except she hadn't been, really, had she? She had only been trying to make things right. She had missed what was important, but I had driven them both away. I had been unable to comfort Vanni or to forgive him, and Julian had borne my resentment and my tacit accusations for months. I had accused him of denying his culpability, but had I not done the same? My sister could be cruel, but how much crueler was I, in my way? How much crueler had I always been? I was equally responsible for everything that had happened since Julian and I had met on our porch in Concord. What were our lives, after all, but a series of things we must forgive one another?

She said, "Addie?" but before I could answer, she put her hand to her mouth and ran to the side of the road, retching helplessly into the straggling wildflowers.

I hurried over to her, waiting until she was finished, helping her to her feet again.

"I'm sorry," she said. "I'm so sorry."

I took her into my arms, and was again swept by my sense of entanglement. She was warm and pulsing, my vibrant, terrible, half-mad sister, but that she loved me was something I could not deny, nor that I loved her. She was mine, as I was hers, and we had found destruction in that, but perhaps we could find redemption in it too.

Louisa whispered, "I've vomited every morning this week."

I drew back.

"And my monthlies are late." Now she spoke bluntly, matter-of-factly, but I did not miss her fear.

"Whose?"

"I don't know."

"Julian's?"

"No! No, how can you think it, Addie?"

"How could I not?"

"It's not his," she said miserably.

"Then whose?" I was relentless. "Bayard's?"

"Perhaps. But he . . . he usually wore a—oh, I don't know what to call it. A cap? And when he didn't . . . he was careful. Not all the time, but . . ."

"Vanni then," I said dully. "It's Vanni's."

"I don't know." She pounded her fists into her womb. "I hope not. If it's his, I want it out. I don't want to keep it."

But now I saw a way to atone for everything I had not done. I grabbed her wrists, stopping her, gripping them so tightly she made a little sound of pain. "Louisa, stop it. Stop it. Look at me."

She raised her eyes to mine.

"You will do nothing to hurt this child, do you understand? If you do, I will leave you. I will never forgive you and I will never have anything to do with you again. Do you hear me? Never."

She stopped struggling against me. "Why, you did love him."

I shook my head.

"You did. Why would you care so much about his child if you didn't?"

"Because I owe this to him. So do you."

"He ruined himself, Addie," she said, understanding too well. "With his temper and his pride. He betrayed Bay first."

"But our betrayal was the last," I said. "And that's the one that matters."

THIRTY-THREE

VANNI

It was three months before I learned that Julian Estes had drowned in Lac Léman, and another two weeks before I managed to put together that it had happened on the day I'd left. I can't say I mourned him, but I knew then that any hopes I'd harbored for Adelaide's forgiveness were gone. Whether or not I was to blame, how could she look at me again? I could only remind her of his death. By then, in any case, my money was gone, and there was no way to return. I'd heard that Bayard was in Rome, and there was no rumor of any woman with him, and so I had no idea where she might be. She was a lost dream, though one I kept dreaming with distressing regularity, so that no matter where I fell asleep—an alley, a tavern, my own poor excuse for a bed—I woke despondent and aching.

I wanted it to end. I wanted to forget her. I never wanted to forget her. I had no idea how long what I felt for her would last, or if it would ever go away. I had never before been in love. I'd made grand passions of nothings—Vera Brest, Mrs. Leporello, others—but what I felt for Adelaide eclipsed those so completely it was as if I'd invented something wholly new.

The day I'd left the Diodati had turned stormy by evening, so that I was soaked by the time I made it to the inn where I stopped that first night—a luxury, because I'd meant to sleep in the open as often as I could to save money. There is nothing like the mountains—and the Alps especially—to make one feel inconsequential. They rose precipitously on either side of the road, jagged and gray and snowcapped, rock strewn everywhere, as if giants had thrown great slabs about, the constant sound of stone splitting—a crack, a distant roar, the thunder that was not thunder but falling rock. I went to the Mer de Glace and Le Jardin just to be sure I'd had them right in my story—not that it mattered. The story was gone, and good riddance, not my story. I stayed in little huts along the way. The Swiss are a hospitable people. Those days, I was despairing and desolate and pining, but I'd had a plan—hadn't I? I thought I'd had a plan.

It was in Milan where I'd heard that Julian Estes was dead, and that the lake had spit out his body and heaven had refused him—or so I assumed. Surely God would not want an unbeliever by his side. The notice of his death was in a newspaper on the floor of the room I rented.

Julian Estes, the writer of Atheist poetry, has drowned. Now he knows if God exists or no.

It was weeks old, yellowed and rumpled with damp, and when I picked up his damned flask, it sent a glare into my eyes as if in deliberate mockery, one more dig leveled from Estes beyond the grave.

"At least I'm not dead," I sneered back. When I was done with Julian Estes and the Wentworth sisters, when I was done remembering, I meant to take the flask to the nearest pawnshop. What satisfaction I would gain from seeing it sit forgotten, ignoble, in some dusty bin, but for now it felt enough of a slight to take up his flask, to toast his death with a sip. One sip became two. Or more. I don't remember. In fact, I hardly remember much beyond stumbling from my room, nor where I intended to go, but I do remember stumbling back in the early dawn hours and crawling up the stairs—literally crawling, because I'd been beaten so badly—by whom, I didn't know—I could not walk. My nose bleeding, my torso riddled with bruises, and two black eyes. I made it to my room and vomited in the chamber pot and fell asleep on the floor to nightmares of ghosts and demons and some joker with a baton telling me I had to leave the gaming table while I hurled insults despite the fact that he was twice my size. The laudanum blurred and expanded everything. No wonder Estes had seen spirits.

Oh, and then there was the small matter of waking to find half my money gone.

So yes, blame Estes for all of it, or blame Adelaide for not bothering to even say good-bye, or Louisa for coming to my room, or Bayard, or me . . . yes, blame me, for daring to believe I could be something other than I was.

I decided to eschew the laudanum—obviously I did not handle it at all well, and my father and the monks had warned me a hundred times about the dangers of such things. Still, I was melancholy and bitter and as prone as always to losing my temper. Another small incident in Milan, and I was asked to leave by the authorities, not that I could blame them; I'd been to the court three times by then for fighting, and frankly I was weary and bruised so deeply there seemed to be no end to the pain. I wrote articles on my travels, sold some, managed to find my way back to London, where all I thought about was my father and how I could not go home a failure. I stayed as far away from Bethnal Green as I could, avoiding the places he might go, and wrote him letters. To explain the London postmark, I lied that I'd forwarded them to a friend there for delivery, as I was moving about so often, and instructed him to direct any replies to London as well. I told him I was in Lausanne, and then Bern, a denizen of Rome, and then Venice—Adelaide's cursed city—and after that I was just willy-nilly choosing without much thought of an itinerary that made any sense. His letters back were loving, joyous. How glad he was that I was traveling the world, and I should look up my uncle Beppo in Sicily and he thought my mother's sister might still be alive in Naples, though he wasn't sure and he couldn't remember her married name. I sent him the few articles that were published, and his pride in me was a torment. The articles were nothing, stupid, pointless. I was practically incompetent. Why should he be so proud? I was capable of so much more; how could he not see it? Who else ever had, but Adelaide?

I argued with a porter when he wouldn't step out of my way on the walk. I got into a fight at a faro table, which erupted into chaos and ended with me arrested for the night until I sobered up, though I wasn't drunk, not really, but it brought me some unwanted attention, and three days later, Colburn's men found me. I managed to evade them both, but I couldn't stay in that room, not that I was all that attached to it, and so I moved into one that was, if possible, worse.

Still, I had hope. My father waited for my grand success, and so I tried at another novel, and meanwhile I daydreamed about Adelaide. That soft, quiet smile as she sat at my desk. *I see you. I know you.* I would see it again, I knew. One day, when I finished a novel, and published it, she would pick it up somewhere and read my name and come searching for me. I would pass her on the street. She would stop and turn, a double take, and then her eyes would light with pleasure, and she would rush into my arms and say, *Vanni, how I have missed you! How I love you!* But it was becoming harder and harder to write; I felt restless, angry, unable to sit still long enough to form a sentence.

I'd been in London four months, and was walking down the street, hoping to find a decently cheap pork pie, when I passed John Murray Publishers, and noticed the line of people going inside, all emerging again with printed pages they were already reading devotedly.

"What is it?" I asked one of them.

"Bayard Sonnier's new story," he told me.

I hadn't known there was a story. The novel, yes, he'd been working on it then, but it wouldn't have been printed yet. "What's it called?"

"'The Witches,'" he said.

I began to feel a vague misgiving, but then again, that was what Bayard's story for the contest had been called. Perhaps he'd finished it. I stood in line and bought a copy with coins I could not spare, and when it was in my hands, I saw that the actual author's name was not Bayard's at all, but *Anonymous*.

My misgiving grew stronger. I drew back against a building, out of the way of passersby, and opened the cover. The story was prefaced by a letter.

Dear Sir,

In the summer of 1874, I was staying with good friends in the Château Orsini on the shores of Lac Léman, only a short distance from the Villa Diodati, the house that sheltered Lord Byron and his friends Percy and Mary Shelley in 1816, and where the novel Frankenstein *was conceived. Some sixty years later, that house was rented by Bayard Sonnier. I was pleased to know him when he visited Count Orsini's salons, and he told me that he and some friends who were visiting him at the Diodati had decided to hold a contest of their own in homage to the one that so inspired Mrs. Shelley. The result of this contest you hold in your hands: his story, "The Witches," which I think you will find—as I do—to be a work of genius in its depiction of two sisters who are bound by both benevolent and sinister forces. Brilliance is in every word, and though his name is not on the pages, I have*

been assured by those who know Mr. Sonnier best that this is indeed his work. This came to me through a friend who was anxious to keep Mr. Sonnier from throwing it into the fire—he deemed it not worthy of publishing! I would feel myself negligent if I allowed such a story to fall into obscurity, and so I send it to you, his publisher, in the hopes that the rest of the world will appreciate it as I do.
— *a Lady and an admirer of Mr. Sonnier*

Now my misgiving had turned to dread. I turned the page.

For Adelaide W—No man has been so blessed by inspiration as I have been by yours. You are a flame in a dark and cold world. May you ever burn beautiful and fierce.

My hands began to shake; I felt sick. The words leaped before my eyes, so familiar, yes, of course, because they were mine. What the hell had Vera Brest done? Bayard would be furious—writing about his life had been bad enough; he would never forgive that I'd stolen his work. I thought I'd escaped this, at least. There must be a way I could mitigate it, something I could do before he discovered it . . .

I hurried back to the office, pushing my way past the line, inside, despite the protests—"Wait your turn!" "Hey, mister, you can't do that!"

The bookseller glanced up tiredly. "You'll have to stand in line like the others."

I said, "I'm here to see Hanson."

"Oh then." A shrug. "Upstairs."

I knew the way well enough. I had been here dozens of times on business for Bayard. When I went upstairs, Hanson's secretary said, "Calina! It's been some time. Is Sonnier back in town?"

I shook my head. "I need to see Hanson."

"You don't have an appointment."

"Do I need one?" I asked, leveling him my best I-work-for-Bayard-Sonnier stare, despite my slovenly appearance. I don't think he'd heard that I was no longer in Bayard's employ. In any case, he noted the papers in my hand and went suddenly wary.

"We had it on the best authority that it was his."

"Whose authority?"

The secretary swallowed.

I said, "Have you heard from him?"

"He's denying it, but no one believes him."

There it was, the nightmare I'd been hoping to avoid. If Bayard already knew . . .

"Let me see Hanson."

The secretary motioned to the door.

I knocked and was bidden to enter. When I did, Hanson looked up from his desk and frowned. "Calina. What brings you here?"

"This," I said, leaning to wave the pages in his face. "This story."

"What about it? We were told—"

"It's mine," I said.

Hanson rose. "Now, there's no attribution."

"It's mine. Reid out there says you've heard from Bayard already."

Reluctantly, Hanson admitted, "We're printing his retraction. Soon."

"You mean after it sells a few thousand copies."

He said nothing.

"You can pay me for it, as it seems to be selling so well. And you can give me proper attribution."

"It's not selling that well," he protested—a lie, of course. I'd seen the waiting line. Not that I was surprised. Publisher excuses had always been Bayard's great frustration. "And I can't just go handing out money to anyone who comes in."

"I'm not just anyone. I wrote the bloody thing."

"Can you prove it?"

"Yes, of course. That is . . . I think so. What do you need me to do?"

Hanson reached for a file. He opened it, drew out a piece of paper, and handed it to me.

It was Bayard's denial, written in perfect penmanship—obviously he had a new secretary. *Not me.* I should not feel so jealous and forsaken over it, but I did.

It has come to my attention that a story called "The Witches" has been attributed to me. Not only do I deny that I wrote it, I condemn thoroughly the thief who has. It is true, as the letter states, that I started "The Witches" as part of a contest in the same spirit as that played in the Diodati with Byron and Shelley. My story does bear a resemblance to this one, but only in its opening scene. What I wrote follows; you will see that it has not much in common with this scurrilous attempt to make money in my name. He who has stolen it knows that I hold him in the greatest contempt. It is deeply distressing to me that this amateurish tale can be in any way intuited to be mine, and the author, whom I once thought a minor talent, has disabused me completely of that notion. He is clearly nothing more than a plagiarist and a fraud, and I wholly and completely deny that any part of this story can be mine, and challenge anyone who has the effrontery to think I would write something of such inferior quality to think otherwise.

I felt I had been flayed. All my hopes that I had escaped this punishment . . . I should have known I could not. I handed the letter back to Hanson, who watched me cautiously.

"Do you still wish to claim it?" he asked. "We mean to attach his letter to a new printing, along with his unfinished story."

If my name was on it, my father would see it, even if I didn't send it to him. He would see this letter. To be so damned by words . . .

amateurish, plagiarist, fraud . . . The shame he would feel . . . I did not want to imagine it.

"No." I threw the pages I'd bought onto his desk and went out of his office, down the stairs, and into the street, where the line of those waiting to see the new story by Bayard Sonnier stretched down the block.

I made my way back to my boardinghouse. The streets were crowded, the people changing from well-dressed businessmen and their wives to laborers, sailors, a few children kicking loose cobblestones down the street. The front door dragged across the floor as I pushed it open, announcing my arrival as loudly as any foghorn. Mrs. Dance screeched from the parlor—tiny, crowded, a collection of sagging settees and fraying chairs shoved into every spare space so there was barely any room to move—"Who is that?"

"Calina," I answered, and then hoped she would leave me be, but no, she came hurrying out, her grease-stained apron still around her ample waist. She was already raising the spectacles that dangled between her breasts.

"There you are. Some men come to see you a few hours ago."

I sighed. "Really."

She reached into her apron pocket, drawing forth a crumpled, folded paper. "They left this for you."

I didn't want to look at it, but she was waiting as if she'd been told to make sure I read it, and so I opened it to find a demand letter from Colburn and Sons Publishing, on a lawyer's letterhead. He'd found me again. I would have to move. But just then the thought of it was exhausting.

I gave Mrs. Dance a thin smile and went to the stairs, ignoring her disappointment that I wasn't sharing whatever news she'd given me, though I had no doubt she'd already looked at it.

"Bad news, Mr. Calina?" she called after me.

My room was nearly barren. No more beaver hat—that had already gone to a secondhand clothing shop—as had the waistcoats. The pocket watch, the chain, the ornaments were long pawned. I took off my coat and sat on my sagging mattress. All I wanted to do was sleep, but my mind spun, humiliation—again, and fear, disappointment. I felt betrayed by Vera Brest, by Bayard himself, and that was the worst thing, that he should so scorn me, that he should tell the world how he reviled me. The only good thing was that he hadn't used my name, but those who were important to me would know exactly of whom he wrote. Adelaide would know it. My father.

Those days with Bayard, attending the salons, drinking wine, discussing his plots and his characters, his good-natured insults interspersed with advice, seemed so long ago it was almost as if they hadn't happened but in my imagination.

I lay back, closing my eyes. My mind bit at me, pricking, blaming, a litany of my sins, and finally, unable to manage another moment, I rolled over and grabbed that silver flask, which I still kept, unable yet to relinquish it.

I shook it—still laudanum inside, months old now, who cared? I twisted off the cap and sniffed; it smelled the way it always smelled. But I hesitated before I drank, remembering Milan, and then . . . well, what could be more disastrous than what had already happened? How was it possible to ruin anything further?

I stared at empty pages while the last of my ink dripped uselessly from my pen. Ideas played about in my head, but the words . . . the words eluded me, and finally I lost them in wild nightmares of Adelaide and Louisa, Bayard and my father, where I woke shaking and sweating to see them standing before me, disappearing when I tried to touch them. Staying in my hovel of a room, where those blank pages mocked me— *amateur, fraud, a minor talent*—was impossible. The streets were more interesting, in any case; there were a hundred stories there. That man lounging in the alcove was a merchant who had lost everything to a confidence man. The rag-and-bone man had been a sculptor cheated of his commission by an untalented rival, and those women over there were sisters—a bit of a recurring theme, wasn't it?—respectable once, fallen on hard times when their diplomat father died and their uncle set them out, and sometimes we sat around a paltry fire in the evenings in their tiny parlor of a flat, and they would tell me stories of how they'd traveled to the Orient when they were young.

They would all be characters in my newest novel once I found those bloody words again. How did they escape me so easily? The days blended together, one day sunny and then raining, and then snow. Too cold to sit on the streets, and I'd somehow lost my hat, though at least my face was warm—one good thing about having no soap to shave—though itchy . . . lice, I supposed, or fleas. The place *was* a hovel. Ink was precious, but still I couldn't fight the compulsion to put something—anything—on paper, though I no longer had the will to write to my father, and I seemed to have lost the ability to form sentences. I drew designs, swirls and cross-hatches that turned into words before my eyes, Adelaide's *"Brilliant!"* in my head, Estes's flask by my side, nearly empty—I would need to buy more, but I'd run out of things to sell, and the last bit of money I'd earned from helping a coalman unload when his boy hadn't showed up was all but gone. I took a sip and tucked it into my coat pocket.

The knock on the door—not really a knock, more a scratch—and I was back in Geneva again, looking up, expecting Bayard to step inside; *"Here are the newest pages, and be sure to send the last ones to Hanson; he's complaining again,"* but instead of Bayard there were two men I didn't recognize.

"There you are," said one of them, burly, mustachioed, bulbous nose. "Watcha doing, Calina?"

"Why, he's writing!" said the other, just as burly, clean shaven, shaggy haired. "Let's see what it is, yeah? Somethin' for Colburn, I hope?"

I scrambled from the mattress, but before I'd gone two steps, the clean-shaven one grabbed my arm and threw me against the wall, and when I gasped, sinking to the floor, the other grabbed me and slammed me back again, his fist in my gut—*stomach, Vanni, remember who you are*—and I jackknifed, retching. They began to tear apart the room, tossing things about. I ran at one of them and he hit me hard in the face and tossed me out and suddenly I was crashing down the stairs, tumbling—who was groaning so loudly?

I heard them behind me, and doors opening, other lodgers coming out to see what the commotion was about, the landlady screaming, "Hey now! This is a respectable house!"—something only the unrespectable ever said. I staggered to my feet, pain so sharp I retched again, nearly falling out the door into the street. I'd had a back exit scouted for weeks, as Colburn's men had become less and less accommodating, and now the bailiffs had become involved too.

I caught the glances of people on the street as I limped by, half bent, my arm—aching, useless, broken?—held tight against my chest, which hurt so badly I could hardly breathe. I found my way to a street not far distant, lined with shops, people everywhere shopping for . . . Christmas? Could it be Christmas again so soon? Someone near was making moaning, mewing noises. My arm was excruciatingly painful, nauseating. Finally I could go no farther. There was a bench before some café, the snow coming down, the walk slippery. They would send me away soon enough, I knew from experience, but I had a few moments, and I could not go another step.

The bench was cast iron and so cold I felt it through my coat, but the pain made it as nothing. I gathered close into myself, trying to think of what to do. Tears came to my eyes, blurring a scene that was already rather blurry, lights in storefronts blending to create a series of halos, garlands of holly and ivy and mistletoe, snow and shoppers like a Currier & Ives litho.

And then, like an angel, there she was. I knew her from across the street. Her way of walking was so familiar to me that I would have spotted her in any crowd. That fluidity, that sway, uncorseted, natural. My gaze sharpened, nothing in focus but her, everything else in hazy aura around her, and I told myself *no. No, it couldn't be her, not after so long. Not here, not now, it's just another hallucination.* I blinked, trying to dispel it, but she was still there. Stopping to look in a shop window, her hair gleaming darkly, a small hat and a half veil, some kind of bobbing thing, leaves or berries, decorating it.

Adelaide.

She had been sent just for me, I knew, and I tried to rise, to go to her, but pain struck me gasping down, and so I tried to call out, "Addie!" My voice was hoarse; it got swallowed by the street.

She turned from the window as if she were searching for something, for me. She'd heard me somehow, she knew . . . *Adelaide.*

She looked across. Everything in me shuttered and stopped. *Now,* I thought. *Now.*

Her gaze landed on me, paused. I waited for the double take. I smiled and waited for her to run across the street, into my arms. I wanted to wave, but I could not take my good arm from my broken one. I could almost hear her voice in my head. *I have missed you so. I love you.*

But there was no double take. No running into my arms. She turned away, walking quickly, and in stunned disbelief, I stumbled to my feet, I tried to go after her, halting, staggering, a sharp pain in my chest, my arm, that stopped me, so I had to press my hand against a window to keep from going to my knees, nearly falling against a slovenly man with hair past his shoulders, greasy and stringy, a face so gaunt it was nearly skeletal, a filthy coat, blood dripping from a cut on his cheek into his unkempt beard—homeless, derelict. I lurched away with a grunt of pain, trying to escape him, and he lurched away too, and it dawned on me that it was no man, but my reflection.

The man I was trying to escape was me.

She could not have recognized me. I did not recognize myself, and this evidence of what I'd become . . . The soft blur of delusion melted away; I was suddenly sober. The world became sharp edged and dangerous. Who was I trying to fool? I had written nothing for months. All the stories I'd thought to tell, the characters in the streets waiting for my pen . . . The homeless man in the alcove had been as drunk as I when he told me the lie of his life. The women I sat with were drugaddled prostitutes who sucked desperately at the few drops of laudanum I offered and then sucked me after. The rag-and-bone man had seen in me a fellow pretender—why not? I was, wasn't I? I would be writing no novel; there was nothing to save me. I was the fraud Bayard had called me, a counterfeit. My father would be ashamed to see me now. I was ashamed of myself.

I reached into my pocket for Estes's flask, and it seemed to glow in the ambient light of the shops, a beacon—or no, a curse. I was under one just as she had once told me she had been, but mine was of my own making. I could not stand the sight of it anymore. I could not stand the memories, or the knowledge that I'd had everything and thrown it all away, and perhaps one only got a single chance at that. Perhaps God, or fate, or whatever ruled this world, had already watched me squander mine, and had no more to offer. I was nothing and I'd left nothing to show I'd existed. I was already gone; I just had not realized it yet.

The pain was agonizing. I forced myself to walk, to keep walking, until I passed a pawnshop, a light leading me there as if I were meant to find it—something working in my favor at last. I could not open the door; I could only pound on it with my good arm until the owner came, and then when he saw me, he tried to close it again until I held up the flask and said, "Please. This."

The exchange took moments. All this time, and I'd thought I would feel some satisfaction when it was gone, some thrill of retaliation, but I felt only a deep weariness, only pain, only that gnawing shame. The only place I knew to go was back to my room, and if Colburn's men were waiting for me, so much the better, though I would have preferred a less painful way to die. I stopped at the chemist near my boarding-house. He was used to me by now, and his distaste too was familiar when I entered.

"No more credit, Calina."

I went up to the counter and slammed down the handful of coins and said, "I'm paying my bill. Then give me as much as the rest will buy."

I left with a bottle and tears in my eyes. The door of my room was already open. On the floor were my papers. Invisible words, stories untold, all in my head, never to be set down. I closed the door with my foot and collapsed onto my bed, every movement hurting, my head throbbing, my arm, my face . . . She had been on the other side of the street. She had looked at me.

I uncapped the bottle and thought of those times in my bedroom, writing companionably, when the words had come in such a torrent I could not get them down quickly enough. I thought of drifting with her in the gentle currents of Lac Léman, watching a sunrise in the shadow of the mountains, where, for the first and only time in my life, I'd been everything I had always wanted to be. I had loved her, but more than that, I had found myself in her company and her quiet encouragement, in her soft smile that told me I was understood, that told me I was seen. I could not bear to be invisible again.

I brought the bottle to my lips, and I drank long and deep.

THIRTY-FOUR

ADELAIDE

The lecture hall was full. Louisa had made certain, as always, that the newspapers had all printed notices, and that broadsheets were plastered on nearly every telegraph pole and wall in London.

ADELAIDE WENTWORTH

AUTHOR OF *LORD CLAIRMONT'S MUSE*

7 P.M., THE EGYPTIAN HALL

DISCUSSING

THE VILLA DIODATI AND THE SUMMER THAT INSPIRED *LORD CLAIRMONT'S MUSE*

Her Life with the Atheist Poet JULIAN ESTES,

Free Love,

Transcendentalism,

and SPIRITS

I had protested mentioning Julian at all, but Louisa insisted. "He's as infamous in his way as Bayard, Addie. More so, even. It's how we'll lure them in."

She was right. They came to discover if the gossip they'd heard was true; they stayed because they were interested in his theories and the hope of an enlightened society; and they left with copies of *Lord Clairmont's Muse*. The tables near the doors were piled high with books, and already lines were forming to buy, cashiers at the ready.

I had never suspected that I might be a good speaker, and I had surely never suspected that Louisa had any touch of managerial genius, but in these past months our combined talents had enabled us to pay back Bayard's many loans, and to rent rooms in London. I spent my nights speaking, and my days working on another novel, and I was more content than I could have ever imagined being. Even on my best days with Julian, I had never thought such things possible.

"Funny, isn't it," Louisa mused. "All this time, I thought it was Julian who would change the world, when really it was you."

Her equal pride and astonishment made me laugh. Whether Louisa would eventually decline as our father had was impossible to know. But that she had found a talent necessary to our lives gave her a kind of balance. Or perhaps it was that she was no longer afraid I would abandon her. We had always been bound, but this new chain was one we both knew I would never break. My obligation now ran too deeply to escape, nor did I wish to.

I thought of Julian often. Not only did the lectures make certain of it, but, as his theories and his philosophies fell from my mouth into receptive ears, I was glad to give him a voice, and glad that in some way I was atoning for what had happened between us, and fulfilling his dream, which had once also been mine. Yet my life with him seemed another life. He was not the one I grieved.

I watched for Vanni. He had been from London, and I wondered if he might be living here again. If he were, surely he would come, out of curiosity if nothing else? So many months had passed; no doubt his love for me had faded, but we had been friends, and I thought he must miss that as I did. I imagined seeing him in the audience. He would sit quietly until the crowd dissipated, until those last admirers who lingered to ask me questions had finally gone. I would step down from the lectern and see the uncertainty in his dark eyes, and I would say, as if nothing had ever come between us, *"I wondered when you would appear."*

"I couldn't stay away any longer," he would answer. *"I've missed you."*

"I'm glad you're here. I've missed you too. So much."

He would smile, and hold up a copy of *Lord Clairmont's Muse*. *"You dedicated it to me."*

"I'm only returning the favor," I would tease. *"But you deserve it. It would never have been written without you."*

"You would have written it eventually."

"No, it needed you. Will you come for tea? I have a surprise for you."

Or so my fantasy went. But "The Witches" was the last trace I had of him. I had expected him to come forward and say he wrote it, and when he did not, and I read Bayard's terrible insult, I understood why, and I pleaded with Bayard to retract it.

"He doesn't deserve the things you said," I'd told him.

"Really? He stole it from me. Along with several other things."

"The story is good, and you know it. It's unfair and unworthy of you to condemn it."

"Unworthy?"

"Or perhaps you're jealous . . ."

"You must be joking."

"You said he had talent. You said you were trying to make something of him. Do him this favor now, Bayard. You're not a vindictive man."

"Don't be so certain."

But he'd written a letter to the newspaper, and another to Hanson, retracting his insults and giving the author of "The Witches" a name, and when next I saw it printed, Giovanni Calina had been proudly proclaimed the author.

The story had sold six thousand copies in the first weeks, Bayard said in admiration, and though I waited nervously and hopefully for Vanni to acknowledge it, he never did.

"Hanson said Vanni showed up the second week," Bayard told me, a bit guiltily. "But when he saw my denial, he left. Hanson hasn't seen him since."

"Can you blame him? How could he admit to writing it after that? You should be ashamed."

"Thank God I have you to keep me on the righteous path," Bayard said sarcastically. "What would I do without your good example? You did, after all, accept his apology so gracefully."

I flushed. "I was angry."

"As was I. And I think I had more reason, didn't I? I deserve some credit for trying to make it right. Though frankly, he should count himself lucky for it."

"Perhaps he doesn't know," Louisa said to me when I worried over it. "Perhaps he's not in London, and he hasn't seen it—oh, Johnny, no, no, no! Give me that!" She swooped in on her son, snatching from his hands a pen that had rolled to the floor, and handed it to me in exasperation. "You will end up choking him if you're not more careful."

"I think he wants to be a writer," I said, grabbing him up, smothering him with kisses until he giggled in my arms. "Like his father."

"One story does not a writer make," Louisa said darkly. "He should have been Bay's—then perhaps you could claim that talent runs in his blood."

But he was not Bayard's. That had been obvious the day he was born, with his swath of nearly black hair and his nearly black eyes and olive skin that could not have come from anyone in that villa but Vanni. It was for him that I'd finally taken the five hundred pounds Vanni had left for me. For his son. Of all the gifts Louisa had given me, all the strawberries and beach stones and paper flowers, this was the best of them, and one we both treasured.

"Oh, his lips are so perfect." Louisa had sighed; I could not tell if it was with dread or admiration. Perhaps it was a bit of both. "He has his father's mouth."

I spoke forty times that year, not just in London, but in France and Italy and Germany. In Switzerland too. Everywhere I looked for him. I searched faces on the street. I waited. The new novel was coming along well, but I wanted his advice. I wanted to see him.

"Why?" Louisa asked irritably. "Why is he so important?"

"You don't want John to know his father?"

"I don't care if he knows him," she said honestly, too much so. "It's only that it seems to matter so much to you. Why?"

"Because it's unfinished," I told her. "Because I was wrong, and I want to apologize. Because he should know he has a son. Because everything we have now is due to him."

"Due to you, Addie," she said, as insistent as she'd often been when she used to speak of Julian's genius. "It wasn't Vanni who wrote *Lord Clairmont's Muse*. It was you. You've done what even Jules couldn't do. Papa and Mama would be so proud. And Julian too. How does Vanni matter?"

But my debt to him was too large to ignore. He was gone so entirely it was as if he had not existed, and I began to feel a quiet desperation, as if some catastrophe had happened that I had not seen or heard but that somehow belonged to me.

Bayard no longer sent pages for me to transcribe; I no longer needed the money, and he had hired another secretary, a mild and unassuming man who had been a tutor and did not wish for more. But he wrote often, and so when his next letter came, I had no reason to think it anything other than his usual witty entertainment.

My dearest A—

Bad news, I'm afraid, but it's so old now that there is no mending it and nothing you can do. Poor Vanni is dead. I heard the news this morning from Hanson, who finally sent someone to his father to deliver royalties, as Vanni never tried to get in touch—don't ask me why Hanson thought to do it. He had no obligation. Guilt, I imagine. Ah well, I suppose there is hope for publishing yet.

In any event, I know very little. It was some months ago—in December, Hanson thinks. Vanni was found in his room—not a good part of town, I'm afraid. Laudanum overdose. Hanson thinks perhaps a suicide but no one of course will admit to that, and there was no note so who can say? Hanson had no idea where he is buried.

Now . . . I know what you will do and that Louisa will complain, but tell the little fiend to be compassionate for once, and let her know that I am in agreement with you. Mr. Calina was very proud of his son, as I think I've told you, and no doubt is devastated. It can be no small thing for him to know he has a grandson.

The neighborhood is dangerous for a woman, so please—for God's sake listen to me and do not go there alone. I would never forgive myself if something happened to you.

With affection, as always,

B.

Louisa looked up from her ledgers and her schedules, frowning. "What is it? What's wrong?"

"He's dead." The letter winged to the floor, where his son grabbed it with a cry of triumph and crumpled it in his little fist.

Louisa hurried over and gathered me in her arms, and I sobbed against her shoulder as she comforted me. She whispered, "But look, Addie. He's not gone, not completely. Look at the wondrous boy he's left behind."

It was another thing I had not expected: that Louisa might have the words to soothe what felt like a broken heart.

The next day, I hired a carriage. When the driver heard the address, he looked at Johnny in my arms and opened his mouth to protest.

I said, "I have to go there. Please."

He shut his mouth again and patted his coat pocket. "All right then, I've got a pistol."

I dandled Johnny on my knee, and he gurgled contentedly as I looked out the window at the changing scenery, small shops and taverns and peddlers pushing carts, hollow-eyed children and wash strewn over balustrades, gray already from coal smoke. The carriage stopped before a small cobbler's shop, **CALINA & SON**. I stared at the name. *"If not for that story, I would have become a cobbler like my father."*

"We're here, ma'am," the driver called. The carriage rocked as he jumped down from the seat and opened the door, and it was only then that I noticed that people had stopped what they were doing to stare at a strange carriage, a fashionably dressed woman, a baby boy.

"I'll pay you an extra crown if you wait," I told the driver.

Then I went inside. The walls were lined with shelves crowded with shoes and boots, leather samples, lasts. It smelled of oil and glue and dust. At the back of the shop was a counter, and an older man rose slowly from behind it. His hair was as dark as Vanni's, though heavily threaded with gray. He looked tired and worn, weighted by sorrow. He also looked surprised to see me.

"Ma'am?" he asked, obviously confused by the visit of a well-to-do woman. "Can I help you? Are you lost?"

"I've come on behalf of your son," I said.

He deflated, putting his hand on the counter to steady himself. "I'm afraid Giovanni is with God now."

His grief deepened my own. For a moment, I could not speak through it. Johnny grabbed at my earring as if to remind me of Louisa's words, and to say, *Don't be sad. I'm here.* Gently, I plucked his hand away and said, "Yes, I know. I am so very sorry, Mr. Calina. So very sorry. But I came because I thought you might like to meet his son. Your grandson. This is John Wentworth."

"John—" Mr. Calina stared at the boy in my arms. "Giovanni's boy?"

I nodded. "As you can see, he looks very like his father."

Mr. Calina seemed stunned. Then he came to me, his eyes filling with tears. "Is this . . . can this be true?" He touched Johnny's chubby arm as if he were afraid to find his grandson was an illusion. "And you are . . . you are his mother?"

"His aunt," I said. "I'm Adelaide Wentworth."

"Adelaide." His blurry eyes flashed with recognition. "Adelaide. You. You're the one. He wrote to me of you. The American sister."

"One of them, yes."

"His story—" He reached behind him to a thin book on the counter. It was an oft-read copy of "The Witches," the cover worn at the edges. He opened it to the second page, the dedication. "'To Adelaide W—' That is you, yes? He wrote this for you."

"He was my friend," I said, my own eyes blurry now. "I knew him when he was Bayard Sonnier's secretary."

"Ah. Gio-Gio was so very proud to work for him. He wrote of him often. Mr. Sonnier thought him talented, you know. A great man such as that!"

"Yes, he did." I thought of Bayard in the kitchen. *I am trying to make something of him.* The worry on his face as he stared out at a lake in the midnight dark.

Mr. Calina closed the book, fingering it lovingly. How tender was his expression. They told me he was beaten. His arm was broken. Some ribs. He took laudanum for the pain. Too much, he . . ." He choked on the last and reached into his pocket for a handkerchief. "My clever boy. Such a special boy. Who would not have been proud of a boy like that?"

He wiped his eyes and reached out a gnarled finger to John, and my nephew curled his own small fingers around as if he recognized his grandfather and meant never to let go. As I should have done with his father. Johnny understood already what had taken me months to realize.

"You will be special too, yes? How can it be otherwise, with such a papa?" Mr. Calina said to him. He looked up at me. "Does he have a temper?"

I laughed. "Oh, with his parents, how could he not?"

"You must teach him to control it. It will cause him only trouble. That was the problem with Gio-Gio. He was like lightning. Angry in a flash, never stopping to think."

Lightning in the mountains. Spirits rising to the stars. I felt Vanni's presence all around me here, in this little shop where he had been a boy, comforting and reassuring, and I knew he had forgiven me before he'd reached the road that morning, even as I'd watched him, too angry to call him back, nourishing my own cruelty. I wanted to cry for what I'd lost, for the terrible mistake I'd made.

"I may not be the best one to teach him," I admitted. "So I had hoped perhaps you might help. I've come to ask if we might bring him by now and then: my sister and I. Or you could come visit him. We would like him to know his grandfather. Perhaps you could tell him about Vanni . . . we knew him for such a short time, after all."

"Me? Look at this shop, Miss Wentworth. I am no gentleman."

His words summoned a memory with painful clarity. The steamer from Villeneuve, the sun sparkling on the water and Vanni speaking of how his father had wanted him to be clear of a life he feared was Vanni's destiny. I said, "I want Johnny to be the man his father was—who better to teach him than you?"

Mr. Calina straightened. With a quiet smile and a quieter dignity, he said, "Thank you. I would like that very much."

I had wanted forgiveness and redemption. I had wanted a finish to everything that was unresolved, but now, with his words, I realized that it was not really what I wanted. Nothing was really ever over. Nothing was ever really done, and that was how it should be. Those loose strings dangled, every mistake I'd made that I'd hoped to atone for, to erase, and yet those mistakes had birthed everything I had now. Had I not run off with Julian, I would not have realized that the life I longed for was too small. Had I not brought Louisa, we would never have gone to Geneva to meet Bayard; I would never have met Vanni. Had I not rejected him, there would be no dark-eyed boy with his father's perfect lips on my hip now, and I would not be filling lecture halls and writing novels, and Louisa and I would not have found our way back to one another; the knotted skeins of our lives might have come unraveled after all.

"I don't think we can truly know the impact we might have on anyone."

No, we could not, and while Julian had spoken of unhappy souls lingering, I thought perhaps he had actually been seeing something altogether different, proof that the souls that touched ours never went away, but became a part of us. We could never know what even our smallest gestures might mean, what a smile on a bad day might ease, or a hand put out to keep a stranger from falling, or a word spoken one night in a garden by a man limned by gaslight, who'd stood on tiptoe to reach for me a star.

AFTERWORD

My first introduction to *Frankenstein*—and by that I mean not the culturally ubiquitous, staggering, and incoherent creature popularized by Boris Karloff, but the haunting philosophical novel—was through a two-night TV miniseries called *Frankenstein: The True Story*, starring Leonard Whiting, Michael Sarrazin, and a very young Jane Seymour. While *The True Story* was neither true nor a particularly faithful adaptation, it did begin with a scene depicting how *Frankenstein* was conceived during the stormy 1816 summer that Mary Shelley (then Godwin) spent at Lake Geneva with her lover and soon-to-be husband, the poet Percy Shelley; Lord Byron; his doctor, John Polidori; and Mary's stepsister, Claire Clairmont (who was also Byron's lover). After a night telling ghost stories, they decided to hold a contest to write their own.

The result of that contest was *Frankenstein*, and also John Polidori's "The Vampyre," the first modern-day vampire tale, introducing the vampire as we know him today—an urbane, cultured gentleman with undeniable sex appeal. Mary Shelley was nineteen; John Polidori, twenty-one.

By the time I saw this miniseries, I'd already decided I was going to be a writer, and the thought of these Romantics sitting around discussing philosophy and literature was something I could not forget. With my friend Debra Schultz, who was equally consumed—or perhaps forcibly dragged along (and who gave me my very first copy of *Frankenstein*, a New American Library mass-market paperback, which I still own)—I explored Byron, Shelley, and all things *Frankenstein*. For me, it became a fascination—all right, call it obsession—that never died, and one that has been richly rewarding.

Byron said of his time in Geneva: "Between metaphysics, mountains, lakes, love unextinguishable, thoughts unutterable, and the nightmare of my own delinquencies . . . [I would have] blown my brains out, but for the recollection that it would have given pleasure to my mother-in-law."

Byron's words reflect some of the emotional turmoil, resentments, and jealousies of that summer. He was coming off a disastrous marriage and very humiliating public separation rendered more horrifying by the rumors (true) of his love affair with his half-sister. He had escaped to Geneva, and Lac Léman, to lick his wounds, and did not expect Claire Clairmont, who had briefly been his lover in London, and who was determined to keep him, to show up with her stepsister, Mary, and Percy Shelley in tow. Fortunately, Byron and Shelley became good friends, and Byron was prepared to be charmed by Mary, who was the offspring of two respected philosophers, William Godwin and Mary Wollstonecraft.

Though neither Mary Shelley nor Percy Shelley mention Claire or Polidori in either the 1817/18 or 1831 edition preface/introduction to *Frankenstein*, the two were emotionally and intellectually tangled with the others, and the effects of those relationships would be enduring. Claire would bear Byron's illegitimate daughter and rue the day she met him ("I am unhappily the victim of a happy passion . . . it was fleeting, and mine only lasted ten minutes, but those ten minutes have discomposed the rest of my life . . . my heart wasted and ruined as if it had been scorched by a thousand lightnings"), and her relationship with Byron, as well as Shelley's support of her, would lead to the death of one of Mary and Percy's children, and cause an irreparable rift in the Shelley marriage. For the entertainment of a lady friend, John Polidori would riff on the fragment of a story Byron wrote (and abandoned) for the contest, and would end up ruining his reputation and earning Byron's contempt. He would commit suicide only a few years later, and die in obscurity.

This true story is the inspiration for my reimagining, *A Drop of Ink*. I cannot explain why my fascination with these people should be so persistent. Perhaps it is because they were all larger than life, despite—or perhaps due to—their terrible flaws. Percy Shelley was reviled and belittled for his beliefs, and yet he still insisted upon living them, no matter the damage he caused to those he loved. Byron wrote poetry that was not only immensely popular, but is still relevant today. He was one of the first celebrities, scorned for his lifestyle by his contemporaries, and yet he lived exactly as he wanted, on his own terms, even as it forced him into exile. He never returned to England, but remained in Italy and Greece, eventually dying of a fever fighting for Greek independence in Missolonghi. Though John Polidori's story is the least known and the most pathetic, he was precociously intelligent, earning a doctor's degree at nineteen. He was the uncle to the famous Rossettis: William, Christina, Dante Gabriel, and Maria. Not only is he credited with creating the vampire genre, his influence on *Frankenstein* is still debated today.

And as for Mary Shelley—she and Claire Clairmont were women ahead of their time. Raised by the precepts set forth by Mary's famous mother, Mary Wollstonecraft, who wrote *A Vindication of the Rights of Woman*, and educated by her father, William Godwin, as men would have been, Mary and Claire lived lives of passion and creativity at a time when it was nearly impossible for a woman to make a choice other than marriage. Mary Shelley raised a son and wrote several novels beyond *Frankenstein*. She kept Percy Shelley's flame burning by editing his poems and introducing his writing and his theories to the world. Claire Clairmont took Shelley's teachings to heart, traveled widely, spoke several languages, and chose to never marry. She died in Florence, Italy, at eighty, having long outlived all the others, and was the inspiration for Henry James's *The Aspern Papers*.

If it is true that we can never know the impact that we might have on one another, then it is also true that I cannot begin to estimate how greatly these people influenced my own life and writing—a full two hundred years after the summer they spent together on the stormy shores of Lac Léman.

ACKNOWLEDGMENTS

Many, many thanks to my very talented and insightful editors, Jodi Warshaw and Heather Lazare. As always, working with them has been a privilege and a delight, and I am so grateful for their perception, enthusiasm, and professionalism. I never doubt that their suggestions will make a book better—and that is a gift. Thanks must also go to Kristin Hannah for not only pointing me in the right direction during the brainstorming phase of this story, but also for telling me tactfully (okay, maybe not *tactfully*) that I needed to throw out the first draft completely and start again, regardless of how much I loved it. I hate to admit it, but she was right. I am not sure what I would do without her, and I hope I never have to try. Also, thanks to my husband, Kany Levine, not only for his love and support, but for reading this book at an earlier stage than usual, and offering some very crucial and helpful suggestions, as well as much-needed encouragement. I've been wasting his editorial expertise until now, but no longer! As always, I am grateful for all that Kim Witherspoon, Lena Yarbrough, and everyone at Inkwell Management do on my behalf. Gabriella Dumpit, Dennelle Catlett, and the marketing and publicity teams at Amazon Publishing/Lake Union are wonderful to work with. In this industry, it is easy to become cynical and jaded, yet their excitement, support, and efficiency never flag. Thank you all for that. And, of course, I must thank my family, and my husband (again) and daughters, Maggie and Cleo. I think it is not easy sometimes to live with a writer, and their patience, support, and love give me someplace soft and safe to land after a hard day of tilting at windmills—and that means more than I can say.

ABOUT THE AUTHOR

Photo © 2012 CMC Levine

Megan Chance is a critically acclaimed, award-winning author of historical fiction. Her novels have been chosen for the Borders Original Voices and Book Sense programs. A former television news photographer and graduate of Western Washington University, Chance lives in the Pacific Northwest with her husband and two daughters.